Date Due

AUG 29	SEP 22	OCT 7	NOV 18
SEP 25	DEC 12	OCT 20	MAR 22
NOV 4	DEC 29	JAN 2	APR 5
DEC 6	OCT 28	SEP 4	JUN 11
DEC 20	NOV 23	DEC 20	AUG 2
FEB 7	DEC 30	JAN 5	NOV 1
MAR 19	22 NVP	APR 19	FEB 10
APR 23		SEP 20	
SEP 5	MAR 1	SEP 11	

LUCIUS

The Adventures of a Roman Boy

HE HAD HIS DAGGER OUT IN A MOMENT AND RUSHED AT ME

Page 325

LUCIUS

The Adventures of a Roman Boy

BY

A. J. CHURCH

Author of "Stories from Homer,"
"Stories from Virgil," etc.

BIBLO and TANNEN

New York

Carnegie Public Library
Robinson, Illinois

Reprinted, 1960
by
BIBLO and **TANNEN**
BOOKSELLERS and **PUBLISHERS,** Inc.
63 Fourth Avenue   New York 3, N. Y.

Library of Congress Catalog Card Number: 60-16706

Printed in the U.S.A.

Noble Offset Printers, Inc.
New York 3, N.Y.

PREFACE.

T HE main action of this story belongs to a critical and interesting period in the last years of the Roman Republic. In 72 B.C., when my hero is represented as starting to take up an official position in Sicily, Italy was slowly recovering from the effects of the internal struggles which had distracted the state for many years; of the Social War in which Rome had been fighting for her supremacy among the kindred Italian peoples; and of the Civil War, the long conflict between the nobles and the people, terminated, at least for a time, by Sulla's victory in the year 82, and by the bloody proscription which followed it. Many of the evils of these terrible times still remained. Italy, in particular, abounded with ruined and desperate men. With these and with the fugitives who were always trying to escape from the cruelties of slavery, Spartacus, a gladiator, who in 73 led a revolt at Capua, recruited his army. In the following year this man was at the height of his power. In the same year the insurrection of Sertorius, who had defied the power of Rome in Spain many years, was brought to an end by his assassination. In

Asia Mithradates, king of Pontus, had been driven out of
his dominion, and had sought shelter in the dominions
of his son-in-law, Tigranes, king of Armenia. He was not,
however, at the end of his resources, and it was not till
nine years afterwards that his final defeat and death took
place. During the greater part of this time the pirates
held almost undisputed possession of the Mediterranean
Sea. Pompey put them down completely in the year 67.

In the postscript to my story affairs have changed completely. The Republic has passed away, and the Empire
is divided between Antony in the East and Augustus in
the West. I may remark that the old gardener of the
last two chapters is not an arbitrary invention of my own.
Virgil, in his fourth Georgic (that in which he treats
of bee-culture), speaks of having known "an old man of
Corycus" who had a garden near Tarentum. As there was
a Corycus in Cilicia, it has been suggested that this old man
was one of the pirates whose lives Pompey spared after his
victory, and some of whom he is known to have settled in
Italy.

A writer who has been engaged in teaching for the
greater part of his life can hardly help trying to make his
book useful. I hope, however, that my young readers will
not find this story less entertaining because it may help
them to realize the period to which it belongs. They will
certainly not find it overloaded with learning — a fault
which, indeed, it is only too easy for most of us to avoid.

HADLEY GREEN, *June*, 1885.

CONTENTS.

LUCIUS
ADVENTURES OF A ROMAN BOY

TWO THOUSAND YEARS AGO: or, THE ADVENTURES OF A ROMAN BOY.

CHAPTER I.

A START IN LIFE.

TWO lads, each of whom carried a fishing-rod in his hand and a roughly-made basket of willow-work on his shoulders, were making their way up the left or eastern bank of the Liris, near Arpinum. The elder of the two was a lad of about seventeen, though his tall and well-developed frame made him look considerably older; the younger may have been his junior by about three years. The time was about an hour before sunset of a day in the latter half of March.

"Come, Caius," said the elder of the two lads to his companion, "we have had about enough of this tiresome Liris. I hate this dull, thick water. There is not much fun in catching these fish; and when they are caught they are so muddy and flabby that they are scarcely worth the trouble of carrying home. Let us see whether we cannot get something out of the Fibrenus. At home they always say that a Fibrenus fish is worth twenty out of the Liris. Now that the sun has got so low I think that we may do something."

The two friends had just reached the Fibrenus, a little stream that, after running a short, swift course from the hills among which Arpinum was situated, mingled its clear waters with the slower and more turbid current of the Liris. It broadened out just before the point of junction into a reach which had something of the look of a small lake. Most of this pool was covered with water-weed, which was then just breaking out into flower, but a narrow channel in the middle was kept open by the force of the stream. The water was remarkably bright, and curiously cold to the touch. The first peculiarity made the fish particularly difficult to catch ; the second gave them, it was supposed, the firmness of flesh and the delicacy of flavor for which they were celebrated through the whole country-side. Only the most skilful of the neighboring anglers found it worth while to try their hands on the shy perch and still shyer trout which inhabited the Fibrenus, and even these returned more often than not with empty baskets. At the upper end of the pool which has been just described was one of the most favorite spots for the exercise of the angler's craft. The river here made a little fall. The water was therefore broken ; commonly, too, it was covered with foam, which sometimes helped the angler by concealing the fall of his bait. The elder of the two companions, whom we may without further delay intro- duce to our readers by the name of Lucius Marius, had often taken a fine fish out of the little eddies that were formed by the cascade, and he now resolved to try them again.

The younger lad, who had a modest distrust of his powers,

stood at some distance from the water's side, and contented himself with watching the operations of his more experienced comrade. Putting a new bait, the largest and freshest worm which he could find in his bag, upon his hook, he waited for a little puff of wind to help him in his cast, for the breeze was, as usual, dying away as the sun sank towards the horizon. The puff, the approach of which was signified by a gentle rustling of the tree-tops behind, came in due course, and Lucius threw his bait with all the skill which he possessed, and, as it happened, exactly at the right moment. It fell on the centre of the deepest eddy, about four or five feet below the fall, and had not sunk more than half-way to the bottom when it was seized by a large fish, heavier and stronger, as Lucius, with his well-practised hand, felt in a moment, than any that he had before had the chance of securing. The place, he knew, was one in which it would require all his skill to play a large fish with success. The water for some five or six yards below the cascade was clear and deep. If the fish could be kept there all would be well, if only he had been securely hooked, for the tackle was both new and strong. But beyond this distance the water began to shoal, and the weed-beds afforded a refuge by help of which, as the anglers of Arpinum knew to their cost, many a fine fish had escaped. The trout, a fine fellow of three pounds, for such he had shown himself to be by a frantic leap into the air almost immediately after feeling the hook, would infallibly make for this shelter. It was the choice which the angler knows so well, and which he always finds so difficult to make between two dangers, the danger of losing the fish by checking him in his rush, the danger of losing him by allowing him to reach some place from which it is impossible to get him out. In this instance fortune favored the angler. The fish, as a heavy fish sometimes will, seemed to prefer to keep his head up against the stream; and for the first two or three minutes, always the most dangerous time in such an affair, wasted his strength, now in rushes down to the bottom of the pool, now in wild leaps out of the water. When he changed his tactics and began to make for the weed-beds he was sensibly weaker, and it became less dangerous to check his course. Once, and once only, he managed to get the line round a weed, and Lucius' heart, to use a common phrase, was in his mouth. Happily for the fisherman, the weed had not reached its strongest growth, and yielded to the pressure which he ventured to put upon it. The trout was not yet taken, but he was practically vanquished. Once and again he showed his broad spotted side, his rushes became weaker and shorter, his leaps out of the water ceased altogether. Lucius skilfully piloted him to a place where the bank overhung the water. Then, shortening the line as much as posble, and handing the rod to his young companion, he threw himself at full length upon the bank, and, reaching out his hand, thrust his fingers into the trout's open gills. A strong and skilful jerk landed the creature on the bank, where it lay, glittering with purple and gold in the slanting sunbeams, the most splendid prize that Fibrenus had yielded for many a year to the angler's skill.

"My best fish," said Lucius, after looking at his captive in silent delight for a few seconds; "and, I strongly suspect, my last out of Fibrenus for many a day."

"Your last!" replied his young companion; "why your last? What is going to happen to you?"

"Happen to me! That I don't know: 'all these things lie upon the knees of the gods.' But I know that I have got to go out into the world. Arpinum is a dear old place, but one can't stay here all one's days. The farm is not enough to satisfy one; and besides, there is not really work enough for me. My father can manage it very well with his bailiff, and I must do something for myself. Do you know, Caius, sometimes I like the idea of going, and sometimes I hate it. At this moment I am envying you with all my heart. You will go back to school and have the jolliest time of it, the working for prizes, the games — I never knew how jolly these things were till I had left them behind me. And then you will come back here, and there will be the fishing, and the hare-hunting, and the harvest, and the vintage. Yes; just now I should like to be a boy again. Now you, I dare say, are almost ready to give one of your eyes to put on the man's gown,[1] and be, as people say, your own master. Well, it is a good thing, perhaps, that wishing has nothing to do with it. I can't go back, and you can't go forward — at least, as fast as you wish. The thing is to be content with what one has and where one is. Somehow or other I have a kind of presentiment that I shall hear something to-day about my future. Marcus Tullius — the great barrister at Rome, you know — has been

---

[1] At an age varying from fifteen to seventeen a Roman boy put on the plain white gown (*toga*), which was the dress of the citizens, leaving off the *prætexta*, or gown bordered with a purple stripe, which he had been accustomed to wear, as well as the round ornament of leather or metal (*bulla*) which had hung from his neck.

looking out for something for me, and he is expected home to-night, and may very well have something to tell me."

"Oh, don't you hope," eagerly cried the younger lad, "that it will be something to take you across the seas? Wouldn't you like a commission under Lucullus, and to get a cut at Mithradates, or to make a cruise against the pirates? Then there is always something going on in Gaul, and Spain, and in Africa against the blacks.   Oh ! it makes me mad to think that I shall be tied to those stupid books for two or three years yet.   It is all very well for you to preach to me about being content.   You were just as bad yourself six months ago, and now you do nothing but talk about 'happy school-days,' and 'the delight of being a boy again,' and such rubbish.   But promise me that if you hear of a chance you won't forget me.   Father would very likely take a year off my time.   You know Pompey was a soldier before he was sixteen."

The two companions had by this time reached the house of Lucius' father.

"Come in, Caius," said the elder lad, "and help us to eat the big trout."

"My dear Lucius, I should be delighted above all things, but it is impossible.   You know my dear mother.   By this time she is probably in the agonies of bereavement.   It is the same thing every time I go out.   She sends me away with her blessing ; and as she likes me to enjoy myself she is really cheerful for about an hour after I have started. Then she begins to be a little anxious.   Her fears increase as the sun goes down.   At sunset, if by any chance I have not yet returned, they become positive despair.   At this moment, I dare say, she is dismally reckoning up the cost of the wood and spices for burning me, and of putting the slaves into mourning, and of a neat little monument in the family burying-place with an appropriate inscription to the best of sons! No; I must go, or she will positively have given out the contract for my funeral. Farewell; and don't forget to look out for me."

"Farewell! I doubt whether I should not be doing you an ill turn by taking you away too soon from your books; but, depend upon it, I won't forget you."

Lucius found on entering his home that the preparations for the evening meal were far advanced. The great fish was duly admired; his tail-fin was cut off to serve as a witness of his size against the incredulity of future times — for anglers were even then the victims of the cruel suspicion which doubts the accuracy of their weights — and he was then consigned to the gridiron under the clever hands of Ofella, the old Sabine cook, a freewoman whose honest and skilful services the house of Marius had been fortunate enough to enjoy for many years past.

The apartment in which the household was collected was a long, low room, not unlike the kitchen of an old-fashioned English farmhouse. Hams and flitches of bacon hung from the rafters, and a great log of beech wood was burning cheerily in a large open fire-place. On the mantlepiece were quaint images of a highly antique appearance. These were the household gods, and were almost the only peculiar features of the room. A long table of polished oak ran down the middle of the room, its only ornament being a silver salt-cellar of considerable size, the old-fashioned shape of which showed that it was an ancient possession of the family. At this table the whole family sat down to the evening meal; the older slaves, among whom were two or three gray-headed men (for the elder Marius did not hold with Cato's cruel counsel to the farmer that he should sell his worn-out slaves), joined from time to time in the conversation of their masters. Smoking bowls of pease-porridge, a dish of young cabbages stewed in a savory gravy, huge loaves of rye and barley bread, with one of wheaten flour for the upper end of the table, and a cheese made from goat's milk, were the principal viands. There was also a knuckle of ham, which had already seen some service, and some salt fish. The trout made, as may be supposed, a welcome addition to the fare of the evening.

Lucius, who had commonly all the healthy appetite of youth, sharpened by exercise, could hardly eat for excitement. His presentiment had been correct: he was to hear something of his future that day. "Marcus Tullius wishes to see you to-night," his father had said to him before they sat down to their meal. In the impatience of youth he was for starting off at once, but his father insisted on his taking some food. "Have your supper in peace," he said, "and let our friend have his."

The lad was content to obey, but he waited for the time to start with manifest impatience.

The house of the great advocate, to which he soon made his way, had evidently been in former times very much the same kind of dwelling as that which has been just described — a simple farmhouse; but it had had additions made to it as its owners grew richer and came to have more wants and more refined tastes. The room into which he was introduced by the young slave to whose guidance the porter at the outer door committed him, was evidently one of these additions. It was a handsome chamber, fitted up with book-cases on the three sides which were not occupied by the windows. Each book-case was surmounted by a marble bust of some philosopher or poet, while the spaces between them were occupied with pedestal statues of Mercury and Minerva.

In this room four persons were sitting when Lucius was announced. One of these was an old man with a remarkably pleasing and refined face, who sat by the fire reading a parchment roll, and occasionally making a remark to a lady who faced him on the opposite side of the hearth, and who was busy embroidering a little child's cloak. The lady was a handsome woman, somewhat fair in complexion for an Italian, of five-and-twenty or thereabouts, simply dressed in a matron's robe of white, reaching to her feet, and confined at her waist by a crimson girdle. Her hair, which was abundant and of a rich chestnut color, was fastened in a Greek knot, through which a silver arrow was run. Two silver bracelets on her left arm, and two or three rings, one of which contained a particularly fine sapphire, were her only ornaments. Marcus Tullius himself, whom our readers will recognize by the more familiar name of Cicero, was walking up and down the room, dictating to a secretary, who sat busily writing at a table. He was a man of about four-and-thirty, slightly above the middle height, spare in figure, with a long, rather sallow face, generally somewhat grave in expression, but able to light up occasionally with

a pleasant smile. On hearing the slave announce Lucius'
name he suspended his dictation, and came forward with a
frank and hearty greeting.

"Welcome, my dear Lucius. I made sure that we should
have you here directly. I got home last night for my
holiday. You have not left school so long as to have forgotten that these are Minerva's Five Days.[1] The good people at Rome are busy with the shows, which, I own, are
not very much to my taste. So I have stolen away for a
breath of country air, and I don't know where one can get
this fresher than at Arpinum. But I can't get quite quit
of work, and am busy revising my last speech for the
booksellers."

Then turning to his secretary :

"That will do for the present, Tiro. Read it over and
mark anything that does not seem to you to run quite
smoothly. And now for your business, my dear boy. You
will remember, I dare say, that I was in Sicily two or three
years ago. I was quæstor there in the western division of
the island, and I think I may say, without flattering myself,
did pretty well. Now, my friend Manilius is just about
starting to take up the very same office, and he wants some
one to help him. I thought of you at once. You will not
be a mere clerk, you understand, though you will, of course,
have to do a good deal of clerk's work. You will live with
the quæstor, go with him on his journeys, and be in fact a
sort of aide-de-camp to him. It is a kind of work that
will give you a great insight into how things are managed

---

[1] Minerva, the patroness of learning, had a feast of five days (March 19–23)
which was always kept as a school holiday.

in the provinces; and you could not be under a kinder, more good-natured man than Manilius. Don't be vexed," added the speaker, fancying that he noticed a shade of disappointment on the lad's face, "that it is not a bit of soldiering I am sending you to. That will come soon enough. A Roman is not likely to suffer for want of fighting. But to learn something about business is a chance that does not come every day. It is much easier, though you may not think it, to conquer a province than to govern it. No one can blame Rome for the way in which she has done the first business; but the second — that is another affair altogether. And this reminds me of something I want to say to you. I don't hear altogether good reports of what is going on in Sicily just now. I must not prejudice you against any one; but still I must put you on your guard. You have but just ceased to be a boy here, but there you will have a man's work. You will have some power, and the people in Sicily will fancy that you have a great deal more than is really the fact. They will always be wanting you to speak a word in your chief's ear, and will be ready with their bribes. Whatever you do, keep your hands clean. You come of a race that never cared for money, and you will not disgrace it. And there is another thing for you to remember. They are poor creatures, many of these Sicilians. In their best days they were always falling out of the hands of one tyrant into those of another, and they are very little better than slaves now. But remember that they are Greeks; their ancestors were educated gentlemen when ours were little better than barbarians. Almost every scrap in our literature that is worth having comes from them. Remember this, and try not to despise them. And now about your journey. The quæstor is going by land as far as Laüs in Lucania. There he takes ship. It is a choice of evils, you know. There is Spartacus with his gladiators on the land, and there are the pirates on the sea. You see, my boy, you have got a fair chance of adventures. Spartacus, however, is at present at Thurii, and I should think that you may easily get as far as Laüs without being troubled by him. However, the quæstor has business in the South that must be attended to, and he has made up his mind. The voyage from there to Messina is not a long one, and as safe, I fancy, as any voyage is nowadays. He starts from Rome to-morrow, so it will be of no use your going there. You must join him at Capua, where he is to stay till the 5th of April. And now good-night. Come and see me again while I am here, which will be for four days more. But stay; here is a little keepsake and companion for you."

He went to one of the book-cases and took down a parchment roll, which he handed to Lucius. It was about eight inches long and five or six in diameter, and the page which he unrolled to exhibit to Lucius showed that it was covered with Greek writing, small and close, but exceedingly clear.

"There," he said, "is the best part of the equipment with which Alexander went out to conquer the world. You have heard, I dare say, that he always slept with the *Iliad* under his pillow. I know you love Homer, for the last time that I was here I overheard you reciting him to your young friend Caius Frentanus. You had been fishing in the Fibrenus, and I was in my reading-room on the island. And very well you gave it, I must tell you. It was Hector's speech to Polydamas. I never appreciated it so much before. You remember the lines :

> " ' His sword the brave man draws,
>   And owns no omen but his country's cause.' [1]

If you are not in too great hurry to get home I should like you to stay and hear a little translation I have made of the passage into our own language."

Lucius, who knew, as indeed did all his neighbors and friends, the great man's weakness for his own verses, professed himself of course anxious to hear. He listened to the translation, which, to tell the truth, was of not more than moderate merit, with deferential attention, and praised it possibly beyond the strict limits of truth. His admiration was certainly not so sincere as his gratitude for Cicero's kindness. This he expressed in the heartiest way. Then, after saying good-night to the elder Cicero, to Terentia, who kindly invited him to pay a special visit to her and to her daughter, his little playfellow Tullia, he made the best of his way home.

---

[1] The reader must suppose these lines (which are really from Pope's translation) were said in Greek.

CHAPTER II.

AN ADVENTURE.

LUCIUS did not fail to present himself on the day appointed at the residence of the Prefect of Capua. He was perhaps a little disappointed with the appearance and manner of his superior. The quæstor was a man of about thirty-two, sufficiently good-looking, but already somewhat unwieldy and corpulent, foppish in his dress, and with a drawling, affected voice, which was not a little irritating to any one who was compelled to listen to it. Just then he was full of the grievance of having to leave Rome at such an inconvenient time, and began at once to pour his griefs into the ears of his subordinate.

"It is perfectly monstrous," he said, "making one leave Rome in April! If it had been in December, now, it would have been different. I am told that Sicily is very pleasant and warm in winter, while Rome is so cold that one can hardly keep one's self alive. But now, at the very best time of the year, when it is neither too hot nor too cold, when all the best people are in town and there are entertainments every day, it is cruel to be banished in this way."

These complaints were repeated again and again at every

stage of the journey. Lucius was soon exceedingly weary of them, and was not much better pleased when the quæstor varied them with anecdotes about himself and his friends. According to his own showing there had never been a man so popular and so ill-treated.

" I should have been on the highroad to be consul," he would say, " if I had had my deserts. But there are some great people whom I didn't please; too independent, my dear lad, too original for them. If you want to get on you must be commonplace."

His talk, however, was not always so empty and conceited. He had lived among great people, and had seen great events; and though he did not really understand either the one or the other, the personal details which as an eye-witness he could sometimes give were often remarkably interesting. He had been a spectator of some of the most dreadful scenes of the civil wars, and he made his young hearer's blood run cold by describing how he had seen the market-place of Rome almost ankle-deep in blood, with human heads piled up in heaps against the walls of the houses. All his reminiscences, however, were not of so dismal a character. He had been a boy of ten when Lucius' great kinsman, Caius Marius, came back from his victory over the barbarians from beyond the Alps, and had had such a triumph as Rome had never seen before. Lucius was intensely interested in hearing all that he could recollect about it.

" I can see it all," he said, " as if it had happened yesterday. How the streets were crowded ! I remember my father saying that all Italy seemed to have emptied itself into them.   And what shouting !   And then the procession itself !   Of course it wasn't so splendid as some that have been seen.   The barbarians hadn't much gold and silver and jewels to make a great show ; but all that there was was so strange, it seemed as if it came from another world. There were the great wagons lumbering along, drawn by such oxen as never had been seen, with horns five feet long from root to tip.   And then the prisoners !   If the oxen were big, what were the men !   Our tallest Romans seemed children beside them.   One could not imagine how the sol- diers had managed to make a stand against them and actu- ally conquer them.   And they were as like to each other as so many brothers, all with yellow hair and ruddy faces, and eyes as blue as the sea.   The king was an absolute giant, nearly eight feet high.   I remember being almost afraid to look at him, and dreaming of him for weeks and weeks afterwards."

The quæstor had also much that was interesting to say about Marcus Tullius.   For the most part he was far too fashionable a person to show anything like enthusiasm ; but for Tullius he did seem to have a genuine admiration.

"Ah !" he said, "you people at Arpinum ought to be proud of your townsman.   You have never heard him speak?   Well, that is a real treat in store for you.   I don't care much in general for law or politics ; but I never miss a chance of hearing him.   He is absolutely irresistible. There is nothing that he won't talk you into believing. You may know that he has got no case ; but before he has done he makes every thing so plain and clear that you can't imagine how you ever thought otherwise."

For two or three days the travellers pursued their journey without interruption; but as they went farther south they found a general feeling of uneasiness along the road. At an inn which had been built just where a branch road turned off to Pæstum, the host, who had been much gratified by the quæstor's loudly-expressed appreciation of his fare, especially some fat beccaficos and a haunch of roebuck, was very emphatic in his warnings about the dangers which threatened all travellers in Southern Italy.

"My dear sir," he said, "be advised by me, if you don't want to fall into the hands of Spartacus. Since the spring began he has been on the move, and the roads are not safe. I had a couple of merchants here the other day, and they told me all about him. He does not seem such a bad sort of fellow, though he is a rebel. They were taken, it seems, on the road near Laüs, and of course gave themselves up for lost. But they got no harm after all. They were marched up to Thurii, where Spartacus and his men have been all the winter. The place, they said, was a wonderful scene, as much like a fair as a camp. People were thronging in from all the country to buy and sell, and the harbor was full of ships. You see, sir, these people have picked up a pretty lot of plunder from one place or another; for they have run over nearly the whole of the east side of Italy from north to south, and they are ready to sell what they have got very cheap. There are some capital bargains to be had there, I am told, and I can very well believe it. My friends the merchants made a very good business of their trip, even according to their own account, and one does not expect a trader to be quite correct when he gives you the credit side of his account. You see they had six mules' loads of arms with them, swords and daggers of the very best quality from Corsica and Spain, and these are just what Spartacus is always ready to buy. He gave them pretty well their own prices, and I don't suppose they spared him. And then they did a little business on their own account. They might have bought any amount of silver plate, but that wouldn't have suited them. You see pieces of plate can be recognized, and that would not have answered their purpose. They did buy a few gold cups for about half the price of the metal, as I understood, and had them melted down. But the chief business they did was in jewels and fine stuffs, linen and silks (the new textures, you know, that they bring now from the far East). They sold two of their mules, and came away with the others pretty well laden ; and if you will believe me, sir, they did not lose a pennyweight of goods or a penny's worth of money. And Spartacus gave them a safe-conduct too. If it had not been for that, they told me, they would have been taken half-a-dozen times or more upon their journey back."

"Well," said Manilius, " I don't particularly wish to make this gentleman's acquaintance. I have nothing to sell, you see, and I am in a hurry. But what would you advise, for I must get on, you understand ? I want, as I think you know, to make the best of my way to Sicily, and I should best like, for more reasons than one, to go as far as I can by land."

The landlord considered a while. " I have it. Wait here two or three days. I will answer for it you won't repent it, for I see that you are a gentleman who knows what is good. This will give you time to send a messenger on to the nearest camp, and to get an answer back. Varro the prætor has got a very fair force with him at Velia — two legions, I understand, and about as many more auxiliaries, encamped about thirty miles to the south from here ; and I did hear of his intending to march as far as Laüs. Well, if he does, you might go with him, and the rebels will think twice before they meddle with a force like that. Will that suit you ? "

" Exactly," answered the quæstor. " Laüs is the very place I want to go to. I have business of importance there which I should not like to neglect. That done I can take ship."

" Very good," said the landlord. " Then I will send off a messenger to the prætor, if you will write a few lines for him to carry. It is now about an hour to noon, and he will do the thirty miles, barring accidents, in five hours. Give him three hours to rest, and he will be back long before you are out of your beds to-morrow, for he is as active and long-winded a young fellow as ever I saw. You will see from the answer he brings back what you had best do. You can, if need be, by making an early start, reach the camp to-morrow. But if there is no need for hurry, I should strongly recommend you to stay."

The letter was written and the messenger despatched, with strict injunctions to lose no time upon the road. The man, a spare young fellow, whose legs seemed to have been developed out of all proportion to the rest of his body, started at a good round trot. He made indeed such excellent use of his time that he was back at the inn before dawn the next day. He brought a despatch addressed to the quæstor, which, as it was marked "urgent" on the outside, that official, not altogether to his liking, was roused to receive. It ran as follows : —

"*Marcus Terentius Varro to Tiberius Manilius Quæstor greeting.*

"*It will be very grateful to me to afford you the protection which you seek for your journey, and, if I may speak as a friend, to have your companionship. Know, therefore, that it is my intention to set out, if the auspices be favorable, at daybreak the day after to-morrow. It will be necessary that you should reach the camp to-morrow. If you can arrive in good time, which, indeed, is a thing to be desired for other reasons, the road being not altogether safe, you and your friend will, if it is pleasing to you, dine with me. Farewell.*

"*Given at my camp, at Velia, the tenth day of April.*"

The party started at early dawn. Two traders, who had business in towns farther south, had asked and received permission to join them, and the party numbered about twenty, the greater part of whom were, of course, slaves. All were armed. Though unable to resist any serious attacks from the rebels, if they should be unlucky enough to fall in with them, they might count on being safe from any chance marauders, bands of whom infested the country, making a profit out of its disturbed condition. As it turned out they met with no molestation. A number of ill-looking fellows, in parties of two or three, were hanging about the roads, who probably would have robbed and murdered a single traveller, but felt it prudent to have nothing to do with the quæstor and his well-equipped company.

The prætor's camp was reached about an hour before sunset; and Manilius found awaiting him a message from the general, renewing for him and his companion the invitation to dinner. They had just time to enjoy the luxury of a bath, and to change their clothes, when the dinner hour, which, for their accommodation, had been fixed unusually late, arrived. They found a numerous party assembled in the prætor's tent, a spacious erection which was used only on occasions when he gave an entertainment to his officers. Six tribunes and about twice as many centurions of the first rank were present, and the party was completed by two or three young men, none of them much older than our hero, friends or connections of the prætor, who lived in his quarters, and had much the same relation to him as an aide-de-camp in the present day has to the general to whom he is attached. The talk turned, of course, very much on the prospects of the war, and Lucius found that those who were best qualified to judge thought that it would be a serious matter. One of the youngsters, his tongue possibly loosened by copious draughts of the prætor's wine, began to talk in a loud and boastful tone of the short work which would be made with the rebels.

"I can't conceive," he said, "how it is that these fellows have been allowed to make head against us so long. It is a shame to think of a parcel of slaves beating consuls and their armies. Don't you think, sir, that we might do what I heard some fellows did with their slaves some hundreds of years ago? My tutor, who was a Greek, read the story to me out of one of his books, and I have never forgotten it; it seemed to me such a capital way of dealing with such rascals. I remember it was something of this kind. The masters had been away, fighting somewhere for years and years; and when they came back they found that their slaves had rebelled, and had taken possession of their houses and every thing else, and were encamped on the border of the country with a regular army, ready to fight. Well, they did fight; and the first day neither got much the better of it, and the masters saw that if they did win in the end there would not be many of them left, and of their slaves none at all. Well, sir, the story went on to say, they went out the next day, not with arms in their hands but with whips, and the slaves, as soon as ever they saw them, gave in and begged for mercy, the old habit was so strong. I vote we go out against these rascals with whips."

"My young friend," said the prætor, "that is a very good story, and I am very much obliged to you for telling it. But, depend upon it, we shall have to use our swords, and use them with all our might, against Spartacus and his peo-ple. You may call them slaves, and so in a sense they are; but there are few of them who were not born free. Sparta-cus himself was a Thracian shepherd, taken prisoner in some foray; and a number of the others have come to be what they are in just the same way. We pick out from our pris-oners of war the very best and strongest we can find for our gladiators, teach them all we can, make them as strong and brave and skilful as is possible; and now we find ourselves matched to fight them. I tell you, gentlemen, it is no trifle we have before us. Man for man these fellows are better than we are ; as brave, for they have been used to hold their lives in their hands ; and stronger, for they are all picked men ; and better swordsmen, for they have handled nothing else but the sword all their lives. We shall beat them in the end, but we sha'n't do it to-day or to-morrow."

The young Roman made no answer, though he whispered to Lucius, who was his neighbor, " The old fellow is rather a croaker ; but he is as good a soldier, they say, as there is — thirty campaigns, and pretty nearly as many wounds. He will tell you the story of them whenever he has had a cup more than usual, but commonly he is as modest as a girl about them. That cut over the left eye he got from Sertorius himself. You see he has lost the little finger of his left hand ; it was cut off by a Teuton at Raudium. Yes ; he has a right to talk ; but I don't see, for all that, why we should not make mincemeat of these ruffians a little quicker than he thinks."

Lucius was soon to see whether the old man or the young was in the right. The army moved, as had been arranged, early the next morning. The prætor marched with all the caution of a veteran who knew his business, and who did not despise his enemy ; but the line of march was one which it was not easy to reconnoitre. The first day and the second the progress of the army was unimpeded. Not a single enemy showed himself from morning to night ; and, consequently, though the vigilance of the commander was not relaxed, some of his subordinates began to grow a little careless. It was late in the afternoon of the third day that the advanced guard of the army, which was moving without scouts properly thrown out, found itself suddenly attacked.

A squadron of cavalry was in the extreme front of the line of march. Its commanding officer was unluckily ill, and was being carried in a litter; his next subordinate was ignorant and careless, and the men, who were not kept in hand as they should have been, and had been making free with the wine-casks of the farm where they had made their mid-day halt, were half asleep upon their horses. In a moment a body of two or three hundred men, which had been lying ambushed in a valley on the left side of the road, threw itself between the horsemen and the infantry which was following them. The squadron was left without orders, for the officer in command had lost his head, but the instinct of safety made them turn their horses' heads and try to regain their connection with the main body. They made a charge, but it was languid and spiritless, and made little impression upon the enemy. Only a few troopers, who happened to be particularly well horsed, or especially good swordsmen, cut their way through; the rest were either taken prisoners or killed. The alarm passed quickly along the whole line; a halt was immediately called; and as but little daylight was left, the prætor resolved to encamp for the night where he was, and to make his position as safe as he could. Such a camp as the nature of the ground allowed was hastily made, an hour's labor from the practised hands of the Roman soldiers rendering it sufficiently strong to resist any but a most determined attack. The night, however, was spent in the midst of continual alarm, and every one was glad when the light of the next day appeared. At first it seemed that the enemy had disappeared, and that their advance was not to be disputed. The prætor, who had now taken up his position with the van, moved cautiously forward, and had accomplished a march of about six miles by noon when the scouts came racing in from the front, with the news that a formidable body of the enemy were in posi tion about half a mile farther along the road. A few minutes brought the prætor in view of this force. The line of march was here crossed by a river, narrow but deep, and now swollen by the spring rains. There was a bridge across this stream, so strongly built of stone that the enemy had not been able to break it down, as they would probably have done had it been possible; but they had occupied it in force. The prætor's disposition was already made. Two squadrons of cavalry were in advance, with about an equal number of men carefully picked from the infantry among them; behind there was a number of catapults, and behind these again the main body of the legions. At an arranged signal from the prætor, who had foreseen an obstruction of this kind, the advanced force divided, making room for the action of the catapults. These poured a storm of stones and bullets upon the defenders of the bridge. The range had been carefully taken, and almost every missile took effect. A retreat, which was almost a flight, was the result, and before many moments had passed the bridge was clear. The cavalry took immediate advantage of the opportunity and charged, the infantry following them at the double. Before the enemy could rally, or could be joined by reenforcements from their main body, the passage was secured and a strong position established, protected by the catapults, which were now posted on the river bank on either side of the bridge. Meanwhile a ford had been discovered higher up the stream, a not very easy one certainly, and indeed almost dangerous, but still available for the cavalry and for the light-armed troops, and relieving the pressure on the narrow thoroughfare of the bridge. Rafts, too, were hastily constructed, and some of the Spanish auxiliaries attached to the legions made the passage in the way with which they were familiar in their own country, swimming across by the help of inflated skins. Early in the afternoon the whole of the fighting men had crossed, excepting the guard which protected the baggage, and the non-combatants. These could hardly be transported before nightfall. Orders had been issued that the men should take their midday meal as opportunity served. This had been easily done, many finding a convenient time while they were waiting for their turn to cross. The men, their strength thus recruited, and greatly inspirited by the brilliant success at the bridge, were eager to fight. It soon became evident that they were not to be disappointed. The enemy, whose numbers were roughly guessed to be about a third greater than the prætor's army, had made their dispositions for a battle, and were manifestly determined not to give way. The ground on the farther side of the river was such that there would be little room for strategy, and that the two armies would have a fair trial of strength. It rose gently to a height of about three hundred feet, with an incline which may have measured a mile in length. It was unenclosed and open, except for a few small copses scattered about it.

About three o'clock the legions began to move up the slope, the skirmishers being in front, and the cavalry moving along at a foot's pace on either wing. Lucius was of course eager to do his part, and begged the prætor to employ him in any way or at any place where he might be of use. The general answered with much good sense and kindness :

"My dear lad," he said, "you must be guided by me. It is your business to make the best of your way into Sicily. It is not your business to fight in South Italy. You have to help Tiberius Manilius the quæstor, and not Marcus Varro the prætor. I might order you to go to the rear and get out of the way of danger. But I won't. You might take it as an affront. But I do order you not to strike a blow if you can help it. I have got foot-soldiers and troopers enough to win the day if we are to win it, and one more would make no difference. Stay with me. I may make use of you as a messenger. If the need comes I sha'n't scruple to do it, for the work of the republic must be done somehow. Meanwhile stay with me, and be content with looking on. You shall see something, I promise you, worth seeing. My men are pretty good, and these fellows there are not to be disposed of in such a hurry as our young friend thought the other night. We have begun well. You see they were not prepared for the catapults. I fancy they have none themselves, and could not make much of them if they had. I only hope that we shall end as well as we have begun."

The battle had now fairly begun. The skirmishers had fallen back on the main body, which was now within a few yards of the enemy. The heavy javelins which the Romans carried were discharged with great effect, and the rebel line began to waver. But when the two opposing armies actually closed the advantage seemed to be the other way. The fact was that man for man, as the prætor had foreseen, the enemy were superior. Wherever the Romans could act in a body, could keep their military formation and advance in an unbroken line, their discipline and the power it gave them of acting together told heavily in their favor. Whenever, on the contrary, the battle became a series of hand-to-hand conflicts, they suffered severely. The ordinary foot-soldier, often fresh from the plough, was no match in strength, or stature, or skill in arms for the gladiator, always a practised swordsman, and often a giant in stature, with whom he was matched. On the whole, it was true, the ground favored the better-disciplined troops, and the Romans slowly advanced. The experienced eye of the prætor saw, however, that this advance was not made without serious losses, and, aware that his own forces were outnumbered, began to grow anxious for the result. Meanwhile he continued to follow the movement of his troops, directing, by messages conveyed by his aides-de-camp, the manœuvres of his subordinate officers. It was nearly sunset when an incident occurred that compelled him to use the services of Lucius. His quick eye discerned an admirable opportunity for throwing his cavalry, which hitherto had taken little part in the action, upon the left flank of the enemy.

"Ah!" he cried to Lucius in a cheerful voice, for he was one of the men whose spirits rise under the excitement of danger, "now is your time. I must use you, whether I will or no. Ride as fast as you can to Lucius Verus, prefect of the cavalry, and tell him to charge. He is to make his way up that hollow yonder on the left of the enemy. It will pretty well keep him out of sight till he is close upon them.

Then he is to charge and do his best. But, mind, you are
not to go with him. On your obedience now, promise."

Lucius started off at full speed and delivered his message.
He found the cavalry fretting at their inaction, and delighted
to receive the order to charge. The young aide-de-camp
whose vain self-confidence had been so severely reproved
by the prætor had been told off to do staff duty with the
prefect of cavalry, and recognized our hero.

"Ah!" he cried; "well met. Come along with us and
see what these fellows are made of."

"I must go back to the prætor. He strictly commanded
me not to charge, and I gave him my promise."

"Very good!" cried the other lightly; "and glad to
give it, I dare say. Farewell, then, till we meet again."

It was carelessly said, without much thought of the meaning which it might bear; but Lucius's blood boiled at what
seemed to him an intolerable insult. For a moment obedience and promise were forgotten. Then the old training
regained its power. He turned his horse's head away and
rode slowly back, tears of vexation and rage slowly running
down his cheeks as he went. From these bitter thoughts
he was roused by a sound which seemed to show that the
battle was coming nearer to the route which would take him
back to the prætor's side. A hasty glance showed him that
this was indeed the case. The left wing of the Roman
force had given way. A column of the enemy had broken
the front, and were now driving it back in something like
a rout. At the head of this column was a man of gigantic
stature, who, wielding a sword of enormous length and
weight, seemed to cut down a Roman at every stroke. His

followers were little inferior in strength or stature, and it was evident that a serious danger threatened at least a part of the prætor's army. Before Lucius could collect his thoughts he saw that his way of return was intercepted. It was not without a certain feeling of pleasure that he found himself free from his promise. His blood had been heated by the sight of fighting, and was now raised to boiling point, so to speak, by the young aide-de-camp's insult. He had now, it was clear, to defend himself, and he prepared to do so. But the fates had ordered that his time for fighting should be yet a while delayed. He had drawn his sword and was preparing to ride at the nearest of the enemy, when a heavy javelin struck his horse upon the ear. The animal, maddened by the blow, reared and struggled, and threw him heavily on the ground with a force which made him unconscious.

CHAPTER III.

SPARTACUS.

IT was late in the night when Lucius recovered his senses. He found himself in a large plainly furnished tent. A lad of about his own age sat by his side, more than half asleep. He roused, however, when the patient whom he had been set to watch moved on his couch and attempted to sit up.

"Hush!" he said, putting his finger to his lips, and gently preventing the young Roman from rising. "You are not to speak or move. These are the general's orders, and no one thinks of disobeying him. If you are thirsty you may have a draught of milk, and then you must go to sleep again as fast as you can."

Lucius was ready enough to do as he was told. He was weak and giddy, and was almost surprised to find how little he seemed to himself to care what had happened to him or where he was. While he was lazily guessing at the answers to these questions, and trying to bring back the last thing he could remember before his senses left him, he fell asleep again. When he next woke it was about an hour after sunrise. The lad who had spoken to him the night before, now wide awake, was still at his side.

"Tell me," said Lucius, "where I am and how I came to be here. I remember getting a terribly hard knock on the ground, and after that nothing."

"Hush!" said the boy; "you shall hear every thing when the general comes. And here he is."

As the words were spoken the giant of the battle of the day before pushed aside the curtain that hung over the entrance to the door, and entered, followed closely by a little gray-haired man, whose short spare figure was in curious contrast to his companion's huge frame. The little man was evidently a physician. He stepped up to the side of the couch, felt the patient's pulse, looked at his tongue, and asked the young attendant how he had slept.

"I warrant he has done pretty well in that way," he went on without waiting for an answer; "or we should not find you, my young friend, looking quite so rosy and fresh this morning. He has slept well, I am sure, and you not so badly. Well, sir," he said, turning to his companion, "I shall not have to bleed him, and he will get better all the quicker. Give him as much milk and bread as he fancies, and, if he cares for them, a bunch of raisins, but for the present no flesh or wine. And when he has had something to eat and drink, you may tell him what you want to say, but, remember, not before."

Lucius, who felt little inconvenience from his tumble beyond bruises and a general stiffness, and who was by this time exceedingly hungry, enjoyed with the heartiest appetite the jug-of goat's milk and the loaf of coarse brown bread which, together with a bunch of raisins, were now put before him. As he was eating his meal, soldiers continued to enter the tent, and, after respectfully saluting the giant, to deliver some message with which they had been intrusted, to receive their orders, and to depart. It was evident that the giant was a person of consequence, and Lucius, recollecting the descriptions which he had heard of Spartacus' remarkable stature and great personal strength, had no difficulty in concluding that he was in the company of the rebel general himself.

Spartacus meanwhile, for Lucius was right in his guess, watched the young Roman disposing of his bread and milk. with something of a kindly smile upon his face. When the meal was finished he spoke, his accent and language being surprisingly refined.

"Now, young sir, we may talk without disobeying the good physician's orders. Doubtless there will be one or two things which you will be anxious to know. First about the battle; well, it was drawn; perhaps your friends will say they won. Certainly they made their way past us; there is no denying that. But then they left fully twice as many dead on the field as we did. So we will call it drawn. And now as to yourself. You were thrown from your horse. Perhaps you remember that. And then you were taken prisoner. But don't be uneasy. An exchange has been arranged. Three or four of my officers were taken; and we, on the other hand, laid our hands on seven or eight of yours. About nightfall there came a messenger with a flag of truce from the prætor, who, by the way, is as good a soldier as I have ever met, inquiring after you and the others. I did not stand out for terms, and, to tell the truth, I didn't want prisoners myself, and I did want the men that your people had taken; so the matter was soon settled. I have just got my officers back, and your companions are gone, and you shall go after them as soon as you are fit. But the physician says that you must not travel for a day or two. Meanwhile, I will treat you as hospitably as I can, if you can put up with the hospitality of a slave."

These last words were added with some bitterness of tone. Lucius replied with the frank and engaging smile which was one of his chief charms, "I have heard too much of Spartacus not to be proud to be his guest."

"Well, then," said the general, "you will amuse yourself as best you can till dinner-time, when we shall meet again. I, as you may suppose, have plenty to do, and must ask you to excuse me. You can take a little stroll if you feel strong enough, but don't go far from the tent. The physician would not approve, and perhaps there are other reasons."

Lucius, interested as he was at thus meeting with one of whom he had heard so much, was at first disposed to grumble at being detained. But when he attempted to rise he found that he was weaker than he had thought, and he was glad to stop and rest himself more than once during the process of dressing. This at last accomplished, he made his way out of the tent, supported by his attendant of the night before. There was a considerable open space in front, which seemed to be used as a sort of playground by the soldiers, and Lucius watched them with interest as they wrestled, jumped, and ran foot-races. He was struck, when he remembered that there was scarcely a man of the whole number but had been a slave, with the good order which prevailed. The good humor, too, of the contending parties was remarkable. Not an oath or angry word was to be heard, and the young Roman could not but feel that the rebels set an example which the camp which he had just left might profitably have followed. Shortly after noon he received another visit from the little physician, who prescribed another light meal, but promised him, if he would give a pledge to be moderate, somewhat better fare at dinner. About four o'clock in the afternoon the attendant conducted him to a bath tent, which was simply but comfortably furnished. The bath was followed by a short sleep. A little before sunset he was summoned to dinner. The meal was of the simplest kind. There was a soup of the kind which would now be called hotch-potch, two or three kinds of vegetables, and a roast pullet. There was a flask of wine upon the table, but Spartacus himself drank nothing but water. No other guests were present, and all the waiting was done by the lad whom Lucius had found watching by his bed the night before.

"I thought it best to be alone," said the host. "To tell you the truth, though I have some excellent officers they are not exactly the guests whom you would care to meet. I wanted too to speak to you. You are younger than any of the prisoners who have hitherto come into my hands, and perhaps have not yet learnt to think that there can be no good in a man who ventures to say *No* when Rome says *Yes*. Something too in your look makes me feel that I may be frank with you. You shall hear my story, and possibly some day you may speak a good word for me. In one way it won't matter to me, for I shall be gone. Yet I should like there to be some who will believe that I was not a mere robber. Well, you shall hear and judge.

"I was a shepherd, as my father and my grandfather had been before me. I worked on a big farm near Byzantium, as they had done in their time, and should have been content, I dare say, to go on in the same way to the end of my days. Well, my master — he was a Greek by descent — was ruined. How it came about I never rightly understood To tell you the truth, I thought little in those days except about boxing and wrestling and such things, for as far as these were concerned there was no one to beat me in the whole country-side. I remember hearing something about taxes not being paid; I can only say that my master was an honest man if ever there was one; and I should not like to say as much for the Roman — for it was a Roman — who got possession of the farm after him. Well, I did not care to take service with the new man. Few of us did. So then there was a choice before me; I might become a robber or I might enlist. Most of us chose the first. People at Rome wonder, I dare say, at the number of robbers there are in the provinces. This is the way in which they are made. Here were some eight honest men, men who had worked for their bread all their lives, turned adrift; and more than half of them took to the hills. And that sort of thing is going on, believe me, nearly all over the world. I have talked with men from all parts since I have been in command here, and I have heard the same story over and over again. If I were to go out into the camp here and bring in the first man that I found, you would probably say that he was a scoundrel, and perhaps you would not be far wrong. But then he could tell you such a story of what has made him a scoundrel that you would begin to think there was something wrong somewhere. Well, to come back to myself. I became a soldier. It was just a dog's life. You see, I was not a citizen of any kind, but, as they were pleased to say, a simple barbarian. So I had no rights, it seemed. I put up with it as long as I could, but there is an end to all things, even to a soldier's patience, which has indeed to be pretty long. One day an officer struck me with his stick. He had been drinking, and chose to think that because he was too confused to manœuvre the cohort it was my comrades' fault and mine. It made it all the worse to bear, that he was a little fellow who did not nearly come up to my shoulder, and whom I could almost have blown away with a breath, let alone using my hands. I felt as if I could have killed him, but I didn't. I just took him up and dropped him into the river, and then when he was half drowned dragged him out again. Of course I was arrested. They would have killed me, but you see I was the show soldier of the legion, the biggest and strongest man in it, and when they had their games used to carry off most of the prizes. So I was to be flogged. That I was not going to put up with; so before the time came I ran away. So it came to the first choice after all; I had to be a robber, for there was literally nothing else for me to do. Of course we called ourselves patriots, and we also preferred to rob a Roman or a Greek rather than a native Thracian, and a rich man rather than a poor man. I see you smile. It wasn't only because we got good plunder out of the one and little but hard knocks from the other. We preferred to set things right, to take away from the rich to give to the poor, and so forth. And we tried to do it, but it didn't always work quite right. We had to live, you see, and sometimes, as, for instance, in the depth of winter, there was very little doing. We were obliged then to live upon the poor. We had to make them give up their corn, and we took their sheep. And we had always to keep them in terror of us. If a peasant seemed to be any thing like friends with the soldiers, he had to have a pretty sharp warning, have his house burnt over his head, for instance, some night, if he did not have a dagger in his heart. Of course there were some who did try to make their market both out of the soldiers and out of us. And after about two years of it, when, to tell you the truth, I was getting pretty well tired of the life, one of these fellows trapped me and sold me. He sent a little lad one day up to a hold we had in the hills, with a message that a party of traders would be going past his house in the afternoon with a load that would be worth taking, and that we were to lie in wait in a place that he told us of. We need only send a small party, he said, for it would be an easy job. Well, the party of traders was really a party of soldiers, who had their armor and their swords and so forth under their long cloaks. And the scoundrel had hidden another party of men in his house. He *was* a scoundrel, sir, for we had paid him well for every thing we ever had from him; only he thought that our game must be up sooner or later, and that he had better make his market while he could. Well, *he* got no good out of it, for I had the pleasure of cleaving his head open with the last blow that I struck before I was taken. Taken we all were ; we might have got away from the first party, but the others took us in the rear, and we were fairly trapped. Well, of course I looked for nothing but the cross. A deserter and a robber could hope for nothing else. But it wasn't to be. Just then there was a special demand for gladiators ; a good many are always wanted, but this was something out of the common. I suppose some fine gentleman at Rome who wanted to get himself into office and hadn't done much to get a name was going to give a very splendid show — tigers fighting against lions, and bears against panthers, and of course men against men, two or three hundred pairs, I dare say, it might have been. The men, sir, are what really please. I have the best reasons for knowing it. The people will cheer a fine lion or a tiger, but their silence, their dead breathless silence, with their eyes fixed and their teeth set, when they see a man's life on the turn of the wheel, that shows what they really care for. I have watched them over and over again, for I was at the trade myself, as you shall presently hear, for a couple of years and more. Well, as I have said, there was just then a particularly great demand for gladiators, and word had been sent to the governors in the good provinces to be on the lookout and get all they could. By the *good* provinces I mean the provinces from which they get their supply — Gaul, and Spain, and Thrace. They like men from Europe, you see. Our fencing-master used to say that the fellows from Asia were hardly worth the carriage, though he did allow that he got some stout fellows from Africa. So it came to pass that I had the choice, death on the cross or to be a gladiator.

Well, life is sweet, even to a slave, and I chose life. Again
and again I have cursed the hour when I did it. Two or
three days' pain, — yes, sir, you look surprised, but it lasts
as much as three days sometimes, especially with a stout
fellow like me, — and it would have been all over ; as it is,
what I have suffered no one knows. Well, I was taken to
Rome and set to learn my trade. There were some seventy
or eighty of us, and we were trained and taught like so
many schoolboys. There were teachers for the beginners,
and the great man himself, the master of the school, for
they called it a school, gave us the finishing lessons. I was
a pretty apt pupil, I fancy, and had learnt nearly all he had
to teach in three months' time. Well, there was another
man in the same school that I made great friends with. I
was a fool to do it ; a slave should never love, he is sure to
break his heart if he does ; he should have neither friend
nor wife. But he can't help having a heart, and I was
young, and, as I said, a fool. My friend was as unlike me
as a man could be. Like to like, they say, but it often goes
by contraries in friendship, I find. He was a slim fellow,
tall as men go, but about a head shorter than I am, with
yellow hair and blue eyes, and cheeks like a rose, as fair as
a woman and as beautiful as a god. He came, I found,
from somewhere in Gaul, from near a great river there is
there that they call the Rhine. He was the very nimblest
and most active fellow that ever I saw in my life ; and we
two were the old master's chief favorites. Well, by great
good luck we were both in the same set. You know they
have different kinds of gladiators. One will have a net and
a thing with three prongs that they call a trident, and an-

other will have a shield and a sword, and so forth. They
don't commonly put two of the same set to fight together;
it amuses the people better to match one kind of arm against
another. We two friends then were in the same set, and
we never were beaten; he, as I have said, was as nimble as
a deer, and you wouldn't easily find my match for strength.
So there was nothing, you see, to hinder us from being
friends, and we began to hope that we should both get out
of that accursed school alive, and that is not a thing, I
assure you, that many do. How we used to talk over what
we would do if only we could get away! I was to go back
with him to his own country. You see I could scarcely say
I had a country of my own to go to. And we were to hunt
bears and wild boars and stags, bigger, he said, than were
ever to be seen in the south. And I was to marry his sister,
that was one of his dreams, poor dear fellow. He had left
her a girl of seven or eight some eight years before, and he
was never tired of telling me how beautiful and how clever
she was. They make much of their women in those parts,
I could see from what he told me. Well, one day there
was a very splendid show, for some great man's funeral I
think it was. Anyhow no expense was spared, and every
thing was to be of the best. But it happened, by bad luck,
that the supply of gladiators fell short. We two, as usual,
had had it all our own way. Each of us had fought two or
three times and had beaten our men. The time wasn't up,
and the people hadn't had their fill of blood. And so some
evil demon put it into the mind of some one of the crowd
to cry out 'Spartacus and Arminius' (that was what they
called him — his real name was Hermann). And in a mo-

ment all the theatre took up the shout. You see they wanted to pit us against each other. Neither of us had ever been beaten, and they thought it would be a rare piece of sport to see which would be the better man. Of course we hated to do it, but it had to be done. And there was reason to hope, too, that it might not end so very badly after all. We were both as good swordsmen as there were in Rome — perhaps better than any — and it would not be difficult to make a pretty play of fighting that would amuse the crowd without either doing the other any harm, and that is what we tried to do. You would have thought that we were fighting for our lives, for we struck and parried till the whole place rang again. It did well enough for a time, but then the people want blood. Pretty sword-play amuses them for a while, but it doesn't satisfy them. So they began to shout 'They are mocking us;' and I knew, and so, I saw, did Hermann, that it would be dangerous to go on any longer in that way. But what was to be done? Well, if one of us could get a wound that would be enough to put an end to the fight, but not enough to be dangerous; we might both escape. I say 'might,' for it wasn't certain even then. You have heard, I dare say, that when a man is wounded it rests with the people to say whether he is to die or not. But we hadn't much fear on this score. We were both favorites from having been champions so long. But who was to have the wound? who to give it? We daren't speak to each other. Every one was watching us, and there was a silence like as of death over the whole place. But we looked at each other, and if ever I read any thing in a man's eye I saw in his 'Let me have the wound,' and I am sure that I put into mine 'Let me have it.' Well, we stood a few minutes taking breath. Then we set to again. I knew what I meant to do, and I guessed pretty well what he meant; we had both of us the same thought. It was to slip, as it were, by accident, and wound himself on the other's sword. But you see it had to be done without letting any one see that it was done on purpose. Well, he managed it more cleverly than I; he was quicker and nimbler than I was by a long way. He contrived that we should get to a place where the sand was covered very thinly over the blood in a place where a man had bled to death — a young Spaniard he was; it was his first battle. I remember him well, and I remember how those gentry in the seats laughed when he tried to hold the wound together with his hands. Well, Hermann slipped in the blood in the most natural way in the world, so that my sword ripped an ugly-looking wound in his side before I was aware. But though it was ugly-looking it wasn't a really bad wound, and I thought it was well over. But — by all the gods it makes me mad when I think of it — it was all wrong. What made the people so savage that day I don't know. Any trifle will do it. I have seen days when they would spare nobody, not the best fighter in the school, and days when any bungler would escape. Perhaps it was the weather; there was a bitter wind blowing, and these Italians hate being cold above every thing. But whatever it was, when I looked up, expecting of course only to have to sheathe my sword and make my bow, I saw all their thumbs pointed towards poor Hermann — that is the way they have of saying 'Kill him.' If they want to keep him alive they turn them down. **I** had to kill him; yes, sir, kill my friend, my brother. I threw my sword on the ground, and there went up a roar, like as of so many wild beasts, round the theatre. Hermann heard it and said, 'You must do it. Kill me. I would sooner die by your hand than by any other man's. And if *you* don't kill me they will butcher us both. Give me the stroke, dear Spartacus, give it, and, if you will, avenge me afterwards.' And I did it, sir; yes, I killed him."

As Spartacus spoke these last words his emotion, which had been increasing for some time, entirely overpowered him. He started up from his seat, and threw himself on the ground, while his huge frame was shaken with convulsive sobs. Lucius watched him with something like terror. After a while he grew calmer and resumed his story.

"Young man, I sometimes wonder that after that day I ever remembered what mercy meant. Think what it was. You may have to kill an enemy; you may kill a friend who has turned enemy; but to kill a friend whom you love — The gods, if there are gods, which I sometimes doubt, or if they have any concern with a world in which such things can happen, the gods cleanse me of that blood! In a way, I know, he killed himself, for he took hold of my sword and drove it, pulled it, I should rather say, into his own breast. Well, that was all over; and the crowd shouted, and threw flowers to me, and couldn't make enough of me. Oh! how I longed that the earth would swallow them up — them, and me, and all the accursed city with us.

"From that day I thought of nothing but vengeance. The first thing to be done was to escape. Before long there came a new batch of learners to the school, and there were some among them whom, by carefully sounding them, I found to be bold and determined fellows. We laid a plot, but were very careful whom we let into the secret. Before long came the opportunity. There was to be a show at Capua, and some five hundred of us were marched off there to make sport for the provincials. Seventy of us broke away from our guards, who were very weak, and made for Mount Vesuvius. There is a large hollow on the top which makes a famous place for our encampment. Italy is a place, where, if you have a carcass, you will pretty soon have the eagles, or vultures, or whatever you will, gathered together; all sorts of recruits came flocking into my camp. There were men who had been sold for slaves when the provincials had been finally beaten by Rome — men of as good birth, some of them, as any noble of the Romans, who had been working in farm-gangs or in mines; ay, and there were Romans, too, who had lost their all, some of the conquered in the civil war, who had had every thing taken from them, and some of the conquerors who had spent all their plunder; and there were slaves without number. All that I had to do was to choose. Well, sir, I needn't tell you the story of my wars; most likely you know it. But I will tell you one thing: it is not of my own free will that I am here. When I was in Northern Italy, and had my way clear, as I had after beating the consul Lentulus in Picenum, I wanted to get across the Alps and let my men disperse to their homes. Some of them were willing enough, the Gauls and Spaniards and Germans among us; but the majority were against it. Some of them had no homes to go to, and a good many did not like to leave Italy. So they compelled me to come down south again, — yes, compelled me; I am only half master, you see. I can keep discipline; there is no more quiet camp than this in the world; no single man dare set himself up against me, but I can't control the whole. Well, they loved the vineyards, and cornfields, and gardens, and all the pleasantness of Italy, and made me come here. I know what the end will be; I am not fool enough to suppose that in the long-run we can win, and that is why I wanted to give those that I really cared for, the true gladiators, not these vagabond adventurers who call themselves such, a chance of escape. Sooner or later you must crush us. But we shall want a pretty strong net to hold us; and the dogs, and the hunters too, for the matter of that, will have one or two deep bites to remember us by. But caught, sooner or later, we shall be. For myself I don't care. I wouldn't ask to live, now Hermann is dead. If you could put me where we often talked of being, by his father's cottage on the Rhine, could I show myself there with his blood upon my hands? No; my days are numbered; and to die like a soldier is all I ask, and that is a prayer that a man can answer for himself. But I should like to know that there is some deliverance for these poor creatures. When will it come?"

"One of the greatest men in Rome," answered Lucius, "says that he hates these shows."

"Does he!" said Spartacus; "then I honor him. Well, it will come some day. Meanwhile do you remember my story; and now it is time for you to sleep."

CHAPTER IV.

PHILARETÉ.

AFTER two more days of rest Lucius felt his strength perfectly restored, and was ready for the start, which it had been arranged that he should make on the following morning. He continued, of course, to be the guest of Spartacus, and was charmed with the ex-gladiator's courtesy, good sense, and good feeling. He was just about to take leave of his host on the night before his departure, when a message reached the general, informing him that some prisoners had just been brought into the camp. Spartacus left the tent to inquire into the matter, and in the course of about half an hour returned, followed by the party. It was evident that he was disturbed and perplexed in no common degree.

The captured party consisted of two women and a man. The younger of the two women was a girl who might have numbered about sixteen years. (She was really, as Lucius afterwards found, about a year younger.) Her dress, simply made and without ornament, but of the richest materials, her tall and graceful figure, and her noble bearing, showed that she was rich and well-born. Her beauty was remarkable. Her face was of the purest Greek type, save that the

line of the nose and forehead was not quite as straight as
might sometimes be seen. No one, however, would have
hinted a fault in the delicate curve, from which an outline
that might otherwise have seemed too severe gained a certain softness. The cheek was exquisitely rounded, though
it still kept something of the fulness of childhood. The
mouth was small, with a certain firmness about the lips
which would have made a sculptor feel that she would have
suited better as a model for a Diana than for a Venus.
Her hair was tied in the usual Grecian knot, but her hasty
journey had somewhat disarranged it, and a lock dropped
over the collar of her purple mantle, against which it made,
with its rich golden brown, an exquisite contrast. Her
agitation as she stood, the object of all eyes, was evidently
great, but it was caused, one might guess, as much by anger
as by fear. Her bosom, which had a girlish delicacy of
outline, rose and fell quickly, and her face was pale ; but
her eyes, which were blue and clear as sapphires, were fixed
unflinchingly on the general's face, and were full of an angry
light. Her companion was a stout, middle-aged woman,
apparently an upper attendant. She was almost senseless
with terror, and swayed herself helplessly backward and
forward — a motion which she only interrupted from time
to time to wring her hands. The man appeared to be of
the same rank and of about the same age as the older
woman. He was, in fact, her husband.

"Lady," said Spartacus in a kind and gentle voice, "will
you tell me your name?"

"I am Philareté, daughter of Theron, a citizen of
Tarentum."

"You were ill-advised to travel in this country except with an army for escort; and even then I do not know that you would have been quite safe."

"So they told me, but I could not choose but go."

"Why so, lady, if I may ask?"

"How could I stay when my father was ill, perhaps dying?"

"The gods reward you for your piety, my daughter! Meanwhile," he added in a low voice, "I wish one of them would condescend to give me a hint of what I am to do."

He marched up and down the tent several times with huge strides, biting his nails and muttering to himself. The girl's courage never seemed to falter for a moment. As for the older woman, she had sunk in a shapeless mass upon the ground. The man stood as he had done from the beginning, in stolid silence, his eyes fixed upon the girl.

Spartacus spoke again. His voice was now harsh and rough, not, as it seemed to Lucius, because he was angry, but because he felt an agitation which he could not conceal. "You cannot stay here. I cannot have women in my camp; much less such women as you. But how are you to go? I cannot send an escort with you, and you cannot go alone. Stay — I have it; if you have the courage of your looks there is a way. You must change your sex for the time. There is a lad here of about your height. His clothes will suit you to a nicety, and you must condescend to dress yourself up in them; and here is your escort," he went on, pointing to Lucius. "By the greatest good fortune in the world here is a Roman citizen, an exchanged prisoner who was going to leave the camp to-night or to-morrow morning under a safe-conduct. The lad of whom I spoke was to have gone with him as a guide. You must take the guide's place. These two, your attendants I suppose, must stay. There will be no trouble about them. What say you, lady?"

The girl was silent for a moment. Her bearing had greatly changed while Spartacus was speaking. The proud eyes were drooped to the ground; the pale cheek was crimson with shame. She cast a look, half inquiring, half imploring, at Spartacus and the young Roman. Something in their looks seemed to re-assure her. "I will do it," she said; "perhaps, if the gods are kind, I may see my father again."

"There is no time to be lost. Make yourself ready as quickly as a woman can. But I must first get you your clothes."

He stepped to the door of the tent and called, "Cleon." When the lad appeared he gave him some whispered directions, adding in a louder voice: "Be silent as the grave; you know that I do not speak in vain."

Cleon left the tent, and speedily re-appeared carrying a bundle of clothing in his hand. This Spartacus handed to the girl, pointing as he did so to one of the sleeping compartments of the tent. When she was gone Spartacus turned to the young Roman: "I will go with you to the camp gate and see you safely out, and I will give you a safe-conduct which will take you past my outposts or any out-lying bands that may belong to my army. But you have others to think of. There is always a fringe of rascals hanging on to any business of this kind. There are fellows whom I have turned out of my army, and there are fellows who have never been in it, and they both use my name for their own villanous purposes. They rob and ravish and murder, and of course it is all put down to my account. Well, you'll have to reckon with these. You may escape them altogether; you are more likely to fall in with some of them. Get out of their way if you can; if you can't, I won't say to a Roman, Do not be afraid of them; but I say, Be hopeful. They are mostly great cowards, and happily they seldom go about in more than twos and threes. You told me, I think, that you were a pretty fair swordsman. Very good; that will serve you in good stead. Take this sword with you. You can use it or your own, as you think fit, though mine, I think, is a handier weapon. In any case it will be of no harm to have a spare one at hand. One hears of the things breaking just when they are most wanted; mine, I will warrant, will not break. I had it from a man who had been with Sertorius, and it is made from the very best Spanish iron. See now how splendidly tempered it is."

He took it and bent it round his neck till the point touched the hilt.

"And take this," he went on, giving Lucius a dagger. "If some fellow does get you down somehow, you will find this useful. And now sit down and write the safe-conduct, for, as you may guess, writing is not one of my arts."

Lucius accordingly sat down and wrote at the general's dictation:

"*Spartacus, Commander-in-Chief of the Army of Freedom, to all whom it may concern.*

" You will take notice by this that you are to pass on, assist, and succor, Lucius Marius, a Roman prisoner duly exchanged, who bears this letter, and Theron, one of my servants, who is acting as his guide."

The general then dipped his signet-ring in the ink and marked the document.

Philareté by this time had finished her toilet, and appeared in the main tent ready equipped for her journey. She wore a tight-fitting tunic, girded at the waist with a leathern belt. Happily for her purpose it had long sleeves adapting it for the use of a wearer who might be exposed to weather. This had made it easier for her to retain her own under tunic, the superfluous length of which she had contrived to conceal by deftly fastening it up over her shoulder. She wore a short cloak of some woollen material. Long riding-boots, which would have been inconveniently large had it been necessary for her to walk, completed her costume. The two men stood dumb with astonishment, so complete was the transformation. Who was this slim handsome youth that stood before them? The girl's spirits had risen when she had boldly faced the inevitable. She said to Spartacus, with the first approach to a smile that had been yet seen on her features:

"And how will this do?—But I must first ask you to do the barber's office for me."

As she spoke she drew out of the knot into which her hair was gathered the golden arrow which kept it together. "Give this," she said, "to poor Theron, whose clothes I am taking so unscrupulously. He will think mine a poor exchange, but this perhaps will help to recompense him."

As she spoke the mass of her hair fell, a wealth of rippling tresses, far below her waist, its golden hue glistening in the light of the lamp which hung from the roof of the tent. Lucius thought as he looked that he had never seen any thing so beautiful, and something seemed to whisper in his heart that this was an eventful day in his life. It was just upon his lips to say, " How monstrous to spoil such hair ! " when Spartacus, who felt that there was no time for senti- ment, stepped forward with a pair of shears, and with a touch that was gentle though decided shortened the beauti- ful tresses to such a length as a somewhat foppish young lad might wear. " There is one thing still to be done. You are too fair, lady, for the character you are to play. We must tone down this too brilliant hue."

He took a little flask containing a brown dye from a little receptacle of various articles of disguise ; for disguise was an art in which the spies of Spartacus were particularly ex- pert. A little of this applied with a napkin to the girl's face, neck, and hands still further completed her disguise.

" And yet another touch," said the general with a smile. " Theron has a budding growth on his upper lip of which he is not a little proud. A little charcoal will imitate it passably well — at least while it is dark ; and it is only here, till you get out of the camp and beyond the outposts, where he is likely to be known as my servant, that you will need it."

The girl applied the charcoal, readily supplied for the emergency by a burnt stick from the fire, with skilful fingers. She had now regained her spirits and almost her gayety. Nature had given her, as an inheritance, it may well be, from past generations, a singularly fearless temper; and this perilous adventure began to seem to her more and more like a frolic.

"Do I satisfy you now?" she said with a playful salutation to Spartacus.

"Yes; we can do no more. And now not a moment must be lost; the farther you can get from the camp before it grows light, the better. The horses are ready, I hear, and we will start."

Lucius would have helped the girl to mount, but she sprang lightly into the saddle before he could reach out his hand, whispering at the same time: "Beware; remember that I am your servant." In this character she kept her place behind while Lucius rode on in front, Spartacus walking by his side. A few minutes brought them to the southern gate of the camp. At the sight of the general's well-known figure it was opened without question, and the party passed out. When they were out of earshot of the sentinels, Spartacus took leave of his two guests.

"Farewell, young sir," he said to Lucius; "we shall never meet again, but you will think kindly of the gladiator. Do your best for this maiden, and the gods reward as you deserve!" He laid his hand as he spoke with a kindly pressure on the young man's shoulder. Then turning to Philareté he said: "And you too, my daughter, farewell! If you can ever do a kindness to a slave you will repay me for any thing that I have done for you. The gods preserve you! If they fail, as they sometimes will, here is something that will help you in your need."

He put a dagger into her hand as he spoke.

"I have never asked you which way you wish to go, but I have no doubt that your safest and easiest plan will be to go to Heraclea. It is a strong place, and you can make your way from it by sea anywhere you please. You must go at first due east; keep the Great Bear on your left hand — that will be one guide if the night keeps clear, as it promises to do; and let this wind, which is, I know, due south, blow on your right cheeks — that will be another, unless it should change. It will hardly be that both will fail you. This road will take you nearly straight, but of course there are turns and branches where you will have to use your wits. You will strike the river Siris where it is not very large. When you have crossed it turn south. It is now an hour before midnight, and there are still six hours of darkness. Before they are passed you will, I hope, be safe. And now again, farewell! The gods keep you!"

He pressed the hands which the two reached out to him and turned away. They never saw him again. He had still victories to win, but the fate which he foresaw for himself was not far off. Before another year was out he fought his last battle near the head-waters of the Silarus, and fell covered with heaps of slain. Even in the confusion of that terrible rout some of the faithful followers whom his rare qualities had bound to him contrived to carry away and bury his body.

The two strange companions pursued their way. For the present no danger was to be apprehended. The outposts of Spartacus were extended as far as three or four miles from the camp. So far the general's safe-conduct was sufficient protection. Beyond these the utmost caution would be needed. The veteran centurion who commanded the farthest outpost gave them a word of warning. "There are scoundrels hanging about, sir," he said, "who don't care a speck of wool for one side or the other."

They were now on the highest ground over which their road would take them. Behind and somewhat lower, marked by the dim light of its watch-fires, was the camp which they had just left. Before was the darkness into which they were about to venture. It was a brilliantly clear night, just stirred by a breath of the mildest air. The height on which they stood gave them a view, almost unbroken, of the horizon on every side ; and Lucius, who had been taught from his boyhood to watch the rising and setting of the stars with a care which we, used to other ways of reckoning time, can scarcely appreciate, felt that his chances of finding the way were excellent.

"It looks well for us, lady," he said. "I know the stars almost as well as I know the road up to my father's house. We shall make our way all right to Heraclea, which can hardly be more than thirty miles away, by daybreak. It will suit you, I trust, to go there ; but the general seemed to leave us no choice."

"It will suit me excellently," she answered. "My foster-mother lives there, and I cannot do better. And now let us ride as fast as you think we can. I shall not cry 'halt.'"

"Good !" said Lucius ; "but mind, if we are pursued and my horse fails, or any thing else happens, you must go on. It is no good for both to perish."

"Sir, you do not know me, or you would not say such a

thing. I am a Spartan, and we are not accustomed to leave our friends."

"The gods grant that there be no need! And I have the best hopes. This beautiful night seems an omen of hope."

They rode on at a moderate pace. They had plenty of time for their journey, and it was necessary to reserve the strength of their horses for a great effort, if such should be called for. The words that passed between them were but few. The intense interest of their journey filled the thoughts of both of them, and seemed to make it almost impossible to speak on any other subject. Lucius too had to watch carefully the direction of the road by which they were journeying. Every mile or so it was necessary to choose between two ways, either of which seemed to have something to recommend it; and it was necessary to know precisely in what direction they had been moving before they reached the doubtful point.

Three hours' riding brought them to a spot where Lucius judged that it would be advisable to make a brief halt. A little rill here crossed the road, widening out into a shallow pool just below it.

"We must give the horses a short rest. We have time enough for that, and indeed even in time we shall lose nothing. I judge that it wants about two hours to sunrise. Do you see that star in the west almost straight behind us? It sets about sunrise at this time of the year, which is, as you know, about twenty-one days after the equinox; and I calculate that it is still about two hours' distance from the horizon. We will let the beasts have a mouthful of grass and a little — but, mind, a very little — water. It seems hard not to let the poor creatures drink their fill, but if we did we could get no speed out of them afterwards. But surely you need something yourself?"

Philareté at first protested that she wanted nothing, but was persuaded to eat one of the hard-boiled eggs with which Lucius had provided himself. The draught from his wine-flask which he offered she positively refused. "You remember," she laughingly said, "in Homer — you have read Homer, I suppose?"

"Yes," answered Lucius, "and have the *Iliad* this moment in my pocket."

"Well, you remember how Hecuba offers Hector the wine-cup, and he will not take it? You must let me follow his example; and indeed I have never tasted it."

Half an hour's rest was as much as Lucius deemed expedient. Mounting again they proceeded at the same steady pace as before. The road now began to descend considerably, and the travellers had little doubt that they were approaching the valley of the Siris. Once across this river they would, as Spartacus had given them to understand, be in comparative safety; and they now began to hope that they might reach it without being attacked. But this was not to be. They were about two miles from the river when they had to pass a little cross-road, which, as they glanced down it in going by, was made impenetrably dark by closely-overarching trees. But though they could see nothing they had themselves been seen. Their figures had shown clear and distinct against the sky to the man of a party that was bivouacked in the lane. For nately some little time was lost before the man could rouse his companions, and again before they could mount their horses. Our two travellers had got, therefore, a little start; and the stillness of the night enabled them to hear the clatter of the horses' hoofs as soon as their pursuers had turned on to the high-road.

"There is some one behind us," cried Lucius. "We must not wait to see whether they are friends or foes. Friends, indeed, I fancy, do not ride about at night."

They urged their horses at once to the top of their speed, and for a while at least had the satisfaction of feeling that the sounds did not come nearer. But three or four hours of riding, even at the moderate pace which they had used, had of course taken something from their horses' strength, and after a mile had been passed it was evident that the pursuers were gaining. The road, however, continued to descend. This was to the advantage of our travellers, as even a weary animal can go rapidly down hill, and they were consequently about two furlongs in advance when they reached the river-bank. Here an unexpected difficulty presented. Philareté's horse refused to take the water, and there was no time to coax it into doing so.

"Mount on mine," cried the lad in an imperious voice which silenced the objection that the girl was about to offer. She obeyed without a moment's delay. Happily the other horse was better trained, and entered the river without difficulty. The passage at first was easy enough, the water being well within the depth of both horse and man. Then it suddenly deepened, and both were compelled to swim. Lucius was a bold and strong swimmer.

Putting the bridle round his left arm, and thus leaving his motions unimpeded, he struck out for the opposite shore. The distance was not great; but the landing seemed to be difficult if not impossible. A steep bank of ten or twelve feet in height confronted them. Lucius at once guessed what had happened. He had mistaken the direction of the ford. It lay obliquely down the river, and he had supposed it to be straight. Turning the horse's head down stream with a slight bend to the shore which he had left, he soon found his footing again, and had no more difficulty in making the passage. But he found on landing that he could no longer see the point from which he had started, and so could not tell what his pursuers were about. And how was he to resist them, if, knowing the place, as they probably did, they should keep to the true direction of the ford, and so make their way across? The situation was almost desperate. It was something, however, to know what was going on. The cliff, if it was any thing like a solitary rock, would give him an advantage if he had to defend himself against odds. Quickly slipping the reins of the horse around the bough of a tree, he hurried to the cliff, Philareté, with her clumsy boots, doing her best to keep pace with him. He was not a moment too soon. The foremost pursuer had already entered the water and was making his way across. Happily he made the same mistake as Lucius had done, and left the ford, swimming his horse to within two or three yards of the cliff before he saw that a landing was impracticable. Just as he turned, Lucius saw and seized his opportunity. A stone of some five or six pounds in weight happened to lie at his feet.

He took it up, with a recollection, which made him almost laugh in the very crisis of the danger, of his favorite Homeric heroes, and threw it with all his force at the head of the swimmer. The man had not caught a glimpse of his assailant, and made no effort to avoid the missile. It struck him on the back of the neck with stunning force, and he slipped from his saddle into the water. His horse, losing the guiding pressure of its rider's hand, turned to the shore which it had left, which it reached as two other riders came up. The men were astonished and alarmed at the sight of the dripping, riderless animal. What had happened to their companion? Had a river-god dragged him from his saddle? For such things could still be believed by the vulgar. The darkness too, always a cause of terror to the ignorant, frightened them; and possibly their conscience, if a conscience the hardened ruffians still had, made cowards of them. They remembered, too, that they had no longer odds on their side. They were but two to two, and their antagonists would have the advantage of meeting them when they were struggling out of the water.

There were now some faint streaks of dawn in the eastern sky. Lucius and his companion, as they crouched behind the brushwood on the cliff, could just see the two horsemen as they stood motionless on the further bank, and could hear their voices in whispered consultations. If they should determine to attempt the passage of the river, it would be his policy to remain where he was on the chance of their coming within reach of such a missile as had disposed of their companion. That failing, he might either await their attack where he stood, or oppose as they came up from the ford.

the end of which he could easily reach before them. Fortunately he was not called upon to decide the point. After
a few minutes' hesitation the two men tied up their horses
and walked down the side of the river, apparently looking
out for their companion's body. Lucius, still keeping out
of sight, followed down his side till he reached the ford,
and from that point watched the brigands till they were out
of sight. He then determined to push on for Heraclea, for
which they would have to take some road tending south,
that might seem to have sufficient traffic on it to be the
approach to an important city. He was not long left in
doubt. A gentle ascent of about a couple of miles brought
them to just such a road as they were looking for. They
had already made up their minds to follow it, when they
heard the sound of approaching footsteps. Lucius deemed
it prudent that they should hide themselves till they could
see who the new-comers might be. He was soon satisfied.
A flock of sheep was seen coming along the road, followed
by eight or nine armed men on horseback. Laying aside his
weapons he stepped out into the road, and addressing the
person who seemed to be the leader of the party, briefly
explained that he was an exchanged Roman prisoner on his
way, with a companion, from the camp of Spartacus to the
town of Heraclea. When he related his adventure at the
river, the farmer (for such he turned out to be) asked him
whether he could describe the man whom he had struck
with the stone.

"As far as I could see," said Lucius — "but you will
remember that it was very dark — he was a big man with a
bushy head of hair and beard."

"Then, sir," said the farmer, grasping his hand, and shaking it heartily, "I congratulate you on having rid the country-side of the very worst villain in the south of Italy. He has harried the other side of the Siris, for he did not often come across, the gods be thanked, these ten years. They have sent out, I was going to say, legions against him, and to think that at last a boy should kill him with a stone! Pardon me, sir, for calling you a boy; after all you cannot be much more in years. But anyhow you will take rank from to-day as a man."

The rest of the journey was accomplished without any further adventure, and about eight o'clock in the morning the party reached the gates of Heraclea. Philareté's foster-mother, who had been a poor fisherman's wife when she nursed her, was now a lady of some importance in the town. Her husband now owned several vessels of his own, and lived in a comfortable house near the harbor. Eutimé (for this was her name) was at home, superintending the tasks of her two handmaidens, and was not a little surprised when a handsome boy, in wet and dirty clothes that made grievous stains upon her floor, threw himself into her arms. But the voice awoke her memory at once. The girl, whose courage and endurance had never failed when danger and fatigue had to be met, broke down when she found herself in a safe haven of rest. She burst into a passion of tears, and her foster-mother wept and sobbed for sympathy. Lucius thought it best to leave them to themselves, and finding the husband, told him the story of his adventure. This done he reported himself to the prefect of the town, with whom he found a hospitable welcome.

It was a matter of course that he should call next day and inquire after his companion. He was told that she had rested well and was much recovered, but he was not invited to enter the house. When this reception was repeated three or four days in succession, he began to be seriously disappointed and annoyed. It did not occur to him that the girl would hardly like to show herself in the boy's costume which she had worn during the night of their memorable ride, and that she had no female clothing but what she could borrow from her foster-mother or the slave girls. On the fifth day, however, Lucius was admitted, and soon forgot that he had ever been disappointed and vexed. He had half feared, though reproaching himself for his fears, to find a masculine young woman; and the blushing, timid girl who rose to receive him charmed him the more by the exquisite maidenliness of her looks. The eyes, which were but seldom raised, and then only for a moment, were soft and tender. Lucius could not have believed that they could blaze with courage if he had not seen the sight himself; her voice was sweet and low, and the lad found himself remembering with wonder the ring of daring that he had once heard in it. At first she was very silent and reserved, and left all the talking to her foster-mother. It was evident, however, that in her private talks with this lady she had not spared her praises of the young Roman. Eutimé fairly overpowered him with her thanks and blessings, and would not allow for a moment his modest disclaimers of merit. On taking his leave he was heartily invited to return.

A few delightful days followed. Philareté's anxiety about her father had been removed by good news, and Lucius,

for the present at least, had no cares. He had sent messages both to Laüs, where his superior might still possibly
be, and to Messana, which town he would probably make
his landing-place in Sicily, announcing his arrival at Heraclea and asking for instructions. Till an answer could
arrive his time was his own, and he asked for nothing better
than to spend it in Philareté's company. The girl had been
brought up with something of the Spartan tradition of freedom, and met him with a charming frankness that was yet
entirely modest. The two soon became excellent friends.
Lucius told Philareté about his family, his friends, his
school-days, his plans for the future; and the young lady,
who was the daughter of a prosperous merchant in Tarentum, was equally confidential. The good foster-mother
spun or slumbered at her wheel as the two talked together.
Sometimes an excursion on the water was planned, the old
sailor being delighted to put all that he had at the disposal
of the beautiful girl whom he loved as a daughter. When,
at the end of a fortnight, Lucius received a message from
the quæstor bidding him repair, without delay, to Messana,
he felt that he should carry away with him from the charming Greek town an impression which he never should lose.
Like most lads of his age he had rather looked down upon
girls, and his feelings were still vague and dim; but there
was now a glow and color in his life that were new to it,
and he felt that they came from the eyes of the beautiful
maiden whom he had guided across the Calabrian hills.
He could not speak — indeed he did not know what to say;
but when he went the day after his summons came, to say
farewell, he felt that she must know something of what was

in his heart. And she did know it. Few words passed between them, and they bade each other farewell, an onlooker might have thought, almost coldly. But when, that same evening, he stepped on board the ship that was to take him to Messana, a young slave put into his hand a small packet. It was a locket of gold, with a little curl of golden brown hair, and engraved in Greek letters upon it the two words, COURAGE, FAITH.

CHAPTER V.

AGRIGENTUM.

WE shall not follow our hero's journey through Sicily. It will suffice to say that he met his chief, and in his company reached Agrigentum, which was one of the chief towns of his district. They found it a busy place, its streets thronged with passengers and vehicles, its harbor filled with vessels, big and little, many of which were occupied with taking in cargoes of sulphur. Lucius had of course seen sulphur before, but he had never thought whence it came and even what it was. "This stuff," said his elder companion, "shows us where we are. I showed you Ætna the other day, with its cap of smoke upon its head. It is far away to the north-east; but we are in its country, so to say. You know the old fable, how the giant lies with Ætna on his breast, his right hand stretched out to Pelorus, his left to Pachynon, and how he shakes the island when he gives a turn in his bed. You have never felt an earthquake, I suppose. Well, you won't like it when you do; and the oftener it comes you will like it the less. It is a curious thing, that while men get used to other dangers they never get used to this. A native is always more frightened than a stranger. But let us hope that the giant will sleep sound for the present."

All the lions of the town were duly visited, the chief lion, if the phrase may be allowed, being of course the brazen bull in which, five hundred years before, the tyrant Phalaris had been accustomed to roast his victims alive. The town was vastly proud of this curious monument of the past, though it was not much to its credit that it should ever have submitted to so abominable a tyranny. Men, however, are not very particular about such things, and a curiosity, like even the most discreditable ancestor, is sure to be valued if it can be traced back to a time sufficiently remote. Every visitor was at once taken to the Bull. The principal inn was known by this sign. The silversmiths did a brisk trade in little bulls of silver or bronze; and even the first and second founders of the city were not more gratefully remembered than the great Scipio who had brought back to it this precious possession after an absence of three hundred and fifty years. This and the other sights having been duly inspected and admired, the two companions made their way to the house of the mayor, if we may so style the chief magistrate of the town, where it was usual that distinguished visitors should be entertained.

The dinner, to which they sat down about six o'clock in the evening, the luxuriously early hours of Rome not having yet made their way into the busy trading town, was sufficiently sumptuous. The Agrigentine merchants were rich, and no one was more affluent or more hospitable than the mayor. In the course of their after-dinner talk he inquired of his guests whether they had happened to notice a house by the harbor, which was called the "*Ship*."

"Yes," said Lucius; "it was pointed out to me, and my

guide seemed to take it for granted that I knew all about it. There seemed to be some joke; but the house looked common enough, and I could not understand."

" Yes," replied the host. "There is a joke, and we think it a good one in Agrigentum. I will tell you the story. It happened about a hundred and fifty years ago, and an ancestor of mine, I have always heard, was concerned in it. There was a young fellow named Doricles, belonging to one of the best families in the town, and he was going to be married. It is a custom here, and I dare say it is in most places, for a man to give a dinner to his friends a few days before the wedding. They call it bidding good-by to their freedom, though a good many of them, I fancy, have pretty nearly as much freedom after they are married as before. Well, Doricles gave his dinner to some ten or twelve friends, and they drank, as they do at such times, pretty hard, and kept at it till it was close upon morning. By that time some of them were past noticing any thing, and the rest were ready for any nonsense in the world. One of them makes his way across the room to the window to get a breath of fresh air. As you may suppose, he was not very steady on his feet, and the floor of the room seemed to go up and down, as it will to a drunken man. He was always a mad kind of fellow, and now he cries out, ' Ho, there, mates, rouse up! This is a terrible storm, and we shall be wrecked if we don't take care.' It was rough weather, as it happened, and there was a great gale blowing from the sea. ' Let us lighten the ship.' The notion just caught the fellows' fancy, and they set to work with a will, throwing chairs and tables and mattresses, every thing, in fact, that they could lay their hands on, out of the window. By this time it was beginning to grow light, and the people were going to their work. It was not long before there was a crowd about the house, and such a shouting and laughing as never was heard. It was a good day's work for some of the loafers. If the town had been sacked they could not have made a better harvest. Well, before long the magistrates heard of the uproar, and made their appearance on the scene. They called for Doricles, and he came to the window with a garland hanging down over one ear, and generally not a little the worse for wine. 'Doricles,' shouted the senior magistrate, 'what is the meaning of all this?'—'Gentlemen Tritons,' he said, 'I am very glad to see you. You will excuse my messmates; the weather has been too much for them, and they are terribly sea-sick. To tell you the truth, when I heard your voice I was lying under a bench half dead with fear. We had done our best to lighten the ship, but I thought that it was all over with us. But now that you have had the goodness to appear, things, I am sure, will go well.'—'No more of this nonsense, Doricles,' said the magistrate. 'A man does not get married every day, and this once we will look over it; but don't do any thing like it again.'—'Thanks, Gentlemen Tritons. We won't forget your kindness. If ever we get into harbor, and I begin to hope that we may, you shall have a sacrifice, as sure as my name is Doricles. Your coming in this way, in your cloaks and all, just as if you were so many mortal men, is most uncommonly kind, and you won't find us ungrateful.' And he shut down the window. That was how the house came to be called the *Ship*.

"Ah!" said the host after a pause; "it was pretty well the last merrymaking the poor fellows had. Our poor town was the lamb for which the wolf and the fox were fighting — excuse me, gentlemen, but you Romans boast of having something of the wolf in you, and Carthage, every one knows, was a fox. Well, Agrigentum was supposed to be on the side of Carthage, not that it really wanted any thing but to be left in peace. Then some scoundrel of an African — you can buy any of them, I believe, for a handful of silver — opened the gates to that butcher Lævinus — pardon me, I forget myself — to the proconsul, I should have said, and of course the people who had to pay for it all were, not the Carthaginians, who cleared out in good time, but our poor citizens, who could not run away. Doricles, who had not been married more than a year — he was a magistrate himself by that time — was sent to the stone-quarries at Syracuse, and my ancestor and some twelve or fifteen others, all the best-born and richest men in the place, bore him company. You never saw the stone-quarries, gentlemen? The most terrible prison in the world, as black and as hot as Tartarus, and pretty well as hard to get out of. Doricles did get out, and my ancestor too, or else I should not have had the pleasure of entertaining you to-day, but it cost their families pretty nearly every drachma they had to ransom them."

"Well," said Lucius, "I suppose those days are gone for good. Nothing of the kind could go on now; there could not be another Lævinus."

"Hush!" said the host; "we may talk about the past as much as we please, but the present is another matter.

Somebody may be listening;" and he went to the door to satisfy himself that nobody was near.

"I have as good a set of slaves as any one, and I try to be kind to them, but I don't care to trust them further than I can help. You see, it is a terrible temptation to a man to put a rope round his master's neck when he can get his freedom for doing it, and perhaps a talent as well, to set him up in business. Well, gentlemen, there are awkward rumors about the governor. We haven't suffered much in Agrigentum here, but I have heard strange stories of his doings elsewhere. You are pretty safe, anyhow, to hear a good deal about him before you leave the island — but he is coming here to-morrow; you will see him and judge for yourselves."

It was about three or four o'clock in the afternoon of the next day when the governor made his expected appearance. He was certainly very unlike all that Lucius had looked for. Instead of a dignified official, majestic with his robes of state and insignia of power, he saw an effeminate lounger, who seemed as if he could have no thoughts beyond his dress and his dinner. The Roman costume he had entirely discarded. His tunic was of Greek fashion, and he wore a gay upper garment of purple embroidered with gold, which might have become one of the dandies of Ephesus or Corinth, but looked strangely out of place in the ruler of a Roman province. This languid exquisite — who, however, could show energy enough when the occasion demanded some act of audacious robbery or violence — was clearly incapable of any thing like the exertion of riding on horseback. He was carried in a litter by eight bearers, stout

Bithynians, who were just then the fashion for this kind of service. A cushion, covered with muslin so fine and transparent that the roses with which it was stuffed could be seen through it, lay on the floor of the conveyance. Roses, indeed, seemed to be the great man's special fancy; he had a garland round his head, and another hanging loosely from his neck. He was a man of between forty and fifty, stout in figure, with a red and bloated countenance which bore the tokens of excess. The exertion even of alighting at the gate and walking to his chamber seemed to be too much for him, for his bearers carried him in his litter straight to his apartment, while he bestowed a careless salutation on his host, who stood obsequiously at the door with something like terror in his face. Lucius and his chief he honored with a supercilious stare.

Three or four wagons followed, conveying the baggage of the governor and of his staff, one of them being specially devoted to his travelling kitchen, another to his wine-cellar, and a third being loaded with masses of snow from Ætna.

That evening our hero saw nothing more of the great man. The Agrigentine magistrate was a worthy fellow, and though he could not escape the unwelcome necessity of witnessing, if not sharing, the revels of the governor, had far too much good feeling to bring his young guest into such a scene. Lucius had his meal with the two sons of the house, one of them a year older, the other a year younger, than himself. They had plenty to talk about. The young Agrigentines were as fond of sport as Lucius himself, and had had better opportunities of following it. Hares and roedeer were common in the woods near the town, and it was not unusual to find a wild boar, a possible peril which gave a flavor of danger to the experience. The lads were anglers, too, though the Sicilian streams were apt to shrink in a way that sadly interfered with their sport. But they astonished Lucius with their accounts of the sea-fish which they took in the bay and along the neighboring coasts. The size, the variety, and the number of their captures fairly made his mouth water. From exchanging these experiences of sport they turned to draughts, and fox and geese, games in which Lucius found himself very much outmatched by his more nimble-witted companions. Late in the forenoon of the following day Lucius received, somewhat to his surprise, a summons to the presence of the great man. Verres was sitting in a room that looked out upon the garden. By his side was a jar of water tinged with fruit sirup, and buried up to its brim in snow. His dress consisted of a fine under-shirt and drawers of silk, with a loose wrap of the slightest and most transparent material over it. He was busy examining with the eye of a connoisseur a small bronze. It was the figure of a satyr, carrying over his shoulder a wounded deer. The tense sinews of the satyr, who was evidently putting out his strength to support his burden, contrasted vividly with the slackened limbs of the animal. The Agrigentine host was standing by in an attitude of respectful attention, but with uneasiness manifest in his face.

"And this you say is an Euphranor?" said the governor.

"The pedigree, my lord, is undoubted. The artist made it for an ancestor of my own, who was one of the first settlers in the new foundation, and it has been in the family ever since."

"That sounds very well; but do you feel sure that the master did it all himself? These great men have a way of doing a great deal of work by the hands of their pupils. The satyr's head and neck are very good; but the rest of the piece seems hardly up to Euphranor's mark. Still it is worth having, and I shall be very glad to buy it."

"Excuse me, my lord, but I should be very sorry to part with it; it has been a long time in the family. In fact, it is an heirloom, and not mine to sell."

"Never mind that, my good friend; I will hold you blameless. The prætor's receipt will be quittance enough in any court of law, heirloom or no heirloom. Come, I will give you two thousand sesterces for it."

"Two thousand sesterces, my lord! why, my ancestor gave ten times that for it three hundred years ago!"

"Then he was taken in. No; two thousand is quite as much as the thing is worth."

"My lord, I really can't sell it for that," stammered out the magistrate, roused to assert himself by seeing the most valuable work of art that he had about to slip out of his hands. "You could not get a copy done for that money even in common bronze, and this is the best Corinthian."

"Two thousand is my maximum. I never go beyond it; and mark you, sir, I have got some better things than this for no more."

The expression on the governor's face changed as he spoke from an easy, careless gayety to a sternness which it was not pleasant to see.

"I don't always buy," he went on; "I have had many fine things given to me."

Beckoning to the magistrate to approach, he whispered a few words in his ear. The poor man grew pale. Lucius heard afterwards what they were. " I find that a week or two in the stone-quarries has a wonderful way of opening a man's hand or loosening his purse-strings."

"You shall have it, my lord," the magistrate stammered out.

Verres scratched a few words on a piece of paper, which he tossed carelessly to the merchant. It was an order on the quæstor for the money. He then clapped his hands, and a slave, who was waiting outside the door, came in. "See this is packed up," he said, pointing to the bronze, "and see that it gets no damage. If it does, so much the worse for you," he added, with a scowl which made the man visibly tremble.

It was now Lucius' turn for an interview.

"You are a Roman?" said Verres, with a smile that was meant to be re-assuring. "Your name, if you please, and your birthplace?"

"Lucius Marius of Arpinum, my lord."

"Marius of Arpinum!" repeated the great man. "Any relative of that"—

He was going to say something disparaging of the great soldier who had delivered Rome from the barbarians, for Verres, though low-born, was a hanger-on of the party of the nobles, to which Marius had been any thing but a friend. But he checked himself. He had a purpose to serve, in which he wanted to make the young Roman useful. He was struck, too, by something frank and bold in the lad's expression, and though it was not in his nature to feel any

genuine admiration for these, or indeed for any good qualities, he felt that it would be inexpedient to give offence —
" of the distinguished general," he forced himself to say.

" I am his great-nephew, my lord."

" And you are come, I understand, to be quæstor's clerk
to my good friend Manilius. Surely, my son, that is a poor
employment for a lad of your inches. Any cripple can write
and cipher. But a straight well-grown lad, with such shoulders as yours, should do something better worthy a Roman,
and the nephew, too, of Marius, perhaps the very best soldier we ever had. You can throw a javelin as far as most, I
warrant, and have learnt your sword-play pretty well ! "

Lucius would have been something more than mortal boy
if he had not been somewhat moved by this condescension
and flattery. He had heard little, it is true, about Verres,
and that little was not favorable ; his frank and pure nature,
too, had been repelled by the cruel and sensual expression
of the governor's face. But first impressions often pass
away. The courtesy of a great man is powerful with every
one, and with the young is almost irresistible. Verres exerted himself to please, and he could scarcely fail of success.
He showed the keenest interest in all Lucius' tastes and
pursuits, made him relate some of his sporting adventures,
questioned him in the kindest, pleasantest way about his
plans for the future, in a word laid himself to win the young
fellow's heart, and, of course, won it.

" I am intending," he said at last, " to fit out a fleet
against the pirates. These fellows are becoming perfectly
intolerable, and they must have a lesson. A particular
friend of mine is to have the command. He is an excellent

fellow, as brave a man as ever stepped, and a good sailor.
But, unfortunately, he is not a Roman. In fact, he is a
Syracusan. Of course there is a good deal of jealousy about
the matter. You will hear, I dare say, some very disagree-
able things said about it. Pray, don't believe a word of
them. When you have lived a little longer in the world
you will find that there will be people whom nothing and
nobody can please. Still I should like my friend to have a
Roman officer near him. There might be a difficulty about
asking an older man to go, but with you it is different; besides, I don't mind asking you a favor. Will you go? You
will be something like second in command, a pretty bit of
promotion to a lad of nineteen."

"I am a little more than seventeen," interposed Lucius,
dreadfully afraid that the appointment would be revoked
when the governor heard the real state of the case, but
fully determined to tell the truth.

"You astonish me! I could have sworn that you were
at least nineteen. But never mind. Pompey was in command of a division when he was no more than you. These
things go a great deal by luck. Your uncle, you will remember, was nearly forty before he got his tribuneship.
But the chance comes sooner or later. Yours has come
very soon. The thing is to take it when it comes."

Lucius was eloquent with his thanks. The prospect, in
fact, delighted him beyond measure. He had been chafing
a little at the thought of confinement to the desk, and here
was an opportunity of freedom and distinction far beyond
his wildest dreams.

"Well, that is settled," said Verres. "I will make it all

right with Manilius. Report yourself to me at Syracuse in a month's time."

Lucius broke out again into thanks. Verres listened with courtesy till he had exhausted himself, and then dismissed him with a courteous farewell. Our young friend would have been less pleased than he was if he could have seen the sneering smile which settled on the governor's countenance when he found himself alone. "Let us hope that you will like it, my young friend," he murmured to himself as the door shut behind the lad.

Lucius was of course nearly out of his senses with delight. He seemed to himself to be at least some inches taller, and, though naturally a modest lad, could scarcely help giving himself some airs. His young friends of the night before viewed him with an admiration not wholly free from envy. Their father was somewhat guarded in his congratulations, and the quæstor was almost discouraging. "You will wish yourself back before long," he said ; a prophecy which the lad received with the incredulity which such unwelcome predictions generally meet with.

CHAPTER VI.

VERRES.

PUNCTUALLY on the day appointed (the month named by Verres expiring on the fifteenth of June) Lucius presented himself at the gate of the governor's palace in Syracuse. He was a little surprised to find it closed, for it was an hour (about seven o'clock in the morning) when a great man's house at Rome would have been thronged with callers. A kick at the gate produced no effect, and it was only when this had been repeated at least half a dozen times that a slave, whose unwashed face and garments hastily huddled on showed that he was but that moment risen from his bed, slowly opened the wicket.

"What do you want, young sir?" said the man in a surly tone.

"I am come by appointment to see the governor," replied our hero with as much dignity as he could assume.

"And, pray, who sent you here to see the governor?" retorted the man. "It was a fool's errand anyhow. The governor is not at home." And vouchsafing no further information he slammed the door in the visitor's face.

Astonished and indignant at this reception, Lucius was about to recommence his attack on the gate when a passer-

by, who had stopped by the way to listen to the dialogue,
courteously accosted him.

"You are a stranger here, sir, I imagine, and don't know
the ways of the place. His Excellency finds the palace
too hot for him in the summer time, and lives in tents on
the shore. The sea air, you will understand," he added
with a smile, "is necessary for his health. You will find
him there; but you must not go too early — we don't keep
up your early Roman habits here. In fact, you had better
send a messenger with a note, and ask him to fix the time
for an interview."

Lucius thanked his informant, and followed his advice.
The note was duly written, despatched, and delivered, but
the great man vouchsafed no answer. Three days had
passed, and Lucius, uneasy at this unaccountable silence,
had begun to fear that he had made a mistake in not at
once presenting himself to the governor, whether he was
living in his palace or in a tent, when he received a note,
which ran thus:

"*Lucius Verres to Lucius Marius, greeting.*

"*I invite you to dinner to-day at three o'clock, when you
will meet your superior officer. If you have any companions
who are likely to be good company, bring them. Write back
and say how many there will be of you. Farewell.*

"*From my palace by the sea, June 18th.*"

It was already past noon; for the messenger had loitered
on his way for one gossip at the baths and another at the
wine-shop. Lucius wrote back an acceptance, adding that
he had no companion to bring. That done he promptly

put himself into the hands of a barber, who curled his hair and shaved off the slight traces of down which his youthful chin presented. These important operations concluded, he had little more than the necessary time to make his way in one of the carriages which plied for hire in the streets to the governor's seaside quarters. The row of tents in which the luxurious Roman was accustomed to spend the hot summer months formed something like a camp, and had been pitched as near to the water's edge as the necessity of allowing for an occasional rise of the sea (due to wind rather than to tide) permitted. It was the largest of these which served as a dining-room, and into which Lucius was ushered. It was a spacious apartment, measuring as much as fifty feet each way, and rising in the middle to a height not very much less. These were the dimensions as viewed from within; viewed from without they were considerably larger, for the tent was double throughout, and there was a space of six feet between the outer and the inner coverings. This arrangement considerably mitigated the heat of the sun. Openings, which could be closed or enlarged at pleasure, had been arranged on the north and south sides. Both could be opened when the wind was not blowing strongly enough to produce an inconvenient draught. On this particular occasion, as there was a brisk breeze, they were open towards the south only, affording a delightful view of the bay. The walls of the tent, to the height of eight or ten feet, were hung with purple. The floor was of tessellated pavement, with patterns of fishes and birds upon it.

Lucius arrived almost exactly as Verres and his guests were preparing to take their places at the table. The gov-

ernor, who, contrary to his usual custom, wore the dress of
a Roman magistrate, the white toga with its broad edging
of purple, occupied a couch at the top of the horse-shoe
table. At his left hand was a chair in which sat a lady of
remarkable beauty, clad in a graceful but perhaps too gayly
colored Greek costume. On the lady's right hand again was
another couch with a single occupant, evidently a fop of the
first order. His Greek dress was of the newest and most
fashionable cut; his hair was elaborately curled and almost
dripping with perfume; his fingers were loaded with rings,
and he had even condescended to the feminine ornaments
of a necklace and bracelets. His features were pleasing,
but had a weak expression; while the flush upon them
showed that, young as he was, intemperance had already
begun to leave its tokens behind it. Lucius found his own
place next to this fashionable young gentleman. His neighbor on the other side was a lad of about fourteen, who still
wore the boy's dress (which closely resembled the official
costume). The party was completed by two freedmen,
who occupied a fourth couch on the left hand of the
governor.

Verres introduced his new guest with a careless but not
uncourteous brevity. Lucius learned that the handsome
lady was named Niké; that his fashionable neighbor was
her husband, Cleomenes, his future commander, a fact that
surprised and did not altogether please him; and that the
boy was the governor's own son. The two freedmen were
not thought worth an introduction. These were invited to
amuse the other guests, and in fact were professional per-
formers, who considered themselves sufficiently paid by

their dinner and by other gains, not always of a respectable kind, which they picked up by the favor of their host.

The talk turned at first on the merits of the various dishes and wines, which were more sumptuous and varied than any thing that Lucius had ever seen or heard of. Accustomed to the simple fare of a country-house, where the old habits of Italian frugality had been scrupulously retained, he was simply amazed by the succession of delicacies, some of them wholly unknown to him even by name, which the slaves in waiting continued to offer him. His young companion, however, boy as he was, seemed thoroughly acquainted with the merits of every thing. The ignorance or indifference of his neighbor excited his unbounded surprise. " Is it possible that you don't like oysters? " he cried, as Lucius passed, without helping himself, a dish of the shell-fish which a slave had offered him. " These came all the way from Misenum. Perhaps you thought them Sicilians, which, I must confess, are somewhat flabby. But you may rely on these being genuine."

Lucius owned that he should not know the difference. " In fact," he said, " I never tasted an oyster. We get fresh-water mussels at home, but I confess that I don't much like them."

" I should think not," cried the boy. " Mussels indeed ! Who ever heard of such a thing? Never to have tasted an oyster ! And you have put on the man's gown ! "

He seemed lost in astonishment to think that a fellow creature's education had been so neglected. " But," he continued, as he caught sight of a new dish which the elderly man, who was in command of the waiters, was bringing in with some pomp, "here comes something that you are sure to like."

It was a peacock, as was evident from its gorgeous tail-feathers. It was evident from the state with which it was served, the dish on which it rested being of silver gilt, that it was regarded as one of the principal ornaments of the banquet.

"And what do you think of that?" cried the lad when Lucius had finished his portion.

"To tell you the truth," said the other, "it seems to me a little tough and dry. A common pullet is just as good, and, but for the look of the thing, even better."

The boy looked at him as he might have looked at a savage. "Well," he said, after a pause, "try that white wine. It comes from a vineyard near Ætna; a little fiery, perhaps, as it should be, coming from such a soil, but with a very fine flavor. You shake your head! Perhaps you are right. I was forgetting. 'A white wine with boiled meats, a red with roast,' I have heard my father say so often, and I ought to have remembered. Fill your cup — stay a moment and have a clean cup — with that Cæcuban. It is thirty years old, and you can't get a better wine in Sicily."

Lucius began to feel himself very much out of place. Being little more than a boy he was ashamed to make a confession, which he knew would rouse his young companion's contempt. However, he screwed up his courage and said:

"The truth is I seldom drink any wine."

"What, in the name of the twelve gods, do you drink?"

"Why, water, or milk, and sometimes, when the vintage is going on, a draught of the must before it goes into the vat. Two or three times in the year, on my father's birthday, or Saturn's days, we have a jar of real wine put on the table, but I must say that I care very little for it."

The boy looked at him with a mixture of curiosity and contempt. "And if this is your drink," he went on, "pray what do you eat?"

"Pulse porridge, and cakes baked in the embers, and any vegetables and fruits that may be in season, and a slice of mutton-ham or salt pork on most days. Sometimes we have a hare roasted. Sometimes we get quails or partridges. Once or twice in the year we have a haunch of venison or a fore-quarter of wild boar. That is our bill of fare; and I can tell you," added our hero, who was a little nettled at his companion's airs of superiority; "I can tell you that it is no bad training for a soldier."

"A soldier! Hercules and Venus, who wants to be a soldier? When you have been here a month you will see that there are better trades than a soldier's." With this remark the lad turned away and applied himself seriously to the business of dinner. He had done his duty to a guest whom he felt to be under his special care; but now it was evidently useless to waste any more trouble upon him.

Lucius' other neighbor had overheard, with not a little amusement, some of this conversation.

"You are quite of the primitive sort," he said with a

pleasant smile; "one of the Romans who have conquered the world, which our young friend there," he added in a lower voice, "certainly never will be. I haven't the good fortune to be one of your countrymen, but I have the good sense to admire their virtues. At present I am delighted that you are going to serve under me. You are just the man that I want. Things are not quite in the good order that I should like to see them in; but with your good help we will alter all that. But 'business to-morrow.' Come and see me — every one knows where I live — and we will talk over what is to be done." By this time the tedious succession of dishes, for such it seemed to one at least of the guests, had come to an end, and the wine was set on. Verres took from the table before him a two-handled cup. "To Jupiter, good and great; to Venus, to Bacchus," he said, pouring, at each name, a few drops of wine upon the pavement. "And now," he went on, "let us drink to our new comrade, Lucius Marius. 'Tis a name that smacks of victory, and I have good reason to know that it is worthily borne. These rascally pirates shall be taught something that they don't know at present. By right this is a toast that should be drunk in bumpers; but we would be merciful to women and children; and my guests will please themselves." The cup was passed round, Verres first taking a deep draught, Niké just touched it with her rosy lips, the Greek's potation also was moderate. Young Verres had by this time nearly reached the limit of his powers. Lucius felt himself absolved from drinking to his own health, and passed the goblet at once to the freedmen, whose well-practised throats easily drained it to the bottom. For a

short time the conversation turned on the pirates, their
recent doings, and the chastisement that was in store for
them. The subject, however, did not seem one interesting
to any of the company except Lucius. Art was the next
topic introduced, and Verres discoursed, with the eloquence
of a *connoisseur*, on pictures, marbles, bronzes, gems, and
the varieties of Samian and Tyrian ware. When the conversation flagged the freedmen felt that the time was come
for them to earn, or rather to pay for, their dinner. They
pretended to quarrel, and set to work to abuse each other
with a flow and variety of language which seemed vastly
diverting to their entertainer and his guests. As they went
on their jokes grew broader and coarser; Niké hid, or pretended to hide, her face with her napkin; and Lucius, who
was really a modest and well-conducted youth, felt himself
more awkwardly placed than he had ever been before in
his life. At this moment an opportune diversion relieved
him from his difficulty. Young Verres, who had been de-
voting himself with more than usual diligence to the wine-
cup, turned to him and whispered in unsteady tones:
"Help me out." Lucius was only too glad to seize the
opportunity of escape. He helped the boy to rise from
his couch, and supported him out of the tent, handing
him over to a young slave who was apparently waiting to
receive him, and who showed no surprise at his state. An
elderly man, in whom Lucius recognized the bearer of the
peacock dish, was standing by. "Will the governor expect
me to return?" he asked, devoutly hoping that it would
not be expected of him. The steward, for such he was,
a little surprised to see one of his master's guests so thor-

oughly master of himself, thought that his absence would probably not be noticed, and Lucius gladly escaped. It was still early in the evening, and there was time for a stroll about the great harbor, a scene of bustle and activity, of which it was impossible to tire.

CHAPTER VII.

A CRUISE.

L UCIUS was of course all impatience to enter upon his new duties, and grudged every moment of delay. He guessed, however, that it would be a waste of time to make a very early visit to Cleomenes, and, as he found when about two hours before noon he called at the young Greek's house, guessed right. Cleomenes had but just finished his first meal, and was amusing himself with two young friends who had breakfasted with him, at a game which our hero could not help regarding with some little contempt. A number of small earthenware saucers were floating in a large basin of water. The players stood about six yards off, each with a cup holding a small quantity of wine in his hand. Their object was to throw the wine in such a way that it would fall into one of the saucers and sink it. Each saucer so sunk was worth a gold piece to the fortunate or skilful player who contrived to send it to the bottom. When the game began there had been nine saucers afloat, and each of the three players had put three gold pieces into the pool, and would take one out for each saucer he might secure. Four had disappeared when Lucius was announced, and Cleomenes was in the highest spirits because three out of the four had fallen to his share.

"Good-morning!" he said. "For Heaven's sake don't interrupt me! I am giving my friends here such a beating as they never had before in their lives. I can aim like Cupid himself this morning. Look here!"

As he spoke he threw the wine again, and, to his unbounded delight, a fifth saucer disappeared.

"Come," he cried to his competitors, "I will wager fifty drachmas that I get two out of the four that are left. There is nothing like following up one's luck."

The young men were not disposed to take the bet. It was clearly their host's day, and they felt that the less they risked the better. Cleomenes in fact did sink two more of the saucers, and consequently pocketed six of the nine gold pieces. Then turning to Lucius with an air of triumph: "What an omen," he cried, "for you and me! Could the Twin Brethren have sent a better? Don't you see?—the saucers there are the pirates, and I, with you to help me, am the man to sink them. You shall have your revenge," he continued, speaking to his friends, "if you will come to-morrow. Meanwhile farewell! My young friend here and I have business to transact—business of the state, you will understand, which cannot be neglected."

And he endeavored to assume an air of dignified importance, not a little to the amusement of his friends, who knew him a great deal too well to be so taken in.

"You must not suppose," he said to the young Roman when they found themselves alone, "that I am given to these trifles. But one should not apply one's self to business immediately after meals. My physician expressly forbids it. But now for our affairs. We are tolerably well prepared for a cruise—in fact about as well as we are likely to be. You won't find things, perhaps, quite as you might expect or wish. We have not got many stores on board. You see this is not like a long voyage. We are always near our base, as the soldiers say, and can pick up pretty nearly what we want as we go along. The crews, too, are not *quite* complete. It really is no use feeding and paying a lot of idle fellows when they are not wanted. We can always get them when they are required. I reckon that we shall pick up the men as well as the stores as we go along. We will press the fellows out of two or three forts that I know of. What is the good of their kicking their heels all day long and looking out to sea? A bit of a cruise and a little service — no running into danger, you will understand, but something that will bring plenty of credit without much risk — that will do them a world of good. Well, if we are ready we had better set out at once. We generally have settled weather about this time of year. The pirates, too, are getting a little impudent. Of course they will be off at once as soon as we show ourselves. When can you be ready? Will three days be enough?"

"I don't want more than three hours," said Lucius.

"Admirable! What energy! This is how you Romans have conquered the world. But I have some little matters to settle. A married man, you see, can't leave every thing at a moment's notice, as a gay young bachelor like yourself. Shall we say the day after to-morrow, about two hours before sunset — that is, if the weather still looks fine? Will you try your hand with the Cottabos? — no? You Romans like something more energetic, I dare say. Farewell, then,

for the present. Our ship, you will remember, is the
Chimæra."

When Lucius presented himself, punctual to the moment,
at the rendezvous, he found the *Chimæra* as gay as paint
and varnish and gilding could make her. A huge figure of
the monster from which she got her name — a mixture of
lion, goat, and snake — adorned the bows. A small pent-
house on the stern covered gilded images of the Twin
Brethren, under whose protection she was supposed to be.
An old sailor greeted the young Roman on his arrival with
a respectful salute. "We do not sail, sir," he said, "till
to-morrow. The captain thinks that there is a little too
much wind; and besides, he dines with the governor.
Meanwhile, sir, you are to be in charge, and I hand over
the ship to you."

The old salt's face, as he spoke, was perfectly grave, but
there was a twinkle in his eye which showed that he had his
own opinions about the delay. As to the weather, indeed,
Lucius, landsman as he was, could see that the excuse was
ridiculous. A fair breeze was blowing just strongly enough
to touch the waves with white. Small fishing and pleasure
boats were going in and out of the harbor; in fact the
weather was fair, and promised to be still fairer as the day
went on. Lucius found occupation and amusement enough
in thoroughly inspecting the ship. It was a decked vessel,
and though it would have seemed small to modern eyes,
was reckoned to be of unusual size. Its new lieutenant was
a little surprised to find so few seamen on board, but concluded that the men, like their commander, had been given
or had taken an extra day's leave. They were probably loi-

tering in the town ; they must be recalled in good time the next day. This must be his first duty as second in command ; for it would not do for his chief to find, when he came on board, that any of his crew were missing. When he announced his intention of calling the roll early next day and of sending a guard on shore to bring in any stragglers, the old seaman listened with a half-suppressed smile, which Lucius perceived but could not understand.

The next morning, about half an hour after sunrise, the ceremony of the roll-call took place. Demarchus (that was the old sailor's name) called over the names. Every one was duly answered, but the lieutenant soon perceived a suspicious resemblance in the voices that replied. Before long in fact, he became certain that one man was doing duty in this way for a good many ; and stepping a little aside to where he could command a view of the place from which the voices seemed again and again to come, he saw that there was a man who sometimes answered to as many as five or six names in succession. He thought it best not to interrupt the call, but to demand an explanation as soon as it was finished.

"What," he said to Demarchus, " is the meaning of this? There are about one hundred and eighty names on the list ; but there were, I am sure, not a hundred at the call. And what did that fellow behind the mast mean by answering name after name? Are the men loitering about in the town? If so, we must fetch them."

"Sir," said the old sailor, " it is all a queer business, but you will have to know it sooner or later, and I had better tell you at once. To put the matter quite shortly, *these*

men are nowhere. Some of them died years ago, some ran
away ; some I never saw, and I have been on the *Chimæra*
a matter of five years. You look surprised, sir, and well
you may be. But listen and you will understand." As he
spoke he dropped his voice to a whisper. " They are nowhere, but they *get their pay* all the same, or somebody else
gets it. The town that finds this ship pays for one hundred
and eighty men ; and we have, as you see, something less
than a hundred. Say each man gets half a drachma a day.
There you have forty drachmas in somebody's pocket. It
is not for me to say whose pocket, but I am pretty sure that
not a single drachma goes back to the town. Then there
is an allowance for food. The missing men, of course, want
food just as much as those that are here ; and to tell you
the truth, those that are here don't get much more than
the missing. Yes, sir, we haven't food for fifty on board
— I might say a score — let alone a hundred. Some of
the men bring a supply on board ; and then when we
touch anywhere — and we touch, as you may guess, pretty
often — they are exceedingly nimble in picking up any
trifles that may come in their way. Then there is something to be done in fishing when the weather is fine. No,
sir, they don't starve ; but you can't say much more. And,
sir, we are better off in the *Chimæra* than they are in any
of the other ships. We haven't got much more than half
our crew, but they haven't a quarter. You see, our captain
is a favorite at headquarters, and he is better treated than
some ; but you wouldn't believe how short-handed some of
the others are. Do you know the real reason why we didn't
sail yesterday? The weather was all right — you saw that.

sir, though I doubt whether you have been much to sea before; but the wind was blowing into the harbor mouth, and *we could not* get out. We had not enough men to man the oars, and so we had to stay at home. You see people suspect something, but they don't *know;* and it would never do to show our weakness publicly. We shall go to-day, sir. The wind has shifted and blows out of the harbor, and we can do without our oars. The *Chimæra* makes a brave show, sir; and the others look pretty well too when *they are under sail,* but I don't like the look of things. And if the pirates do show fight — and I am told they will — it may turn out a very ugly business. And now, sir, I have told you the whole truth, as far as I know it; for I seem to see in your face that you are one to be trusted. But mind, you must not seem to know any thing. See, here comes the captain."

Just as he finished speaking Cleomenes stepped out of a litter, which had been carried by the bearers down to the water's side, and came on board by a gangway. He greeted his lieutenant with much friendliness and warmth.

" My excellent Lucius, I am delighted to see you. I felt sure when we first met that you were exactly the man that I should like to have with me. You have every thing ready, I see." He saw something in the young Roman's eye that seemed to say that every thing was *not* ready, and hastened to anticipate any remark. " Ah! there are some things you want to speak to me about. Very good. We shall have plenty of time for that when we are out of harbor. That is the first thing to do. Demarchus," he added, turning to the old sailor, " signal to the rest of the squadron that they are to follow me out of harbor under sail."

The order was duly given. The *Chimæra* soon had its sails hoisted, and led the way gayly enough. Its consorts, as the lieutenant soon saw, were not in such good case. The start was not so speedily made, the sails were not so skilfully handled, and the canvas, when spread to the wind, looked old, discolored, and worn. Still the squadron, which numbered eight ships in all, made a sufficiently fair show as they passed one after another out of the harbor mouth. Crowds of people had gathered on the piers on either side to see them off. Most of them noticed nothing wrong; and though there were not wanting critical eyes, for Syracuse had plenty of sailors, young and old, among its citizens, there was a strong feeling that silence was safer than speech. The exit safely accomplished, the squadron turned southward, and had the honor of receiving the farewell salutations of the governor himself, who stood dressed in purple cloak and tunic reaching down to his heels, and surrounded by a party of gayly attired ladies in front of his seaside quarters.

In the course of an hour or so Cleomenes beckoned to his lieutenant. "You find," he said, "that every thing is not quite complete. You will remember that I told you so. But we have really got pretty nearly every thing we want, for this will be more of a promenade than an expedition. The pirates daren't show themselves within ten miles of us. Why, the *Chimæra* would sail over any one of their little bits of vessels and not feel it. Still we may as well pick up some more men from the seaside forts. To-morrow I will send you with a requisition to the officers in command. We

shall get some provisions too, I dare say, in the same **way**.
As for to-day we will do about ten miles more or so, and
then stop for the night. I shall have my tent pitched and
dine on shore. It is far more pleasant, I think, than living
on board. You will come, of course, to-night, and whenever you please without further invitation."

Two or three days' easy voyaging in this fashion brought
the squadron to the south-east corner of the island. Lucius
paid his visits to the forts, and duly presented his commander's requisition. His experience at the first of these
places, a somewhat ruinous building about five-and-twenty
miles south of Syracuse, pretty well represented what he
found at them all. " You want some men," said the old
soldier in command, a deputy centurion who must have
seen at least thirty years of service, " and are *authorized to
take as many as are not required for the safe keeping of the
fort.* That is how your document runs. Very good, sir.
I will muster the garrison, and you shall see how many I
have to spare. Very luckily you have come just at the right
time to see them all. They are mostly scattered a good
deal, looking out for something to eat, it may be, or doing
a stroke of work for a farmer in the neighborhood. But
just now they are all at hand."

All at hand they were, and they numbered exactly *nine*.
" Now, sir," continued the old soldier, " I might hold this
place with a hundred men, if the attack was not too brisk.
Of course if the enemy brought big catapults to bear on us,
or came to close quarters with pickaxes, they would soon
have the whole place down about our ears. Still I might
hold out pretty well with a hundred men. Well, I never

had more than *thirty*. This was five years ago, sir, when I came to the place. Since then they have been dropping off one by one. All the young and active fellows have found something better to do, and nobody seems to care whether they stay or no. The district round about here goes on paying for them, I am told, and some one, I suppose, draws the pay. It does not much matter, I fancy. Of course the pirates could take the place if they chose. But it is not worth their while. There is nothing for them to get, and I don't feel uneasy on that score, though this not the sort of thing that a veteran like myself cares to do. But you perceive, sir, I can't do any thing for you in the way of men. I see the requisition goes on : *The commander will also furnish you with any surplus stores that he may possess beyond what may be needed for his garrison.* Well, come this way and see what the men have got for their dinner."

He led the way into an adjoining room, where the men were engaged with their meal. They had a steaming dish before them, which Lucius at first sight supposed to consist of parsneps, but which he found on inquiry to be the roots of dwarf-palms. " There, sir," said the old officer, " that is what my men mostly live on. Happily there is no want of them about here. We do pick up a bird or rabbit now and then, and we keep a few hens, and sometimes we catch some fish on shore-lines ; but if it were not for the palms the men would sometimes come off very badly. No, sir, I have not got any *surplus stores beyond what may be needed for my garrison.*"

This matter disposed of, Lucius had some interesting talk with the old soldier. He had served his first campaigns in

Northern Italy two and thirty years before, when the barba
rians had swarmed across the Alps, and seemed likely to
bring back the times of Brennus and the Gauls. He had
been one of the few survivors of the dreadful day of Arausio,
where eighty thousand Romans and allies lay dead on the
field of battle, and he had shared in the two great victories
by which Caius Marius had delivered Rome from a destruc-
tion that had at one time seemed inevitable. His respect
for our hero was of course immensely increased when he
found out that he was a kinsman of the great consul. But
when the young man, whose blood fairly boiled at the tale
of these monstrous abuses, spoke of trying to get things
righted, he strongly advised him to do nothing. "You will
only be running your head against a wall, sir. These things
will get set right some day, but *we* had best leave them
alone. I am told that the governor we have now does not
care much what he does, so that he gets his own way. He
has scourged men and crucified them, yes, Roman citizens
too, if they so much as ventured to whisper a word against
him and his goings on. Take my advice, sir, and say
nothing, at all events as long as you are in Sicily."

This, as has been said, was a type of what our hero found
at all the forts which he visited on the same errand, and he
began to think that his command was not quite so desirable
a thing as he had once expected.

CHAPTER VIII.

THE RESULT OF THE CRUISE.

EVERY hour made Lucius more dissatisfied with his position. His chief was neither a soldier nor a sailor, had no idea of how to navigate a ship, and no wish, as far as could be seen, to fight it. The other captains were, perhaps, a little better fitted for their places. Of seamanship they had little or nothing; still they were not, like Cleomenes, mere effeminate fops. Lucius believed that they would fight if they had the chance. To tell the truth, though he was as brave a young fellow as ever stepped, he did not particularly wish that such a chance should come. For if the equipment of the *Chimæra* was defective, that of the other ships was simply deplorable. They had one man where they ought to have had five, and even for these scanty crews there were hardly sufficient arms, and scarcely a morsel of food. Lucius could only devoutly hope that the pirates had been so much terrified by the report of Cleomenes and his squadron that they would not think of making any nearer trial of its strength.

The weather was now becoming very hot, and the commander of the squadron was accustomed to spend both his days and his nights in the tents that had been pitched for him on the shore. He drank far into the night and slept far into the day. To his duties he was absolutely indifferent. No watches were kept; there was no exercising, no manœuvring, no drill. In fact the men were pretty well occupied in keeping themselves alive, for such small stores of provisions as, taught by experience, they had brought with them, were by this time exhausted. Lucius found that the palm-roots which he had seen in the guard-room of the fort were their chief means of subsistence. Some hours were daily spent in digging these from the ground, where happily they were found in unfailing abundance; and the rest of the day was often consumed in a search for any kind of game (for the poor fellows were not at all particular in their tastes) with which their fare might be improved. In this state of things Lucius felt himself helpless. All that he could do was to insist upon the arms being kept clean, and the sails and tackle ready for use, and to refuse, as far as courtesy and policy permitted, the unceasing invitations of his chief.

About a fortnight after the departure of the squadron from Syracuse, Lucius, taking a small guard with him, had been paying a visit to a fort on the south coast with the object of obtaining re-enforcements. This at least was the professed end of his journey; but, as a matter of fact, he had no hope of effecting any thing. He had long since found out that Roman credit and Roman resources were at their very lowest ebb in the island; and he could see no chance of a change for the better. The best thing, he felt, that he could do was to be as busy as he could about whatever duties were left to him, and to forget, as far as possible, a shameful state of things for which he was not responsible. He had done as little as he had expected, and was on his way back, when, mounting a height that commanded a view of the little bay in which the squadron had taken up its position, he saw something that made his heart beat with fierce excitement. A strange vessel was making its way from the southward towards the bay, and a sort of instinct seemed to tell him that she was one of the pirates of whom he had heard so much. She was long and low in the water, with three tall masts, too tall, a landsman would probably have thought, for her size. From the middle of the three a black flag floated. Her deck, he could see, was positively crowded with men. She came rapidly on, using both sails and oars. The sails were new and bright; the oars rose and fell with a regular sweep which told of a strong and well-practised crew. Casting a glance up at the shore, Lucius saw that the approach of the stranger had been perceived. The ships, which had been partially grounded, the sterns almost touching the shore, while the prows were afloat, were being hastily pushed into deeper water. There was indeed no time to notice more. The lieutenant felt that his place was with his ship, and that it was a misfortune, though capable, he hoped, of being repaired, that had separated him from it just at the moment when his services were most required. Bidding his guard follow him without delay, he set out at the top of his speed; and as he was a quick and long-winded runner, contrived to reach the shore at the exact moment when the *Chimæra* was gliding out into deep water, and to scramble on board. His companions, who were not so young, and possibly not so zealous, were left some distance in the rear, and judged it best to board one of the other ships.

Cleomenes was in a state of pitiable confusion and terror, bemoaning himself now over the loss of what he had been compelled to leave behind him in his tents on the shore, now on the detestable inconvenience of having to deal with the intruding pirate. "Idiot that I was," he exclaimed, beating his breast, and positively crying with vexation, "idiot that I was to take the best silver bowl on shore, and the Myron cup! There is nothing like it in Syracuse, and now that filthy barbarian will be burying his swine's snout in it. And the wine too! that thirty years' old Chian. I haven't more than two casks in my cellar, and it positively can't be got now for love or money. Lucius, what is to be done? Do you think that we could make terms with the fellow? Would you mind taking a flag of truce and seeing whether you could treat with him?"

"Surely, sir," cried the lieutenant astonished, "the best way will be to fight him. We haven't got, perhaps, all that we could wish; but there are some stout fellows on board. And then we are eight to one. Why, sir, we can run him down. The *Chimæra* is five times as big and heavy as that craft, and sails like a bird."

"Fight him!" screamed the captain; "fight him! we are not fit to fight. You know we're not. I shall do nothing of the kind. It is all very well for a hare-brained young fellow like you to talk of fighting, but I have got the lives of my men to think of."

He turned to the sailing-master and shouted, "Put every rag of sail on; send down all the men that can be spared to the oars, and steer due north."

For a moment Marius was stupefied with astonishment.

"What, sir," he cried, "you cannot mean that we are to turn our backs upon this pirate ! You don't trust your crew. But I am sure that these men will follow you if you will fight."

He looked round at the crew, many of whom had come aft, attracted by the raised voices of the two speakers. A murmur of assent was heard from many of them, though some, who did not care a jot for pirates or Romans, were silent.

"Fight !" cried Cleomenes, "it is impossible. I won't hear of it. I know that ship. It is Heracleo's own, and he is the most dangerous and determined villain in the whole Mediterranean."

Lucius stood in despair. The *Chimæra* was just beginning to catch the wind and to move more quickly through the water. Lucius had seen something of her sailing qualities, and had heard more from the old seaman who had practically commanded her. He felt pretty sure that, unless the wind dropped, she would easily outsail the pirate. But to escape on such conditions ! It was simply intolerable. His mind was quickly made up. The other captains could not possibly be such cowards as Cleomenes. He would throw in his lot with one of them. The nearest ship to the *Chimæra*, which, better manned and better equipped as she was, had naturally got a start of the others, was, as a hasty glance showed him, the *Gorgon ;* and he remembered to have met the *Gorgon's* commander among the guests of Cleomenes, and to have thought him a man of spirit and courage. Without giving his cowardly superior a chance of stopping him, he stepped on the gunwale of the ship and plunged into the sea. A distance of about three hundred yards divided the *Chimæra* from the *Gorgon,* and the distance was nothing to a practised swimmer, especially as the sea was calm and the water warm. Lightly clothed as he was, and carrying no weapon but a sword, he struck out for the *Gorgon,* and reached it in the course of a very few minutes. The crew helped him to scramble up its side, and he stood panting and breathless on the deck.

"Welcome, Lucius Marius," cried the captain, "though I never saw a guest arrive in so strange a fashion! But tell me, what is Cleomenes about? Is this some grand manœuvre that he is practising? Why does he not signal to us what we are to do?"

"Manœuvre!" said Lucius as soon as he had recovered his breath. "There is nothing of the kind, unless you call it a manœuvre to run away. He was screaming and crying like a woman, and shrieked with fear at the very notion of fighting. I told him that he could run down the pirate as easily as if it were a cockle-shell; but he wouldn't listen to a word. He could think of nothing but saving his precious skin. All the furies confound the coward! I couldn't stay with the villain and be disgraced. I am under your orders, sir, if you will take me."

The young captain reached out his hand. "You do me honor, sir," he said. "I am ashamed to think that that coward is a fellow-countryman, a Greek. Anyhow we will fight, and to tell you the truth I don't see what else we can do. The *Chimæra* can outsail the pirate, but *we* can't. And if the wind drops, as it is very likely to do towards sunset, Cleomenes, for all his running away, will find himself in a strait."

The crew was mustered, and Lucius observed with dismay that their numbers scarcely exceeded forty; that nearly half of them were men clearly unfit for service, and that the remainder, though more effective, were but indifferently armed, and bore on their faces the evident marks of privation and neglect. Such as they were, however, the best had to be made of them. The captain briefly addressed them.

"Comrades, the only hope you have is in yourselves and your swords. The pirate knows nothing of mercy. He may spare two or three of the strongest among you to ply his oars; the rest he will drown as a man would drown so many useless whelps. But you can at least die like men. This young Roman, sooner than fly with that runaway in the *Chimæra*, has come to share your fate. Follow him and me, and he will not be sorry that he left a coward to stand by the side of brave men."

The men shouted in reply as boldly and cheerily as any one could have hoped. Meanwhile the *Gorgon* was moving slowly on before a failing breeze, and the pirate was rapidly diminishing his distance. The position of affairs was this. Six of the squadron were in advance of the *Gorgon*, the *Chimæra* leading the way and rapidly gaining on its consorts; the remaining ship of the eight was about a quarter of a mile behind it. The pirate was now close upon this laggard, and Lucius and his comrades watched with intense interest for the result of the encounter between them. Would they surrender? Would they attempt to resist? Had they but been strong enough to man the oars, they would have reversed their course and hastened to the help of their comrade. But they had literally not a single man to spare for the rowing-benches, and the wind was against them if they wanted to go back. It was maddening to have to wait without being able to stir a finger to help themselves, but it was all that they could do. Their suspense was soon over, for they saw the pirates board and take possession of the vessel, apparently without meeting with any kind of resistance. Their own fate could not now be long delayed, as the pursuer was moving with at least double their own speed. A few minutes indeed brought him alongside; grappling-irons attached to light chains of finely-wrought iron, which it would have been difficult to sever, were made fast in their bulwarks, and the assailants prepared to board. Lucius had seen fighting before, but only as a non-combatant, unless we are to except his adventure in Calabria. He was now about to strike a blow for himself, and after one tremor — he hardly knew whether of joy or fear — had passed through him he addressed himself to his work. He felt a strange exaltation and intensifying of every feeling and faculty. Keeping his eyes fixed on the boarders, who were now climbing up from their own bulwarks on to the *Gorgon* (which stood some three or four feet higher out of the water than the pirate craft), he nevertheless seemed to take in as if by instinct the attitude and demeanor of every man in his own crew, and to appreciate in a moment the chances of the conflict. These, indeed, were deplorably unfavorable. Some ten or twelve cravens had already thrown down their arms and were begging for quarter; nearly as many more were evidently failing both in spirits and strength. The knot of determined men who had clustered about the captain and Lucius numbered less than a score, and the assailants were many times as numerous. The pirate leader, a wiry, well-knit man of about forty, led the attack, and engaged the captain of the *Gorgon*. Lucius found himself matched with a gigantic Asiatic, to judge from the darkness of his complexion, who had the advantage over him of nearly half a foot of stature. The young Roman, however, was a practised swordsman, and a resolute temper, inherited from a long line of ancestors who had been accustomed to take to fighting as one of the avocations of life, enabled him to turn the teaching of the fencing-school to good account. His blood seemed to be absolutely on fire, and yet he was entirely cool, if to be cool means to be wary and self-possessed, to see every chance, to use every opportunity, to lose nothing from rage or excitement. His head was protected by a small steel cap, but he had no other armor, and for the single conflict in which he was engaged, its absence, leaving its limbs unfettered, was no small advantage. He had laid aside his short Roman sword, and used a longer weapon of Asiatic manufacture (it came from a Colchian forge). A small dagger suspended from the girdle completed his equipment. His antagonist evidently thought that he could make short work of the affair. He dealt a tremendous blow at the young Roman's head, a blow delivered with such force that it partially broke through his guard, and but for the steel cap would have inflicted a severe, if not a fatal, wound. For a moment Lucius was half stunned, and the feeling of confusion lasted long enough to

prevent him from dealing the counter-stroke to which his
adversary had laid himself open. Two or three seconds
restored him to himself, and the pirate was not long in finding out that he had no raw lad to deal with. Each arm in
succession received a wound that weakened though it did
not disable him. His almost gigantic frame was better
suited for a single violent exertion than for endurance ; and
his courage was not of the kind that holds out against pain.
His blows became feeble, his guard unsteady ; he gave
ground, and would even, if the field of conflict had made
the movement possible, have turned to fly. Lucius, confident of victory, felt something of a playful impulse in
dealing with his vanquished foe, and remembering an old
trick of the fencing-school, gave a sudden twist to his
weapon which wrenched the weapon out of his adversary's
hand, and sent it spinning over the vessel's side. With a
sullen look, in which rage and fear were mingled, the barbarian stood waiting for the deadly blow. A practised
soldier would probably have dealt it at once, but some impulse which he would have found it difficult to name stayed
the young Roman's hand. The battle had been a positive
delight to him ; but now to kill this stalwart fellow, who
but just now had been matching his strength against him,
seemed monstrous. He fancied himself back in the fencing-
school, where to strike an antagonist already disarmed
would have been an impossible act. It was the feeling of
a boy in his first battle, one that would hardly recur in a
second experience, and perhaps would not even then have
resisted the reflection that he must either kill or be killed.
But if the disarmed pirate had reason to thank the impulse

which checked the blow, so also had the young soldier himself. His duel had been brief, but it had lasted longer than the struggle of which it was a part. This indeed had been finished as soon as it was begun. Numbers, arms, and spirit, every thing in fact, had been on the side of the assailants. An unlucky slip of the foot had put an end to the gallant fight which the captain, a brave and skilful man-at-arms, was preparing to make. A lunge at his antagonist, the commander of the pirate vessel, made perhaps with too much vigor, had exposed him to a sword stroke which almost severed his head from his body. His men lost all heart at his fall. A common feeling of the uselessness of resistance made them drop their weapons. Both conquerors and conquered had then turned to witness the duel that was being fought between Lucius and the Asiatic giant. The pirate chief had forbidden interference by a significant gesture, and he now watched the conflict with an amused interest. The giant was known and disliked as being something of a bully, and no one was prepared to be better pleased than his superior if he could be taught to be a little less overbearing. When he stood disarmed and at the Roman's mercy, the captain thought it was time to interfere, and gave a sign to two of the crew. They stealthily approached Lucius behind, and the lad, who had forgotten every thing but himself and his enemy, found himself in a moment disarmed and with his arms tied down to his sides. A single glance round showed him that the battle was over and that all his comrades were prisoners like himself.

"Well fought, young sir!" cried the captain, who had picked up a fair amount of Latin in conversation with not a few Italian prisoners. "Well fought! I haven't a better swordsman in my crew. Inguomar there has met his match, and, perhaps, will crow a trifle less loudly than hitherto. Excuse the indignity of being disarmed and bound. I did not know what mischief a hot young fellow with a sword in his hand might do, but if you will give me your word not to escape you shall be free."

Lucius saw no use in refusing the promise, and gave it with a grace and cheerfulness which made a favorable impression on his captor. No such indulgence was shown to the other prisoners, who were tied hand and foot and lowered into the hold.

The wind had by this time altogether failed, and the remainder of the Roman ships had got out such oars as they could man. They made, however, but little progress, and Lucius began to hope that, thus driven to bay, they would, willing or unwilling, be forced to fight. They might have done so then, as they would probably have done before, but for the cowardice of the commander of the squadron. The course of the *Chimæra* was suddenly changed. It became evident that Cleomenes had given up the hope of escaping with his ship, and was determined to abandon it. Its prow was directed to the shore, from which, indeed, it was not more than two or three hundred yards distant. In a few moments Lucius saw it beached, and watched the captain, whom he could distinguish by his gay cloak, leap from the deck on to the sand, and run inland at the top of his speed. The crew were quick to imitate his example. The other ships followed the lead of the *Chimæra;* all five were soon rocking, empty and helpless, in the breakers. The pirate captain did not apparently think it worth while to search them. He was doubtless aware how very little of value there was likely to be in a Roman ship which depended for its equipment upon Verres. He rowed up to each in turn, ordered some combustibles, of which he seemed to have an ample supply in hand, to be put on board and lighted. In a few minutes the whole were in a blaze, and in a few minutes more, for the ships were dry and rotten, the squadron had ceased to exist.

It was now nearly dark, and the pirates judged it best to remain where they were till the morrow. The prisoners in the hold were supplied with bread and water; Lucius was honored with better fare, some preserved meat, some dried fruit, and a small flask of tolerable wine. This he disposed of without going below. When he had finished, the captain brought him a cloak made of the rough goats'-hair cloth for which Cilicia was famous.

"You will be more comfortable up here than down below," he said in a friendly tone; "but wrap this round you against the dews, and take care to cover up your face from the moon. We sailors on these seas think the moon far more dangerous than the sun. A man won't let his worst enemy sleep uncovered in the moon. And now, good night!"

"Well," said Lucius to himself, "that does not mean very much. He may keep me from being moonstruck to-night, and may cut my throat to-morrow. However, it is no sort of good to anticipate, and he does not seem a bad kind of fellow."

All his anxiety, and of course it was impossible to feel

quite at ease when he found himself in such a plight, did not keep the young fellow long awake. He slept soundly and long, and the morning was well advanced before he opened his eyes. When he did open them he was half disposed to believe that they were deluding him. The pirate vessel was close upon the mouth of the harbor of Syracuse. At the moment of his first looking about him it was almost exactly opposite the place where the tents of Verres had been pitched. The prætor's camp had, it was evident, been hastily struck, and the beach was strewed with the relics of flight. Most men in Heracleo's position would have been content to drive the governor of Sicily from his summer quarters, but he was of a singularly daring temper, and he resolved to brave his enemies in a way that would not easily be forgotten. Three other vessels had by this time joined him. With this little squadron he entered the harbor. It was a thing that no hostile fleet but one had ever ventured to do before, and that one had never returned to tell the tale. The fleet of Athens, three hundred and fifty years before, had found its way in, but had never got out again. The Carthaginians had never been able to do so much ; the Romans themselves, though they had taken the city, had failed here. It was by land, and not by sea, that they had been successful. Lucius had been long enough in Syracuse to know that the town was proud of the harbor which no enemy had ever entered except to his own loss and ruin, and he watched with unmixed astonishment four insignificant vessels which could hardly have withstood one good-sized man-of-war make their way into the sacred enclosure. The sight that met his eyes was strange indeed. The harbor went deep into the most populous part of the city. From end to end its sides were thronged with men and women and children; the windows of the houses and the roofs of the public halls and temples were crowded. Not a sound was heard from the vast multitude as the four pirate ships rowed leisurely up the harbor, keeping about a bowshot from the shore, but otherwise, it would seem, careless of attack. There was both fear and anger in that strange silence. But the silence did not last very long. When the daring little squadron, after reaching almost the farthest point of ·the harbor, turned to leave it, without so much as a finger being raised to avenge the insult, a great roar of hatred and rage burst from the crowd. Men shook their fists at these impudent intruders; they shook them with still greater fury at the prætor's palace, where Verres, for once, it may almost be believed, ashamed of himself, was hiding. A new idea seemed to strike Heracleo when he heard the uproar. He gave orders that the course of his ship should be changed so as to bring it within a few yards of a spot where he could see the magistrates, conspicuous by their robes of office, standing at the water's edge. Astonished at this new piece of audacity the crowd grew silent again. The pirate threw some of the palm-roots which the Roman crew had been reduced to eat, and which had been left in the ship. "See," he cried in a clear voice which was heard far and wide, "see, your men have left their bread behind them." This done, he and his companions left the harbor as calmly and unconcernedly as they had entered it.

CHAPTER IX.

THE PIRATE CAPTAIN.

HERACLEO had now to dispose of his prisoners, of whom there were about thirty in all. It was no part of his policy to feed a number of useless mouths, and he could not dispose of them by sale — the usual way, in those times, of dealing with such property. They were all ranged in a line along the deck, and Lucius had to take his place among them. The pirate captain walked up and down this line several times, carefully inspecting the men's faces and figures. For the most part they were a poor, puny, half-starved lot. Never very strong, bad and scanty food had still further reduced them, while their ragged clothing would have almost looked shabby upon scarecrows. Still there were four young fellows whose frames, large, though ill-filled out, seemed to promise better things. These the captain picked out with the eye of a connoisseur, and beckoned them to stand out from the rank.

"Men," said he, "Rome does not seem to have fed or clothed you very well. Do you feel disposed to try whether I shall treat you better? Look at these fellows here"— the crew were standing in a half-circle watching the proceedings — "and see how you like their looks. We are all free comrades here. Every man has his share of what we earn according to his rank and time of service. When he thinks he has had enough he can retire, and we will find him a bit of land somewhere at home. What do you say?"

Three of the four came forward at once and said, "We agree;" the fourth stood still in his place, but shook his head in token of refusal.

"Very good, my man," said the pirate; "you think us a disreputable lot, and will have nothing to do with us. Perhaps you are right. Stand back; I will dispose of you afterwards."

The poor wretches who had not passed the captain's scrutiny stood trembling and fearing the worst. Pirates always have, and, for the most part, deserve, a very bad reputation, and report had of course been busy with the horrible doings of Heracleo and his companions. The men fell on their knees, stretched out their hands, and begged for mercy. Lucius remained standing, and another who had looked at first inclined to imitate the rest, followed his example.

"Rise up," said the captain with a smile of contempt. "I have no quarrel with you, and would not stir a finger to hurt you. I do not love the Romans; and you, if I may guess from your looks, have no special reason to do so. You shall be set on shore, but I recommend you not to try to earn your living in this way again. You see it is but a poor trade, and it isn't every one would be so merciful to his prisoners as I am, nor will I promise to be so a second time, if I catch sight of your faces again."

He then ordered a small flag to be hoisted from the

mizzen mast. Two or three fishing-boats that were in the neighborhood of the ship seemed to understand the signal, and hastened to approach. They evidently recognized the pirate, but were in no sort of fear of him. It was indeed his policy to be on good terms with the fishermen and all the humbler inhabitants of the coast, while he waged unceasing war against the fleets of Rome whether they were bent on war or on trade. These humble folk furnished him with information which often enabled him to lay his hands on prizes which he would not otherwise have secured, they piloted him through unknown waters, and indeed made it possible for him to defy for so many years all the power that was brought against him.

"Have you any fish for sale?" he began by asking.

An ample supply was promptly forthcoming, of which he purchased as much as he wanted at what seemed to Lucius a liberal price.

"And now," said he, "I want you to do something for me. You see these fellows here. I didn't ask you to take them in exchange for your fish. You might have thought it a bad bargain. What I do ask you is this. Put them ashore at the nearest town. Here is a silver piece for each man's passage-money. Deal fairly with them; you are honest fishermen, so don't behave worse than pirates."

He divided the prisoners among the boats, paying to the captains the sum which he had promised to give for their fare to the shore. He then handed to each prisoner another silver piece. "This," he said, "will buy you a loaf of bread or so till you can get something to do. And here are five pieces for you who were too honest a man to join us. As it is, I don't think we want you. Still I like an honest man though I am a pirate. Good luck go with you."

The fishing-boats went off with their new cargo, and now Lucius and a single companion remained to be dealt with. The elder of the two was taken first, and it was evident from the looks of the crew that a serious matter was in hand.

"Who is this man?" asked the captain; "does any one know any thing about him?"

"I do," said one of the crew, stepping forward and making his salute. "He used to be a tax-gatherer in Lycia; and if he gathered a silver talent for the tax-farmers he gathered a couple for himself. One of his tricks was to put off giving a receipt, and then declaring that he had never been paid. Another was to give no notice, or next to none, claim a great sum which a man could not easily get in a day or two, and sell him up if he was so much as an hour behind. That was how he ruined me. The gods confound him for it! I had as pretty a little farm, corn-land and pasture, and vineyard as there is in Lycia, and this fellow turned me out of it in the depth of winter. My wife and her baby died in the snow, and I lost these fingers from the frost," and he held up his maimed hand. "Yes, I know him."

"Is there any one else to speak to him?" said the captain after a pause.

"I know him," said a gray-haired sailor. "He was a trader then at Rhodes, and I was captain of one of his ships. He was one of a company that made good each other's losses at sea, and he took care that they should have losses enough to make good for him. He sent me to sea with a weak place in my ship's bottom that was bound to

give way as soon as ever it was tried.   I had my little bit of
cargo on board to trade with on my account.   That I lost;
but that was not all.   My two sons were among the crew,
and they were both drowned.   We three held on to a mast
for a day and a night; they, poor fellows, dropped off, first
one and then the other; I was coward enough to see them
die and to live on.   But that is the fellow that did it.   Yes,
I know him."

"Is there any one else?" asked the captain again.

"I know him," said a third voice, and a young man
stepped forward.   "If he has been a tax-gatherer and a
merchant, he has followed our trade too.   You know Cleon
of Coracus?   But do you know how he, one of the cleverest men that ever sailed a ship, was taken like a fool
of a rabbit in a trap?   Why, this man betrayed him, sold
him and his crew to the Rhodians.   He was his lieutenant,
and knew his plans.   He put the admiral of Rhodes on his
track, and was well paid for it too — a quarter-talent for
Cleon and three gold pieces for each of his crew, and there
were eighty of them.   My own brother was one of them;
and I saw them crucified and stuck round the harbor.   Yes,
I know him."

The wretched man turned to each of his accusers as he
rose a face that grew more and more ghastly pale.

"What have you to say for yourself?" asked Heracleo in
a cold quiet voice.

"They have lied," he said.   "I am an honest man."

"Nay," said the captain, "now that I come to think, I
do remember you as Cleon's lieutenant, but you are grown
fat and sleek beyond all knowledge.   That he was betrayed

I know, and I always believed that you were the man that did it. And if you could do that, it would be easy enough for you to sell up a farmer, and send a ship and its cargo to the bottom. What say you, men?"

A low growl of assent went round the half-circle. At a sign from the captain a stalwart fellow stepped out from the ranks and laid a heavy hand on the culprit's shoulder. The man started and screamed with fear. "Take care what you are doing. Any harm that you may do me will be repaid tenfold. Don't touch me. I am a citizen of Rome."

The words produced a singular effect upon the assembly. They seemed to pass in a moment from rage to calm. But it would have been a very careless observer who should fancy that the change boded any good for the prisoner. The smile that passed over the captain's face was grim and mocking. It was not fear, but the eager prospect of a bitter jest that made his crew so quiet. The man that had put his hand on the prisoner's shoulder at once stepped back and made an exaggerated gesture of respect.

"Pardon me, sir," he said; "we were not aware that we had the honor of entertaining so distinguished a guest."

Then turning to the rest of the crew, "Do you hear this, you insolent fellows? Here is a Roman citizen, and we have actually kept him in the hold! Down on your knees, all of you, this moment, and beg his pardon."

The men did as he said, with a ludicrous imitation of dismay and penitence. They seized hold of the wretched man's hand and covered it with kisses, while they implored his pardon and besought his good offices with his countrymen. When they had sufficiently amused themselves in this way they went on to play another act in the farce.

"Don't you see," cried the man who had spoken before, "that our honored guest is not dressed quite as he should be? We did not see at once that he is a citizen. Bring a pair of shoes and a gown."

A pair of shoes in the last stage of shabbiness and decay, and a gown of which one might possibly guess that it had once been white, were brought out. The leader in this tragical sport began to untie the sandals which the prisoner wore and to fasten the shoes in their place with an elaborate show of respect and care. The gown was then carefully arranged, the folds being made to fall with as much dignity as their ragged condition allowed.

"There, sir," said the man, falling back a step and pretending to look at his victim with admiring awe. "There, sir, you are dressed at last as becomes your station. And now I doubt not you would gladly leave us and return to your native country. It overwhelms me with grief and dismay to think that we have detained a citizen of Rome so long. — Make ready there for my lord's departure."

A ladder was let down the ship's side, and the pirate, taking the prisoner's hand, led him with the utmost courtesy of manner to the side.

"I am afraid, sir," he went on, "that there will be a little difficulty about the way. We can take you most conveniently as far as the water; but as to any thing further we really don't see what can be done. You will have to do the best you can. But no harm can possibly happen to so distinguished a person, and in any case we could not possibly

think of detaining you any longer. Will you please to
descend?"

The wretched man cast an agonized glance about him;
but there was not one gleam of pity in any of the swarthy
faces which surrounded him. Then he collected himself.
Vicious and degraded as he was, his nerves shaken by the
excesses of an evil life, he was still a Roman, and like a
Roman he would die. Folding his arms resolutely upon his
breast he jumped from the deck, and in a moment disappeared below the water.

It was now Lucius' turn, and the prospect was gloomy
for him. The ferocious instincts of the crew had been
roused, and they were ready to demand another victim.

"And you too, young sir," said the man who had taken
the leading part in the dismal farce which has been
described, "are you a Roman citizen?"

The captain whispered, "Say that you are not. No one
knows you here."

For a moment Lucius hesitated. Life was dear to him,
as it is dear to every man, even to those whom it has given
little, and promises, perhaps, less. And it had been dearer
than ever to him since that perilous ride across the Calabrian hills with the Tarentine maiden, and the happy following days in which he had learned to love, and had begun
to hope that he was himself beloved. For a moment he
hesitated, but not for more than a moment. If he followed
that poor wretch down to the bottom of the sea he should
never look on Philareté again, but neither, he felt, could he
look upon her again if he were to stain his honor with a lie,
and deny his country. He made up his mind.

"Yes," he said in a clear confident voice, lifting his head as he spoke, "yes, I am a citizen of Rome."

There were a few in the crowd on whom the courage of this frank declaration was not lost; but they were only a few. A pirate's life does not help to cultivate generous feelings. A low growl of "Let him go home with his fellow" ran round the crowd, and the man who had been foremost in the sport stepped forward again. But Lucius' time was not come. The pirate captain stood up in front of the men and spoke:

"Comrades, I don't often interfere between you and your spoil or your sport. You have your share, and I have mine. If there is any one who thinks that he has been unfairly dealt with, let him speak. You are all silent; then I will assume that you are satisfied. But I have a right, which I have seldom claimed, the right to have my first choice out of the booty which we take. I claim it now, and my choice is this lad. And you, I trust, approve."

He spoke in a good-humored tone, but like a man who was not accustomed to have his requests denied. A sullen murmur was heard from some of the crew. In a moment his manner changed. "What!" he cried; "do you hesitate? It is my right, and I will have it. Have I been your captain these ten years, led you to victories more than you could ever have hoped, and made you richer than your dreams, and now my right, I do not say my wish, but my right, is questioned. Who is on my side?"

More than half the crew stepped forward; the rest looked at each other and hesitated. "Down on your knees, mutineers," cried the captain in a voice of thunder, "and beg pardon." He was instantly obeyed. Then his manner changed again. His tone became soft and caressing. "Surely such old friends as we are cannot quarrel about such a trifle as this. It is my whim, and you must honor me. The steward shall broach a cask of Cyprus for you, and you shall drink to our new comrade."

He turned to Lucius and whispered, "You are safe for the present. Come into my cabin. It will be best for you to be out of their sight. We shall have time to talk about your future to-morrow. Meanwhile take a little rest."

The young Roman was glad to follow this advice. His head was beginning to ache most painfully. He had had, in fact, a slight sunstroke. For two or three days he was not able to raise his head from the couch on which he had thrown himself, but passed his time in a half-dozing condition. The pirate ship meanwhile was rapidly pursuing its journey eastward.

CHAPTER X.

AMONG THE PIRATES.

EARLY in the morning of the third day Lucius was roused by an unusual trampling of feet over his head. He found himself on awaking quite free from pain, and with no more remains of languor than might be got rid of by a bucket or two of sea-water. He was about to go upon deck in search of this remedy, when, to his surprise, he found the door of the cabin fastened from the outside. The cabin had a little window in the stern covered with talc, a passable substitute for glass, used much in ancient times. He could just catch sight through this of a vessel which appeared to be about three miles behind, and which, as far as he could judge, was sailing in the same direction. It had a crowd of canvas upon it; whether it was also using oars it was too far off to see. He naturally began to speculate as to whether the appearance of this stranger had any thing to do with his confinement. Looking again through the window in about a quarter of an hour's time he felt certain that the pursuing ship, if indeed it was pursuing, had decreased the distance. At the same time he became aware that the pirates had manned their oars, and he had little doubt that they were being chased. A few minutes later the door was opened, and the captain presented himself. "Excuse me," he said, "for keeping you a prisoner down here. You are looking, by the way, much better this morning. The fact is that it would not be safe for you to be on deck just now. That ship — you have seen her, I dare say, through the stern window — is chasing us, and, unless the breeze gets much fresher than it is now, will probably overtake us. I know her by the cut of her sail. She is the *Apollo* of Rhodes, and is one of the fastest sailers in these seas. And she is very well manned too. If she comes up with us we shall have a very hard fight for it, and I think that you will be the better out of it. I called you ' our new comrade ' the other day ; but I know better than that, and the men know it too. You never could be a comrade of ours. Well, you see, as you could not be with us, my men would hardly believe but that you would be against us. Besides, if we were taken you would be an awkward witness against us. I don't know whether witnesses would be much wanted. As for myself, if ever I am taken my fate is certain, for I am as well known in these seas as the Colossus of Rhodes itself. Still there are some here who are not known, and who might escape if there wasn't some one to swear to them, and that is just what you could do, and, mind you, would have to do. You would have to tell the story, for instance, of that poor wretch yesterday, and that would crucify every man on board. Well, the long and short of it is, that if you were seen on deck you would probably be got rid off. I couldn't save you, and I don't want either any thing to happen to you, or to have a quarrel with my men, especially just now. So I shut you in the cabin for

your own sake, and I advise you, if we come to a fight, to
fasten the door from the inside. I shall do my best to
sink the ship sooner than be taken ; but if it comes to that,
I give you my word to let you out first, and then you must
take your chance."

The captain left the cabin, again fastening the door on
the outside. Lucius continued to watch, and, it may be
guessed, with increased interest, the approach of the *Apollo.*
For that she was approaching there could be no doubt.
The breeze was dying away, and the greater breadth of canvas which the Rhodian spread enabled her to catch every
breath that there was. Lucius could now see the gilded
figure-head under the bowsprit, and the flag bearing upon it
a sun with streaming rays (Rhodes was pre-eminently the
land of the sun), and could almost reckon the number of
rowers that must be plying the two banks of oars. As for
himself, he hardly knew what to wish. The thought of
freedom was sweet, but the risk was terrible. If the captain should be killed — and what was more likely in the
desperate fight that was likely to happen? — who would
care or even remember to give him a thought? He might
easily be drowned without a chance of escape, shut up like
a rat in a trap, and to perish in such a fashion seemed ten
times more dreadful than to fall in fair fight upon the field.
The Rhodian was now within a hundred yards of the pirate,
and commenced the attack by a shower of arrows. But the
distance was still too great. A few stuck feebly in the ship's
side ; most fell into the water. Another moment or two,
however, brought the *Apollo* within a spear's-throw of her
enemy. The antagonists were now so close that Lucius

could no longer see any thing from his post of observation. But a heavy fall overhead followed by a groan told him that the battle had commenced in earnest. It had commenced indeed, but it was not to go on. The Rhodian was within a few yards of the pirate, and its crew were preparing to grapple and board, when an unexpected event happened. Lucius, who still looked through his window, though what was going on had passed out of the range of his sight, perceived that the sea to windward had grown suddenly dark. A squall was travelling rapidly in the direction of the two ships, too rapidly to raise the sea into great waves, but raising and whirling a cloud of foam before it as it went. It took the *Apollo* entirely unawares, so intent were the captain and crew upon the pursuit and the fight, and as every inch of canvas had been spread to catch the failing breeze the situation was extremely perilous. Happily for the ship her mainmast went by the board. Even then she heeled over to the very edge of the water, and it was doubtful for a moment whether she would recover. The pirate suffered less. She was lower in the water, and she had a smaller breadth of canvas. Lucius felt her dart forward like an arrow from the bow, and the next moment saw the damaged pursuer at least a hundred yards astern, and hanging over her side the mass of tangled sails and cordage which her crew were using all their efforts to cut away. He felt that this chance, whether it meant escape or death, was over, and half disappointed, half relieved, he sat down with what patience he could summon to wait for what next might happen.

It was not long before he heard the outside bolts withdrawn. The captain entered, in high spirits as it seemed.

"Well," said he, "that was a narrow escape, and perhaps it was as lucky for you as it certainly was for us. It might have gone hard with you, especially if I had been killed. Now you can come upon deck. The men are in the best of humors. Indeed, we are now so near home that we may feel pretty safe. Don't you feel disturbed at that. You may depend upon me for getting you away from our disreputable company somehow."

Lucius gladly availed himself of the permission to leave his prison, and breathed again the fresh air with the keenest delight. A bath was his first thought, and this was easily managed after a fashion. There was a ladder down the side of the ship. He climbed down this, and stood on the lowest rung while one of the crew dashed over him some buckets of sea-water, a vigorous shower-bath which did him, he felt, an immensity of good, and gave him an appetite which almost astonished himself, for the breakfast of boiled fish and bread, washed down with warm wine and water, which was served to him and the captain under an awning on deck.

"We are not far from our journey's end," said Heracleo to his guest. "If this wind holds good a while longer we shall be there to-morrow morning. We don't go back home till the winter sets in ; but we have a station about half-way between that and our best hunting-ground (which, I may tell you, is the sea about Italy). There we put in some time in the course of the summer, according as it may suit, to repair damages, and refit and divide any profits that we may have made. The place, by the way, is something of a secret. No one who happened to sail by would guess that it was there ; and you will have to swear in the presence of the crew to say nothing about it. Otherwise I sha'n't be able to answer for your life. When we get there we will see what can be done for you."

The west wind continued to blow steadily, and the pirate dashed gayly along eastward. Lucius, though he was a prisoner among men who were commonly thought to be the worst cut-throats in the world, could not help feeling his spirits rise. What the future might bring he could not, did not even try to, guess; but the present, as far at least as its outward surroundings were concerned, was delightful. The sea was of the deepest blue, touched here and there with white as a wave curled over and broke; the sky was cloudless, though a slight haze just veiled the sun and tempered its heat. Sometimes a "school" of tunnies or porpoises would be seen rolling over and over in the water; sometimes a flock of sea-gulls and cormorants would be seen, now hovering in air, now dashing down upon the waves, where a shoal of mackerel moved like the shadow of a little cloud across the shining surface of the sea. Meanwhile the crew, glad to be released from the labor of the oars by a steady stern wind that sent on the ship faster than any rowing could move her, lay on the deck or lounged against the bulwarks, joining in a snatch, now of Greek, now of Latin, and now again of some barbarous song. They were indeed a polyglot collection. The bulk of the crew were Cilicians, and fellow-countrymen of the captain; but they had recruits among them from the whole of the Mediterranean shores, from the Pillars of Hercules on the west as far as the Syrian coast on the east. Whatever the place they came from, most of them had learned to express themselves, if it was but rudely, in both Latin and Greek. How far they had come on their way, Lucius had but little idea. Some high land was just visible in the extreme distance on their left hand, and he guessed, judging by the length of time they had been running before the wind, that it might be the southern point of Greece; and the idea was confirmed, when, after two or three more hours' sailing, a long stretch of land, which seemed as they approached rapidly to rise out of the water, showed itself on their right. Before the light failed he could just distinguish white cliffs, which formed, he could hardly doubt, the western end of the " chalk island," Crete.

"You had best go below," said the captain to him, as he lingered, long after sunset, on the deck, entranced by the singular beauty of the scene. " The wind has brought us on quicker than I expected. Had it been in the daytime I should have had to blindfold you, for we don't care that any stranger should know the secret of our harbor of refuge. As it is, it will be enough if you will go below and sleep. Don't wake, or anyhow don't rise, till I call you."

Lucius promptly obeyed advice which, though spoken with good humor, had all the tone of a command, and was soon sleeping the dreamless sleep of youth. When he awoke he found the captain standing by his couch.

"Well done, my son," was his morning salutation. " You really flatter me by sleeping so soundly. I can't indeed be so bad as they would make me out if my prisoners are so much at their ease. But get up and dress yourself. You remember about the oath. We are going to have a sacrifice, and you can't do better than take it on the victim. For myself, I am quite satisfied with your word; and besides, I don't suppose you have much notion of where you are, or how you got here. Still, the men will have it so, and it is only fair to satisfy them."

"I have no difficulty about swearing," said Lucius; "though, as you say, I know nothing to tell, except that when I last saw the land I guessed that we were somewhere near the west end of Crete."

"Well, that is not much of a clew. I don't mind telling you that you are right so far. But Crete, you know, is a famous place for labyrinths; and this is as pretty a little labyrinth for finding your way in or out of as you will easily see."

It was indeed a curious scene that met the young Roman's eyes when he came upon deck. He found himself in what he knew must be a landlocked harbor, but which, only that he knew that the ship must have found its way in by some channel or other, he would have believed to be an inland lake. Its shores were steep down to the water's edge, varying in height from fifty to sometimes as much as two hundred feet. Above the cliffs rose a perfect circle of wooded hills, the sloping sides of which were now lustrous in the early morning sunlight. On one side only of the harbor was there any level ground. Here a small stream, which found its way down through a ravine in the hills, had made, it would seem, a little delta for itself. An expanse of meadow, still beautifully green, though midsummer was now past, lay on either side of the channel, through which the water, though now shrunk to almost its smallest space, still babbled gayly. It was on the edge of this low-lying part of the shore, that Heracleo's ship, with five others, for Lucius saw that they were not the only occupants of the harbor, were drawn up. They were ranged with their sterns to the shore, being attached by strong cables to posts driven into the ground, while the prows were kept in position by anchors on either side. A crowd of men, which must have numbered at the least five or six hundred, was ranged in a semicircle in one of the river-side meadows. Close to the stream itself stood a rude altar of stone, and a number of oxen, sheep, white and black, and some large swine, were ranged, ready, it would seem, for the sacrificer's knife.

"Come along," said the captain: "they are waiting for us. They will sacrifice that white bull you see there, and you will have to put your hand on the altar, and swear to keep the secret of the island."

They landed by a gangway, and went up to the altar, a loud cry of welcome rising from the crowd as soon as the well-known figure of the captain was seen. The bull, whose horns had been roughly gilded, stood quiet, an omen of good luck, as the crowd did not fail to observe with delight. The first thing was to cut away some of the short hairs which grew upon the forehead and to burn them in the fire that had been kindled on the altar. One of the attendants now brought a bowl of salted meal, which he sprinkled between the animal's horns. Meanwhile another had approached from behind, and swinging a great pole-axe over his head, dealt a mighty blow which severed the spine. The bull fell heavily forward. Another attendant cut the throat from ear to ear, and a fourth held beneath a broad dish which was to catch the blood. Lucius was now called up to take the oath. As it did nothing but bind him to secrecy about

things of which he really had no knowledge, he felt no
objection to taking it. Placing one hand on the stones of
the altar, the other on one of the horns of the victim, he
repeated the words : " I, Lucius Marius, swear by all the
gods of heaven and hell that I will reveal nothing that I
know concerning the affairs of the free Confederacy of the
Seas." The sacrifice then proceeded. Some of the inner
fat and some of the entrails of the animal were burned in the
fire ; the rest of the flesh was kept for the feast, which was
not the least important part of the ceremony. The other
animals were dealt with in the same way, the name of a different god or goddess being called over each. Roman, Greek,
and barbarian deities were thus honored. As may be supposed, a congregation of sailors did not forget to secure, if
they could, the favor of the powers that controlled the
weather. White sheep were offered to the nymphs whose
kindly power was supposed to give gentle breezes, and
black sheep to the storms.

The banquet that followed was a scene of rude enjoyment. An unlimited supply of fresh meat was a luxury
that the company but seldom enjoyed, and which they made
the most of on the rare occasions when it came. Lucius
had seen at home that a Volscian ploughman or vine-dresser,
accustomed to live for the most part on vegetable diet,
could, on the occasion of a feast, dispose of a vast quantity
of flesh, but he had never seen any thing like the feats
which his new companions accomplished in this way. The
sea-air seemed to have given them appetites which it was
impossible to satisfy. These heroic supplies of food were
washed down by equally heroic draughts of wine. Great

casks had been broached; from these the wine had been transferred into pitchers, and mixed with rather more than its own bulk in water. A number of young lads were fully employed in running up and down the ranks in which the guests had ranged themselves round the altar, and filling the cups. These, Lucius observed, were of silver, and in some cases even of gold. Many a private plate-chest, many a public treasury, and, it was said, many a temple in the sea-board cities of the Mediterranean must have been ransacked to make so goodly a show of wealth. The mirth of the day, of course, would not have been complete without song. As the feast was held in the open air, and the company was large, there were few singers who could have made themselves heard by all. The guests, therefore, naturally broke up into parties, who found for themselves the entertainment that they best liked. In one place a party of Greeks, real or so called — for the Greeks had always an astonishing success in giving their customs and language to tribes quite remote from them by birth — listened to a recitation from Homer. In another place a number of Cilician mountaineers joined in chorus with some ballad in their own tongue. Lucius himself, pressed to sing, and yielding to the request on a nod from the captain, gave them an old Volscian war-song, handed down from the time when the little mountain state had matched itself on equal terms with Rome. We may venture to say that none of the audience understood it, but the air and lilt of the words had something spirited and martial about them; Lucius, too, possessed a very sweet and powerful voice, and the effort was received with great applause.

Having thus discharged his duties as a guest, he was glad enough to steal away and refresh himself with a bath. The bath over, he took a *détour* which brought him to the upper side of the meadow on which the feast was held. It was his fancy to follow up the stream through the woods, from which it issued forth on to the plain. This was no easy task, but it amply repaid all the trouble spent upon it. The air, permanently protected from the sun by the over-arching trees, was deliciously cool; and the stream made its way down to the plain by a beautiful succession of cascades and pools, these latter tenanted, as Lucius could see, by some fish of magnificent size. After a while farther progress was barred by a precipice, over which the stream made a sudden leap of more than sixty feet, and which, as far as the young traveller could see, it was impossible to climb.

It was almost dark when he found himself again on the shore. A few revellers were still lingering over the remnants of the feast, but the greater part lay fast asleep about the meadow. It had been arranged that he should take up his quarters at night in the ship, and he was very glad to avoid the noisy or drunken occupants of the beach.

In the course of the next day he made acquaintance with a young Greek of about the same age as himself; and the friendship grew as rapidly as friendships do under such circumstances. Two or three days afterwards the two had been bathing together, and were resting after an unusually long swim, when they heard voices on the other side of the rock in the shadow of which they were sitting. They could not see or be seen by the speakers, but as the distance was not more than a few yards every word uttered was distinctly audible.

"It is all very well," began one of the men, "for our captain to have his fancies; but it does not seem to me the
right way of carrying on our business. To my mind there
is only one safe maxim for this trade of ours: 'Dead men
tell no tales.' I don't take much count of oaths. I have
broken too many myself; ay, and seen others break them
too. I know something much better than an oath for
stopping a man's mouth."

What this something was, Lucius and his companion could
not see, for the speaker explained himself by a gesture; but
they could guess.

"Ay," said another voice, "but what will the captain
say? He has taken a great fancy to the lad, and I shouldn't
care to come in his way if he knew that I had harmed
him."

"There is no need for him to know," returned the first
speaker; "the fellow and that young Greek, who, by the
way, is just another of the same sort, are always wandering
about; and a couple of strokes of a dagger would dispose
of them. Bury their bodies in the sand for the time, and
sink them in thirty fathom of water next night with a stone
round their necks, and we needn't trouble about them any
more. What do you say?"

At this point the two fellows turned back, but Lucius had
heard enough.

"And what do *you* say?" he said to his young friend.

"Why, that we must be off. I have thought so for some
time. I have been here, as I dare say you know, some time
longer than you, and I have heard one or two hints before
that the men don't like any one to be here who is not one

of them. You see, they bury a great deal of their treasure here. That I happen to know for certain. If they knew I knew it, I should have made acquaintance long since with the pleasant things which our friends just now were talking about. But even as it is they are suspicious. We must go, I say."

"It is all very well," returned Lucius, "to say 'go,' but how is it to be done? It seems to me that we might as well try to fly up to the moon."

"Well, we can't go by ourselves. Still, I think that I see a way. There is a man here who goes in fear of his life, and would be rejoiced to get away. He has got a blood-feud, you see, with some of his comrades; and though it is supposed that such things are forgotten on service, it will sometimes happen that on a dark night, when a man is found alone, they will be suddenly remembered. He is a strong fellow, and a capital seaman, I have heard. My idea is that we should get him to go with us; make free with one of the boats, the smallest we can find that will stand any sea, put something to eat and drink on board if we can find it, and make the best of our way off."

"But how about the captain? Shall we tell him?"

"I should say 'certainly not.' He is an excellent fellow, a great deal too good for his company; but it is better that he should know nothing about it. If he were to help us it would be very awkward for him with his men. You see, he is captain, but he mustn't draw the reins too tight. No; we had best go without a word; and, depend upon it, he will be very glad if we can get away, and all the more glad the more kindly he feels towards us. Meanwhile I will see what my friend the sailor thinks. Meet me after sunset. If it is to be done we had better lose no time about it."

At the time appointed Lucius returned to the place, and had not to wait long before he saw the young Greek, whose name, by the way, was Charicles, approaching.

"I have made it all right with the sailor," he said; "he is as anxious to get away as we are. He is in charge of one of the ships, and he can get away with the biggest of the boats without taking much trouble. Don't go to sleep to-night, but keep on the lookout for us. We shall come to your cabin as soon after midnight as possible. The moon will be just rising then, and there will be enough light, but not too much."

Lucius' only anxiety was about the captain. Would he pass the night as usual on shore? Very probably; but once he had slept on board ship. If he did so on this occasion there would be nothing for it, Lucius felt, but to take the chance of letting him into the secret. Luckily the question did not arise. Heracleo slept on shore, where indeed his presence was required to keep a somewhat turbulent company in order.

The hours seemed to Lucius to be lengthening almost into days as he waited for the boat. As a matter of fact, however, it was punctual to its time. The moon was still behind the amphitheatre of wooded hills, though the sky had begun to lighten a little under the influence of its rays, when a boat, rowed by two muffled oars, came stealing silently along. It was not without reluctance that Lucius left his preserver in so unceremonious a fashion. The purse girdle which he wore round his waist still contained a small store of gold pieces. Of these he left three as payment for a small bundle of clothing with which the captain had supplied him, and which he now thought it better to take with him. To these he added a small silver ring, the parting gift of one of his boyish friends at Arpinum. He was unwilling to part with it, but he was still more unwilling to leave one who, pirate as he was, had served him so well, without some token of remembrance. It would be as well, he felt, to postpone as long as possible the discovery of his departure. Accordingly he did not leave the money and the ring on the table of the cabin, where the captain would be sure to notice them, but dropped them into a drawer where they would probably lie for some time undiscovered, but would certainly be found sooner or later. These preparations had been made before the time appointed for the boat's arrival. When it came he had nothing to do but to drop into it with his bundle. The shore on which the ship lay was happily within the shadow of the hills, behind which the moon was rising. By this shadow, which grew darker and less penetrable as the moon began to throw its light on the rest of the harbor, the boat crept along, the sailor looking carefully out for the opening of the harbor, a place which it was very easy to miss. There was a break in the line of cliff; but it was a break through which one saw, not the open sea, but another line of cliff behind. The fact was that the real opening was guarded from sight by a great mass of rock, some two hundred feet in length, and covered at the top with a growth of trees, and separated from the shore by a channel of about forty feet in breadth. Into this channel there was, of course, an entrance at either end of the covering rock, but the sailor, for all the intentness of his watch, missed that to which the boat first came, and had nearly missed the other. Luckily he observed it before it was too late. Creeping round the corner of the rock, a manœuvre easy enough for the boat, but difficult in the extreme for a ship of any size, they found themselves in the channel. A slight motion of the water soon told them that they were near the sea; and before long the sea itself, light with the rays of a moon which had now risen high in the heavens, became visible to them.

CHAPTER XI.

A STRUGGLE FOR LIFE.

FOR some time hardly a word was spoken. The two oarsmen bent to their work, and put all the speed they could upon the boat. Pursuit, indeed, was not probable, for they seemed to have escaped observation, and several hours would probably elapse before their absence would excite attention. Lucius had steered as he had been directed, due south, finding his course by the stars, for the night was fortunately clear. The wind was nearly aft, coming as it did a few points to the westward of north. When about two hours had passed the dawn became visible, and as the light increased the breeze slightly freshened. The sailor, a stout-built man of about forty years of age, now ceased rowing, and with the help of Charicles put up the mast, and spread the one sail, a large fore-and-aft piece of canvas, to the wind. He took the rudder into his own hand, and giving a slightly more easterly direction to their course proceeded to review the situation. He was a native, we may here say, of Lycia, and spoke a broken dialect of Greek, interspersed with some Latin and some barbarous words, which Lucius would have found it difficult, if not impossible, to understand without the help of the young Greek.

"Will you see, sir," he began, "what we have got to eat and drink? I put in what I could lay my hands upon at the moment, but I am afraid there is very little."

The stock was found to consist of a cask holding about twenty gallons of water, a keg of salted mutton, two bags of biscuit — not exactly our modern article, but bread which, to prevent its growing mouldy, had been double-baked — and a skin of wine, holding, it might be, eight or ten gallons. Lucius had made free to add to his bundle of clothing a couple of the captain's fishing-lines. He never forgot a chance of amusing himself with his favorite sport, and there was a hope that they might be of service in replenishing their stock of food.

"Well," said the sailor, "it might be worse, and it might be better. This won't keep us very long; but it ought to do till we strike the land somewhere — Crete ought to be somewhere on the south-east, unless I am quite out in my reckoning — or, better still, till we fall in with a vessel; the gods grant it be not a pirate! This north-westerly wind will hold, I take it, for a good time yet; it always blows about this time of year, and, luckily, is seldom very strong. We can't stand much of a breeze, you know, in this little cockle-shell."

Lucius and his young friend could, of course, do nothing else but hand over the management of the little craft to their older companion; and indeed they had little doubt of his being well capable of it. According to his calculations they could hardly fail to sight some part of the northern coast of Crete within two days, the course that he steered being south-east by south, and the wind blowing steadily from N.N.W., and driving the little boat with its capacious sail gayly before it at the rate of at least seven miles an hour. So confident were the voyagers of this result, that they were less sparing of their provisions and water than they would otherwise have been. When the third morning came, and then the fourth, and nothing was in sight, their position began to be serious. The sailor himself was evidently anxious, and scanned the southern horizon unceasingly for some token of land, but all in vain. He had evidently miscalculated his position, had probably overshot the eastern end of Crete, and had got besides into a part of the sea which was outside the usual tracks of eastward or westward bound traders. Hitherto, indeed, they had not seen a single sail. Still, if they held on in the same course they could hardly fail to come across the route which was commonly followed by Italian and Greek merchantmen when sailing to Alexandria, the only danger being that they might cross it in the night, and so pass into another unfrequented region. This was re-assuring, and they were beginning to recover their spirits when an unexpected calamity reduced them almost to despair. The wind suddenly failed, and they lay under a scorching sun, with not more than a couple of days' scanty allowance of water and food. Lucius tried his fishing-lines, but in vain ; they were in one of the deeper regions in the Mediterranean, where, as, indeed, is the case in all seas where the depth exceeds a certain limit, fish are exceedingly scarce. It was possible, indeed, to make a slight progress by rowing, but so slight was it that it scarcely repaid the exertion. Indeed they soon gave it up by common consent. Their only chance seemed to be to husband their strength to the utmost in the hope that some happy chance might bring them across a ship's path. They arranged the sail as an awning, and cowered under its shade from the heat of the sun, waiting with what patience they could muster for relief. The fishing-lines were still useless, except that twice a sea-bird laid hold of the bait as it happened to float upon the top of the water, and was secured and devoured almost before it could be plucked.

The young Roman, schooled to endurance from his earli-est boyhood, and taught that to bear hunger and cold and heat with patience was at least as great a part of a soldier's and citizen's duty as to be bold on the battle-field, held out against his sufferings, intense as they were, with admirable fortitude. His Greek companion, though not so sternly trained, for he came from one of the luxurious and pleasure-loving cities of the Ionian coast, and was not made of so strong a fibre as Lucius, had yet a brave spirit of his own, and would not be behind his comrade. But the sailor was of a weaker and more vulgar nature. He had had more than his share of the provisions, for the two lads had not failed to remember that he was a full-grown man, besides having to bear the larger part of the labor; but he had never been satisfied. When the last division had been made he had not had the self-restraint to use any economy with the slender store allotted to him, and had been relieved more than once by the kindness of Lucius and the young Greek. As time went on, and the sufferings of the party in-creased, it was evident that he was becoming desperate. On the morning of the fourth day he signed to the young Greek that he wished to speak to him. (He commonly occupied the fore part of the boat, while the two lads sat in the stern.) Lucius had no particular reason to suspect him of any evil design; still he watched the two as they talked, and saw an unmistakable look of horror come over the face of the Greek. An inkling of the truth flashed across him in a moment. The two, though of different races, were, in a sense, fellow-countrymen; he was a foreigner and a stranger. Could the sailor be plotting his death? and how? What would it profit him, if it were accomplished? Whatever it was that the sailor said, after the first look of dismay which Lucius had happened to catch, the young Greek showed no sign of emotion or surprise. He seemed to listen attentively, and to nod now and then as if in assent.

"What was our friend saying?" whispered Lucius in Latin, when he had returned aft.

"Oh, nothing!" lightly answered the other, purposely using the dialect which the sailor spoke, and raising his voice so that it might reach the man's ears; and he sat silent for a time, which to Lucius, who could not help thinking that there was something to tell, seemed to be almost interminable.

The fact was that the Greek had all the diplomatic instincts of his race. To have answered Lucius' question at once, and to have told him all he had heard, would have roused the fury of the sailor, and would have precipitated a struggle which it was better to postpone. As it grew dark the sailor slept, or pretended to sleep, under the sail, and the Greek found the opportunity for which he had been waiting. By speaking in Latin he could conceal his meaning from the sailor, who knew only a few words of that language, and could not understand a connected sentence in it. But this was not precaution enough for the wary lad. A confidential tone might betray him almost as clearly as if the words themselves were understood. Accordingly he began talking in his usual way about the unfailing topic of the chances of deliverance; and then, without the least change of tone or manner, went on, to Lucius' intense surprise, to tell the secret.

"You caught my look," he said, "I noticed that you did; I saw something of it reflected in your face. I was a fool not to keep a better command of my countenance, but it was a horrible thing that that ruffian said to me. Do you know that he actually proposed that he and I should kill and eat you! 'He and I were Greeks,' he said. All the Furies confound the scoundrel for calling himself a Greek, and proposing in the same breath that we should do a thing which the worst barbarians would be ashamed of! 'You and I are Greeks,' these were his words, 'and he is a stranger, a Roman, and our natural enemy. If we go on like this we shall all die. But *that*' — he had the grace, thrice-accursed scoundrel as he is, not to say the horrid word again after he had once mentioned it — '*that* will keep us alive for five or six days at least. Before that a wind must spring up, and we shall be saved, and who is to tell the secret?' Well, I saw that I had better speak him fair. It wouldn't do, of course, to give in at once. That wouldn't have been natural, and he must have suspected me. So I made objections, said you were my friend, that it was a terrible thing, that we should never forgive ourselves if we did it, that we had better wait in the hope of being relieved, and so on — the

usual things that one would say ; and I made him think that
my objections were growing weaker and weaker, and at last
I seemed to give in. The villain had all his plans ready.
I was to arrange to keep the first watch, and when you were
asleep he would come up softly so as not to awake you, and
finish the business. The gods forgive me for seeming to
favor such a hideous scheme ! But anyhow we are prepared,
and we will fight it out. It will be very strange if we are
not a match, together, for that ruffian. I will take the
watch, as was arranged, and you will seem to go to sleep —
I needn't tell you that you had better keep awake — so we
shall be ready for him. I hope to finish him with my sword
before he has a chance ; but if he gets to close quarters you
must be ready with a dagger."

It must not be supposed that all this was said without interruption. So long a speech might have aroused suspicion.
The young Greek accordingly paused from time to time,
and Lucius, taking the cue from him, interposed in the same
indifferent tone of voice some observation or question.
Their plans finally settled, the Greek began the watch, and
Lucius apparently composed himself to sleep.

It was about midnight when the lads heard a slight noise
of movement from under the sail. The night was dark, for
there was no moon, and the stars, though the sky was cloudless, were veiled with a haze ; but now and then, as the slow
heave of a swell passed under the boat, a flash of phosphorescent light would give a momentary glimpse of every object
in it. It was such a flash that showed the sailor to the
young Greek. The man's eyes glowed like a wild beast's
with hunger and rage as he crawled slowly towards the stern,

while the blade of the dagger which he held between his teeth gleamed in the momentary light. Lucius, lying in the attitude of a sleeper, could see nothing; but a touch of the foot from his companion warned him that the crisis had come. The sailor paused for a moment in his approach. "Is he asleep?" he asked in a hoarse whisper. The Greek made no reply, but struck fiercely at him with his sword. Unluckily the darkness deceived his eye and the blow fell short. Before he could recover his weapon the sailor had closed with him. The lad's strength was no match for the tough sinews of the man; still he had an advantage of his own. Like all the well-born youths of his race he had been carefully trained in gymnastic exercises, and he was a skilful wrestler. Remembering just in time a trick of the ring, he tripped up his powerful foe, who fell heavily on the deck, dragging, however, with him the young Greek, on whom he kept a firm hold. Lucius was ready to do his part in the struggle; but the darkness was intense, and he was afraid to strike lest he should harm his friend and not his foe. The sailor's strength soon told in the struggle that followed — in a few moments he was uppermost, and in a few moments more had disengaged himself from the grasp of the lad and was preparing to strike. Lucius saw his opportunity, and threw himself, dagger in hand, upon the man. But the boat was now rocking so fearfully with the movements of the combatants that it was difficult to aim; and the blow, instead of piercing the body as had been intended, only inflicted a slight wound upon the arm. The sailor turned furiously upon his new assailant, and struck at him with his dagger; but his foot caught in the figure of the young

Greek, who was lying half-stunned in the bottom of the boat, and he fell forward upon the gunwale with great force. Lucius, stepping backward to avoid the blow aimed at him, had thrown his weight upon the same side ; and the next moment the danger which had been threatening them for some time was realized, and the boat upset. The sailor, like many of his class then as now, could not swim a stroke, and screamed for help. But Lucius, if he had been disposed to give it, had his hands full already. The Greek, never a very skilful swimmer, was now half-unconscious, and though somewhat revived by the shock of his sudden immersion, needed all the support and encouragement which his friend could give. Nothing could be done but leave the sailor to perish. The wretched man made a frantic effort to grasp the side of the boat, but, utterly unable as he was to make the least forward movement in the water, failed to reach it. He sank with a cry of despair, then for a moment rose again. This time he was too exhausted to utter a sound. Lucius to his dying day never forgot the brief glimpse which he had of that agonized face as it became visible for a moment in the weird phosphorescent light that now and again gleamed upon the sea. His own position was perilous, in fact almost hopeless. The boat was floating bottom uppermost. It was doubtful whether the two lads would have been able to right it if they had had their full strength. As it was, when both were weakened by hunger and thirst, and one was still suffering from the hurt received in the late struggle, it was impossible. All that Lucius could do was to climb on to the boat as it floated and seat himself astride, and to help his companion to gain the same position

A thin rope of some fathoms' length was fastened to some part of the stern. This he cut off with his knife, and used it to fasten his weaker companion to himself. This done, there was nothing left for him but to wait. Faint signs of the day, the "rosy fingers of the dawn," were now showing themselves in the east. He watched them rapidly brighten into gold, and then saw the sun rise slowly out of the waters, unshaded by a single streak of cloud. He was conscious of a dim sense of the beauty of the sight, mingled with the thought, which seemed hardly to terrify or distress, that he should look upon such sights no more. It was his last moment of consciousness. He fell forward, still mechanically grasping the keel, and remembered no more.

CHAPTER XII.

A MEETING.

WHEN Lucius regained his senses he felt that he was no longer on the boat. More than that he was at first too weak, languid, and confused to take in. To sleep on something of which he only knew that it was much softer and more pleasant than the keel of a boat, to lie half-awake with little thought of any thing beyond the sensation that he was comfortable and safe, to take food and drink from some one who seemed to be always at hand to supply them, but about whom he knew and cared to know nothing more — this for some time was enough for him. But by degrees, as the pulse of life, which had been so perilously near stopping, began to beat more strongly, his brain cleared, and he began first to question with himself where he was, and then to look about in the hopes of finding out. His first discovery was that he was wearing a tunic of some very fine woollen stuff, that he was lying on a particularly soft mattress, which was furnished with a fine sheet of linen and a crimson rug. Looking about him a little more he found that he was in a room which it was easy to recognize as a particularly handsome and spacious cabin. The sides were furnished with purple-covered couches, and the floor covered with carpets of a make such as he did not remember to have seen before. The slightly arched ceiling was adorned with festoons of flowers painted on a ground of delicate green. By his bedside was a small table with an ivory slab, on which stood a flagon and a silver cup. No one was visible at the moment; but at the slight noise which he made in moving round to complete his survey of the apartment an elderly woman, who had been sitting behind a curtain, came forward. A look of pleasure came into her face when she saw the change that had taken place in her patient, but she was too good a nurse not to know that the first use he would naturally make of his newly gained strength would be to overdo it. She put her finger on her lips in token of silence, and glided out of the cabin. In a few moments she returned, followed by an elderly man whose dress and bearing seemed to indicate that he was a man of considerable importance. He sat down by Lucius' side, and taking his wrist in his hand felt his pulse.

"I am glad, my friend," he said, "to find you better. Your pulse is steadier and stronger. Of course you want to know where you are and how you came here. But you must wait a while. You must be content to know that you are in good hands, if I may say so much of myself."

"How is my friend?" asked Lucius.

"He is well," briefly replied the other; "but no more questions at present, or the head nurse will be blaming me. And now take this draught and go to sleep again."

Lucius was tired enough even by this brief conversation to offer no objection: he obediently drank the potion which his host offered him, turned his face to the side of the cabin, and was soon sound asleep.

It was late in the afternoon when he woke. The light was softer and more subdued, and a delicious breeze, moderated by the silken curtains which were stretched across the windows of the cabin, cooled the air. Both the nurse and the stranger of the morning were sitting by his bedside. The latter again felt the lad's pulse and put his hand upon his forehead. The result of the examination was apparently satisfactory.

"I find you much stronger than you were this morning; and now I may venture to introduce myself. I am by name Theron, a merchant of Tarentum, on my way to Tarsus, and have had the good fortune, if I reap no other advantage from my voyage, to save your life. And now do you think you can bear a little surprise — I venture to think a pleasant little surprise?"

Something familiar in the look and tones of his host had already struck the young Roman, and while he spoke he had vainly attempted to think of whom they reminded him.

"I can bear any thing, thanks to your kind care."

"Well, then, you shall see an old friend."

As he spoke he raised a small silver whistle to his lips. At the sound the cabin door opened and Lucius saw again a figure which for the last two months had never long been absent from his thoughts, whether he was awake or asleep — the beautiful Philareté. The sea air and the sunshine had given a somewhat richer coloring to her complexion; and her hair, cut almost close to her head when Lucius last saw it, had grown in clustering ringlets down to her neck. She stood waiting at the door till her father — for such, as our readers will have guessed, the merchant was — beckoned

her to approach. She came forward with downcast eyes
and a blush on her cheek; for, to tell the truth, the young
Roman had been nearly as much in her thoughts as she
had been in his.

"And now you two are quits if you choose to think so,"
gayly said the father, who, after the manner of fathers, did
not perceive or did not understand his daughter's emotion.
"You saved her life in that dreadful ride from Spartacus'
camp, and now she has saved yours. Yes, if it hadn't been
for her obstinacy, which I must allow may sometimes be a
good thing, you would not be here. You must hear the
story. Two or three days ago, about noon, when we were
working our way slowly along the coast, in as dead and hot
a calm as ever I saw even at this time of year, we noticed
about half a mile to larboard a small flock of sea-gulls hovering
over something in the water, but what the something was we
could not clearly see, particularly as there was a considerable
haze in the air. One thought it might be a shoal of fish;
the birds will follow a shoal, you know, for a hundred miles.
Another thought it might be a dead dolphin or shark, and
indeed there did seem to be something black on the top of
the water. Whatever it was, it didn't seem worth while for
us to go out of our course to look at it, and we should have
gone on our way but for this girl here. 'O father,' she
said, 'suppose that it should be a boat with a dying man
on it! I am sure it looks like a boat.' How she was sure
I don't know, for I could see nothing of the kind, or the
sailors either. But she stuck to her point. Nothing would
satisfy her but we must go and look. And she had her way.
I dare say you guess she commonly does have her way.

Indeed I verily believe that there would have been a mutiny among the crew if I had not yielded. So we went, and sure enough, when we came close there was a boat turned bottom uppermost and two men upon it, one of them tied by a cord to the other."

"Ah!" cried Lucius, remembering with remorse that in the delight of his own recovery he had almost forgotten his friend. The merchant's beaming face was clouded in an instant with an expression of grief, and Philareté's eyes were filled with tears. Lucius guessed the truth.

"But you said this morning when I asked you about him that he was well."

"My son," said the merchant gravely, "it is well with those who die young and are at rest. I did not tell you the truth plainly this morning, because you were just recovering and it might have thrown you back. But the fact, is your companion was not alive when we reached you. He was still tied to you, but his head hung down almost in the water, and the birds had begun to peck at him. We saved him, anyhow, from their beaks, poor fellow. We were obliged to bury him at sea. So I wrapped him in a tunic with his hands and feet fastened together, and a piece of iron to sink him, and he sleeps as peacefully as he would under the turf. And when we get to harbor he shall have his monument. Let us hope that Charon won't refuse him passage. But let us also," he added in a gayer tone, "be thankful that you have not got to ask the old god to take you across just now. Upon my word I thought at the time that it was all over with you. Only Philareté was determined that you should live; and, as I said just now, she always has her way. Well, to go back to my story, we found you, not dreaming, of course, that you were any thing but a stranger. At first my girl did not recognize you ; and no wonder, when one thinks what you looked like. And, after all, it was not you, but your book — for we found your Homer in your pocket — it was that book, not you, that she recognized. But when we did know who you were — well, I won't say how glad we were. Such things are not put in words, my dear boy. *I* am not quits with you ; no, nor ever shall be ; for if it hadn't been for you I should have been the unhappiest father in the world. But you have had talking enough for to-day. Now you must go to sleep again, or, if you are not quite ready for that yet, shall Philareté read to you? Reading is often a wonderful thing for sleep, quite as good as poppies."

"It would delight me," said Lucius from his heart, resenting at the same time the thought that Philareté's voice could ever send *him* to sleep. The girl sat down by the bedside, and, unrolling the Homer scroll, read in an exquisitely melodious voice, which brought out all the majestic harmony of the verse, one of her favorite passages — how Hector left the battle that he might bid his countrywomen make supplication to Athené, and how there met him his wife Andromaché, and how they talked together, and how Hector blessed her and his child. But for all the music of her voice and the beauty of the matchless verse, and the young Roman's firm conviction that he could listen to such verse and such a voice forever, he was asleep before the reader's voice broke over the pathetic tale how Andromaché and all her maidens wailed for the living Hector as though he were dead, for she thought that she should never see him any more returning safe from the battle.

The girl sat for a few minutes silently watching the sleeper and listening to his regular breathing. Then gently putting her lips to the hand which hung languidly by the side of the couch, she rose and left the cabin.

The next morning Lucius was able to come upon deck.

"Tell us your story," said the merchant as he sat, with his daughter on a cushion at his feet, while the young Roman, who, as an invalid, was still under orders, reclined on a couch. "Tell us your story, or as much as you feel able to get through."

His audience listened to his tale, not without more than muttered maledictions from the Tarentine on the greed and cowardice which had nearly cost the young fellow liberty and life. When it was ended the merchant said:

"And now it is time that you should hear something about us and our plans. I am, as I told you, a merchant of Tarentum, and I am on my way to Tarsus, where I have some important matters to attend to. I shall probably be staying for some time at Tarsus, and I didn't like to leave my daughter behind me. I lost her mother some time since, and we are every thing to one another. And now as to your plans."

"One question," interrupted Lucius. "How about the pirates? How is it that you venture into these seas which are infested with them? And Tarsus is in Cilicia, their headquarters, I have always been given to understand."

The merchant smiled. "I don't wonder at your asking, particularly after the experiences you have had. But you may be re-assured. I feel pretty safe, and for two reasons. First, I have a fairly strong, well-manned ship here, one that the rovers won't meddle with if they can help it. They prefer to bite what can't bite again. And my crew is not only strong and well-armed, but it is faithful. Shall I tell you how I make them so? Well, I give them a share in my profits. They have their wages to begin with, and then, over and above these, they have their share, every one of them, from the captain down to the smallest boy. And, mark you, they are all free. So the ship really belongs to them as long as they are the crew, as much as it belongs to me ; and if they had to fight they would be fighting for their own. That is one reason why I feel pretty safe. The other I will tell you in confidence, and, to speak the truth, I am rather ashamed of it. I pay a tax to the pirate fellows, and they let me go free. I can defend myself from any casual attack, but the main body of them have a sort of commander-in-chief, and don't hurt a ship that has his pass. It is not, I know, what ought to be. But that is not my fault. I pay taxes to Rome, and Rome ought to keep the seas free ; but as she doesn't I am obliged to look out for myself. But now for your affairs. When we get to Tarsus you must write home to your father, and I should say to Marcus Tullius, and of course to your quæstor. Marcus Tullius may very likely put you in the way of getting something to do out here. I know that he is agent for the tetrarch of Galatia for one thing. Meanwhile you will, of course, be my guest. And don't think," he went on, seeing Lucius was about to interrupt, " don't think that I am putting you under an obligation. I understood from my daughter that you were going out to Sicily to help the quæstor with his accounts. Well, if you will only help me in the same way you will more than

repay me for any thing that I can do for you. However, I
don't want your answer at once. Think over it, and let me
know when you have made up your mind."

"There is very little need to think over it," said Lucius.
"You have put the matter so kindly, and I should like the
plan in every way so well, than I may say ' yes ' at once."

"So be it then," replied the merchant. "Then we may
consider that matter is settled."

The days that followed were days of unmixed happiness.
The ship, named the *Argo*, after the most famous craft of
the ancient world, drove gayly along before the summer
trade-winds. To sit under the deck awning listening to the
merchant's tales of a life which, though it had been spent in
trade, had not by any means been void of adventure — for
had he not been beyond the Pillars of Hercules and sailed
on the great Western Ocean? to hear Philareté read Homer,
sometimes to read to her, and be corrected in his pronun-
ciation by the most charming of teachers, every now and
then to change the book for a game of draughts or " fox
and geese ; " when they had had enough both of books and
games, to hold endless talks together, talks in which there
was not a word of love, but which were penetrated throughout with something of its spirit ; these were an untiring delight, and Lucius sometimes felt inclined to wish that the
Argo was bound, not for Tarsus, but for the end of the
world.

CHAPTER XIII.

TARSUS.

THE voyage of the *Argo* was prosperous to the end. The weather was uninterruptedly fine, while the merchant was right, it seemed, in having no fear of the pirates. Several times, indeed, craft that had a very suspicious appearance hove in sight; but they seemed to be satisfied by a nearer sight of the *Argo*. Whether it was the number of armed men whom she could show — once or twice these were mustered for the benefit, it seemed, of a stranger that happened to approach, or the sight of some particular emblem that she carried, and which only a person learned in such matters could interpret, Lucius did not know. About ten days after the rescue the merchant said to the two young people, "To-morrow at dawn, if this wind holds good, we shall be at the mouth of the Cydnus, and from there to Tarsus is not far. Shorten your slumbers, for it will be a sight worth seeing."

The calculation was very nearly correct. The sun had but just showed itself above the horizon when the *Argo*, having successfully crossed the bar of the river, anchored on the inner side. Some custom-house formalities had then to be gone through, and a pilot, acquainted with the somewhat

intricate channel of the river, had to be taken on board.
Later in the day she pursued her course up the river to Tarsus itself, which was distant about eight miles from the sea.
The river up which they were travelling was a clear and
rapid stream, so rapid, in fact, that they were obliged sometimes to have recourse to towing from the bank, and as clear
as a mountain torrent. "The clearest and coldest in the
world," said the merchant, though Lucius was inclined to
put in a word for his own Fibrenus at home. "As for its
clearness, you can see for yourself; and yet here it has
received the drainage of a great city. Above Tarsus it is
literally like crystal. As for its coldness, you remember
how Alexander of Macedon, plunging into it one day when
heated from a march, caught a fever which came very near
to putting an end to his conquests."

Tarsus lay before them, the gilded roofs of its temples
and halls glittering in the sun, and on the sky-line behind
the city towered the heights of the Taurus range, some of
the loftiest summits being still tipped with snow, though
midsummer was now long past. A somewhat laborious passage of about three hours brought the travellers to the city.
Below it the river broadened out into a lake which was used
as a harbor, and in which was ranged a goodly array of
trading-ships. Tarsus itself was divided into two portions
by the river, a division from which, indeed, it took its name
of the wings. Handsome bridges spanned the stream, on
either side of which embankments, massively constructed of
stone, furnished two splendid promenades. A constant
stream of carriages, of riders, and of pedestrians passed to
and fro, for the day was now drawing towards sunset, and it

was the hour for the rank and fashion of the city to show itself.

"'Tis one of the gayest and richest cities in the world, and, what is better, one of the most learned. Young men come here to be taught from all Asia, ay, and from the West too. Indeed, Tarsus holds itself to be pretty nearly as good in the way of learning as Athens itself."

The merchant, as soon as his ship had entered the river, had sent a message to the city announcing his arrival. Hence the house which he had hired, and where he had been for some time expected, was pretty well prepared for the reception of his party, and Lucius found himself in exceedingly comfortable quarters. His first care was to write a long letter to his father, in which he related his adventures, described how he was situated, and asked instructions for the future. He was of course enthusiastic about his host, though he said very little about his host's daughter. The conclusion of his letter ran thus: "You will doubtless in any case set these circumstances before Marcus Tullius, and ask his advice. My host advises this the more urgently because, as he says, Marcus Tullius has intimate relations with certain great men in these parts. Nor am I without hope that as he would have helped in Sicily, though this the Fates have forbidden, so he will help in Asia. I should be sorry to return to Arpinum, which otherwise I should revisit with supreme delight, bringing back nothing but a tale of misfortunes. I pray you, therefore, dearest father, yourself to lay my case before Marcus Tullius as speedily as possible, but assuring him at the same time that I would myself have written to him if I had not feared to make myself troublesome to him with my affairs."

This letter written and despatched, there was nothing for
it but to wait patiently for an answer, which indeed could
hardly arrive before the end of three months. "My dear
young friend," said the merchant when Lucius spoke of his
delay in a tone of complaint which, to tell the truth, was
just a little affected, — " my dear young friend, what do you
want? Here are you not quite eighteen, and you have gone
through more adventures than many men of eighty. I positively can't remember how many chances you have had
already of being knocked on the head or drowned. Let
the Fates have a quiet time with your thread of life. If the
lady with the shears has always got them so close, she may
make a mistake some day and cut it short when it is not
intended. Give yourself a rest for a time, or you will have
lived out all your life before you are twenty. And mind,"
he added, changing his bantering tone to one of earnest
kindness, "mind, not a word of being a burden to me.
Let the letters be as tardy as they will — remember that
possibly they may not be in time to catch the last ship eastward — you will always be welcome here. And now let us
join the fashionable people by the river side."

It was impossible to doubt the sincerity of the merchant's
kind assurances, and Lucius was delighted to accept the
situation. He was far from finding the time hang heavy on
his hands. For an hour or two he was accustomed to help
the merchant with his business affairs. This work was itself
an education. It was like a new world opening before him
when the young Roman began to realize the vast extent of a
great merchant's business. It seemed to have branches
which reached over all the dominions of the Republic, and

even beyond them. The great man had an interest in the produce of the palm-groves of Palestine ; he had mortgages on wheat farms in Egypt and Africa. Thousands of oxen and ten thousands of sheep on the uplands of Phrygia, if they did not actually belong to him, were in pawn for money which he had lent to their owners. Kings were among his debtors, and very often, he used to complain, but indifferent paymasters. " Not that they are not honest," ne was wont to say, " but they seem to have every thing but money, armies of slaves, but not a gold piece." Then he had vineyards in Campania, a marble-quarry in the Ægean, and a silver-mine in Thrace. The varieties of merchandise in which he dealt were positively bewildering. Wheat from Egypt, dates from Syria, silk from the far East, elephants, lions, and panthers for the shows of Rome and of the great Italian cities, purple dye from Tyre, pearls fished out from the depths by Red Sea divers, jewels from Indian mines, works of art from Greek cities, Persian embroideries, arrows from Scythia and swords from Damascus, were some of the goods in which he traded.

The merchant, however, did not demand from his young friend more than a short time daily ; and he took care that he should not miss the more regular opportunities for education which the city afforded. Lucius now found his knowledge of Greek to be of the greatest possible use. The teaching of the professors, for Tarsus was a regular university and had teachers of the greatest eminence, was delivered in this language. At first he had some difficulty in following them ; but he had constant practice at home, and in the course of a very short time could not only understand what was said with perfect ease, but could talk the language fluently if not very elegantly. It was no small help to him that he had to rehearse all that he heard to a most enthusiastic pupil at home. The university of Tarsus was not so far before its age as to open the doors of its class-rooms to women, and Philareté, who was a keen student, was therefore obliged to receive her instructions second-hand. Lucius had no disposition to be idle or inattentive ; had he had it ever so strongly, he would soon have been shamed out of it by the girl's energy and perseverance. As it was he made a progress that was most unusual, and that surprised both his teachers and his fellow-pupils. His Roman pride had at first been grievously wounded by the contempt with which he found himself treated. " Barbarian ! " he would hear his class-fellows mutter when he happened to blunder over an accent or an idiom. He had known, of course, before that to the Greeks all races but their own were barbarians ; but it nevertheless tried his temper not a little to have this practical experience. However, he soon won a place of distinction among his fellows. After about two months of attendance on the rhetoric class, the professor, not perhaps without a mischievous desire to make sport of the young foreigner, proposed that he should take the affirmative side in the discussion on one of the themes on which it was usual to practise the ingenuity of the class. The case was thus stated :

A woman of Smyrna was accused of poisoning her husband. She did not deny the accusation, but pleaded " not guilty" on the ground of justification. This husband, she alleged, had murdered her son born in a former marriage. Was she deserving of death, or no ?

Lucius' first impulse was to decline the office ; but Philareté strongly urged him to accept, and he was unwilling to
refuse.   The side for which he was to plead was not the one
which appealed to the popular sympathies.   But as a Roman
he was strongly impressed with the supremacy of law, and
felt that it ought to be vindicated even against sentiments
that are praiseworthy in themselves.   He bestowed a great
deal of pains on his thesis, and was at the same time in no
small degree indebted to the suggestions and corrections of
Philareté.   His first few sentences were halting and confused ; but he warmed to his subject as he went on, moved
not a little by the eager attention which Philareté, who was
one of a considerable audience from without, fixed upon
him.   A loud roar of applause greeted his peroration, for
the Greeks were always generous in acknowledging merit,
and the "barbarian" never had to complain again of any
affronts.

There were other things, perhaps more effective then, as
they might be more effective now, than his rhetoric, which
made his fellow-students regard him with respect.   In his
own peculiar Roman exercises there was no one in Tarsus
who could approach him.   His horsemanship was admirable
— there was not an animal in Tarsus so unruly that it could
manage to throw him.   His swimming was unmatched both
for speed and distance.   The young Greeks vowed that he
must be another Leander when they saw him swim out in
the bay till they could no longer distinguish him among the
waves.   With the quoit, the javelin, and the bow he soon
rivalled the best, and though he never learned to row as well
as some, yet in the boat-races on the bay his sturdy strength

and unfailing condition never failed to help his comrades to success.

Amidst these employments and amusements the days passed quickly enough. The young man, for such he was rapidly growing to be, would not have been ill content, however much they had been prolonged. The consequence was, that though he was delighted to get once more some tidings of home and friends, it was not without some misgivings that a pleasant time was about to come to an end, that he recognized on a letter which was one day put into this hands his father's seal. The letter had come by the last eastward-bound ship, and the rate with which it had travelled was considered a marvel of speed. After a budget of home news which would be less interesting to our readers than they were to Lucius, the writer went on : " I went without delay to Marcus Tullius, who, according to his custom, was at home during the games at Rome, for as you know he does not love such amusements, and laid your letter before him. He desired me to say that he did not regret your departure from Sicily, even though it had been brought about in so violent a way, seeing that it had ended well ; that things are going ill in that province, and that it can be to no one's profit to be mixed up with the doings of its governor ; that he thinks he can serve you effectually by the letter of com· mendation herewith enclosed. At the same time he was very urgent with me that I should accept on your behalf certain moneys, which you may hereafter repay or no as you may think fit or find possible. This, after some demur, I accepted, deeming it to be the duty of a generous man to accept a kindness which is generously offered. You will therefore receive herewith a bill of exchange for 200,000 sesterces [1] which I have bought of a company of knights trading to Cilicia and the parts thereabouts, for which, I do not doubt, your host the merchant will give you money down. And that you may distinguish that which you owe to my affection for you, and that for which you are indebted to the friendship of Marcus Tullius, I inform you that of this sum I have furnished one-third only. Let Theron of Tarentum and Philareté his daughter know that I, together with your mother, render them most hearty thanks. All the gods preserve you! Farewell!"

The letter enclosed was in the following words:

"*Marcus Tullius Cicero to King Deiotarus greeting. I commend to you Lucius Marius of Arpinum, a friend and fellow citizen. Know that he is of kindred not only respectable but distinguished, and that he shows himself worthy of it by many and great virtues. He has already passed through many dangers unhurt. For this reason I the more willingly commend him to you, knowing that you will find him not only prudent and courageous, but also, what sometimes seems to be of more importance even than these things, fortunate. Farewell!*"

"And who, pray, is King Deiotarus?" asked Lucius of his host, to whom he hastened to communicate his letters and their contents.

"Tetrarch, or, I should rather say, king of Galatia. He has done good service to Rome, and has been well paid for it. To be quite honest, I do not like all that I have heard of him. Still, he will be sure to deal fairly with you, a

[1] About $8,000 of our money.

Roman citizen, and coming as you do with such a recommendation. I should recommend you to go, and to go at
once ; for such a letter as you have from Marcus Tullius loses
much of its weight if it is not presented without delay. You
know, my dear boy, I don't want to get rid of you. You
have been to me like the son whom I once wished to have,
but whom the gods never saw fit to give me. But it is the
best host who speeds the parting guest, and I see here an
opening for you. There will be stirring times in Asia yet,
for Mithradates is not by any means at the end of his resources, and if I know you, you would not thank me if I
were to keep you out of what is going on. And now for
your plans. There will be a caravan starting in a few days
for Pessinus, which, you should know, is the king's capital.
You can't do better than go with it. It is about three hundred and fifty miles, and you will do it before the worst of
the winter comes on. Now as to money. You have got,
you say, a little gold still in your purse ; well, don't take any
more, but let me give you a letter of credit to a correspond-
ent that I have at Pessinus. You might leave a hundred
thousand sesterces in my hands, to see whether I can make
any thing more of them. And you must not be offended if
I settle with the master of the caravan for your passage-
money. I shall make a better bargain with him than you
will ; and if some day you are rich — and there is something
still to be picked up in these parts, though the times are not
what they were — and I am poor, then you shall pay me
back."

When the little party met at the evening meal Lucius
guessed that Philareté had heard the news. Her usual

gayety was somewhat eclipsed, her cheeks were pale, and her eyes had something of the look of recent tears.   But she said nothing on the subject, and Lucius was equally silent. The merchant, too, was not in his usual spirits, and all felt something like relief when the hour for separating arrived. The next day Lucius, who was almost too excited to sleep, was early astir.   Descending to the morning-room for the draught of milk and the crust of bread with which he was accustomed to break his fast, he saw Philareté in the garden and hastened to join her.   She gave him her hand, and he noticed as he raised it to his lips that it trembled in his grasp.   She made an effort to speak in her old tone :

"So you are going to leave us and seek your fortune among the Galatians?"

"Ah, Philareté, you know I am bound to go !   I must go out into the world as those before me went out.   You would be the first to blame me if I held back."

"Yes," cried the girl, with a flash of the old fire in her eyes, "go ; you are not one to choose the distaff when you may have the sword."

"And you will think of me when I am gone," said the young Roman, clasping her right hand between his own, and gazing into her eyes as earnestly as if they held some secret which he wished to discover.

Thinking about him was just what Philareté had been doing for months past, ever since the morning, indeed, when they rode together into Heraclea.   It was what she had been doing as she lay awake more than half the night, and had not ceased to do when, towards daybreak, she fell into a restless sleep.   It was what she was certain to do still more constantly when he should have left them. But to be asked to do so! That was a different thing. The girl had been brought up very much alone. She had had no girl companions to chatter to her about sweethearts, and if she had begun to love she hardly knew it. Lucius was her comrade, fellow-student, friend, perhaps brother. But now she began to have a dim consciousness that he might be, nay, that he was, something more.

"Think of you!" she said, with the instinct of concealment which a woman never seems to lose; "of course. Father and I will think of you till we see you again."

But her eyes, wont as they were to meet his with so frank a gaze, were drooped upon the ground, and her voice faltered. Lucius went on:

"Dearest, may I speak? Every thing between us is unequal. You are the daughter of kings that traced back their line to Jupiter: my grandfather was a peasant. You are wealthy: I have nothing but my sword. And yet I dare to love you. I *must* say it before I go. I don't ask you to answer me. Being nothing more than I am I must not expect an answer. Still, I could not leave you without telling you something of what is in my heart. And if I come back having done something, something more," he added with an effort to smile, "than being taken prisoner and being shipwrecked, perhaps then I shall dare to ask you a question which I dare not ask to-day."

For a few moments he stood holding the girl's hand. He did not ask for an answer, and yet he seemed to hope that an answer would come. Then he unloosed the clasp, and turned as if to depart. The girl joined her hands in a little gesture of appeal, lifted her eyes for a moment to her companion's face, and whispered :

"O Lucius, I will think of you ; and you will come back, will you not?"

The lovers, if we may so call them, had been too much engaged with each other to notice the approach of a third person. The merchant had something to say to Lucius, and, not finding him in the house, had come out to look for him in the garden. A bystander would have been amused to watch the expression of astonishment, and even dismay, that came over his face, as, standing close to the young people, but half hidden by a shrub of bay, he listened to their conversation. When it reached the point to which we have brought it he judged it to be about time to interfere.

"Here is a fine state of affairs!" he cried, in a tone which was meant to be angry, but which was at least half amused. "Who would have thought of a boy and a girl making all this fuss? Pray, my dear sir, how old are you that you must be thinking of a wife, for that, I suppose, is the plain meaning of your fine language?"

"I am eighteen to-day," answered Lucius with as much dignity as he could command.

"Eighteen ! truly a mature age, and fit to undertake all the responsibilities of life ! And this young lady is seventeen, if I remember right. Truly you are not disposed to let life slip by ! And your means, young man? You at least ought to have enough to buy the torches for the procession."

The young Roman stood shamefaced and confused, but after a few moments' silence he plucked up courage to answer :

"Oh, sir! I cannot say that I have not thought of marriage, but I have not spoken of it. I know that it is too hopelessly far off. And I have said nothing to your daughter that I should have been unwilling for you to hear. Nor did I intend to go without asking *your* leave to hope."

"Hope!" said the merchant. "I can't prevent your doing that. But, to be serious, I hadn't thought of any thing like this for my daughter. To tell you the truth, I had not noticed that she had grown up into a woman. And if ever the thought of a husband for her has crossed my mind, it has been of a man of her own race. Still, I do not wish to put an absolute *veto* on this matter. There must be no engagement. This may be a boy-and-girl fancy. She may see, you may see, some one you like better. Ah, you may shake your wise heads and groan, but I have known such things happen! And you must make your way in the world. I have enough for you both, it is true; but you are not one, I am sure, that would like to live on a wife's money. You will have thought, perhaps, that it was very base of me to talk of your means, but we merchants have a way of looking at this side of the question. And now, mind, no more of this, for the present at all events. Come, Lucius, I have some business to talk over with you. And you, my darling," drawing the girl to him and kissing her fondly, "get you to your embroidery, and believe me that I am not angry with you. And," he added in a whisper, "if you *must* think of a young man, I am not sure that our Lucius here is not as good a subject for your thoughts as any."

CHAPTER XIV.

THE CARAVAN.

THE caravan which Lucius was to join started on the 3d of November. It was sent, in the first instance, by the city of Tarsus with presents to the king — a robe of honor and a crown of gold. It was consequently protected by a detachment of the local force which the city kept in its pay. Merchants and other travellers were of course glad to take the opportunity of making the journey in comparative safety. As most of these had armed followers of their own the caravan could muster an imposing number of men, and was fairly safe from attack. The city, too, thought it expedient, not indeed to pay a tax — that would not have become its dignity — but to make presents to the mountain tribes through whose territory the road passed. A handsome supply of wheat and wine, neither of which the mountaineers could produce for themselves, was annually sent to the chiefs, and it was understood that caravans which carried the city's ensign of a flying bird should not be molested. There was sometimes a little trouble when the tribes happened to fall out among themselves, but on the whole the bargain was fairly well kept, and the road was, in consequence, tolerably safe.

The escort was nominally commanded by a citizen of Tarsus. But Anthemius — for this was his name — was now an old man, and, thanks to the city feasts at which he was a regular guest, had grown too fat to mount his horse. His regular practice was to give out his intention of making the journey, to be carried in a litter for the first half dozen miles, and then to discover that business or family affairs, of which he heard from a messenger duly instructed to overtake him at the appointed place, demanded his return. He would then call a halt, assemble the escort, make a little speech expressing his regret that he had been again prevented from making the journey, and hand over his authority to the second in command.

Leucon, the second in command, was a soldier of a very different stamp. He was a man of about forty-five, a spare, wiry, well-knit figure, his face burnt to a deep umber by the suns of nearly thirty campaigns, his short hair and close-cut beard (a long beard, he was wont to say, was most dangerous to a soldier) just sprinkled with gray. He had been struck by Lucius' soldierly figure, and by the grace and ease with which he managed his horse, and he lost no time in introducing himself and striking up an acquaintance. Lucius found him an entertaining companion, all the more interesting because it gave him a glimpse of a kind of life which was quite new to him. Leucon, in the course of their journey, told him the story of his life. It was told, of course, bit by bit, but we may conveniently put it together.

"I come from Nonacris in Arcadia. Fighting has been the profession of my family for I don't know how many generations, and we never cared particularly for whom we fought, as long as the pay was good. The rule was for one son to stop at home and cultivate the little farm which was our hereditary property, and for the others to take service abroad. Very few of them came back; I don't think that they were very welcome if they did. You see, when a man has been fighting for his own hand for thirty or forty years he doesn't quite fall in with peaceable ways. Of late years the trade has not been as good as it was. A hundred years ago there was always fighting going on in Greece and Asia and Syria. But you Romans have put an end to most of this, and a man has to go further afield. I went out when I was eighteen, and took service with King Mithradates. Ah! that is a wonderful man, and unless I am very much mistaken we haven't heard the last of him yet. In these days he hadn't come to blows with Rome, but he was always at war with the tribes of the Black Sea coast and of the Caucasus. Well, I had as much fighting as a man could wish for seven or eight years. Hard work it was, the worst climate you can imagine, the sea frozen over in winter, and the dust and heat intolerable in summer, and the king caring for nothing — he might have been made of iron. Then there was nothing to get beyond one's pay, for the savages had simply nothing that was worth taking away. Still one learned a good deal about soldiering there. Then there came an awful piece of business. The king had been fighting with the Romans, or at least with the Romans' friends, for two or three years, for things were wonderfully confused, and you were too busy quarrelling at home to care much what was going on abroad. He was spending the winter at Pergamos, and he sent for me — he had left me to

look after things at home. When I got to Pergamos I found
I was to go to Miletus with a sealed letter that was not to
be opened till a certain day. And when I opened it I found
my orders were these. Every Roman or Latin in the place
was to be murdered. Well, sir, I would have no hand in
such a business. I am not particular about men's lives;
when it comes in the way of my duty I can take them without any scruple, but then my duty is to be a soldier, not a
murderer. The letter said that I was to go to the magistrates of the town, tell them what was to be done, get their
orders, and then do the work — I had thirty men under me.
Well, I took the letter and showed it to the chief of the
Roman merchants in the town. I knew he would not believe it unless he saw it in black and white. That was all
that I could do for them. I heard afterwards that most of
them took the warning and got off, but others preferred to
stay and take their chance, and I don't wonder at it. They
had lived there half their lives, had married there, and
didn't care to begin the world again. Then I had to think
of myself. I made some excuse about business for the king
that I wanted to do at some inland place, and then I started.
I had my horse, and ten gold pieces in my purse, and that
was all that I had after more than ten years' service. I had
saved something, but I had left it at home — I mean at the
king's court — and then there was a half-year's pay due to
me. All that, of course, I lost; and indeed I thought that
I should be lucky if I got off with my life. Well, on thinking
it over I concluded that Tarsus would be the best place for
me to make for. You see, the king had never got a hold of
the city, and was not likely to get it. So I tried to make

my way by this same road that we are travelling now.
very hard piece of work, for it was winter-time and bitterly
cold, and the snow deep on all the high ground. I got on
my way pretty well till I lost my horse, which was drowned
in crossing a river, and very nearly drowned me, too, along
with him. I found that I was being hunted after, and had
to disguise myself. By the greatest good luck I found one
of the wandering priests of Cybele lying dead — he had
been overtaken by a snowstorm on one of the mountains in
Phrygia. I dressed myself up in his clothes, and buried my
own. That did very well till I fell in with some of my own
craft. You see, that I didn't know their jargon, and felt sure
that they would find out pretty soon that I was an impostor.
Well, I got away from them when they were all tipsy, and
then my good luck came in again. I met a beggar on the
road, and exchanged clothes with him. To be honest, you
might call it robbery rather than exchange, for I made him
give up his own clothes and take mine. But then I gave him
my last gold piece to make it up to him. As for his clothes,
they were not worth a drachma, I am sure. I shudder to
this day when I think how dirty they were. However, they
were as good as a safe-conduct, for nobody thought of
touching me. So at last I got to Tarsus, without a brass
coin in my pocket, my feet so frost-bitten that I nearly lost
them, in fact the most miserable object you can conceive.
Happily I had one or two old friends in the place who knew
me, and took care of me. When I recovered I took service
with the city, and a very good master it is."

The journey was not to be made without some interruption. One of the quarrels among the mountaineers, which,

as has been said, sometimes disturbed the peaceful arrangements between them and the city, had broken out, and about the seventh day the caravan found its progress blocked by a strong force of barbarians which occupied a height commanding the road. A halt was immediately called, and as it was already nearly dark it was determined to bivouac for the night. The commander called Lucius, of whose spirit and intelligence he had begun to think very highly, into counsel.

"We might storm the position," he said, "but I don't feel quite certain about my men. Very few of them have seen any fighting, and this is not the kind of thing to give them for their first experience. You see, get up the heights as quickly as they may, they must lose some men before they get a blow at the enemy, and that is a thing that young soldiers don't like. No, a first fight should always be on equal terms. We might fail, you see, and that would mean the loss of every thing. No, we must use stratagem, and I will tell you what I think of doing, and I look to you to help me. I noticed, before it got too dark to see, that there was another height behind the one on which the mountaineers are posted. Well, I propose to send some dozen men or so to occupy that, and take the enemy in the flank. If there is one thing more than another that barbarians cannot stand, it is the fear of being taken in flank. I have got a steady old officer whom I shall send in command, and you shall go with him. Of course I shall give him instructions; but if he is steady he is stupid, and I want you to *understand* my plan. You have got to make as much of your dozen men as you can. Let them show themselves without being too much seen. Two or three of them shall have bows, and two or three slings. Make as much play with these as you can, and don't spare shouting."

The lieutenant was sent for and duly instructed, and told to look to Lucius for further explanations if they were wanted. About two hours after midnight the party started under the guidance of a merchant's clerk, who happened to know the way, being indeed a native of one of the neighboring villages. They had to make a considerable compass to gain the desired post without running any risk of being observed by the enemy, and their way lay, for the most part, through a very dense and tangled wood. It was close upon dawn when they found themselves on the height. The enemy had not thought of posting any sentinels, knowing that the advance of the caravan would be sure to wake them. They were sleeping, most of them, on the bare ground, wrapped in their rough cloaks of Cilician goat's hair, though there were two or three tents for the accommodation of the chiefs. Every thing favored the commander's plan. The little party could approach the enemy without any danger, at least immediate danger, of being attacked, for the camp was overhung by an almost precipitous height. From this they could discharge their arrows and missiles with effect, while they could show themselves among the trees which lined the edge without letting the enemy discover how small were their numbers. The *ruse* succeeded to perfection. The mountaineers at once concluded that a powerful force was about to take them on the flank and cut off their retreat, and they hastily abandoned their position. The caravan, which had been ready to start for more than an hour, at once moved forward, and the difficult bit of road was passed before the enemy could find out the truth.

The rest of the journey was accomplished without any hinderance, so that before the end of November the travel-lers were safely lodged in Pessinus.

CHAPTER XV.

A HUNTING-PARTY.

THE travellers were to be allowed a couple of days to
rest and refresh themselves after the fatigues of their
journey. Then the king was expected to give an audience,
at which the envoys from Tarsus were to produce their
presents, and at which it had been arranged that Lucius
himself should present his letters of introduction.

The reception was held in the open air, in the court-yard
of the palace. It was a cold day, but the king seemed quite
insensible to the weather. Lucius indeed was struck with
his extraordinary vigor and youthfulness. He must be, he
knew, at least in his seventieth year; but no one, so upright
was his figure, so fresh his complexion, would have put him
down for more than fifty. His hair too, a rich auburn in
color, showed but a few streaks of gray here and there.
Almost the only signs of age about him were the wrinkles
which a close observer might have traced under his eyes and
on his forehead. He stood during the whole of the audience,
though a chair, over which was thrown a rich purple coverlet
edged with gold, stood ready for his use. He wore a riding-
dress, and had no mark of his rank except a collar of twisted
gold about his neck, and hanging from it a sapphire of un-

usual size and brilliancy. His face was not unpleasing, as it was certainly powerful. He looked like a man who was commonly good-natured, but could be absolutely implacable and merciless on occasion. On either side of the king stood the nobles, all of them, with the exception of a few older men, dressed like the king, and wearing similar chains though without the jewel. Lucius was struck with their appearance, which was very unlike that of the ordinary natives of the country. In the first place they were un-usually tall, few of them being under six feet, while some of them must have measured as much as seven, and one gigan-tic chieftain exceeded even this stature, as Lucius afterwards found out, by at least six inches. Their complexions were singularly fair, their hair, which fell in long curls over their necks, varied in hue from the auburn of the king to a deep yellow. He was reminded at once of some of the soldiers whom he had seen in the camp of Spartacus, and of whom he had been told at the time that they were Gauls. It was indeed to this race that both the king and his nobles be-longed. More than two hundred years had passed since their ancestors had left their home in Europe, but they were still European in look. The envoys from Tarsus stepped forward, and one of them delivered a long speech, on which the chief professor of rhetoric in the university had exerted himself to the utmost to flatter and magnify both his own city and the king. The gifts were then presented, the king received them, handed them over to an attendant, and re-turned thanks with commendable brevity. It was now the turn of Lucius to step forward. Quickly bending one knee to the ground, an act of homage which it cost his Roman pride some effort to make, he presented the letter of recommendation from Tullius. When the king had read it he said :

"You are welcome, sir. A friend of Marcus Tullius cannot but be a friend of Deiotarus. Give me a little time to consider how I may make the virtues which, now that they are vouched by so excellent an authority, I know to be in you, most useful both to yourself and to me. Meanwhile you are my guest."

On retiring from the king's presence Lucius was accosted by one of the king's chamberlains, who showed him to the apartment which had been assigned to him, and promised to have his effects transferred from the lodgings at which he had temporarily taken up his abode. He dined with a sufficiently gay company of courtiers, and on his return to his chamber found a billet inviting him to a hunting-party which the king proposed to hold the next day.

Early the next morning the young Roman presented himself at the *rendezvous* of the hunt. The king received his salutation with great courtesy, and said to an attendant, "Bring *Irene* for the Roman guest."

Irene was a singularly beautiful and well-proportioned mare of a bright bay color, just such a mount, as far as appearance went, as the favored guest of a king might feel himself flattered to have. But Lucius happened to be an uncommonly good judge of horses, and his quick eye noticed one or two little tokens that the animal's temper might not be altogether as good as her looks, or as peaceable as her name would have suggested.[1] He noticed that as he ap-

[1] *Irene* means peace.

proached to mount her she gave a peculiarly vicious roll of
the eye, and laid back her ears for a moment. It was only
for a moment, for she had all the deceptive arts which have
been attributed to her sex ; but the significant gestures were
not lost upon her rider. He fancied, too, that he had noticed
something like a twinkle in the king's eye as he gave the
order for the animal to be brought out ; while it was certain
that the hunting-party, which had grown curiously silent in
a moment, were watching him with more attention than the
appearance of an insignificant stranger would seem likely to
excite. All this was quite enough to put him on his guard.
Still Irene permitted him to mount her quietly, and to ride
her round the little meadow in which the hunting-party was
assembled. Lucius felt, however, that the ordeal was by no
means over. His companions were still as silent, and were
watching him as intently, as before. Accordingly he did
not relax his attention for a moment. Still he was almost
taken by surprise when the mare began the manœuvres by
which she was accustomed to dismount her riders. She
first lifted herself almost perpendicularily on her hind-legs.
Lucius threw himself forward in the saddle, and with a
strong sideways wrench at her mouth made her drop again
upon her feet. Her next manœuvre was to rise very much
in the same way on her fore-feet, and she continued to make
variations between these two till Lucius began to feel that if
the contest was continued much longer his strength would
hardly hold out. A happy thought occurred to him. An
old Sabine servant of his father's had had a great reputation
for taming refractory horses ; and his secret, so far as there
had been a secret beyond the man's remarkable knowledge

of the animal's ways, had been a peculiar whisper, which he had taught his young master how to imitate. Its magic consisted not in the words, and indeed a Greek horse could hardly be expected to understand an Italian dialect, but in the peculiar tone. Lucius felt doubtful whether, not having used it for some time, he could imitate it now. To try, however, could do no harm, and accordingly in an interval of quiet he made the experiment. The result was a success beyond his expectations. The mare seemed to tremble when she heard the whisper. He repeated it when she seemed about to renew her efforts to throw him, and she was reduced to quiet in a moment. His victory was complete, and was greeted with a murmur of approval from the assembled company.

Something still remained to be done before the preparations for a start were complete. A priest robed in white, with a chaplet of bay about his head, had been sacrificing a goat to Artemis, the patroness of hunters ; and was now inspecting the entrails, to discover from them whether good luck or bad would attend the proceedings of the day.

"That is always the king's way," said a young Galatian chief who had introduced himself to Lucius by bestowing some very hearty praises on his horsemanship. "If the old priest does not give a good account of what he sees, it is quite possible that we may be all ordered back. I have known a most beautiful scenting-day lost because there was or was not — for I am sure that I cannot remember what it ought to be — some line or other in the animal's shin. Sometimes he won't go out at all ; sometimes he goes, but does not seem to expect any good luck, and of course does not get it. And depend upon it, he wants to know something about you. I have seen a guest sent about his business if there happened to be something wrong with the sacrifice. But see, the priest is showing him the tokens. The king looks pleased. We may take it for settled that we shall go."

The young chief was right. The king raised his hand and made a gesture commanding silence. " The gods promise success," he said in a loud voice ; " do your best to deserve it."

Lucius, who had been furnished by one of the attendants with a hunting-spear and a long knife, with the admirable temper of which he was greatly pleased, rode forward with his new friend. The hunting-ground for which they were making was about seven miles from the city. It was a forest of great extent, far too dense for the horses, which had accordingly to be left outside in the charge of the attendants. Hundreds of beaters had been employed for days in driving the game, which was now crowded together in the portion that had been left undisturbed. In this portion the ground was most favorably situated for the operations of the hunting-party. A wall of cliffs, varying in height from a hundred to fifty feet, divided it from the plain cultivated country outside. This wall was broken in one place by a valley formed by the action of a small stream which, though of insignificant size, had in the course of many ages made for itself a channel of more than two hundred yards in breadth. The bed of the stream itself was but a few feet wide ; the rest of the valley was covered with dense brushwood. It was to this opening that the greater part of the game would natur-

ally rush when the beaters should begin to advance from
behind ; and here it was that the king himself with a number of the party had taken up his post.   But there were two
or three other outlets where the cliff had been broken down
by the action of the weather.   At each of these were placed
two or more of the hunters, according to the size of the
opening.   The younger Deiotarus, the king's only son, had
chosen one of these places for his own station, and had had
Lucius and his companion told off to attend him.   The
prince was a young man of about twenty, pleasing in appearance, but far inferior in vigor and strength, as it was easy to
see, to his father.   A detachment of the party had meanwhile been making the best of their way through the wood to
get into the rear of the beaters.   It would be their business
to dispose, as best they might, of such of the game as might
break back through the line of the beaters.   When these
had reached their place the business of the day began.

For a time all was quiet, except for the occasional cry of
a deer, the bleat of a wild goat, or the growl of some beast
of prey.   Before long the noise made by the approaching
line of beaters reached the expectant hunters.   This noise
was indeed loud and incessant.   The greater the din the
safer the men and the more terrified the beasts, some of
which were, as may be supposed, very formidable enemies.
Accordingly the beaters shouted at the top of their voices,
now reproaching or encouraging each other, now warning
the hunters behind of some animal that had gone back.
Meanwhile the agitation in the densely-crowded region of
forest upon which the beaters were advancing grew more
and more intense.   Cries of fear and rage, in every variety

of note, from the shrillest treble to the deepest bass, went
up without ceasing. The hunters outside were scarcely less
excited as they waited for the wild inhabitants of the forest
to show themselves. The first to appear were the hares and
rabbits. With these the boys of the party busied themselves, using their bows and arrows, weapons which some of
them handled with uncommon skill, or setting their dogs,
which were chiefly of the lurcher kind, and very effective
animals, upon the chase. It was not long before the larger
animals began to show themselves. At first they turned
back into the covert, the danger in front seeming even more
terrible than that behind. Then the still advancing line of
beaters drove them forward again; compelled to face the
new peril they charged the hunters, and the fun became fast
and furious. Each sportsman was accompanied by three or
four slaves, who supplied their masters with javelins, gathered up the arrows to be used again, and gave the *coup de
grace* to animals that were wounded. The old king enjoyed
the day to the utmost. Stationed, of course, in the place
where most game was likely to come, his hand was never
idle, while his aim, which he never exercised on any prey
less noble than a stag, a wolf, or a leopard, was almost unerr-
ing. The prince, with his two young companions, was fairly
successful. If the animals that came in their way were not
very numerous, they were, on the other hand, conspicuously
large; and the native hunter who accompanied the party
was in ecstasies over one or two of the heads, which would
beat, he said, any thing that had been taken in the hunt for
many a long year. There had been a long interval in which
they had found little to do, and were naturally beginning to

grow a little inattentive, when the hunter roused them by a sharp cry of warning. Almost at the same instant a huge panther burst out of the thicket. So huge was he, so far beyond all that even the hunter, with the experience of nearly forty years, had seen, that the whole party stood, as it were, paralyzed with astonishment, and seemed to forget that they had weapons in their hands. The beast saw them, hesitated for a moment whether he should attack or fly, resolved upon flight, and in another moment had again disappeared in the wood.

The hunter was the first to recover his breath : " Artemis ! what a monster ! A panther indeed ! — a tiger, I should have said, only that I never heard of them in Galatia."

" Monster indeed ! " said the prince ; " the very Caledonian boar among panthers. But say, Ambiorix " (this was the old hunter's name, come down from his Gallic forefathers), " say, what shall we do ? It would be intolerable to miss such a booty. I would sooner lose half my kingdom."

" We will wait," said Ambiorix. " He is sure to come back to us."

They waited accordingly, but seemingly in vain, the prince growing furiously impatient as the time went by. One of the slaves came forward, and lifting the hem of the prince's cloak to his lips, stood silently seeking leave to speak.

" What is it, Sciton ? " said the young man. " Say on. "

" My lord," said the man, " I have heard tell of this panther before ; and I have always thought that I saw him once when I happened to be in company with old Gelon, the hunter, who died last year. I have heard the country people, too, talking about a monstrously big beast that has killed

their oxen. And they have always fancied that its den was in the back of the cliff, about three hundred paces to the eastward."

"Can you guide us to this place?" said the prince.

"Yes, if my lord so pleases."

"Very well; and I promise you that if we find him and kill him you shall be free. Yes, on my word as the king's son, you shall be free!"

The man's eyes glistened with delight. "Death or freedom," he murmured to himself; "in any case I shall do well."

He led the party straight into the wood. For the first hundred yards the undergrowth was so thick that it seemed as if no living creature of any kind could ever have made its way through it. But when they had gone so far they came on what was evidently the track of some large animal. Something like a tunnel had been made through the brushwood by some creature which they guessed from the size of the passage to be not less than four feet high.

The slave uttered a cry of satisfaction. "We have found it, my lord!" he cried, and he led the way.

Three or four hundred yards of walking followed, which, so well worn was the track, had little difficulty about it, except the stooping posture which the party were obliged to maintain. They now reached the mouth of a cave. A hurried consultation was held as to what was to be done, and how the attack should be made.

"You are sure," said the prince, "that the cave has no other entrance but this?"

The question seemed to strike the slave with something like dismay.

" Pardon me, my lord, I had forgotten. I remember now the old hunter thought that there was another opening, and that the beast must have escaped so long because both had not been watched."

The question was where this other opening could be. One of the party advanced to the mouth of the cave with a lighted pine torch, and advancing a few steps beyond the entrance peered as far as he could into the darkness. The conclusion to which he came was that the direction of the cave was very nearly straight. After a careful consideration of all the circumstances it was agreed that the other opening, if such there was, would be found about a hundred yards to the left of the spot at which they had entered the wood.

" Go back," said the prince to the slave, " by the way by which we came, and see if you can find any thing like the place. If you can, enter it and sound there two notes on your whistle. If you get the same answered from us at this end, then you will know that you have found the right place. We, meanwhile, will wait here with all the patience that we can."

The slave hastily departed on his errand. At the end of an hour the prince and his party heard, first very faintly, then clear and unmistakable, the sound of the whistle.

" Now," cried the young Deiotarus, " if he is here at all we have him between us. But let us hope that the slave will stand firm. Suppose that the brute should choose to go out at that end rather than this. Never before in my whole life have I wished so much that I could be in two places at once. But let us go on."

The party advanced, the young Galatian noble going first, the prince following, not without some grumbling at being kept out of the foremost place ; and after the prince came Lucius. The attendants followed, carrying among other things some spare lances and a supply of torches. The whistle was sounded at intervals as the party made its way slowly along, and the signal was regularly returned. The cavern, which had at first been about eight feet high and five feet broad, now became narrower and lower. At the same time the air became close and almost stifling. At about two hundred yards from the entrance the leading hunter stopped. " I see him, " he said in a whisper, turning to the prince. Orders were given to the attendants to light some additional torches. By their help it could be seen that about thirty yards in front there was a recess at right angles to the line of the passage, and at the mouth a crouching form could be indistinctly seen. The young Galatian had caught the glow of the creature's eye. The eagerness of the prince now became incontrollable.

" I have the right to be first," he cried to the foremost of the party. " I command you on your obedience to give way ! "

" My lord," said the young noble in reply, " I owe you, and am ready to pay you, all respect. But my obedience I owe to the king, your father ; and it is his standing order that you are not to be put into unnecessary danger."

" Go on, then," said the prince in an angry voice, " and I will follow."

The party advanced till the distance between them and

the animal was less than a spear's cast. "Throw," said the prince, "in the name of all the gods."

The young Galatian obeyed, but it was difficult to aim. The outline of the animal only was visible in the darkness, and this but indistinctly. The spear was heard to strike against the rocky wall of the cavern; but the sound was slight, and it was probable that it had inflicted a flesh-wound on the animal in its passage. An angry growl was heard; and the party, planting their spears firmly against the ground, prepared to receive a charge. It was a formida-ble *chevaux-de-frise* that their weapons presented. If the first defence was broken down there was a second behind, and behind this again a third. But the attack was never delivered. After a moment's hesitation the panther, alarmed by the number of its enemies, whom its eyes, accustomed to the darkness, were able to clearly distinguish, turned and fled, making, it was evident, for the other entrance. The party at once advanced. The rocky passage here took a sudden turn; and two or three steps in advance brought them in sight of the opening, which was now less than a hundred yards' distance. The figure of the slave who had been sent to watch it was plainly visible against the light.

"The gods grant," cried the prince, "that he stand firm, or we shall lose the brute after all!" and he shouted, "Be-ware! Courage! We follow!"

It was easy to say "We follow," but difficult to do, and it was evident that the struggle would be over before the entrance could possibly be reached. Over, indeed, it was so far as the gallant slave was concerned. He had received the panther's charge on his hunting-spear without flinching,

and had driven the point three or four inches into the animal's breast. But the wound was not mortal, and the spear had not checked its rush; and the man had been prostrated by a tremendous blow of the paw, which had torn his right side open with a hideous wound. Still he held with convulsive tenacity to the shaft; and the panther, which might otherwise, having overthrown its antagonist, have continued its flight, was checked till it could disentangle itself from the weapon. The delay, though it could not have lasted long, was long enough to give the pursuing party the coveted opportunity. By right the prince should have had the first stroke; but it was no time for etiquette, and the three knives were buried almost simultaneously in the huge body. At least two of them reached its heart, and with a great shudder it turned over on its side, leaving exposed the prostrate body of the slave. He was still alive, though fast bleeding to death.

"Your promise, my lord," he whispered in a faint voice.

"You are free," said the prince, laying his hand on the dying man's head, "you and yours — I make them my charge."

A smile passed over the pale features. "Dear Glycera," he murmured, "I am happy!" Glycera was his daughter; she was free, and she had now the hope, which was hardly possible for a slave girl, of being a happy wife and mother.

The slaves extemporized a rude litter of boughs, and carried the corpse back to the place where the main body of the hunters had now assembled. The prince had taken his own cloak and thrown it over the dead man, and walked by the side of the litter. The splendid booty which his attendants carried behind — such a panther as had never before been seen in Galatia — had lost half its attraction.

The result of the day's sport comprised thousands of animals, both dead and alive. Conspicuous among the latter were a number of panthers and bears which had been taken in nets, and which the king would send as presents to his friends in Italy, or perhaps sell to the dealers in this kind of ware. Wild beasts always found a ready market in Rome. These were secured in cages which were carried on poles by bearers. The dead game was piled in carts. This done, the whole party moved homewards. The proceedings of the day were concluded by a great banquet, at which Lucius had the honor of sitting at the royal table. Deiotarus, who probably owed no little of his singular vigor to his temperance, left the feast early, after appointing the young Roman an hour at which he would give him audience on the morrow.

At the time appointed Lucius was ushered into the royal presence, and met with a very kind and gracious reception. "In the first place," said the king, after repeating in a few courteous words his desire to serve to the utmost the *protégé* of so distinguished an orator and so valued a friend as Marcus Tullius, — "in the first place, tell me your story." "You are a brave young fellow," was his comment when Lucius came to the end of his adventures, "and, as I can see from your way of talking, as modest as you are brave. Now I should like to keep you with me ; and the best thing that occurs to me is to attach you to the person of the prince, my son. He has taken a great fancy to you from what he saw of you yesterday, and the arrangement will suit his taste exactly. He is too old to be a pupil ; and you, though you look older than what you tell me are your years, are too young to be a tutor. But you can be very good friends. You will talk

Latin to him; and though he can speak the language very fairly he has got much to learn, especially in accent. You are something of a student (I have been inquiring about you from my good friends of Tarsus); and if you can get him to follow your example, to which at present he is but little inclined, I should be much obliged to you. A king nowadays cannot afford to be ignorant of books, even though he is king only of these barbarous tribes. Above all, do your best to make him like yourself. If you can do that I shall be more than satisfied, and no reward that I can offer will be too much. At present I must ask you to be content with thirty sestertia (£270) a year, with, of course, free quarters. It is not much, but we have little money here. However, you will be able to save something out of it to begin again elsewhere when you are tired of us."

Lucius, who indeed could desire nothing better than such a post, gratefully accepted the king's proposal.

" And now that we have finished our business," said the old man, " let us have a little talk together. You are fresh from Italy, and of Italy I am never tired of hearing."

Lucius was accordingly put through a sharp cross-examination, which proved certainly that the old king kept himself tolerably well acquainted with all that was going on. Indeed, many of the questions that he put on politics were quite beyond the young Roman's grasp. At one time the conversation happened to turn upon augury and omens.

" I am told," said the king, " that you Romans don't care so much about these things as you used to do. You keep up the old forms, you have your augurs and all the rest of it. Every fleet or army that goes out has the sacred chickens, and it is supposed that you don't fight except the birds feed properly. But I don't suppose that you believe very much. I have heard that my friend Tullius wonders how one augur can meet another without laughing. Well, now, you will think it strange, perhaps, but I do believe. And I'll tell you why. Nearly fifty years ago, when I was a very young man, I was going to a great feast held in Pessinus. My father was one of the old sort, and was a firm believer. Well, when the morning sacrifice was offered the priest found great signs of trouble at home in the liver of the beast; and my father was so struck that he would not let me go. I stormed and raved, of course; but he had made up his mind, and I did *not* go. Now mark the end. In the middle of dinner the roof fell in, and every one of the guests was killed. And I took pains to inquire, and not one of the whole number had tried to find out what my father had done. That convinced me : I never doubted again. And you must confess that this morning every thing went just as had been expected."

"I suppose, sir," said Lucius, "that the soothsayers commonly make it as pleasant as they can. They would not be welcome if they were always in opposition."

"Ah!" said the king good-humoredly, "I see you are inclined to doubt. Well, you will see. For my part the future is so dark that I am glad to get any kind of light that may be given us; and I cannot help thinking that the gods do give us a hint now and then. Anyhow, men have believed this for more than a thousand years, and I am not going to give it up."

CHAPTER XVI.

AN EMBASSY.

L UCIUS found his new work pleasant enough, and certainly easy. Not very much could be done with the young prince as far as study was concerned. He made acquaintance with Homer, and wanted no urging to improve acquaintance into friendship. He came of a family of soldiers; and the stirring pictures of battle, and the glorious verse which sounded like war-music in his ears, possessed him with a charm that never lost its hold. Among other writers he had only one favorite, Xenophon. To be a soldier and a sportsman seemed to him the very height of human happiness. It was a constant delight to him to compare with his own experience what the old Athenian had to say about horses and dogs, about the methods of hunting and the implements of the chase. Equally attractive in another way was the glorious story of the Ten Thousand. These countrymen of his own — for though of a Gallic race he had Greek blood in his veins — fighting their way to the sea and safety through tribe after tribe of savage enemies, across mountains of which they did not know the passes, and rivers of which they had to find the fords, were a perpetual interest to him. But beyond Homer and Xenophon he would not go, nor indeed did Lucius or any one else expect any more.

Meantime the two young men were constant companions, and in a short time became excellent friends. Hunting was a resource for spending their time of which neither of them ever wearied. Once a month there was a great *battue*, such as has been described in the preceding chapter. More pleasant were the excursions which the two young men made together, with perhaps an old hunter to give them the benefit of his experience, and two or three attendants to act as beaters or carriers. Plenty of game was to be got: partridges and quails, which were to be caught in nets or shot with bow and arrow, and hares to be run down with beagles, of which the king had an excellent pack, or tracked, without the help of dogs, by their footprints in the snow. If they were disposed to go farther afield, larger animals were plentiful. Often they would be absent for two or three days, sometimes contenting themselves with rough quarters in a forester's or peasant's house, sometimes handsomely entertained by one of the neighboring chiefs. These glimpses of the home life of a very strange people, a Western tribe surrounded by the associations of Eastern life, were exceedingly interesting to the young Roman. He was especially struck by the national ballads which he sometimes heard sung to the accompaniment of a rude harp in the hall of some Galatian noble. The Gallic speech was dying out, though it had left many traces of itself in the Greek, which was now the common language of the country, but it still lived in the ballads. The difficulty was in getting them interpreted. The guests for the most part, though they considered them

as a necessary part of the entertainment, listened to them without understanding, and sometimes the minstrel himself knew little of the meaning of what he was singing. One night, however, Lucius was fortunate enough to sit by an ancient retainer who was one of the very few that still spoke the old tongue, and who could himself repeat the ballad from beginning to end. It told the story of how the great king Bran (the Brennus of the Roman legend) had marched to the south, how he had put his enemies to flight and sacked their city, and how he had come back in triumph, carrying with him the gold wherewith the men of Rome had purchased their lives. The last part of the story was, of course, new to Lucius, who had been brought up in the tradition, so flattering to the national pride, which told how Camillus had appeared with his host at the very moment when the shameful bargain was being made, had ordered the gold and the scales to be removed, and, challenging the Gauls to conflict, had restored the honor of his country.

Among these fresh occupations and interests the winter and early spring passed pleasantly away. One day, towards the end of April, Lucius received a summons to attend the king. It was not one of the usual days for an audience, and his curiosity was naturally excited. He found the young prince with his father; the old man seemed to be in high good humor.

" You have been reading," he said, " about the Ten Thousand. Well, here is a chance of seeing some of the country through which they passed on their way back to the sea. You know, I dare say, that King Mithradates is in Armenia with Tigranes, his son-in-law, king of kings, as he calls himself.   He is in no great favor, but is kept as a prisoner, and Lucullus hopes to induce Tigranes to give him up.   You know, I dare say, how very narrowly he escaped getting hold of him two years ago.   The soldiers were as near to him as you are to me, when a mule with its pack-saddle full of gold came in the way, and the rascals thought of nothing but the plunder, and let the king go.   Well, as I said, he made his way to Tigranes, and now Lucullus is going to send an embassy to demand him.   The ambassador is to be Publius Clodius, the general's brother-in-law, and, to make a long story short, my son is to go with him, and you will accompany him.   It is a fine opportunity of seeing a country which it would not be very easy to get at, and you are very lucky, I take it, in getting it.   You will start in three days' time, so that you may be sure to fall in with the embassy on its way."

The start was not made, however, as it turned out, till a couple of days later.   Twice in succession the omens were unlucky, the sacrifice on the first day presenting what the soothsayers considered a threatening appearance, and a raven having unluckily thought fit on the second to caw just as the expedition was starting.   Nothing could have persuaded the old king to let his son start in the teeth of such warnings.   He would far sooner have given up the whole plan; as for being late at the *rendezvous*, it was a matter of quite secondary importance.   On the 2d of May, however, the expedition did get off.   The prince, who considered his father's notions about omens to be more than half nonsense, had a private interview with the soothsayer, which Lucius suspected might have had something to do with the favorable answers which that official was able to give next morning to the king's inquiries. It was necessary, owing to this delay, for the party to hurry on. Happily no obstacle intervened, and the travellers joined the embassy just as it was about to cross the borders of Armenia. Beyond this, indeed, it would not have been prudent to travel, except under the safe-conduct which Tigranes had given to the Roman ambassador.

Armenia proved to be quite as interesting a country as Lucius had expected. Its bleak and dreary plains, scarcely broken by a single elevation or even by a tree, would, he thought, have been a miserable place to live in, but they were full of curiosities for a traveller. The underground houses, especially, for the excessive rigor of the climate and the scarcity of timber, and indeed of all building materials, compelled the inhabitants to excavate their dwellings, were exceedingly interesting. The expedition would come suddenly upon a spot in the unvarying expanse of plain which seemed at first sight to be exactly like what they had traversed for many a weary mile, but which was really the site of a populous city. On looking a little more closely, smoke might be seen here and there issuing from chimneys which were raised three or four feet from the ground. Near these chimneys again might be seen what seemed like wells with steps in the sides, but were really the entrances to the underground houses. Descending one of these, which they were most hospitably invited to do, the travellers found what might be called an underground farm. Not only did the Armenians inhabit these strange dwellings, but they kept there their cattle and sheep. The season, indeed, was sufficiently advanced for these to have been sent into the upper air, but the stalls and folds were there. Here, too, Lucius made acquaintance with the famous barley wine of which he had read in Xenophon, and which he had been very curious to see and taste. It was not kept in casks or jars, but every house had a cistern, varying in size according to the wealth of its proprietors, in which the liquor, the result of the fermentation of barley, was made and kept. From these it was drawn off for use into tubs. Hosts and guests would sit round one of these tubs, each furnished with a reed through which he drew the liquor up. It was not unpleasant to the taste, but exceedingly potent, stronger even than unmixed wine, and unmixed wine seemed to Lucius, as it did to the majority of his countrymen, a drink to be avoided. After his first taste he pleaded to be permitted to mix it with water, and his hosts, pitying the weakness and bad taste of the barbarian from the West, graciously gave him leave.

Of Armenia they saw more than enough, for the guide who had been furnished by the chief commissioned to reach them as soon as they crossed the border led them astray. He had been instructed to delude the strangers in this way, Tigranes desiring to gain time, and not particularly caring if some lucky accident should prevent the embassy from arriving at all. For several days the fellow, acting on instructions which had been given him, contrived, without making the party actually travel twice over the same road, to conduct them in such a way that they made little or no progress. It is difficult to say how long this game might have gone on had not an accomplishment of Lucius, of which mention has been made before, come to the rescue of the party. He made it a practice, when the encampment was made every night, carefully to observe at the same hour the position of the stars, and a suspicion that their guide had either lost his way, which did not seem very likely, or was fooling them, soon came into his mind. After two or three cloudy days, which had given the man an unusually favorable opportunity of carrying out his scheme, he was convinced that his suspicion was correct, and lost no time in communicating it to the ambassador. Clodius, who had the short temper and peremptory manner of his family, made up his mind at once. He summoned the guide into his presence.

"Scoundrel," he said, "you are leading us wrong."

The man protested, invoking the names of all his native gods and of such Roman and Greek deities as he could remember, that he had been taking them the very shortest way possible to the king's capital.

"Make ready, lictors!" thundered the ambassador, whose imperious temper was roused to fury. In a few moments the axes were ready. The wretch fell on his knees and confessed what he had been doing; but, still loyal to the king, laid the blame on instructions which he said had been given him by a chieftain on the border.

"And you have dared, rascal, to make sport of a Roman! Scourge him, lictors, till he can't stand. And now, sir," he went on, turning to Lucius, "you shall be our guide, if you will. How shall we march?"

"Sir," said Lucius, "I know that we have been lately going out of our way, but beyond that I know very little. Do we know for a certainty where the king is? We may go all the tiresome journey to his capital, and after all not find

him. If I may advise, let us strike the Euphrates as soon
as we can, travel down it, and when we come to the first
frequented ford, inquire. And to strike the Euphrates we
must go nearly south from here, at all events for the present."

This advice was accepted and followed, and, much to
the relief of Lucius, who felt no little anxiety at having
this new responsibility put upon him, turned out to have
been right. The Euphrates was reached in due course.
Almost immediately afterwards the party was met by an
Armenian noble who delivered to Clodius a courteous message from Tigranes. The king was much troubled to think
that a distinguished Roman who proposed to honor him with
a visit should have had so much trouble. Would he come
on to Antioch, to which place he had been summoned on
urgent affairs? Even there the king could not at once have
the pleasure of receiving him, but would do so as soon as he
should have returned from a campaign with which he was at
present engaged in Northern Phœnicia.

Clodius was half disposed to regard his absence as an
affront, but, as the king had not invited the embassy, was
obliged to make the best of it; nor, indeed, was the time
wasted. Tigranes was a haughty and brutal tyrant who
thought the whole world made for his pleasure, and he had
many subjects who would be only too glad of an opportunity
of overthrowing him. The Roman envoy had many visitors
who came under the pretext of paying their respects to him,
but really wanted to know what chance they had of getting
the Romans to help them in getting rid of their tyrant. He
was liberal in his promises of help, but enjoined caution.

" Don't stir till you see us ready to move, and that in any case cannot be for some time," was his advice to all.

After three weeks of waiting it was announced to Clodius that the " king of kings " had returned, and would be graciously pleased to receive the embassy at noon the next day. Immediately after the delivery of this message came one of the king's principal chamberlains.

He began, " You will make such salutation to the king of kings as is prescribed by the custom of the court."

" And what is that? " said Clodius.

" It is customary to kneel and touch the ground three times with the forehead," returned the chamberlain, who knew how the proposal was likely to be received, but kept his countenance with an admirable gravity.

" Kneel ! " cried Clodius ; " a Roman kneel ! "

" It is not too much honor," replied the chamberlain, " for the king of kings."

" He may be king of kings, but he is not my king. Sir, I am a senator of Rome, and I own no man in the whole world my better save such as the Roman people may set in the offices of state."

The official argued the point in vain, suggested various compromises with equal want of success, and was at last obliged to depart without obtaining any concession. At the audience of the next day every thing was arranged in the way that might seem most likely to impress the imagination of the envoy. The street through which he passed from his lodgings was lined with troops, gathered, as the variety of their equipment showed, from every part of the kingdom. Within the palace the scene was striking. The hall in which the reception took place was crowded with chiefs in every variety of costume, the chain-steel cuirasses of the Parthian horsemen glittering conspicuously among them. At the upper end of the room Tigranes sat in his chair of state, the four corners of which were supported by as many kings, still wearing, to enhance the dignity of their conqueror, their royal robes and crowns.

Clodius approached the royal presence. The young Deiotarus followed him as far as the middle of the room, where, as he was informed, etiquette required that he should stay. Lucius, as not being more than a private citizen, remained at the lower end. With a courteous salutation, into which he put as much respect as he felt to be consistent with his dignity, the envoy presented his credentials from Lucullus. The letter was taken by an attendant, who, after prostrating himself upon the ground, presented it to the king. A frown gathered on his forehead as he read it.

"Your general," he said, "might have given me my due title. 'King' he calls me. Does he not know that I am 'king of kings'? But let that pass. What is your errand? Speak on."

"My errand, sir, may be briefly told. You have within your dominions, and I believe in your own hands, an enemy of the Roman people, Mithradates, formerly king of Pontus. Lucullus having vanquished the said Mithradates in battle and stripped him of his dominions, and being desirous to show him, according to custom, to the Roman people as a proof of his victory, desires you to deliver him up forthwith. And I have further to say that so delivering him up you will deserve and receive the favor and protection of the Roman people; but that if you refuse, Lucullus, according to the authority committed to him, will forthwith proceed to take the said Mithradates by force of arms."

The speech fell like a thunderbolt on the assembly. Such words had never been heard in that presence before. For five-and-twenty years Tigranes had never had a wish ungratified or an opinion contradicted, and he now listened to the words of freedom for the first time. He made a stupendous effort to control himself, and succeeded. He had begun to listen with a courteous smile, and he contrived to keep the smile upon his face. But it was only on his lips that he kept it, it died out of his eyes; while those who watched, and indeed every eye in the room was fixed intently upon him, saw the blood surge up, so to speak, into his face. For a few minutes he remained silent, struggling to master his rage. Then he spoke in a calm low voice.

"What may be the custom of the Romans, I know not, but the Armenians are not wont to betray their guests. Mithradates has eaten my salt. · That is enough. But if it were not, there is more. Lucullus has forgotten that the King of Pontus is not only my guest but my father. That is my answer. But with you, sir, who have come upon this errand, much, I doubt not, against your will, I have no quarrel. I pray you to honor me with your presence at the banquet this evening. The prince will of course accompany you, and you will bring such others of your suite as you may think fit."

The morning after the banquet, which had been a scene of wild and noisy revelry, the ambassador had another visit from the same official that had vainly endeavored to instruct him in Armenian etiquette. He was now the bearer of splendid presents from the king, all of which, however, with the exception of one silver cup of small value, Clodius had the fortitude to refuse. As the party was leaving the chamber in which the ambassador had received them, one of them lingered for a moment behind the rest, and thrust a billet into the hands of the prince. When opened it was found to run thus :

"*To Prince Deiotarus an unknown friend greeting.*

"*Do not linger in Antioch unless you wish to be a hostage. Think not that, even if Appius is safe, you must needs be safe also. The rights of ambassadors are not always respected, much less of those whom ambassadors may bring with them. Those, too, who would not willingly offend Rome may care little about Galatia. In any case, this is a cause it which it is better to be condemned when you are absent than to be acquitted when you are present.*"

The matter was at once put before the ambassador. His advice was clear. "This is a warning," he said at once, "which you cannot afford to neglect. With you, Prince, in his hands, Tigranes would be able to make such terms with your father as would leave very little for him to possess or for you to inherit. As for me, I feel pretty safe. What a barbarian may do in his rage, without any thought of profiting by it, no one can tell ; but he cannot hope to make any thing of me. He knows perfectly well that Rome would not give up an inch of land for a hundred ambassadors."

The next question was, If they were determined to escape, and this seemed unquestionably the wisest plan, which way should they try?

"The easiest," said Lucius, when his opinion was asked, "the easiest would be to go by sea. But we must not risk it, for we may be sure that the harbor is being watched. The best plan, I think, will be to go back, at first at least, the very way we came. We shall be riding away from home, and if they look for us there, their search won't be particularly keen."

This course was taken. It was thought best to put off the start till just before nightfall, when they had the best chance of getting off unobserved. At nightfall the gates of the city would be closed. It was arranged that two of the ambassador's attendants should ride out early in the afternoon, and that the prince and Lucius should start, as if for an evening stroll, two or three hours afterwards. At an appointed place they were to exchange clothes. The attendants would return to the city, having left their horses for the two fugitives.

The plan was successfully carried out, but only up to a certain point. Neither party was noticed as they left the city, but the attention of one of the keepers of the gate was unluckily attracted to the supposed prince on his return. The man was not sufficiently sure to venture to stop the suspected person, but he told his suspicions to the authorities, and a pursuit was immediately ordered.

Meanwhile, however, the fugitives had got a start, and they reached the Euphrates some time before dawn. But now an unexpected difficulty met them. They were still about half a mile from the river bank when the moon, breaking, almost for the first time in their journey, through the clouds that covered the sky, showed them the presence of a body of horsemen on the opposite side of the ford. It was only for a moment, but the glitter of the steel caps of the riders could not be mistaken. It was evident that the plan of seizing them had been entertained for some time, and that every road had probably been barred against them. At the same time it became equally certain that they would be soon, if they were not already, pursued from the city.

Lucius felt that the chances of escape were now heavily against them, and considered it to be his duty to advise surrender. The prince peremptorily refused to think of any such thing.

" No ! " he cried, " I would sooner die than be made what Tigranes means to make me, the instrument of ruining my country. He hopes to work on my father's affection for me to make him give up, it may be, part of his dominions, or it may be abjure his friendship with Rome. To do either would be to ruin Galatia. But if I were to be a prisoner in the hands of Tigranes, subject any day to torture, he might be weak enough to do either the one or the other. On the other hand, if I were dead, he would find another heir to the throne. My sister has children who would be soon of age to succeed. Even if our house should fail, there are other families in Galatia which would be equal to the honor. No, I will not surrender ! But you shall do what you think best. I have no right to endanger your life ; and the reasons which are convincing for me have nothing to do with you."

" Prince," said the young Roman, " I gave you the advice that seemed to me to be the best if we were two private persons who had to choose between the risks of prison or death. But I acknowledge that the arguments which you use as the heir to the throne are irresistible. As for myself, the king, your father, has appointed me to accompany you, and till you command me, I shall not leave you."

" And now," said the prince, " what is to be done? What do you advise?"

" I see," answered Lucius, " but one chance, almost, but yet not quite, a desperate one. We must give up our horses. With them we can go neither backwards nor forwards, for the road is blocked either way. My advice as to them is to start them down the road to the river, give them each a hard stroke with the whip, and they will probably gallop down to the ford. The horsemen on the other side will be sure to see, or, at least, to hear them; but they will hardly be able to distinguish whether they have riders or no, or anyhow, if they do perceive so much, will not easily understand what has become of us. Meanwhile we must escape by the river. Some provident person has given us, you see, two goats' skins, which, when blown out, would help us to swim across the river. We will use them not to swim across, but to swim down. We could do it without, but they will make it far less fatiguing. It will still be dark for a couple of hours or more. Even when it is light, by covering our heads and the skins with weeds, we may very well look as little like two swimmers as could be. That is all that I can see for the present. After that we must trust to fortune and to what-ever may turn up."

The plan was carried out with success. First the horses were started down the road, then the two companions crept through the wood which bordered the road till they had traversed a distance of about half a mile. They then struck for the river, and judging, when they reached it, that they were out of sight of the party which was watching the ford, committed themselves to the water, having first inflated the skins.

They had made between two and three miles, swimming and floating alternately, and were beginning to feel exhausted by long immersion, when they caught sight of a small boat which a fisherman had fastened to an overhanging bough, intending, it would appear, to use it early in the morning. It was happily furnished with oars, and seemed too good a chance to neglect. Luckily at this moment the sky cleared, and the moonlight gave them some idea of where they were going. The river, too, was high, and carried them over rocks and sandbanks, on which during the dry season they would infallibly have been wrecked or stranded. The strength of the current enabled them to move very rapidly, so that by the time it was broad daylight they had put at least five and twenty miles between themselves and the place at which they had embarked on their singular voyage.

For the present, therefore, they were safe; but they could not hope not to be pursued; and it was certain that they would be stopped and questioned as soon as they should arrive at any roadside town or even village.

"It will never do," said the prince, "for us to get into the hands of the officials of the king. To avoid that we must risk any thing and every thing. I have an idea; it is the merest chance, but still it is better than nothing. You have heard, I dare say, that Tigranes has carried off thousands and thousands of people from Western Asia to colonize these desolate regions. From Galatia itself he has taken not a few; and it is possible that we may find among the inhabitants of the river bank an old neighbor or even a countryman. Anyhow we will make the trial."

Make the trial they accordingly did, and with the happiest results. The next bend of the river brought them in sight of a fisherman, who, with the help of his two sons, was dragging a seine-net over a sandy bay of the stream. The prince and Lucius brought their boat to land and offered their help, which was gladly accepted. The haul finished, and the fish — a take so numerous as to put the man into high good-humor — counted, the two were invited to share the morning meal. The language in which the invitation was given was sufficient to show that the fisherman was a Greek, or, at all events, one of the tribes which had adopted Greek habits and the Greek language. The prince, who spoke in the broad Galatian dialect, which he knew how to use on occasion (Lucius remaining discreetly silent), discovered that his host was a Cappadocian who had been forcibly brought from his native country to increase the scanty population of Armenia. Before long he managed to find an opportunity of speaking to him in private. He frankly told his story, and promised liberal rewards if he would help him and his companion to escape. The man, who knew the king by reputation, and was ready to grasp at any chance of returning to his country, promptly consented, and it only remained to consider how the thing might best be done.

"You must not think of it for the present," said the fisherman after reflecting a while. "The whole country will be raised, and every road will be watched. You must be content to try for a while your employment of this morning, in which, I must say, you were both uncommonly handy. In fact you must be fishermen for a few weeks, perhaps months, till the thing has blown over. I can find you proper clothes. My two eldest sons were drowned, poor fellows, a year ago, and I can fit you out with what they used to wear. You, sir," he said, "can talk just like the country-folk, and may very well be taken for one of us. As for your friend, the less he opens his mouth the better. When things are a little quieter you cannot do better, I should say, than go back to Antioch. They won't be looking for you there. Sometimes, you know, the lion's mouth is the safest place, that is if he happens to be asleep. Then Antioch is a big place ; people are always going to and fro, and strangers are very little heeded. It will be hard if you don't get a passage in a fishing or trading vessel perhaps to Tarsus."

Lucius pricked up his ears at the name of Tarsus, and naturally thought the plan an excellent one. It was clear indeed that for the present nothing else remained to be done. Towards afternoon a troop of horsemen was seen on the right bank of the river, who were evidently on the lookout for the fugitives. Similar parties were seen for some days, but as they could be seen approaching from a distance the prince and Lucius were always on their guard, and took care to be busy at their work when they came by ; nor did it occur to any one to examine them more closely.

Towards autumn it seemed possible to make an effort to escape. Tigranes with his court had left Antioch and was busy with preparations for the war, which, after the refusal to surrender Mithradates, had become a certainty. In the mean time the various articles which were wanted for a second disguise had been gradually obtained, for it had been arranged that the prince should play the part of a merchant, with Lucius for his attendant. About the middle of September they bade farewell, with many thanks and promises, to their host, reached Antioch without any further adventure, took passage in a small coasting vessel, and after five or six more days found themselves safe in Tarsus.

CHAPTER XVII.

CAMPAIGNING.

LUCIUS' friends in Tarsus had almost given up the hope of seeing him again. Nothing, of course, had been heard of him and the prince since the day of their sudden flight from Antioch, and though the old king was positive that a party which had started with such admirable omens could not possibly come to any harm, there were very few either at Pessinus or Tarsus who shared his faith. Philareté refused, indeed, to believe that her lover was dead, but her heart sank within her as the days passed without bringing any tidings. These months of sickening suspense had changed her from a blooming girl into a sorrowful woman ; and her father, who was himself greatly troubled by the event, began to think of a change of scene as a forlorn hope of bringing back her health and spirits. But the girl passionately implored him not to take her away from Tarsus, as long, at least, as any shred of hope remained.

" If he does come back," she would say, " he will almost certainly come back here. And if he should come and find us gone ! He might be very ill and want nursing. No ! I can't go away till I am quite sure that I shall never see him again ; and then you may take me where you please."

It may be imagined then what a welcome the young Roman found, when one afternoon, late in September, he presented himself at the merchant's house. The porter stared at him for some moments as if he had seen a ghost, then seized and kissed his hand, for Lucius was a favorite with all the household.

"Let me announce myself," said the young man, and passed on through the central hall to what he knew to be Philareté's favorite room for study. She was sitting with a roll in her hand — the story of Ulysses — but she was lost in thought, with a sad, far-away look in her eyes. So buried was she in her musings that she did not turn her head as Lucius entered the chamber; and he stood for a minute or two watching her as she sat with her side face towards him. He felt the tears rise to his eyes as he marked the pale cheeks, the dark color almost of violet under her eyes, and the listless air of depression which marked her attitude. He began, too, to wish that he had taken a less abrupt way of making known his return.

He was considering what he had best do when he saw Philareté's weary look change to one of eager attention; and the next moment the figure of the merchant himself appeared at the window. His face showed at once that he had heard the news, and Philareté understood it before he had uttered a word. He leaped through the open window with the agility of a young man, crying out:

"Where is he? Why doesn't he come here? If the ungrateful rascal goes anywhere else, I will " —

What he would have done can never be known, for at this moment his eye fell on the figure of Lucius, who indeed thought that it was time for him to advance. The meeting, the long talk that followed, the questions asked and answered over and over again, the exclamations of wonder and pity and indignation, we shall not attempt to describe. It was an hour worth half a lifetime, and we must leave our readers to imagine it if they can for themselves.

We shall pass rapidly over the next few months. The prince found letters awaiting him from his father, directing him to remain at Tarsus during the winter if he should chance to return that way. The journey across Cilicia was, he said, no longer safe. Though hostilities had not actually commenced there was a state of war between Tigranes and Rome, and no ally of the republic could venture beyond the boundaries of the free city of Tarsus. In the mean time he would be the guest of the governor, and would, his father hoped, make the best use that he could of the many opportunities of so famous and learned a city. This stay was unexpectedly prolonged, much, as may be supposed, to Lucius' satisfaction. During the whole of the next year the Roman armies delayed to advance; and the two friends awaited month after month their summons to the court. It was fully eighteen months after their arrival in Tarsus when the long-expected letter arrived. Lucullus, the Roman commander-in-chief, had at length commenced his forward movement. The forces of Tigranes had fallen back beyond the Taurus range, and it was no longer unsafe for Romans and Roman allies to travel in Western Asia. Orders came that the prince and Lucius were to travel home with all speed, as there was a prospect, which for every reason it would be unwise to neglect, of their being attached to Lucullus' staff.

The parting between Lucius and his hosts was of course painful, but it was one which both he and they felt to be necessary. Lucius had his fortune to make, and would have scorned the idea of taking it ready made even at the hands of such a wife as Philareté. The girl herself, if she could have kept her lover with her by a word, was too much of a Spartan to utter it. Her red and heavy eyes told the tale of many sad thoughts about the approaching separation; but she contrived always to keep a cheerful air. The merchant bade his young friend farewell in these words:

"You must see this business out to the end, if it lasts one year or two, or even ten. My own opinion is that it will take more than the shortest and less than the longest of these times. If your general had a free hand he might finish it off very soon; but he has not, and I should not wonder if after all it should be somebody else and not Lucullus who gets the glory of bringing this war, which has lasted, remember, off and on, for more than twenty years already, to an end. But it is no good prophesying. Come back to us when you can in honor, and you shall have my daughter, that is to say if you and she are still in the same mind. Ah, you shake your head! but I *have* known young people change their minds. Don't think of enriching yourself, it is a sad hinderance to good soldiering, besides being as likely way of getting a man knocked on the head before his time as I know. You would not think of it, I know, for your own sake, but you might to please me. Understand, then, that what I want in a son-in-law is a man of honor who has made other people respect him. And now, farewell, and the gods keep you!"

Philareté's eyes were tearless and her voice firm as she parted from her lover. She might have been a Spartan maiden sending brother or betrothed to the wars. But the tears were close behind the smile in those shining eyes, and ready to choke the gay voice in which she bade him do his duty as a good soldier in the field, and told him that she envied him his chances. And when she had waved him her last farewell and seen him turn round the corner of the market-place and pass, it might be forever, out of her sight, she broke down altogether, and her maidens had to carry her to her chamber, as little like as could be to an iron-hearted daughter of Spartan kings.

Lucius and his company found their way to Galatia without mishap, though the roads were not as clear as they had expected. At the capital some disappointment awaited them. Galatia was to send a cavalry contingent to serve with the Roman army, but it was not ready to start. The fact was that money was very scarce with the old king, whose Eastern provinces had yielded him very little revenue since the King of Armenia had ceased to be friends with Rome. There were Roman capitalists, it is true, who were ready to lend money, but their terms were exorbitant, ranging from twenty to forty per cent, and Deiotarus was too prudent to put himself into their hands. At last he had had recourse to the good offices of Cicero, who was on very good terms with the moneyed interest in Rome. Thanks to the great orator's intervention he got a loan of forty million sesterces (£360,000) at what was considered the moderate rate of twelve per cent. This settled, every thing went briskly on, and a contingent of fifteen hundred horse was ready to start

about the middle of August. It was a considerable time
before they came up with the Roman army, which indeed
had moved with a speed and acted with a vigor which had
not a little astonished the " king of kings." To describe
the earlier operations of the campaign does not fall within
the scheme of this story. It must suffice to say that Lucullus had crossed the Euphrates and the Tigris, and had penetrated into the heart of Armenia, and after defeating the
king in a great battle was now besieging his capital, the new
city which he had called Tigranocerta, after his own name,
and which he hoped to make a rival to Rome itself. About
the end of September the prince with his contingent joined
the Roman forces, which were busily carrying on the siege
of the city. His first act was of course to report himself to
the Roman general, and Lucius, who had been formally appointed to the post of second in command, a veteran officer
of cavalry acting as " dry nurse " to the two young men,
went with him.

Lucullus was a handsome man of about forty years of age,
whose elaborately curled hair, fragrant with the richest per-
fumes of the East, and carefully arranged, might have made
his visitors think him the first of fops, if they had not known
that he was perhaps the best general and most able adminis-
trator of his time. His tent was a marvel of comfort and
even luxury. It was difficult to believe that all its costly
and elaborate furniture had been transported for hundreds
of miles over mountains, deserts, and rivers. The floor was
a richly ornamented tessellated pavement with a curious
medley of subjects, the Graces dancing being portrayed in
one place, a quaintly hideous comic mask in another, a carp

with lustrous scales or a richly plumaged pheasant in a third, and in a fourth, perhaps, a curiously exact resemblance of a half-gnawed bone. The tables were of citron wood, polished and exquisitely carved ; the couches were strewn with rich coverlets of purple, and supported by gilded legs, these also being elaborately carved. A side-board displayed a grand array of gold and silver cups ; on two pedestals on either side of the tent were busts of Apollo and Diana, specimens of the best times of Greek art ; while behind the general's favorite chair was a bookcase full of richly ornamented volumes. When the prince and Lucius entered he had one of these in his hand, and put it down with something of an air of reluctance to receive the new-comers.

"Welcome, prince!" he said in a cordial tone, when he saw who it was that had interrupted his reading. "You have come to see some campaigning, I suppose, and left your father at home. His years are getting too much for him. Well, you will not be disappointed. Tigranes will not let his brand-new city here be taken without a fight. Indeed, I hear that he is getting together such an army as never was seen before, and that we may expect him here before many more days are past. The sooner the better, I say, for I am tired of sitting down before this place. We are but poorly off, as you may suppose, at this distance from our base, for siege implements ; and if something does not happen pretty soon we shall have the cold weather upon us. How many men have you brought me?"

"At the muster yesterday morning there were five short of fifteen hundred," answered the prince. "And now let me make known to you my second in command and friend, Lucius Marius, a Roman citizen."

"Your name commends you to a soldier," said Lucullus to our hero with a courteous inclination of the head, "and I have had besides letters from Rome which make me glad to have you in my camp. The prince will dine with me to-night, and you, of course, will accompany him. Till then, farewell ! "

The dinner was in keeping with the apartment in which it was served. Lucullus had already developed some of the luxurious tastes for which he became famous in after life, when the cost of dinner in one of his rooms was never less than four hundred and fifty pounds. Lucius wondered where the dainties which he saw before him, the oysters, the sea-urchins, the lobsters, the turbot, the guinea-fowl, the old wine of Falernum, could have been got in the heart of Armenia. Every moment increased his wonder at the curious mixture of gluttony, foppery, and genius which he saw in his host. It was not diminished by the conversation after dinner, in which Lucullus showed himself as much a lover of books as he was of fine furniture and dainty dishes.

"This," he said, producing a roll from a fold in his robe, "was what made you for a moment this afternoon less welcome than you deserved to be. I had just got it by a messenger from Rome, and was deep in it when you were announced. Listen, and I am sure you will excuse me if I seemed for a moment wanting in the courtesy of a host."

He began reading a passage which describes the sacrifice of Iphigenia, and which may be found in the First Book.

" 'Tis part of the beginning of a new poem about 'The

Universe,'" he went on, "which a friend of mine at Rome is writing, to prove that every thing made itself, as far as I can make out his meaning, for I must own that he is not always so clear or so fine as in what I have just been reading."

He was just going on to give his guests some more specimens, when the officer of the guard came in with a despatch which had just arrived. The general's face brightened as he read the document. "Ah!" he said in a joyous tone, "we shall have the chance of trying our strength with the barbarians quite as soon as I had hoped. This comes, I may tell you, from the tribune Petilius, who has some light-armed infantry and a troop of horse some eighty miles away on the slopes of the Taurus. He tells me that Tigranes is moving on this place with an army that is variously reckoned somewhere between one hundred and two hundred thousand men; he is determined, the spies say, to fight a battle for his capital, and will do so without waiting for Mithradates, who is behind him with another army. That is all right; I don't care for Mithradates' army; it makes little odds whether we fight two hundred thousand or three hundred thousand; but I should be quite as well pleased as not to see the old king out of the way. He knows what he is about, has given Rome one or two great falls before this, and will, I dare say, do so again; whereas this Tigranes is eaten up with folly and conceit. Doubtless we shall see something of his advanced guard within eight days, but these great armies move very slowly."

The anticipation as to time was pretty nearly fulfilled. Petilius with his reconnoitring force fell back before the ad-

vancing army, and came into camp about five days after
the arrival of his despatch. Tigranes was then, he calculated, distant about three days' march; and accordingly late
in the afternoon of the 8th of October the van of the barbarian forces could be seen making its way down the nearest
pass of the Taurus range. The movement went on all night,
which happened to be bright and clear, for the following
morning a vast host could be seen drawn up at the foot of
the mountains. The besieged city was in a state of the utmost excitement. Many of its inhabitants, who had been
violently transported from the cities of Western Asia to fill
its empty streets, wished well to the Romans. But these had
to keep their thoughts to themselves, because the majority
of their fellow-citizens looked upon Tigranes as the man who
was to make their fortunes by turning his new city into the
capital of the world. They thronged the walls, shouting,
singing, and dancing, and yelling out to the Roman outposts,
who had advanced to within earshot of the walls, that they
had better surrender at once.

Lucullus had made up his mind what to do; but he followed the usual custom of calling a council of war. It flattered his officers to have their opinions asked; and as it was
tolerably certain that these opinions would be any thing but
unanimous, no one could be offended that his advice was not
followed. The prince and Lucius were both summoned to
the assembly, which they found divided into two parties.
Some could think of nothing but the siege. It would be
madness, they cried, to give up that, when they had spent
upon it so much time and labor. And what a thing it
would be to have such a place for their winter quarters if

they should be compelled to stop in Armenia until the next spring! Others were equally taken up with the army that seemed advancing to attack them. How can we be talking, they said, of besieging a place when the very next moment we shall probably have to fight for our lives? No; let us dispose of Tigranes and his army first, and then think of the city. Lucullus rose last to address the council. His manner, which was sometimes haughty and cold, was now full of courtesy and conciliation. He thanked the speakers for the advice which they had offered, and praised them highly for the clearness with which they had set it forth, and the admirable reasons with which they had supported it. He then reviewed the situation, as it appeared to him, and finally concluded in these words: "The gallant officers who think that we ought on no account to abandon a siege on which we have now spent much time, much labor, and, I am sorry to say, some blood both of Romans and allies, are certainly in the right. Right also, on the other hand, are my friends who declare that it would be madness to neglect the enemy who is at this moment advancing against us with forces so numerous. Both are right, but both also, I would say it with the good leave of gallant and distinguished soldiers, both are wrong. It seems to me that it is expedient neither to abandon the siege nor to neglect the army of the enemy. The gods of Rome favoring me, I will press on the one and defeat the other. My gallant friend Muræna, with six thousand men, will keep up the siege; I myself with the rest will march against Tigranes. And this, if the sacrifices favor us, we will do this very day."

The distance between the camp of the besiegers and the

outposts of the army of Tigranes was about eight miles, the Tigris being between them. Lucullus felt that a march of eight miles with a river to cross at the end of it would be too much for men who were afterwards to fight with an enemy many times more numerous than themselves. Accordingly he left his camp before the walls of Tigranocerta late in the afternoon, marched as far as the Tigris, and bivouacked for the night on its right or western bank. The next morning the enemy was to be seen full in sight. It was a vast host, such as seldom had been collected since the day when Xerxes led the flower of Asia to perish in Greece. Besides his own Armenian subjects, the king had collected allies from far and wide, from the Indian plains, from the Persian mountains, from the dreary lands which border on the Caspian on the north, from the Persian Gulf on the south. For miles and miles of front stretched the long array, showing every variety of formation and equipment. The king himself stood in a chariot in the centre of the army's front line, with his body-guard in gilded armor round him. The infantry, which numbered, it was roughly calculated, one hundred and fifty thousand, was drawn up on either side. The tall mitre-shaped head-gear of the Medes was to be seen in one place; in another, the sunshine flashed on the steel helmets of the Caspian tribesmen and of the mountaineers of the Caucasus. Clouds of slingers and archers were spread out in advance of the main line; and on either wing were posted two enormous bodies of cavalry, numbering between them more than a third as many as the infantry. Many thousands of these were cuirassiers, and had the chests of their horses protected with armor. No part of the vast host had a more formidable look than these heavy riders, whose weight the strongest line of infantry seemed unable to resist.

The army of Tigranes numbered in all more than a quarter of a million. Lucullus had ten thousand infantry, and perhaps a third as many cavalry. It might have seemed, it did seem to many, absurd that he should dream of giving battle with such odds against him. The Armenian king thought so, for he is reported to have said when he saw the little army " like a flock of kids " in the middle of the vast plain : " On my word, if they have come as ambassadors, there are too many of them ; if as soldiers, there are too few." But there were some, and Lucius was among them, who thought of another ten thousand, who on the plain of Marathon, some four hundred years before, had charged at a run, " like so many madmen," a Persian host at least twenty times more numerous than themselves. These daring tactics, which look indeed like madness, but which are really the bidding of the soberest sense, were what Lucullus was going to follow that day. At early morning the advance began. At first, indeed, it looked like a retreat, for where the Roman camp was pitched the river was too deep to be crossed, and the army had to move a little higher up before it could find a ford. This movement increased the distance between them and the enemy, and for a moment Tigranes thought that it meant flight. " Ah ! " he cried — they heard the story from a Greek prisoner who had been in attendance upon him — " these cowards of Romans are running away." " Sire," said an old noble who stood by him, " I could wish that your good fortune might bring you the impossible ; but

I know these Romans; and when they dress themselves in their best, and have their shields rubbed bright, and their helmets uncovered, and all their arms at their brightest, they mean not running away but fighting." Even as he was speaking the eagle of the Roman vanguard came full into view, for Lucullus had given the order to the army to wheel and cross the river. Tigranes looked on like one stupefied till the first cohort had entered the water, marched through it in as unbroken an order as if it had been dry land, and deployed on the nearer bank. Then and then only, like a man recovering from a drunken fit, he seemed to regain his senses. Three several times he cried out, "The men are upon us;" and issued hurried orders to his generals to set their forces in order.

It was high time that they should do so, for indeed the Romans were upon them. One of the timid advisers who are always ready, if they can, to ruin the bold ideas of greater minds, would have stopped Lucullus as he was crossing the river.

"Take care, my lord," he cried; "take care, this is the ninth of October, an unlucky day, for it was to-day that Cæpio lost eighty thousand men at Arausio in battle with the Cimbri."

"Unlucky is it?" said Lucullus, with a gay laugh. "Then I will make it lucky hereafter. Standard-bearer, lead on."

And following close upon the eagle he himself plunged into the water, and in a few minutes stood on the opposite bank. He was on foot, wearing a highly polished cuirass of scale armor, and a bright-colored cloak with tassels. He had drawn his sword, and was holding it aloft, a significant token to his men that the day's battle was to be a battle of the sword, fought at close quarters; and, indeed, for that small company to let themselves be made a mark for the fifty thousand archers and slingers that were arrayed against them would have been sheer madness. When about two thirds of his little army had crossed the river he determined, without waiting for the remainder, to order an advance, which, a quick march at first, was to be increased to the "double" when they should come within three hundred yards of the enemy. After giving these directions he summoned Prince Deiotarus to his side.

"Thank the gods, prince," he said, "for giving you a chance of striking the first blow at the enemy. You see these cuirassiers there with their armored horses. If that mob of slaves over there has any fighting stuff amongst it at all, it will be there. You and the Thracians will charge them. They are six to one, but what of that? At them as quick as you can."

The prince heard with delight, and galloped off to put himself at the head of his force. It stood drawn up in two squadrons, each consisting of about seven hundred men. The prince briefly addressed his Galatians, giving them the instructions which he had himself received.

"Advance," he said, "at a trot. When we are about two hundred yards from the enemy I will raise my sword above my head. That will be the signal for you to put your horses to the gallop. Don't stop to throw your javelins. Close with them, and strike at the riders' legs. The cuirasses may turn your swords."

The commander of the Thracians spoke to his own men

to the same purpose. The signal to advance was given, and Lucius, who, being the junior officer, was on the extreme right wing, for the first time in his life felt himself in the middle of what is perhaps the most exciting experience in the world, a charge of cavalry. The rapid, yet orderly movement of the lines, whose steel caps, and swords laid back over their shoulders, glittered in the fresh morning sunlight, the measured rhythmical tramp of thousands of horse-hoofs, filled him with such a passion for conflict as, though he was now no novice in fighting, he had not dreamt of before. A kind of intoxication of courage seemed to possess him. Fear was as far from his thoughts as if no such emotion existed. He could hear in the intense strain of his senses the hard breathing of the troopers who were closest to him, and caught a glimpse of their fiercely flashing eyes and hard-set teeth. He felt that with them beside him and behind him he could fling himself without hesitation on any host.

The actual issue of the charge was something of a disappointment. As long as the squadrons advanced at a trot the serried ranks of the enemy's cavalry stood unmoved, and seemed likely to present a firm front to the attack. But when the officers who led the charge raised, as had been settled before, their swords above their heads, and the whole body with an answering shout quickened at once into a gallop, something like a shudder passed through the dense mass of men. In another moment they were hopelessly broken into a wild confusion of struggling fugitives. A few of the chiefs indeed disdained to fly, and awaited with the courage of despair the shock of the advancing squadron.

One of these, a man of huge stature, spurred his horse, itself an animal of unusual size and of a dazzling white color, at the young Roman. But before he had time to strike or to receive a blow he was swept away by the tide of horsemen, and Lucius, as he galloped on, caught a glimpse of rider and steed stretched helplessly on the ground.

The flight of the cuirassiers was followed in an incredibly short space of time by the rout of the whole army. The lines of Armenian infantry were broken by the furious rush of the fugitive horsemen, and, once broken, made no effort to form themselves anew. It was no battle, for five only of the Roman army were killed and not more than a hundred wounded, but simply a scene of slaughter and plunder. Lucius saw with disgust how his comrades went on slaying the unresisting enemy till they could hardly lift their arms to strike, and never ceased from their hideous debauchery of blood except to spoil some corpse that seemed to be more richly accoutred than usual. He had sheathed his own sword, and busied himself in persuading the Galatian troopers under his command to spare the lives of some of the wretched creatures who stood helplessly to receive the final stroke. It was not more than twice or thrice that he succeeded. One young man of two or three and twenty, whose face had caught his attention by some likeness which he vaguely felt, but could not account for, he saved at no small risk to his own life. It was, we shall find, a curious chance that brought the two together, and one that was to have some influence on the young Roman's after life.

Towards evening Lucullus recalled his troops from the

pursuit. That night the victorious army bivouacked on the field among the crowded corpses of the dead, of which, it was said, there were in all as many as a hundred thousand. The next day he recrossed the river, and returned to the camp before Tigranocerta.

CHAPTER XVIII.

CAMPAIGNING — *Continued.*

ONE important result of Lucullus' victory was that Tigranocerta immediately fell into his hands. Though the battle had been fought at some distance from the town, it had been possible for the inhabitants to see from the walls so much as to make them sure that the king had been defeated. There were, as has been said before, two parties in the town, those who wished for the success of the king, and those who were ready to welcome the Romans as deliverers. During the night that followed the battle the greater part of the king's friends fled from the town. Muræna with his six thousand men could not pretend to keep up any thing like a blockade or stop the fugitives, and as he had with him only a handful of cavalry he did not attempt to pursue them. Very soon after his return Lucullus was waited on by a deputation from the town. They had been unwilling subjects, they said, of Tigranes, Greeks, compelled to serve a barbarian. They had always prayed for the success of the Roman arms. Now the gods, who hated tyranny and insolence, had overthrown this upstart, who was not afraid to arrogate to himself the very title of Zeus, and to call himself king of kings. The Romans had only to stretch out their hands and lay hold of his treasures. They would themselves open the gates, and welcome them as their deliverers.

The town which the prince and Lucius entered in the train of Lucullus was a curious sight, for it was wholly unlike any other place they had seen. A town commonly grows up and keeps about it some signs of the various stages of its growth. It has old houses, and it has new. It has been altered and added to, to suit the wants and wishes of various generations. Tigranocerta was altogether new. The caprice of the king had called it into existence, and it bore the marks of its origin. It had been laid out on a regular plan ; the streets crossed each other at right angles ; all the houses in each were of a uniform size and pattern, some being assigned as the dwellings of the rich, and being proportionately large and handsome, others belonging to the middle class, and others again to the poor. As Tigranes had made his plans on the scale of his hopes of what the population would be, rather than of what he had actually ready to settle in his new capital, whole quarters of the city had never been inhabited, and had already begun to fall into ruin. The flight of a part of the population had made the place look still more desolate, in fact the impression on every one was that there was not a drearier spot on earth than Tigranes' new city, and that the sooner it was permitted to sink again into the desert from which it had been called forth, the better it would be for mankind.

The conquerors, however, found attractions in the plunder of the place. The houses of the Greek inhabitants were protected, but everything else was given up to pillage. Besides what they could thus secure the soldiers had a handsome sum distributed to them out of the royal treasure which had been found in the palace, each man receiving between $150 and $200 in our money. Amusements too were not wanting. Tigranes had determined to have a city complete according to the best models of civilization, and he had taken great pains to get together a company of actors, bribing some, and kidnapping others. There was a theatre, too, built after the pattern of that in Ephesus, as far as the skill of a young architect who had had the misfortune to fall into the king's hands had been able to carry him. Lucullus ordered a play to be acted, choosing as suited for the occasion the *Persians* of Æschylus, as being the story of another great victory which in times past the West had won over the East. It was not the least strange of Lucius's experiences, that in one of the most unlikely places in the world, the desolate plain of Armenia, he realized what had been one of the dreams of his life, to see one of the masterpieces of the Greek drama actually put upon the stage.

He was not so well pleased with another amusement which the general provided for his army. The taste for Greek tragedy was, as may be supposed, not very general among the Roman legions, and for these a very different kind of spectacle had to be provided. Several hundred prisoners had been taken in the late battle, the soldiers having spared their lives, not so much out of any feeling of pity as out of sheer weariness of slaying. These were to be turned into gladiators, though the connoisseurs in this kind of amusement did not expect any very exciting sport from such spiritless creatures. There was, however, another resource.

Among the treasures of the royal palace was a menagerie of wild beasts. Tigranes had been accustomed to make part of the tribute which came in from outlying provinces payable in these creatures, and had got together a great collection. The Roman managers saw in the beasts excellent material for increasing the splendor and excitement of the exhibition. Beasts might be made to fight against each other : a lion, a panther, or a bear might be matched with so many dogs ; best of all, if any of the new gladiators should seem disposed not to do their duty of killing or being killed, they might have a lion let loose upon them, and have to fight in earnest for their lives.

With all these combined attractions the entertainment proved, it was generally thought, a great success, the soldiers applauding the various spectacles with great enthusiasm, the greater the more cruel and bloody they were. Most of the Greeks, to whose more refined tastes such amusements were odious, kept away, though some of the chief citizens thought it politic to attend Lucullus, who, of course, presided, and sat, pale and shuddering, during the long-drawn-out hours of horror. Prince Deiotarus, who had something of Greek culture and feeling, excused himself from attending, and Lucius also was glad to stay away.

It was now that he made a curious discovery about the prisoner whose life he had saved on the field of battle. Until this time he had been able to hold very little communication with the young man, whose dialect, though it seemed to contain a certain number of Greek words, he could not understand A piece of good fortune now threw an interpreter in his way. By his help he learned the youth's story, of which, as it is a fair specimen of what had happened to multitudes of others in those days, we may give a brief outline.

"I was born," he said, "in free Cilicia. By rights I should have been a sailor. That has been the employment of my family for generations, and my father is a great man in his way. But somehow I never could take to the sea. Three seasons, one after another, did my father take me with him, and try to accustom me to it, but it was hopeless. Let there be the least breath of wind to raise the waves, and I was helpless. So he gave it up, though it was a great grief to him, and left me to look after things at home, cultivate the little bit of land we had, and look after my mother and sister. Well, about a year ago comes one of the king's lieutenants on a great kidnapping expedition. Most of our people had time to carry their wives and children to our hill-forts, many of which have never been taken. But he came upon our village unawares. We went to bed one night not dreaming of any danger, and the next morning we found the place surrounded by the Armenian soldiers, and we were as helpless as fish in a net. They did not treat us badly on the whole; the king wanted inhabitants for his new towns, and if people would not come into them of their own accord he had to make them. For myself I did not care very much. That summer my mother and sister had both died of a fever that broke out in the village, and I had felt the old house terribly dull and lonely. Besides, I had got tired of farming and stopping at home; and thought that if I could not be a sailor I should like to be a soldier. So I was ready to make the best of it, and when the king's officers saw that I was not sulky like most of the kidnapped people they were kind enough. In the end I was made some kind of a captain in the army ; all the rest of my story you know."

As soon as the prisoner had said that he had once been a sailor Lucius seemed to understand the mysterious resemblance which had struck him in the man's face.

" Can it be true, by chance," he asked him through the interpreter, " that your father's name — you say that he is a great man in his own line — is Heracleo? If it is, I know him very well."

The young fellow was not a little abashed at the question. He was not in the least ashamed of his father's calling as a pirate, which seemed to him just as proper and praiseworthy a manner of getting one's livelihood as any of the occupations which men commonly followed. But he knew enough of the world to be aware that there was a common prejudice against it. He looked in a confused and embarrassed way on the ground, and remained silent.

" Don't trouble yourself," said Lucius ; " if I know your father, I know nothing but good of him. He saved my life, and I think it a great chance that I have been able to do something towards paying him back in kind. And now for yourself. You want to be a soldier ; well, come with me. You have no particular reason to love Tigranes, or his father-in-law King Mithradates ; and I take it that on the whole it is better to be on the side of the Romans than to be against them."

As we are not relating the history of the wars with Mithradates, except so far as our hero was concerned with them, we shall not attempt to describe the events which followed the battle of Tigranocerta. It will suffice to say that the Galatian cavalry were sent home before the winter set in. Many of their horses had died, many more had broken down from excessive fatigue, and on the whole the force was no longer effective. The prince was anxious that Lucius should accompany him in his return, and the young Roman, though he would gladly have seen a little more active service, did not like to refuse. But here Lucullus interfered. Lucius was a valuable officer, and he refused to part with him. The prince therefore departed without him, carrying letters which he promised to forward to Tarsus and Rome, and also taking charge of a sum which Lucius had received as his share of prize-money. It amounted to about a thousand pounds, and the general's secretary of finance gave him in exchange for the coin a letter of credit which would be payable at Rome. This Lucius enclosed in a letter to his father, begging him to use or invest the funds as he might think best. A few of the Galatian troopers had become strongly attached to their second in command, and asked and received permission to remain with him. These were drafted into the Thracian cavalry whom Lucullus still retained, and Lucius received the same appointment in the consolidated force that he had held before.

CHAPTER XIX.

CAPTIVITY.

THE campaign of the following year took Lucius into very different scenes. The Roman general was busy with Tigranes, whom he again defeated, when tidings reached him of a formidable diversion of the enemy in his rear. The great Mithradates himself, one of the most powerful foes that Rome had ever encountered, had marched into Pontus, his hereditary kingdom, and had been gladly welcomed by his old subjects. Half of the province was already in his hands, and the rest would soon be so unless the feeble Roman force which had been left to protect it should be speedily re-enforced. Lucullus determined to send, for this purpose, the main body of his cavalry, which, as he was at the time engaged in what promised to be a tedious siege, was of little immediate use; and by the middle of July the Thracian horse had joined the army in Pontus, then under the command of a certain Fabius.

Lucius was not long in finding out that things were not looking well in Pontus. Fabius was an incompetent general, brave enough, for a Roman was seldom wanting in courage, but weak and irresolute, and, as such persons not unfrequently are, ludicrously jealous and touchy on the subject of his own position and authority. This failing, making him, as it did, particularly unwilling to take advice, was the chief cause of the disasters that soon followed.

Lucius was not satisfied with the demeanor of the cavalry under his command. Since their arrival in Pontus they had become sullen, and at times almost insolent. Unluckily he had never been able to gain the confidence of his chief, a veteran who had served for nearly forty years in the armies of Rome, and who looked upon the young Roman as a mere boy put by favor into a place for which he was not fit. He felt himself bound to tell the old man of his suspicion that something was wrong with the troop, but was treated almost with rudeness. The old commander was furious at the bare notion of his men being capable of treachery. A Roman by birth, he had become a Thracian in habits of life and ways of thinking.

"I would ten times sooner trust them," he burst out, "than I would so many of my own countrymen. They have no politics, sir. That is the chief thing I admire in them; they won't sell their country to serve their party. They are soldiers and nothing more. No, sir, if you want to slander them you must not come to me."

Lucius still continued to listen and watch. The men were now to be seen from morning to night gathered in little knots about the camp, always said by those who know the ways of soldiers to be a suspicious sign. At what they were talking about, Lucius could do little more than guess; but a few words that chanced to reach his ears, and which, having picked up some little knowledge of the Thracian language, he could partly understand, were enough to alarm him.

There were suspicious talks too with the country people. It was impossible to keep any watch upon what was said by the people who crowded into the camp to sell their produce — upon the men with their sheep and oxen, and the women with their poultry and baskets of fruit. Still these men and women had had a king of their own, and had admired if they had not exactly loved him; and no one could tell whether some of them at least might not be plotting to help him. Nothing, however, could be done. Lucius was not more successful when he had an interview with Fabius. The general was very polite but very unbelieving.

"I like zeal," he said, "in a young man; some do not, but they are mistaken, I think. But surely, my young friend, you are letting your imagination run away with you. What should these men want with Mithradates? They have seen us beat him for the last twenty years. Why should they go over to him when they must know that he is on the very brink of ruin?"

Lucius had not to wait long for the dismal satisfaction of seeing that he was right and his superiors wrong. The enemy had become increasingly bold. Time after time foraging parties from the camp were cut off, and almost every night one or other of the sentries was found killed at his post. Fabius announced his intention of giving the enemy a lesson, struck his camp, and after a fatiguing march of about fifteen miles came in sight of the army of Mithradates. The Romans numbered in all about twenty thousand men; the enemy were about twice as numerous. There was nothing really formidable in these odds, had they represented the real truth. But little more than half the Roman army was

trustworthy.   Opposed to them was one of the best generals
of his time, who was now fighting, as he well knew, for his
last hope of power and even of life.   Fabius, who was not
without some of the instincts of a general, saw that the king
was changing the position of some of his troops, and that an
opportunity was come when his cavalry might act with effect.
He ordered the Thracians to charge.   They received the
command in silence, broken now and then with hoarse mur-
murs of dissent, and refused to stir an inch.   The order was
repeated ; and they wheeled round so as to front, not the
enemy, but the Roman army.   Their gestures, their cries,
the direction in which they levelled their weapons, could not
be mistaken.   They had taken sides with the enemies of
Rome.   For a moment Lucius remained rooted to the
ground, unable to realize what he had yet in a way expected ;
then, putting spurs to his horse, he dashed forward with the
idea of seeing what his personal influence could do.   In a
moment he felt himself seized from behind, pulled from his
horse, and handcuffed.   His commander fared worse.   At
first the movement of his men was evidently unintelligible to
him.   When its meaning dawned upon him, he threw himself in their way, almost beside himself with mingled grief,
fear, and rage.   He had recourse at first to entreaties, then
to threats.   Words failing him, he rode furiously at the nearest trooper and struck at him a ferocious blow.   The man
contented himself with parrying it.   The old man was a
favorite with his soldiers, and they were unwilling to hurt
him.   But he would have refused to escape even if he had
been able.   All that he had to live for was gone when his
regiment became traitors.   At a concerted signal from the

king the Thracian cavalry began to move forward. The old commander sat on his horse stolidly in the way, and without attempting to escape went down before the advancing squadron.

Lucius, who was ready to share his fate, escaped by the help of some friends among the men. He had been able sometimes to do some little services to two of the troopers on their way to Armenia, and these they now repaid. They knew enough of him to be sure that nothing would tempt him to break his faith, and that the only chance of saving his life was to make him helpless. Hence the treatment, seemingly so insulting, which he had received. Looking on with his hands bound, he saw but could not avert his commander's fate. For many a year afterwards he never could banish from his mind the sight of the old man, as he lay trampled under the horses' hoofs, his white hair dabbled with blood, and his face still distorted with the wrath and despair with which he had seen the whole fabric of a lifetime's work disappear in a moment.

The treachery of the Thracians disorganized the whole army, and but for the steadfastness of the legions would probably have destroyed it. The auxiliaries almost without exception either fled from the field or stood without striking a blow. The legionaries never lost courage. Forming themselves into a solid body they slowly retreated, facing round to receive the enemy whenever he ventured to approach. Their wounded they contrived to carry with them, the dead they were compelled to leave behind. At last, weary and distressed, but without any very serious loss, they reached the fort of Cabeira. Lucius was spared the painful sight, as he had been hurried to the rear of the king's army. He was considered to be too important a prisoner to be allowed any chance of escape. Indeed he saw nothing more of that year's campaign, but spent the rest of the time till the two armies went into winter quarters in a dreary imprisonment in the remote fastness where the king had fixed his head-quarters. It was with a sense of relief that he heard that Mithradates had arrived, and that he was to be brought before him the next day, though he knew perfectly well that the interview might very probably end with his being handed over to the executioner. One thing, however, gave him some hope, and that was the sudden improvement in his treatment which had begun from the moment of the king's arrival. The chain with which he had been fastened to a staple in the wall was immediately struck off, a comfortable change of clothing was provided, and his food was changed much for the better.

Early the next morning he was conducted into the king's presence. Mithradates was a man of little more than sixty years, who looked in some respects older, in some younger than his age. His spare and active figure, still equal, it seemed, to almost any exertion, might have been that of a man still in the vigor of life. But his face, pale with a death-like paleness such as Lucius had never before seen in living man, was seamed with the lines and wrinkles of extreme old age. Yet here again the eyes, deep sunken as they were beneath the bushy white eyebrows, flashed forth with the fire of youth.

The king, when Lucius was brought into his presence, was just dismissing the envoys from one of the Greek cities on the Black Sea coast. This he did in easy and fluent Greek. Then turning to Lucius he addressed him in Latin which would not have been out of place in the Forum of Rome. Never, indeed, in all Lucius' experience of him — which, we shall see, was prolonged much beyond what he desired — did he see the king at a loss to reply to any man, whatever his nationality, in his own language, even in his own dialect of a language.

" They have treated you well, I hope, during my absence ? "

" I do not wish to complain."

But those keen eyes had already perceived that the young man was more pale and wasted than two or three months of ordinary imprisonment should have made him. " Turn up your right sleeve," he said.

Lucius turned it up, and in so doing showed the mark of the chain.

" What ! " thundered the king ; " they have chained you without my orders — you, a citizen of the great Empire of Rome ! "

Lucius thought to himself of the eighty thousand citizens of the great empire whom the king had doomed to death on a single night, but of course said nothing. The king, for some purpose, doubtless, of his own, chose to be friendly ; and it would be of no use to doubt his sincerity.

" Pardon the stupidity of these fools, who do not seem to know the difference between a barbarian and a citizen of Rome. You will doubtless give me your promise not to escape. Your friends shall hear of your being here — which, indeed, I had forgotten till yesterday. Meanwhile let me try to make your captivity as easy as possible."

Lucius gave the promise required. It would, indeed, have been folly to refuse it. After a few more polite speeches he found himself dismissed. Attentions were now showered upon him. A horse was placed at his disposal, and he was permitted to ride when he pleased, though he had a shrewd suspicion that he was never out of sight. He was removed to comfortable quarters, and his fare was made as sumptuous as the resources of the country would allow. After a few days of this improved treatment he was summoned to a private interview with the king. No one was present but a young Greek who acted as secretary, and a huge body-guard, whose fair complexion and yellow hair proclaimed him to be a Galatian. The man stood as solid and immovable during the conversation as if he had been made of wood.

"Your name is Marius," said the king. "Are you a kins-man of the great Marius of whom I have heard so often?"

Lucius replied that he was.

"Of all your countrymen," continued Mithradates, "he was the greatest. I have always felt that the gods favored me in never matching me against him. If they had I should not be where I am to-day. And you have inherited his beliefs — you are for the people, you are against the nobles?"

"Sire," said Lucius, "I hope that these divisions have passed away. We are all the people."

"That is a great change," answered the king with a smile. "It is not so long ago since the days of Sertorius. He was a Roman, but how many years did he not fight against the armies of Rome? But to speak again of your kinsman. His family and friends were massacred. Do you ever think of revenge?"

"Sire, those were evil days and are best forgotten. When my uncle and his friends were in power they showed no mercy to their enemies. When those enemies again got the upper hand they in their turn showed no mercy. Most of the men who dipped their hands in blood in those bad days are dead and gone. If any remain I would not harm them. The gods will punish them if they deserve punishment."

"And you have no ambition? Your name would be a spell with the people, who have not forgotten the man who was their brother; with the allies, who have not forgotten their friend. You see I know something of your politics. If you have any such thoughts I could help you. I have still old friends at Rome, and I have that which will always make new ones."

"Sire, you mistake me altogether. I have no wish or thought to be more than a simple citizen. If you could offer me my uncle's career, his seven consulships and all his honors, this moment, I would not take it. I have my hopes, but they are not for such things as these. Honest employment, such share of honor and rewards as the gods may think fit, and a peaceful home when my work is done — that is my ambition."

For some time the old man, whose restless ambition had wasted Asia with fire and sword for the last twenty years, looked at the young Roman in silence. When at last he spoke it was in a gentler voice than Marius had yet heard from him.

"Ah! I have heard that word 'home' before, and have tried to think what it means. I have had wives and children, but I never had a home. The gods do not think fit to give to kings the blessing which every peasant may have. But it is too late to speak of that. Nor need I complain of the gods," he added with a bitter smile, " for I suppose that, if they had given me the choice fifty years ago, I should have said 'king,' not 'peasant.' But I shall leave you to think of these things. Meanwhile, you can send tidings of yourself to your friends. I will take care that your letters shall reach the Roman camp. An exchange I cannot promise, for, to tell you the truth, there is no one whom I care to get back. My soldiers I can trust ; but as for my chiefs and my children, I had sooner that they were with the Romans than with me. But if I keep you, as keep you I must, you will have nothing else to complain of."

The king did not give up his hopes of making a tool of his prisoner. He did not believe the young Roman, when he disclaimed all wish to trade upon his name. He knew that party feeling was still strong at Rome, so much so that Lucullus was hampered in his movements, and might even lose his command because he was a noble. He felt, too, that the chances were terribly against him ; that though he might hold out for one year or two years he could not long resist the power of Rome, and he clung desperately to the faintest chance of a division in the ranks of his enemies. All the winter he treated his prisoner with the most considerate kindness, making him an almost daily guest at his table, and putting the best of his stores at his disposal. He even tried a weapon that had been useful to him in the past. His daughters were the most beautiful women in Asia, and he had been able to gain more than one great alliance as the price of their hands. And now the idea seemed to occur to him that love might succeed where ambition had failed. Our hero was no coxcomb, ready to fancy that women were in love with him ; but he could not help thinking that it was no mere accident that not once or twice only the veil of the fair princess Cleopatra slipped down as she passed him in the palace with her maidens. The little notes, too, delicately perfumed with attar of roses, and written in indifferent grammar but in the most elegant Greek characters — the little notes that told him that a brave soldier could not place his love too high — he did not wrong the princess by supposing that she had written them ; he felt pretty sure that, for the best of reasons, she could not have written them : but he knew that the harem was too diligently watched to allow such messages to come without the knowledge of the watchers. We know, however, how he was armed against such assaults. No Eastern princess, however beautiful, could dwell even in his fancy for a moment when he remembered that free, clear-souled maiden who had won his heart long ago in the Calabrian hills, Philareté of Tarsus.

The winter and early spring passed without incident. In the early summer vague rumors that gradually grew more definite began to reach the place of Lucius' imprisonment, of a great defeat which the Romans had sustained. The first certain tidings reached him in a way that he certainly had not expected. A young stranger, he was told one morning, desired to speak with him. As he was allowed to see anybody that he pleased, the young man was introduced. Lucius recognized him in a moment as the Cilician whose life he had saved in the battle of Tigranocerta, and who had been so fervently grateful.

"You here, Chromius!" he cried; "what brings you to this place?"

"It is not strange that I should be where you are, and indeed I reproach myself that I was not here long ago. But you shall hear my story. Lucius Triarius has been defeated — routed, I should say. In one word, there is now no Roman army in Pontus. I thought it was going to happen. No scouting, no guards, no knowledge or care of what the enemy were doing or going to do, but boasting and loud talk. That was what I heard from morning to night in the army, and though I am not an old soldier I knew pretty well what would come of it. Then the general thought of nothing but how to bring off a battle before Lucullus could come. He hoped just to carry off the harvest where others had ploughed and sowed. Well, I did not wait for the end. You know, sir, that there was nothing to bind me to the Romans, except you, and you were gone. So I deserted. Ah! you frown, sir, but I had taken no oath. Well, the battle was fought the very next day after I ran away. The king took the camp by surprise, just as the men were fortifying it one night, weary after a long day's march. Of course the cavalry ought to have scouted in front, but Triarius never cared about such things, and the end of it was that the Romans were taken quite unprepared. Many of the men positively had only spades and pickaxes at hand, so utterly unprepared were they for an attack. Their officers did their best, and I don't know how many of them were killed — an hundred and fifty centurions, they said, and more than twenty tribunes. I had done my deserting just in time. Of course, men who came over after the battle were not wanted very much. I had had the good sense to go before, knowing pretty well what was going to happen. And I don't mean to leave you again, if I can help it."

The next day a message came from the king that Lucius was to join him. Reaching the camp after a ride of three or four days, he found Mithradates in the highest spirits. And indeed his recent victory had been so complete that he had some reason to be confident. The army of Triarius had ceased to exist; the terrible loss of officers, in particular, had shown that the men had lost discipline and courage. And the effect of it had been that the king was in possession of nearly as much territory as he had when he fell out with the Romans more than twenty years before. His spies, too — and he had spies everywhere — brought in information of the mutinous and disaffected condition of the Roman armies throughout Asia. On the whole, his prospects were more cheerful than they had been for years; and the unsubdued spirit of the old man revived again his old hopes and schemes.

"You see," he said when Lucius was brought into his presence, "I shall be king of Asia yet. You Romans make all the world hate you, and you don't seem to love each other. I shall raise Spain, Gaul, Africa, Greece against you; yes, and Italy too, for you have treated the Italians as badly as you have treated us. That is what I am going to do. And now for yourself. Will you help me? Have you thought over what I said to you last winter? You shall have every thing I can give you. You shall be my son-in-law. I will put you above my sons. I cannot trust them; I can trust you."

"Sire," said the young man firmly, "you could not trust me if I were to do what you ask. I have only the same answer to give you now that I gave you before."

For a moment the ghastly paleness of the king's cheek flushed with rage. He half turned to one of the gigantic guards that stood behind his seat, as if to make the sign which would have doomed the young Roman to instant death. Then by a great effort he controlled himself. It was not conscience or pity that checked him. Conscience and pity, if he had ever known them, had long since been strangers to him. But even in his most violent rage he seldom forgot policy, and policy bade him spare the life of his prisoner. He probably, as has been said before, put more value on the name of Marius than really belonged to it. It might be useful to have such a prisoner. If it came to the worst — and he never forgot that his power might crumble again, as it had crumbled before, at the touch of Rome — this life might be made a ransom for his own. This thought suggested what would be the best way of disposing of his prisoner.

"So be it," he said coldly, when his brief passion of rage had passed. "You don't know your interest; some day, perhaps, you will wish that you had made me a different answer."

CHAPTER XX.

A CHANGE OF SCENE.

EARLY next morning Lucius was roused by the news that a party of horsemen were waiting for him. He was to rise at once and start with them. When he was about to mount his horse a written message from the king was put into his hands by the commander of the party.

"*Mithradates the King to Lucius Marius, Citizen of Rome, greeting:*

"*You will renew to the bearer of this letter the promise not to escape which you made to myself. If you refuse to do so, he has orders to put you immediately to death. Your promise given, you will accompany him. No harm is intended against you, nor shall you lack any thing which my kingdom can supply. I trust that you will show to me the same good faith which I have shown to you. You will have many solicitations, for there are many traitors, especially among those of my own household. Be honest and firm. I shall see you again; possibly, if it so please the gods, at Rome. Meanwhile, farewell.*"

It was a long and tedious journey on which Lucius now set out. At first its direction, as Lucius could tell by his observation of the sun and stars, was nearly due west. After about fifteen days' riding the party made a turn northward, and a few days more brought them within sight of a great expanse of water on their left hand which Lucius at once perceived must be the eastern extremity of the Euxine. Almost the next turn of the road brought a prospect which to the young Italian was a far greater surprise and delight. They had been riding for days with a somewhat steep wall of cliff on their right hand, shutting out all further prospect. At this moment there came a great gap in this wall, and through it the travellers could see in the far distance the towering heights of the Caucasus. Range behind range they rose high against the eastern sky, broken now and then by some depression in the line, now by some summit which rose far above its neighbors and seemed to pierce the clouds themselves. It was late in the afternoon when this prospect opened upon them, and the sun was just disappearing. Lucius had not been trained, as is the youth of the present day, to admire the beauties of nature, but he had a susceptible nature, and the first sight of these snow mountains, tinged as they were with the rosy light of sunset, stirred in him an emotion which he could not have described.

The leader of the party, it may be safely said, was wholly free from any such touch of sentiment. The sight did nothing but remind him that they had reached a country where they might expect attack, and must take every precaution against surprise. Hitherto they had gone on their way in the secure fashion of travellers passing through a friendly country; now they moved in military order. Two horsemen rode a couple of hundred yards in advance; and any thing that seemed suspicious was reported to the leader. Lucius felt that he was watched. Indeed the leader explained the situation to him in the frankest manner possible.

"You will not escape," he said, "I know, for you have given your promise. But I am not to let you be taken alive, at least if I can help it. That is the king's order. You will understand then that it will be your interest that we should make this journey safely."

As it turned out they had to fight once only. After accomplishing two days' journey from the place at which their dangers had begun without any thing worse than a few alarms, they found the road, which happened at this point to pass through a village, barred by a force which they roughly estimated at about four times their own number (this was twenty-five, including Lucius). A brief consultation was held between the leader and his two oldest troopers, and Lucius was invited to assist at it, though he could hardly understand the barbarous Greek in which it was carried on. Asked for his opinion he managed to convey it in some such terms as these :

"We cannot force our way here, it seems to me, except by making these people believe that we are much stronger than we really are. The first thing will be to wait till night. The day will infallibly betray us. But we mustn't use the darkness to try to steal through. We must multiply ourselves by its help, waving torches, making as much noise as we can, and then charging boldly at their line. They won't believe that so small a party would dare to do such a thing. They will think that we are the advanced guard of an army, and will give way.   Anyhow this, I take it, is our best chance, for there seems to be no way round."

The plan was carried out exactly, except that, on the suggestion of one of the troopers, some of the baggage animals were employed in a stratagem which was to deceive the enemy.   The most valuable part of the baggage was stowed on the back of three or four of the best and most valuable beasts.   These were, if possible, to be taken along with them by the party.   The others were to be left behind tethered by long ropes to trees by the roadside, and having lighted torches fastened upon their heads.   Their movements, agitated as they would be by their terror at the fire, would give the enemy, it was hoped, the idea of a numerous force.   The device succeeded.   The night, fortunately for the execution of the stratagem, was pitch dark.   The enemy, who did not expect any movement on the part of the strangers, was taken by surprise, and gave way under a sudden impulse of alarm, which was increased by the sight of the flaming torches.   The party took immediate advantage of the chance, dashed through the opening, and, riding at the top of their speed through the village, were soon in the open country beyond.

After this adventure they pursued their journey without any further interruption.   The party, indeed, was just of the kind that might hope to travel with as much safety as ever was possible in that wild region.   It was not large enough to alarm the inhabitants, who would certainly have gathered in force to oppose the advance of any thing like an army ; and it was too strong, too well armed, and showed too little prospect of booty, to provoke the attack of small bands of robbers. There was a general feeling of relief, however, when, coming to a little fishing village on the coast, the line of which they kept as closely as possible, they found it possible to hire two vessels of moderate size which might carry them to their destination. Their horses, which would be of little or no use to them in the town for which they were bound, were left behind in the charge of the principal man of the village, who was to dispose of them at his discretion. The party, with all the effects that they had been able to carry so far, then embarked. They rather overloaded the crank little ships, which were not constructed to carry more than seven or eight apiece, and Lucius could not help anticipating another experience of shipwreck. The weather, however, favored them, blowing with very moderate strength from the south-west, and bringing them in the course of two or three days, during which they were never more than a mile from the shore, to the Greek colony of the *Twin Brethren*, a town with which the king had always maintained the most amicable relations. Here they were hospitably entertained, besides obtaining a well-appointed ship which was to convey them to the appointed end of their journey, Phanagoria, another Greek town on the eastern shore of what is now called the Straits of Yenikale, but then went under the name of the Cimmerian Bosphorus.

Here and in its more important neighbor on the other side of the strait, Panticapæum, now called Kertsch, it was our hero's hard lot to spend as much as four years of his life. It was a wearisome time for the young man, who felt that his best opportunities of making a name and a place for himself in the world were slipping away from him. Still it had its consolations. The young Cilician had been allowed to accompany him from Pontus, and proved to be as fine, brave, and honest a young fellow as could have been wished. The country had considerable resources in the way of sport. There was bear and wolf hunting in the winter. Hares were to be found in abundance, and could be run down in the warmer months of the year with the dogs of the country, a kind somewhat resembling the beagle, and tracked in the snow during the winter. This latter season, too, introduced Lucius to an amusement of which he had never even heard. He had known frosts in Italy severe enough to damage the olives and vines, but he had never seen one so severe and so long continued as to freeze a large body of water; and though the winter in Armenia had been hard enough for this purpose it had so happened that there was no lake in the neighborhood of his place of abode in that country. He now became familiar with the sight of the sea itself covered with a thick sheet of ice for months together, and soon learned the native custom of skating. The skates of those days were bones fastened beneath the boots, and though they were not suited for the cutting of intricate figures and the graceful evolutions of the outer edge, they enabled the skater to enjoy the excitement, or, as some one has called it, the "poetry" of rapid motion. The town, too, was not without some society. It was a Greek settlement, dating from between four and five hundred years before, and the descendants of the original colonists still struggled hard to keep up the traditions of their race. They pretended indeed — it was little more than a pretence — to look upon a Roman as being just as much a barbarian as any Colchian or Scythian tribesman ; but, as a matter of fact, they were glad to make friends with a civilized stranger. Lucius, too, had by this time learned to speak Greek with ease and fluency. His Greek, indeed, was not a little better than that spoken by the colony, which, during its residence of four hundred years and more in the midst of barbarians, had admitted into its daily talk not a few of the native words.

Occasionally too he had the consolation of getting news from Italy and even from Tarsus, though indeed it took nearly a year for a letter to make the double journey to and from that place. The letters came by sea, being brought by traders who penetrated to the remote eastern shores of the Black Sea for some of the products of the country, beaver-skins among other things, and the admirable iron tools which were wrought on the forges of Colchis. The young Roman was free to communicate with his friends, though, even if he had not been bound by his promise, he would probably have found it impossible to escape. As Mithradates had been courteous enough to send information to the Roman commander in Pontus of the place to which his prisoner had been sent, the young man had the happiness of receiving letters with home news in the year after his arrival, as soon as the season was open enough to allow the traders to approach the coast.

In the course of this year (which, we may remind our readers, was the year 66 B.C.) Lucius received a letter from his father which contained some very important tidings. We omit the details about domestic affairs, and about certain neighbors and friends with whom we are not concerned in this story, and give the intelligence which so interested the prisoner. This part of the letter ran thus :

"*And now for yourself and your prospects, my dearest son. Know therefore that the invincible Pompey has been appointed to command the armies of Asia, and that Lucullus, who had ceased to have the control of his soldiers, has been recalled. The fame of Pompey is indeed so great that there is nothing which the Roman people is not willing to commit to his hands. And the reason of this fame is to be found in a matter of which it is possible that you, dwelling in the very confines of the earth, have not heard, though indeed it somewhat concerns you. Last year this same Pompey having been appointed by a special law to have as his province the sea [1] and all the coast within fifty miles, with soldiers and ships as many as he might see fit to demand, in order that he might wage war with the pirates, did within fifty days clear those pirates from the sea, so that at this hour there is not so much as one of them left. Wherefore, when tidings came to the city that things were not altogether prosperous in Asia, one Manilius, a tribune of the people, proposed a law which should give to Pompey the rule of all the legions and fleets in Asia, and this rule he has already taken upon himself. May the gods turn it to your deliverance!*"

Lucius broke the news as gently as he could to the young Cilician, knowing that it probably meant the death of his father. For some days the youth seemed lost in thought. He had apparently something on his mind which he wished and yet could not resolve to tell. Several times he began

---

[1] The writer means the *Mediterranean Sea;* he would speak of the Atlantic as the ocean.

to speak, and then relapsed suddenly into silence. At last he seemed to make up his mind.

"I have a secret," he said one day, "which I can no longer keep to myself. It can hardly be but that my father is dead; and if this is so, then no one knows of this matter but myself. You told me of the island and the harbor to which my father took you. These, as you know, are not easy to find. But there is in the island itself a secret which, if indeed my father is no longer alive, is known to me only. He was accustomed to bury a large portion, not of the general booty, for that was divided among all, but of his own share; his father also had done the same before him; and when I first went to sea with him he told the secret of the place of this treasure to me. Now I mean to tell it to you; and I leave you free to do with it as you will. You will remember that there is a stream which runs into the harbor. Step three hundred paces eastward from the mouth of this stream along the shore. You will know that you have stepped them right if they bring to a little bit of sand which is always wet. Then turn with your back to the sea and go exactly the same distance inland. This distance you will not be able to measure by pacing it, for you will have to go over some rough ground; you must have an actual measure, and lay it along the ground as you go. My father, of course, knew the place well, and could find it without any help; but he told me this to guide me. At the three hundred paces then up in the wood you will find an open space, about sixty feet each way. The spot you have to look for is in this; of course you might dig it all up; but you will find the exact place by this — that there is a little gap in the hills on the opposite side of the harbor, and that exactly at midnight, on the last day of August, the constellation of the Pleiades is just visible from the right spot. If we both get away from this place we will, if you please, go together and search. If I come to my end here, and sometimes I feel that I shall, you will go yourself. You will remember that the island itself lies a little to the north-west of the eastern end of Crete."

Lucius noted down the particulars, but the matter did not make much impression on him ; he was far more interested in speculating on the chances of freedom, which the coming of a new general, and that the most notoriously lucky man in Rome, might bring him. We shall see in the next chapter how he fared.

CHAPTER XXI.

THE DEATH OF MITHRADATES.

TIME went on without bringing much change to our hero. The Roman armies under their new leader had been victorious everywhere ; but still his deliverance seemed not any nearer than it had been. At times he even began to fear that it was farther off. Mithradates had gathered all the troops that were left to him, had made his way, partly by force, partly by persuasion, through the wild tribes that dwelt about the eastern end of the Black Sea, and was now, it seemed, secure in the possession of his kingdom of the Bosphorus. For Pompey, as yet at least, had not seen fit to follow him. There was still plenty to be done in more accessible regions, and to pursue the king to the place in which he had taken refuge could not be done without the sacrifice of many lives.

Happily for Lucius, who might otherwise have spent half his life in imprisonment, the restless spirit of the old man, who had never enjoyed, or indeed cared to enjoy, a year of peace from his boyhood, would not allow him to remain quiet. The scheme which he had conceived was magnificently large and bold. He had failed, he argued to himself, because he had not used the right materials. It was useless to match Asiatics against Europeans. He might gather hundreds of thousands of Armenians and Syrians and bastard tribes, half Greek, half barbarians, from Western Asia, but they would not be able to stand against Roman armies of only one-fifth their number. But there were enemies to whom Rome had been obliged to bow her head more than once. The Gauls under Brennus had actually taken their capital, and had had to be bought off with gold; only thirty years before the Cimbri and Teutones had reduced her to her last army, and it was only the supreme genius of one man that had saved her in that extremity. Here was material enough out of which to raise a tremendous conflagration. Why should he not march along the north coast of the Black Sea, calling all the nations to arms as he went along? They would be ready enough to answer, for there was not one which did not fear and hate the power of Rome. An army would thus be gathered as he advanced : there would be no limit to its numbers, except his own convenience. With these new forces joined to his own — and the latter he was straining every nerve to increase — he would do as Hannibal had done before him, burst through the barrier of the Alps, and make Rome fight for her life before her own gates.

It was a splendid plan, but it was too great for his means. And just at the time, too, when all his powers were most wanted his health failed him. For more than a year he suffered from a disease which not only weakened him in body and mind, but was so horribly disfiguring that he could not bear that any one should see him, but sent out all his orders through the two or three attendants who alone were per-

mitted to approach. Still he persevered. He had accumu-
lated enormous treasures of gold and silver, coined and uncoined ; and he spent them profusely in making preparations
for this last effort. Crowds of the men who were always
ready to sell their swords to the highest bidder came to take
his pay. From these and from the veterans who had served
under him in many campaigns a large army was raised, to
be increased, it was hoped, manifold as it went westward,
calling the wild tribes of the interior to war against Rome,
or, an object that would probably attract them more, to
plunder the rich countries of the South. To the chiefs of
such tribes as could be approached envoys were sent with
rich presents. Meanwhile, in all the Greek towns upon the
coast the docks were busy with ship-building.

At last, in the summer of 63 B.C., nearly four years after
Lucius' arrival at Phanagoria, every thing was ready for a
final effort. The king, too, had recovered his health, and
intended himself to unfold his plans to the army. Lucius,
who, like every one else, had been excluded from his presence, was now sent for to the palace at Panticapæum. The
king's manner to him was sterner and colder than it had
ever been before.

"To-day," he said, "you shall hear my plans, and you
must decide your own part. I have waited long enough."

The assembly to which the king intended to set forth his
scheme of a grand war against Rome did not, of course,
comprise the whole army. No man could possibly have
made his voice heard by so vast a multitude ; but it consisted of all the officers of every degree, with as many of
the private soldiers as could find standing-room in the place

where it had been summoned to meet, the market-place of the capital. The officers of superior rank stood in front. As to the others, pains had been taken to bring into the neighborhood of the king such as were most devoted to him ; these were to lead the applause when he should begin to unfold his scheme, and it was hoped that the rest would follow their example. The scheme itself was unknown, though rumors of it were in the air. Mithradates was carried down to the market-place in a litter. A platform had been erected for him on the flight of steps leading up to the temple of the Twin Brethren. His appearance was greeted with a shout of welcome, for it was many months since he had been seen in public ; but the welcome was hardly as hearty as Lucius, who had been bidden to take his place behind him on the platform, expected to hear. He bowed his thanks to the assembly, and then proceeded to address them. His speech, which was delivered with remarkable fervor and energy, we shall not attempt to give. It set forth the plan that has been described above, of raising the nations of the North against Rome, and avenging on Italy the miseries which Italy had inflicted on the world. It was listened to in profound silence, and when it ended with a glowing picture of the prizes which Rome, full as she was of the plunder of the world, would furnish to her conquerors, there was some sound of applause ; but Lucius, who watched the faces of the crowd with an attention which the orator, rapt in his subject, could not give, saw that they gathered an expression of astonishment and even of dismay as the wild scheme was unfolded before them. Whether the king perceived or no that he had not carried his hearers with him,

Lucius could not tell; anyhow his policy and his pride alike forbade him to acknowledge any thing like failure. He had expressed his will, and it was their duty to fulfil it. He gave the crowd a dignified salute, entered his litter, and, signing to Lucius to follow him, returned to the palace.

"I told you," he said, "that you would have to decide your own part to-day. The time is come. It is now war to the knife with Rome. I have offered peace, even submission, but your general has demanded that I should go myself, and lay my neck upon the ground for him to trample upon. That, then, is over. Henceforth every Roman is my enemy. Make your choice between Rome and me; but remember that if you choose Rome, you die. Do not be in a hurry to answer. I have never seen one of your countrymen for whom I felt so kindly as I feel for you, and I should be sorry to harm you."

Lucius did not waver for an instant in his resolution. Yet a man may be excused if he hesitates for a few moments before he pronounces his own death-warrant. For a brief space he remained silent; then bidding farewell in his thoughts to all that he held dear at Rome and elsewhere, he prepared to speak.

"Sire," he began, "there is but one answer" — He had got so far when he was interrupted by a succession of loud shouts. The market-place, which could be seen from the window of the chamber, was crowded with a multitude of people, soldiers and citizens being mingled together in the greatest confusion. As they looked, a figure, which was at once recognized as the king's son Pharnaces, appeared upon the platform from which the king had addressed the soldiers.

Pharnaces was the favorite son, and had been declared heir to the throne. In spite of this favor he had plotted against his father. The plot had been discovered. Still the old man, who spared neither child nor friend when they stood in his way, had kept a soft spot in his heart for this favorite of his age, and had pardoned him. His appearance on the platform was received with a roar of applause; the soldiers waved their swords above their heads; the citizens threw their caps into the air. The applause became more frantic than ever when an officer, in whom Mithradates recognized one of his most trusted generals, stepped to the youth's side and placed upon his head a large crown, which had been cut for the occasion out of a paper roll. The king ground his teeth together with rage as he looked on. "Curse the viper!" he said. "Fool that I was not to crush him when I had the chance!"

Still his anger did not make him lose his mastery of himself. Power had slipped from his grasp, but he might still save life, and while life remained there was always the chance of power. He sat down and hastily wrote on a scroll of paper these words:

"*Mithradates resigns of his own free-will the kingdoms of Pontus and the Bosphorus to Pharnaces, and engages not to disturb the said Pharnaces therein, if he on his part will grant him a safe passage to whatsoever place without the said kingdoms of Pontus and the Bosphorus he may choose.*"

The scroll was taken by a messenger. The man could be seen to force his way with difficulty through the crowd, to reach Pharnaces, and to put the message into his hand.

The young man read it, seemed to reflect for a moment, and tore the paper. The messenger did not return.

Mithradates had not yet lost all hope. He hastily indited another scroll :

" The father implores his son, in the name of the gods that protect and avenge the family, to suffer him to depart unharmed."

This second message, it could be seen, made Pharnaces hesitate for some time. He read it again and again, and then showed it to two or three of the officers that stood near him. It could be seen that there was a debate ; from the vehemence of gesture in the speakers it might be guessed an angry debate. But the result was too plain to be mistaken. The second scroll was torn like the first, and thrown upon the ground.

Mithradates now hesitated no longer. The game had finally gone against him, the chances were past all retrieving, and he had nothing more to do but to pay the forfeit. He would at least do it without useless complaining. He turned to an attendant and said :

" Go to the princesses and bid them come hither."

To another he said : " Fetch a flagon of wine and three cups."

He then took a casket, undid the fastenings, which Lucius noticed to be curiously intricate, and took from it a sealed earthenware jar, holding it might be half a pint. The persons present in the chamber were the king, the gigantic Galatian body-guard of whom mention has been made before, two attendants, Lucius, and the young Cilician. The princesses now entered the room. They had neglected in their haste to put on their veils, and Lucius could see that neither of them was the sparkling young beauty who had used the artillery of her eyes upon him four years before. Both indeed were handsome women, for they had inherited the clear-cut features and brilliant eyes of their father; but they were past the first bloom of their youth. They had indeed the worn and faded look of women whose lives have been a failure, and in truth their lot had been an unhappy one. Both had been betrothed to kings; Nyssa, the elder, to the King of Egypt, Mithradatis, the younger, to the King of Cyprus. But the alliances planned in the days of their father's prosperity had been broken off when his fortunes suffered a change; and for the last ten years they had dragged on a weary, purposeless life, only relieved from time to time by their having to share one of their father's perilous journeys.

"My children," said Mithradates, "I am no longer king. There is your ruler," and he pointed to Pharnaces, who still stood upon the platform in the market-place, receiving the homage of the soldiers and the citizens. "I will not live under him even were he willing that I should live. What will you do? Your choice is free. Only remember that the man who has betrayed his father will not hesitate to sell his sisters. Pompey will pay a high price to have such ornaments for his triumph."

The women's eyes flashed with a fire that seemed to bring back to them their lost youth.

"Father! we will die with you," they said in one voice.

"It is well, my children. You have decided as becomes the daughters of a king. And now, there is no time to be lost. Unless you make haste, Pharnaces may come and compel you to live. Here is the readiest and easiest way of escaping from him. I have some experience in these matters," he added, pointing with a smile to the jar of poison, "and you may trust me. It will not cost you a pang. But that you may be sure, let me take it first, and you will see that I have not deceived you."

"Father," said Nyssa, "pardon us if we seem to oppose your will; but you have given our choice to live or die, and we have taken death. Grant us the favor that we may die before you."

"Let it be as you will," said Mithradates. Breaking the seal of the jar, he poured a small portion of the poison into two of the cups which he had just half-filled with wine. Lucius started forward when he saw the women take the cups, with a half involuntary impulse to dash them from their hands. The king checked him by a gesture of the hand, and he felt that it was not for him to interfere. Trained, too, in Roman ways of thinking about suicide, he could not but confess to himself that they were right. With untrembling hands they took the cups and drained them. They then kissed their father's hand, and covering their faces with their mantles, sat down. The poison did its work as swiftly and as painlessly as had been promised. They drew two or three deep sighs. Then, at almost the same moment the head of each drooped upon her shoulder. They were dead. Mithradates felt the wrist of each, lifted the mantle, and closed the staring eyes. Lucius, who watched him closely, could not see a sign of emotion in his face. He then emptied what remained in the jar into the third cup.

"This must not fail me," he was heard to mutter to him-self. He had reason to doubt its power. Living in con-stant fear of poison he had so fortified himself with antidotes that he had become proof against this danger. Still he hoped that what he had taken, a potent drug which few but himself possessed or even knew of, might have the desired effect. For some time he sat waiting the result. Finding that the poison was not acting he rose from his seat and walked rapidly to and fro. His skill taught him that move-ment might increase its power. All, however, was useless. "Happily," he said to himself, "there is yet another way. Against that at least there is no antidote."

He turned to the giant who stood, still impassive in the midst of all these horrors, by his chair.

"Man," he said, "you have served me well many a day. I want one service more. I have fortified myself too well against poison. I have not fortified myself against the treachery of friends and children. Against this your sword is the only antidote. Strike here." He pointed out the very spot where the dagger could pass between the ribs and pierce the heart without an effort. The Galatian, still stolid and unmoved, did exactly as he was bidden, and drove the steel well home. But when he saw his master fall a sudden fury seemed to seize him, and he turned furiously upon Lucius. The young Roman's eyes were fixed intently upon the king, and he was entirely off his guard. But for his Galatian attendant his days had been numbered. The young man threw himself between the giant and his victim, and received in his own heart the steel that was aimed against his master. At that very moment the door of the chamber was burst open, and a party of soldiers sent by the new king entered. The body-guard hastily withdrew the steel from the body of his victim, plunged it into his own heart, and fell dead across the body of Mithradates.

CHAPTER XXII.

RETURN.

"WE are come in time," said the commander of the party whose arrival had been so opportune, "though I am afraid we were too late for this poor young fellow."

It was too true; the young Galatian was dead.

"The king," continued the soldier, "bade me say, if we had the good fortune to find you alive, which, to tell the truth, none of us expected, that he desired to see you as soon as possible."

Lucius was very kindly received by Pharnaces.

"We can hardly hope," he said, "to keep you here any longer with us. Doubtless you are anxious to get home. I propose, therefore, to put you in charge of an embassy which I am about to send to the general. You will take with you the body of my late father, which the embalmers will receive orders to preserve. There will also be various presents which I will intrust to your care. You will proceed to Amisus in a ship which shall be at once made ready for you; and will do well, if the general should not have arrived, though, indeed, I expect that he will, to await there his further orders. Meanwhile I beg you to receive from me for yourself some token of my good-will."

In about four or five days' time every thing was ready for

a start. Pharnaces sent some handsome presents to Lucius, among them two swords of Colchian manufacture, exquisite in workmanship and of surprisingly fine temper, some magnificent pieces of amber, two handsome gold cups set with amethysts and topazes, and about £2,000 in gold, coined and uncoined. So he had the satisfaction of feeling that as far as money results were concerned the four years of imprisonment had not been wholly wasted. He had seen the body of his companion decently buried, and gladly turned his back, as he hoped forever, on the inhospitable shores of the Bosphorus.

An opportune north wind carried the ship without any accident or delay to Amisus, which lay in an almost due southerly direction on the opposite shore of the Black Sea. Pompey had arrived there the day before, and Lucius at once waited upon him to receive his instructions. Pompey was most cordial in his greetings and congratulations.

" I have heard," he said, "much good of you both before I left Rome and since I have been in Asia, and I am delighted to see you returned safe and sound. And you have brought, you say, the body of Mithradates. Why should Pharnaces have sent it? Does he think that a Roman likes to glut his eyes with the sight of his dead enemies? The gods forbid that I should do such a thing ! No ! I will not see the body. It would be horrible, and perhaps unlucky. Still, as it is here, we had better assure ourselves that it is indeed he, that I may report the matter with the more confidence to the senate. This I will ask you to do. When it is done bring back your report ; then I shall have more to say to you."

It was a painful duty that Lucius had to perform. The face of the king was changed beyond all recognition, for the embalmers had neglected to take out the brain; but there were other and sufficient proofs of identity. Two slaves who had been the dead man's constant attendants during life swore to certain scars which they declared would be found on the body, and which were found accordingly. Their evidence was put into a formal report; and the corpse was then sent back to Sinopé, to be buried in the tombs of the kings of Pontus.

"I have much to do here," said Pompey at his second interview with Lucius, "and shall certainly not be able to return to Rome this year, and hardly the next. If you care to stay with me I can give you plenty of employment, which would not, I may assure you, be wholly unprofitable. But you have been away from home, you tell me, for nine years and more (Lucius had given the general, at his request, an outline of his adventures), and you will be probably glad to get back. Is it so?"

Lucius said that it was.

"It that case," said Pompey, "you shall have a passport which will help you on your way. But remember, I shall expect to see you at my triumph. No one better deserves to be present than you. And I shall not forget you when the prize-money is distributed. You shall have your full share just as if you had been in the field."

The next morning Lucius received the promised passport. It ran thus:

"*Cneius Pompeius, commander-in-chief, to all whom it may concern, greeting*

"*I notify by this to all persons holding authority in colonies, towns, free and allied cities, and all other places, that Lucius Marius, a citizen of Rome, is travelling on public business, and I hereby command that they furnish him such entertainment as he may require, and forward him on his journey, charging all expenses to the account of the Roman people.*"

Armed with this document Lucius made his journey comfortably and quickly, reaching Rome early in November. His first days were of course given to his home at Arpinum. Our readers will easily imagine with what affection on the part of his father and kinsfolk, with what enthusiasm and delight from his fellow-townsmen, he was received, what a "lion" he found himself, what endless demands were made upon him to tell and tell again his story. He might indeed, had he chosen, have received the highest honors which the town had to bestow. There happened at the time to be a vacancy in the local senate, and he would certainly have been elected to fill it had he not steadily declined on the ground that all his plans for the future were uncertain.

And indeed his stay at home was soon cut short. Great events were going on at Rome, and it so happened that Arpinum was especially interested in them. Cicero, whose rise to fame and power his fellow-townsmen had naturally watched with the greatest interest, was now consul, and was struggling with all his might to crush a most dangerous conspiracy. This is not the place to tell the story of Catiline ; but we may remind our readers that it was at the close of the year (63 B.C.) in which Lucius returned to Rome, that the struggle between the revolutionists and the party of

order came to a crisis.   Lucius had not been at home more
than three days when news reached Arpinum that the life of
its great citizen was in danger, that two murderers had actually presented themselves at his door in the early morning
of the 7th of November, under pretence of wishing to pay
him their respects, but that the servants, happily warned
beforehand of the danger, had refused them admittance.   A
number of young men belonging to the chief families in the
town at once hurried to Rome, and offered their services as
a personal body-guard to the consul.   Cicero had more vol-
unteers for this office than he could possibly employ.   Accordingly he declined the offer with warm thanks, not only,
he said, because his safety was already provided for, but
because he might give offence to the Roman youth if he
called in help even from his native town.   Lucius, however,
whom he was delighted to see again, he asked to remain as
his guest, and Lucius, though not formally enrolled in the
guard, took care to be always near him as long as the danger
lasted.   He remained in the outer court of the temple of
Jupiter the Stayer while the great orator was unfolding to
the senate assembled within, with Catiline sitting pale and
dismayed among them, the details of the plot which he had
discovered ; and he stood immediately in front of the hust-
ings in the market-place on the following day when Cicero
told the people from what he had saved them.   A strong
remonstrance from his father, backed up by Cicero himself,
prevented him from joining as a volunteer the army which,
when the conspirators left behind in the city had perished,
marched against Catiline.

"You really have had your share of honors and dangers,"

said Cicero to him, "and must not grudge their share to others. Don't try the gods too often. They may get weary of saving your life if you call upon them so often. You have heard, I doubt not, the old proverb about the pitcher and the well. You have gone and come back often enough already. Be content to stay upon the shelf while you are still uncracked."

The young man had no choice but to yield to these remonstrances, but he remained in close attendance upon his powerful friend till after the defeat and death of Catiline. He then felt himself at liberty to finish his interrupted visit at home, intending to sail for the East as soon as the spring equinox was past (the sailors of these days being very unwilling to risk any acquaintance with the sea in winter). Accordingly early in April he set out, first making his way to Corinth, and then taking ship for Tarsus, at which place he arrived about the end of May.

CHAPTER XXIII.

IN HARBOR.

THE meeting between the two lovers, after a separation of nearly eight years, we shall not attempt to describe. The young lad to whom Philareté had given her girlish af-fections was now a veritable hero, one whom great generals had honored and trusted, who had been praised by men who were themselves praised by all, and now she admired him almost as much as she loved him. And he had never forgotten her. That, the young man would have said, had he been asked, was nothing to be wondered at. Who could have forgotten so peerless a creature? But the woman, living quietly at home, and remembering how her lover had been courted and flattered, and had been the guest of princes and kings, put a higher value than he did himself on his constancy and faithfulness, and loved him for it all the more. As for Lucius, the woman whose image he had carried with him in his heart through all these years seemed to him far more lovely and admirable even than he had fancied. And indeed Philareté's beauty had not in the least waned. It had grown, on the contrary, riper and more thoughtful; full of the spirituality and tenderness which love, disciplined as hers had been by years of unselfish care, can alone produce.

The one drawback to the joy of their meeting was the failing health of the merchant. He had overstrained his powers. Without feeling the vulgar desire to grow inordinately rich, he had had great ambition in his own occupation. To spread the empire of his trade over the habitable world, to make his ventures in every country, to have his ships in every harbor, his merchandise in every market, this had been the ruling desire of his life, and had possessed him as strongly as the passion for conquest had possessed a Pyrrhus and an Alexander. But this made a tremendous drain upon his strength. While he was still in the vigor of manhood all went well; had he had a son to take up at least a part of his work as his years increased and his powers diminished, no harm might have been done, though it would have been a singular piece of good fortune if the son had been a capable colleague and successor in that vast kingdom of commerce; but as it was he was alone. The burden increased, and the strength with which it was to be borne diminished. His memory, his grasp of facts, his presence of mind, failed him. Then came mistakes, ventures which might be called unlucky, but were probably ill-judged. And there were disasters, real misfortunes which no prudence could have foreseen or averted. Commerce in those days had not the protection of insurance, which now gives a certain safety to its ventures, and at the same time its perils were greater. A gale of wind might send a fleet of merchantmen to the bottom, and there were no underwriters to pay for the damage. Every merchant had bad times; the Tarentine had had them in the past, and, when both his strength and misfortunes were more elastic, had got through them easily enough;

now, when they came upon failing powers and means, they were almost overwhelming.

Fortunately he was still enough master of himself to understand the situation and to meet it. He made no desperate efforts such as a gamester might make to retrieve his losses; he accepted and made the best of them. He contracted his operations, and, so to speak, made no more ventures. Still all this trouble and disappointment told upon him. The spring and hope were gone out of his life. He seemed to have nothing to look forward to, and there is nothing that does more than this to make a man look old before his time.

The return of Lucius was a great delight to him for many reasons. He had himself a strong affection for the young man. He saw his daughter made happy beyond expression; and he saw at hand a long-desired opportunity of laying down a burden that was too heavy for him. He would not disturb the first few days of re-union by introducing any unwelcome business, but when these were past he set the whole subject before Lucius.

"And now," he went on, after exactly explaining the position in which he stood, his means and his liabilities, "and now what will you do? Things are not hopeless; a vigorous hand might take up the threads which a failing one has dropped. You might win back all that I have lost." As he spoke something of his old fire kindled again in his eye. "You have capacities for commerce. I saw that even in the short experience that I had of you. I should be here, for a time at least, to help you; and though I am too old and feeble now for a sovereign I am still equal to being an adviser. My name, too, has not lost its old power. I have still credit, I may say, in every market of the world. What say you?"

"My father, if I may call you so," said Lucius, "I hope that you will not be disappointed if I say that I have no ambition of the kind. I think that I understand the interest you feel in these things, and I respect it; but I don't share it. And not sharing it I am sure that I should not succeed in the life which you suggest."

"Let it be so," said the merchant in reply; "doubtless you are right. I fully expected that this would be your answer, and have made up my mind accordingly. When I was a young man I used to dream of building up an empire of commerce and bequeathing it to a line of successors who should raise it yet higher and higher. But the gods have decided otherwise, and they are wiser than we. And now about business. I know that you have never counted upon marrying the daughter of a rich man, and so you will not be disappointed by what I have told you. But you will not have a wife without a dowry. As soon as my daughter was born I set aside a sum for her portion, put it in a safe investment which I will explain to you hereafter, and have never touched either principal or interest. This amounts to about three million sesterces (£27,000). What may be the remains of my own fortune after all my affairs are settled and all my accounts closed, I cannot say, but I am sure that there will be something not inconsiderable in my favor; enough, at all events, to keep me for the rest of my days. Then there are the sums that I hold for you, what you left in my hands, and what you have remitted from time to time.

These I have managed as well as I have been able, keeping them separate from the rest of my affairs. They amount to four hundred and fifty thousand sesterces (£5,000), to which must be added two hundred thousand more (£1,800) which King Deiotarus paid to me on your account. And you tell me that you have brought back three hundred thousand (£2,700) from your campaigns, and that Pompey has promised you a share of the prize-money. We may fairly reckon that as two hundred thousand more. You will not be dangerously rich, but you will have enough for all reasonable wants."

"I am content, and more than content," said Lucius, "but I have something more to tell you which may have a little to do with the subject."

He then told the merchant the secret of the buried treasure in the pirates' island, just as it had been communicated to him by the young Galatian.

"But I have been thinking," he went on, "whether, supposing that we find the treasure, it would be really ours. It seems to me that it would belong to those from whom it was taken, if we could find them."

"Undoubtedly it would," said the elder man. "Our best course, it seems to me, would be to go, if you consent, to the magistrates of Tarsus and put the whole matter before them. That the treasure should be recovered is quite clear, and that you are the man to recover it; what should be done with it when recovered is not quite so evident, and is indeed too important a matter to be decided by any private individual. I say most certainly, go to the magistrates. But have you told Philareté? I trust a woman's judgment in such matters as much as I would that of the cleverest and most upright man alive."

Lucius gladly accepted this last suggestion, and Philareté was taken into their confidence.

"Above all things," she said at once, "you must keep your hands clean. Put it out of people's power to say that you want to keep this treasure for yourselves. By all means, I should say, go to the magistrates."

The merchant and Lucius accordingly lost no time in waiting upon the provost of the city, and told him the whole story. The provost immediately called a meeting of his colleagues, and after administering the oath of secrecy which it was usual to take in matters of great importance which it would be dangerous to divulge, introduced Lucius into the council-chamber, and bade him repeat what he had already told himself. A brief consultation in private followed. When this was finished Lucius and the merchant were summoned before the meeting.

"You have done well," said the provost, addressing them, "and as becomes the men of honor whom we before this knew you to be. The council has deliberated on the matter which you have put before it, and has come to this conclusion. You are requested to undertake the discovery of this treasure. We leave you to find your own means of doing so at your discretion, offering on our part to give you such help as you may desire. If it so please you we will send a commissioner — one of ourselves — to be present at the search. As to the disposal of what may be found, it is not possible, while all things are so uncertain, to speak definitely. But it seems to us that not less than a tithe of the value of the whole should be paid to you."

No time was to be lost if the island was to be reached at the proper time. The distance from Tarsus to Crete, in the neighborhood of which it was, was considerable ; and though fine weather might be counted on with something like certainty the prevailing winds would not be favorable to a ship travelling westward, and the tedious labor of the oar' would have to be greatly used. Preparations for the voyage were therefore made with all speed. The trustiest men that could be found were chosen for the crew, some being found by the merchant, some by the city authorities. A veteran captain was put in command. Philareté, whom it was at one time proposed to leave behind, made a point of being of the party, and neither Lucius nor her father was disposed to object. The other passenger was the city commissioner, of whose presence the merchant and Lucius, determined to put themselves in all respects above suspicion, made a great point.

Early in August all the preparations were complete. The distance to be traversed was, roughly speaking, about five hundred miles ; and it was not safe to reckon on more than thirty miles a day. They might have to struggle all the way with head winds. The island, too, might not at once be identified, nor the entrance to the harbor immediately discovered. Lucius had only seen it once, and that some years before, in an uncertain light, and when he was thinking more of the chances of getting away than of coming back.

The voyage was made without accident, and with more speed than the travellers had hoped for ; and August was not much more than half over when they sighted the eastern headland of Crete. Then began the difficulties of their search. There were several small islands answering more or less exactly to the description of that for which they were looking. One after another these were examined; but the entrance to the harbor, as Lucius remembered to have seen it, could not be found. Nearly ten days had been spent in vain, and the hopes of the party began to wane. The weather, too, began to look threatening; and it was possible that they might be compelled to put into harbor, and practically to postpone the search to another year. At last Philareté made a suggestion which Lucius always declared helped them out of their difficulty.

"Don't you think, dearest Lucius," she said as they were sitting over their evening meal on the last day but one of August, "that you do wrong by always looking for this place in broad daylight? You have only seen it once, and then it was the early morning twilight. You know how the aspect of a place is changed by different lights and shadows. Why not search for it when it looks just as it did when you saw it before?"

"Madam," said the city commissioner with enthusiasm, "I have always been thankful for the happy thought which prompted you to give us your company on this voyage; but now my gratitude to the gods for what was, beyond all doubt, their inspiration, is increased tenfold. You have found us the clew out of, or perhaps I should rather say into, this confounded labyrinth."

The vessel's course was at once directed to the most likely of the islands, which was happily not so far but that it could be reached before sunrise next morning. The experiment was at once successful. Lucius recognized the spot which he had left behind him in his escape nine years before, and could only wonder that he had not recognized it before.

After this a very short time was enough to bring them to the object of their search, or, if this must be considered to have been the treasure rather than the island, to the first stage in its discovery.

The harbor, when they made their way into it, presented a desolate aspect — very different from that of the busy scene which Lucius remembered on the last occasion. It was evident that no one had visited it for some years. Two or three ships, drawn up on the beach by the little stream, were almost covered by the vegetation which had grown up about them. The grass in the meadow was long and coarse, and evidently had not been trodden for some time past by the foot of man. It was at least probable that no one had anticipated them in their search.

It was now necessary to communicate the secret to some of the ship's crew. The captain, who had all along been in possession of it, was intrusted with the choice; and he selected two who were to assist in the search. It was arranged that the passengers, who might reasonably be expected to like a change from the somewhat close quarters of the vessel, should spend the night on shore, and that the captain and the two men selected should act as their escort. The rest of the crew were to remain on board the ship.

The party accordingly landed, the sailors carrying what was necessary for the bivouac which they proposed to make. The measurements directed by the pirate captain's son were carefully made while it was still day; and the open spot in the woods, as described by him, was found without much difficulty. There remained some anxiety about the weather. Till within half an hour of sunset it was still overcast; then a gentle breeze from the north-west sprang up and cleared the sky. Throughout the evening, which seemed to all one of the longest which they had ever spent, little was said. As midnight approached every eye watched eagerly for the appearance of the constellation which was to be their guide, and when it was seen exactly in the spot indicated all felt that success was assured; and so, indeed, it was.

Nothing was done during the night; but as it began to be light the spot that had been marked in the darkness was excavated. A few minutes' labor sufficed to show that the earth had been disturbed before. Two or three hours' labor brought them to what appeared to be a door; and this, when broken through, was found to open into an arched passage. This again led them to a natural cavern, which appeared to be about fifty feet high and about sixty or seventy every way.

It was not entirely dark in this place. A little light made its way in by the passage through which they had entered, and a little more by some very narrow chinks in the roof. This roof, they now perceived by what they had observed of the ground outside, must be the top of what had seemed to them an inaccessible rock.

When the eyes of the party had become sufficiently accustomed to the dim twilight of the cavern they could see that they were in a treasury. Rows of large chests, sometimes piled one upon the other, stood by the walls. As those who had stored them there had relied for the safety of their contents on their hiding-place, these chests were not fastened in any difficult way. When opened they revealed a vast variety of wealth, collected, it was evident, from many places and through a course of many years. Much was sacred property, small images of gold and silver, some of them strangely antique in shape; sacrificial bowls and plates; knives in which the primitive flint, used in all ages long before all record, was incased in massy gold, and cups richly chased and jewelled, and often inscribed with the names of the pious who had presented them. Secular spoils were still more numerous, and presented indeed almost every conceivable variety of ornament. Besides an enormous amount of gold and silver plate, there were massive rings and jewels, often unset and sometimes even uncut and unpolished; of works of art not in the precious metals there were very few. Those who had stored away the treasure had evidently looked to what could easily be turned into money. The quantity of gold and silver in bars and coins was enormous. The chests were rapidly sealed by the city commissioner as soon as their contents had been examined, and were left to be taken down by degrees to the ship. This could not, of course, be done altogether without the knowledge of the rest of the crew. But though some suspicion was raised that valuables were being taken on board, the secret was fairly well kept, and no one but the trusted few knew of the enormous value of the cargo which was being carried on the return voyage; and these, it may easily be imagined, felt not a little relief when they reached the harbor of Tarsus in safety.

When the treasure came to be accurately examined and valued it was found that the tithe reserved for the finders would not be less than four million and a half of sesterces (£50,000). Lucius reserved half of this for himself, and after handsomely rewarding the few intrusted with the secret and doubling the pay of all the crew, presented the rest as a charitable fund to be at the disposal of the city government. It was found that after all the property that could be identified had been restored to its lawful owners, and large grants had been made to towns which had been injured in former years by the ravages of the pirates, a great sum remained, which fell to the share of the city.

The return voyage had been speedily accomplished by the help of uniformly favorable winds, and the merchant, who had for some time been busy winding up his affairs in Tarsus, proposed to leave for Tarentum before the end of September.

"I should like," he said to Lucius, "that your marriage should take place in Tarentum. It is my daughter's birthplace, and the few kinsfolk that we have are there. We shall have ample time to reach it before the 6th of November, the day that we sea-going folk are wont to say is the last for safe travelling."

Lucius had nothing to object to a plan which promised a speedy end to his long courtship, and Philareté was delighted with the prospect of seeing her old home again. The voyage was made in safety, the party reaching Tarentum on the 25th of October. A week afterwards the lovers were united.

The next year Lucius was summoned to take part in Pompey's triumph. Our readers can find elsewhere, if they will, the description of this the most splendid show that the world had ever seen. All that concerns our story is the fact that our hero received as his share of prize-money, which, by the kindness of Pompey, was calculated as if he had been a military tribune, nearly twice as much as he had expected.

The morning after he had returned from Rome the merchant summoned him to his chamber, which, indeed, he now rarely left.

"I have," he said, "a little surprise for you which will not, I hope, be wholly unwelcome. After providing, as I know you would wish me to do, for some old clerks and dependents, I have invested what remains of my property in an estate in the Peloponnesus. It is called Scyllus, and it was once, as doubtless you know, the residence of the Athenian Xenophon. I have reserved the enjoyment of it to myself for my life, though, indeed, I shall never see it, for I hope to end my days here. In fact, I have given the late owner a lease which will be terminated by my death. Till then you must be content to be owner only in prospect. I say 'you,' for I have left it to you, not to Philareté. I think that a man should live in his own house, not in his wife's." The old man lingered for about a year after this, and then calmly expired, having first had the happiness to embrace and bless a little grandson, who was pronounced by common consent to be the most beautiful child in Tarentum.

In the summer of the same year Lucius and his wife set out for their new home in Greece, and there for the present we will leave them.

CHAPTER XXIV.

FOUR-AND-TWENTY YEARS AFTERWARDS.

THE time is the early morning of a day towards the end of February, when the short winter of Southern Greece is nearing its end. A young man and a girl, both of remarkable beauty, are watching the sun as it rises from behind the snow-capped hills of Arcadia. At the first glance one would fancy that the four-and-twenty years are a dream, that this youth is the very same Lucius Marius whom we have followed in many a perilous adventure by sea and land; this girl the fair Tarentine, Philareté, whom he had won for his bride when we last bade him farewell. Looking a little closer, we see a difference that was not at first sight perceptible. They are indeed a young Marius, a young Philareté, but each has caught something from the other parent, the boy something of a Greek fineness of feature and figure from his mother; the girl, something of Roman strength from her father. He is, perhaps, less sturdy, she, perhaps, less beautiful, but they are certainly not degenerate. But see, here comes our old friend himself. Now we see that the four-and-twenty years are no dream. His figure is somewhat fuller than it was when we last saw him, his beard just streaked with gray, his step a shade slower. The young people seem, indeed, to have outstripped him.

" Ho, youngsters ! " he cries, " have you no pity on an old man, that you climb the hill at so merciless a pace? Lucius, you might win the foot-race at the games next midsummer, but that your barbarian father has unluckily spoiled your pedigree.[1] Rhodium [this, meaning Little Rose, was the girl's name], you are as swift of foot as Atalanta. But let us halt a while, and wait for Sciton and the dogs."

The spot where they stood was one of remarkable beauty. Just below them was the wooded valley up the eastern side of which they had climbed, with a river showing here and there its gleaming pools amongst the trees and brushwood. Behind was a long stretch of forest, still full, as in the days of the old soldier and sportsman who had once been the owner of the place, of game, great and small. On the east rose, ridge over ridge, the mountains of Arcadia. In front was the most famous place in Greece, the plain of Olympia, with its river, its groves of plane and olive, and its temples and treasure-houses just catching on their gilded roofs the first rays of morning.

It was a view of which the father and his children were never weary ; still they had not come to look at the prospect. A glance at their dress and equipment will show that they have a more practical purpose. The elder of the two men has a stout hunting spear with a broad point in his hand, the younger a staff and a sling in his girdle, an implement with which he is singularly expert, being able to hit a flying bird of moderate size not less than nine times out of ten. Even the girl is prepared for the chase. A light bow is

---

[1] No one was permitted to contend in the Olympian Games except he could show unmixed Greek descent.

slung at her side; over her left shoulder hangs a quiver gayly adorned with purple and gold; meant, we may perhaps guess, for ornament rather than use, for, huntress as she is, she has a woman's heart, and loves all beasts both great and small.

They have not waited long before Sciton comes up with the dogs in two leashes. There are four of them, not unlike the beagles of the present time, but somewhat stouter in build, somewhat bow-legged, and with curiously long ears.

"I have set the nets, sir," says Sciton, "one between the two rocks at the south end of the wood, the other in the old place by the spring. A hare has been there, I could see, not later than last night."

The party now moved forwards about a hundred yards, till they came to the edge of the wood. Here the dogs were uncoupled, and the search for game began, the animals, encouraged by Sciton, who acted as huntsman, searching the thick brushwood in a most methodical way. The party had not to wait long. In a few minutes' time a short bark was heard, soon taken up by other voices.

"Diana be thanked!" cries the young man; "that was Warder's voice. He has found something, and something worth hunting. I never knew him taken in."

In a moment the hounds are in full cry, heading away, it may be guessed from the direction of their voices, for the wildest part of the wood.

"You had best stay here, Rhodium," says Lucius Marius: "the country yonder is too rough for you to follow. But very likely the hare will double back this way. Don't wait too long for us; if we are not back by the time that the sun has got behind the pine-tree yonder, make the best of your way home. I shall leave the hunting spear here. Don't trouble yourself about it. Some one shall come for it if we should not come back this way."

The girl was not in the least disconcerted at being thus left alone; nor did she seem likely to be dull. Her first care was to gather two large bunches of flowers, one of violets, blue and white, the other of anemones and narcissus. Her mother always expected her to bring home at least this spoil from her hunting. This done she took a scroll from a fold in her tunic, and seating herself under a lime-tree that was just bursting into leaf, prepared herself to read; for reading was at least as dear to her as hunting. She was soon engrossed in her book, one which she knew almost by heart, but of which she was never tired, the story of how Sparta and Athens, with more than half Greece either false or indifferent, turned back the hosts of the Persians.

She had been thus engaged for about an hour, closing her book every now and then to dream of what she might be if the old days could come back, when the silence was broken by a faint sound in the distance. The hunt, it seemed, was coming back. It grew louder as she listened till she could distinguish, she thought, the voices of her father and brother as they cheered on the dogs. But what is this that comes crashing through the bushes? Manifestly it is something much larger than a hare. Is it a stag, or possibly, for such visitants are not unknown even close to the house, a bear or a wild boar? She is not long left in doubt. A boar, one of the largest of his kind, with shining white tusks at least nine inches long, the bristles on his back erect with rage, his small eyes shining with a fiery green light, bursts out of the thicket. She sees that he is making straight for her, and there is just a hundred yards of open ground between the wood and the seat under the tree before he is upon her. The brave girl showed herself worthy of her race. An observer might have seen that her face was a little paler than its wont, but that her eyes flashed with a fire which no one would have thought hidden in their violet depths. She sounded the whistle that hung from her neck three times, the usual signal of urgent need. Then catching at her father's hunting spear, with an inward thanksgiving to the gods that had inspired him with the thought of leaving it, she prepared to receive the attack. Kneeling on one knee, she planted the end of the spear on the ground and rested the haft on her leg, holding it firmly with both hands, so that the point was about two feet from the ground. She had small hope of being able to stop the brute's charge, but she might check it for a few moments, and meanwhile, though it was but a slender hope, her whistle might have brought help. The boar was now close upon her, but she saw with delight that two of the dogs were in close pursuit. The animal, blinded with rage, charged full upon the spear. Held in the sinewy, practised hands of a hunter it might have pierced him to the heart; as it was, she had pointed it too high, and of course had not held it with sufficient strength, and it made only a slight wound in the monster's tough hide. But it did her a more useful service in a quite unexpected way. When the rush of the brute pushed aside the point, the shaft caught her on the side and threw her on the ground, somewhat roughly it is true, but at least out of the direct path of her enemy. The moment's delay was worth every thing. The dogs were now upon him, biting fiercely at his hocks. He turned first upon one assailant, then upon the other, and inflicted rather an ugly wound on Warder, who was older and less nimble than his comrade. Meanwhile, Rhodium, who had received no worse hurt from her tumble than a little loss of breath, recovered her spear and prepared to resume her attitude of defence. Happily it was not needed. Her brother, who was unmatched for speed and wind in all the country-side, had been but a few yards behind the dogs, and now appeared upon the scene. He had, indeed, a dangerous task to do, such as no hunter would venture on, save under the pressure of the most urgent need. He had no available weapon but his long hunting knife, and if he failed to drive that home at the first blow his own chance of life was small. Fortunately the boar was busily engaged with the dogs which were attacking him in front, and did not notice the hunter's approach. He seized the opportunity, and drove the knife with all his might behind the near foreleg. No second stroke was needed, as none certainly could have been given. The fierce brute, with one great shudder, fell dead upon its side.

Rhodium, now that the peril was past, felt the usual re-action, and could scarcely stand. Lucius, who had forgotten that girls are not made of stuff quite as strong as men, and that even for a man a first encounter with a wild boar is a somewhat exhausting experience, was admiring the magnificent proportions of his prey, when he heard a deep sigh behind him. Turning he saw that his sister was pale and trembling. Happily a remedy was at hand. A flask was

then as now part of the usual equipment of the hunter.
That which Lucius carried held a small quantity of potent
wine of Chios, so prepared that it was nearly as thick as
treacle and as strong as brandy. He poured a few spoon-
fuls of the cordial into the girl's mouth. It acted like
magic, a result not to be wondered at when we remember
that she had never tasted any stimulant before. Philareté
had kept up for herself and her daughter the tradition of the
best times of Greece, that wine was not for women. By the
time her father had come up — and his anxiety had very
nearly made him keep pace with his fleet-footed son — she
was herself again, and could tell the story of her danger and
escape with gayety and spirit. In fact it was he who now
trembled and turned pale, though he tried to hide his feeling by a laugh and a jest.

"Well, my daughter, Atalanta herself could not kill the
great boar [1] without the help of the heroes. She gave him
the first wound, just as you did to the beast yonder, and I
dare say was glad enough to have a Meleager at hand to
finish him. And now, as we have had enough hunting for
the day, let us turn homeward."

A walk of about two miles brought the party to their
home, a plain one-storied house, charmingly situated at the
upper end of the valley. Philareté stood under the porch
waiting for their return. Time had touched her too as
lightly as her husband. The complexion of "roses and
milk" was less brilliant than of old; the tell-tale sun might

---

[1] The great boar of Calydon, for the hunting of which all the heroes of Greece
assembled. According to some accounts Atalanta, the virgin huntress of Arcadia, was
the first to wound it, while Meleager gave it the death-blow.

have showed a faint line or so upon her forehead; but her figure was as straight and almost as delicately outlined as ever.

"What has happened?" she cried at once, the keen mother's eye discerning at once that there was something unusual, perhaps because the gayety was just a little over-done.

"Nothing new, except, if that is new, that you are the mother of heroes. We have been in the wars, but no one is the worse, except poor Warder, and he will do well I do not doubt. Come, Sciton, let the mistress see him."

Sciton, who had skilfully sewn up the poor beast's wound, and was now carrying him in his arms, brought him forward; and all were glad to see that the faithful creature was not too weak to lick Philareté's hand, and even to dispose of a little honey-cake which she produced from her pouch.

In the course of a few minutes the family was seated at breakfast. Some broiled fish of the trout kind, a pile of bread made into loaves of every variety of shape, a cheese very much like what is sometimes called *cream* but should be called *curd* cheese among ourselves, a dish of grapes dried in the sun, apples whose rosy cheeks were just beginning to wrinkle, and a great bowl of milk made up the meal. A small flask of wine was placed by the seat of the master of the house, but any one who had watched it from day to day might have noted that it was taken away, time after time, untouched. The story of the morning's adventure was duly told, not without some tremors on the part of the mother, who could hardly be satisfied that Rhodium had escaped unhurt from so terrible a foe.

" My darling," she cried, " you must never run such a risk again."

" Oh, mother," answered Rodium, " and you a Spartan ! This is not like ' with your shield or on it.' " [1]

" Hush ! Rhodium," said her father, " you must not answer your mother. Still we won't keep you spinning at home, but we must see that your hunting is a little safer than it was to-day. The truth is, we ought never to have left ·you. But who would have thought to find a wild boar within a mile of the house ! I have never heard of such a thing before."

The day was not to pass without further excitement. Breakfast was just finished when a young slave entered the room.

" My lord," he said, " a letter-carrier is here, who says that he has come from Tarentum, with a letter for the lady Philareté."

" Bring him in," said Marius.

The next minute the messenger was ushered in. He was a spare, well-knit man of thirty or thereabouts, so curiously sunburnt that he might have been taken for an Asiatic, though he was really a Spaniard from one of the northern districts. He had boots of untanned leather, with leggings of the same material, a short tunic like a kilt just reaching to the knees, and an upper garment somewhat resembling a Norfolk jacket, belted at the waist, with a pouch hanging over the left hip. He made a low reverence to each of the party as soon as he was in the room, and then, approaching

[1] The famous parting counsel said to have been given by a Spartan mother to her son as he was setting out for a campaign.

Philareté, knelt on one knee and lifted the hem of her garment to his lips.

"Rise," she said; "and now for the message!"

The man took a small parcel from his pouch. It had a wrapping of purple cloth fastened together by a cord of the same color. This cord was tied in an elaborate knot. Untying this with skilful fingers he presented the enclosure to Philareté, again bending his knee as he did so, but returning to an upright position. It was a small roll of parchment, stained of a yellow color on the back. A cord had been passed through and round it, secured with a seal of clay that had been stained of a vermilion color.

After a look of inquiry to her husband, answered by him with a smiling nod, Philareté cut the cord and began to read.

Marius dismissed the letter-carrier, saying at the same time to the slave who was waiting for orders outside the door, "See that he has all he wants, and let me see him again a little before sunset."

Philareté meanwhile had been reading her letter with eyes that opened wider and wider with astonishment. "Come, dearest," she said to her husband, "and tell me whether I am in my senses or not."

The letter which was so astonishing her was written in Latin strongly tinged with Greek idiom. We shall take the liberty of giving it in English.

"Lucius Atilius, Notary of Tarentum, to the Honorable Lady Philareté, greeting:

"It is my duty to inform you that the honorable citizen, Marcus Plautinus, for many years one of the senators of

this place, departed this life on the thirty-first day of January last. The said Plautinus, by a will which I myself prepared three years ago, and which was duly signed and
witnessed as the law directs, has made this disposition of
his property :

"To the city of Tarentum four hundred thousand sesterces
(£3600), to be lent out, at the discretion of the senators,
to good names, the interest thereof to be paid monthly and
distributed to the poor.

"To the town of Brundisium the same sum to be invested
and employed the same way.

"To the Lady Philareté, wife of Lucius Marius, all that
shall be left after payment of the above legacies, whether
of lands, houses, money, jewels, furniture, and all other
property whatsoever.

"I inform you with the greatest pleasure that this inheritance is of very great magnitude. The said Plautinus died
possessed of eighty million sesterces (£720,000), lent out
on excellent security to owners of land, to merchants, and
to certain municipalities, of which Brundisium is the chief,
owing ten million sesterces secured upon the harbor dues.

"He also possessed fifty thousand jugera[1] of land; the
fourth part of a fleet of twelve merchant ships, the half of a
dyeing factory in this town, and certain smaller properties
of which you shall have full information in due time.

"It will be my greatest pleasure to assist you now and
for the future in any thing that may concern this property.
Meanwhile I would suggest that you should either come
yourself or send some trustworthy person to look after

---

[1] About 35,000 acres.

various matters which must of necessity be referred to you.

"I send herewith a letter, written by the testator to yourself, which he wished to be sent to you after his death.

"Written from Tarentum, the 6th day of February, in the Seven Hundred and Fifteenth Year of the Building of Rome."

"What does it all mean?" said Marius. "Do you remember this Plautinus at Tarentum?"

"Yes, I think so," replied his wife. "I remember him as already an old man when I was quite a child. He was once a friend of my father's, but they quarrelled on some matter of business and never spoke to each other again. I remember having heard that his mother was a Greek, and, I think, a Spartan, of one of the royal families. Perhaps we shall find something in his letter."

She opened the letter, and, after glancing over its contents, read it aloud. It ran thus:

"Marcus Plautinus to Philareté, wife of Lucius Marius, greeting:

"I have left you a great inheritance, because you are of the same race as my mother. She was the best of women, and there cannot fail to be something of good in you. I have not cumbered it with any conditions or burdens, deeming that when a man has lived his life he should loose his hold upon his possessions. Alive, I did not stint the gods of their due, nevertheless, I have not charged that property that once was mine but now is yours, with any due of tithe and offering (the charge of four thousand sesterces yearly to the Temple of the Twin Brethren which lies upon my house in the Forum lay thereon when I bought it, nor have I been able to redeem it). I charge you also to be bountiful while you live; but think not to win the favor of heaven by gifts of that which costs you nothing after you are dead. Be merciful to the poor; be lenient to your debtors; and, if it be possible, suffer not yourself to be corrupted by good fortune. I sometimes doubt whether I have done ill or well to you and yours in leaving you this wealth. May the gods turn it to good! Farewell!

"Written on the first day of January, in the third year of the 185th Olympiad."

The young people had begun to gather their thoughts, and were all excitement; Lucius Marius and Philareté had the look of people who had heard bad tidings. Whatever else the news might mean, it meant a great change, and in middle life changes are seldom welcome. The young man was the first to break the silence.

"When do we start for Tarentum? The mother must go to look after the inheritance, and we will go to look after the mother."

"Start!" cried his father. "Start, my dear boy! not till after the equinox; no, not for all the inheritances in the world. A month ago we might have gone unhurt, but now — You remember what the old merchant says in the play:

"Ever have I heard of Neptune from the famous men of old,
He is gentle to the beggar, ruthless to the lords of gold."

Besides there are many things to be settled here, for when we shall see dear Scyllus again who knows?"

That afternoon a letter was written, informing the notary that Philareté and her family intended to arrive at Tarentum as soon as possible after the beginning of April. The letter-carrier started with this in his pouch on the following day, carrying also with him twenty gold pieces securely fastened in his girdle. He had never before carried a letter to such good purpose.

CHAPTER XXV.

AN OLD ACQUAINTANCE.

EARLY in April Marius and his family arrived in Tarentum. One of the merchantmen belonging to the fleet owned by the late Plautinus had taken them on board in the harbor of Pylos, and had conveyed them without mishap to their destination. It had been descried in the offing early in the day by some of the loungers that spent their day on the harbor piers, and as its approach had been delayed by light and baffling winds, time had been given to organize something like a triumphal reception. Tarentum was all alive to see the strangers who had thus become in a moment its wealthiest citizens. It did not accord with the dignity of the senate to be present officially to welcome even the richest of private citizens, but there was not a senator but was present. Atilius the notary, a wizened old man with a keen but not unkindly face, was of course on the spot, conspicuous with a newly washed white toga, edged with a purple stripe of unusual breadth (he held the high office of town-clerk). That day he had the proud position of introducer. It was he, and he alone, who, for the time at least, could determine who should and who should not have the pleasure of making acquaintance with the wealthy Philareté.

And he had accordingly the satisfaction of having persons of distinction, who were commonly somewhat cold and distant, claiming a familiar acquaintance with him. He had small opportunities, however, of dispensing his favors. He had barely introduced himself when Marius, rather alarmed by the crowd, to which the loneliness of Scyllus had not accustomed him, whispered in his ear, "My dear sir, let us have nothing of a procession. Say whatever is civil and right to our friends, but let us get home as quickly as we can."

"You must at least greet the senators," answered the notary; and Marius, promptly concealing his weariness and anxiety to be gone, spoke a few courteous words to the ten gentlemen whom he proceeded to introduce. "I hope," he said with a polite inclination, "I hope to receive my friends very speedily. Meanwhile we all want rest."

A litter, carried by eight stout African slaves, was in waiting for the ladies. Marius and his son followed on foot, accompanied by the notary, who did the honors of the town with much ceremony. It was indeed a town of which its citizens might well be proud. The streets were broad and well kept, the houses stately, shining with white marble, which, in that fine climate, was still almost as bright as on the day in which it was hewn into shape. More than one towering temple struck the eyes of the strangers as they passed along, the most conspicuous among them being that of the great Twin Brethren, the deities under whose special protection Tarentum was supposed to be. But for all its splendor the city had something of the air of decay. There were few vehicles in the streets; these few were for the most part not wagons or carts engaged in trade, but the carriages of the wealthy. On the footways there was no throng of passengers; in the least frequented streets grass might be seen growing.

The house for which our party was bound stood on the south side of the market-place. Its outside appearance was unpretending and even mean; but when the porter, who had evidently been watching for the arrival of the new owners, threw open the outer door the scene was changed as if by magic. The vestibule was paved with variegated marbles, and lined on either side by statues in white marble. Beyond this was an open court, with a fountain rising in the middle so high that its topmost jets were touched by the evening sun, and with orange and lemon trees, on which the fruit was just beginning to form, round the sides. Opening out of this court were a library, lighted from above, with its four walls lined with bookcases; a winter dining chamber, looking upon the bay, with its windows so arranged that they could catch every ray of the sun from its rising to its setting; another for summer use, looking to the north; smaller chambers meant for sitting-rooms and boudoirs, and two ranges of bed-chambers, intended for summer and winter use. Our friends had brought only three or four personal attendants, but they found all their wants carefully and promptly attended to. A large and, it was evident, a carefully drilled, army of slaves was at their command. The notary, who continued to play the part of host, whispered a few directions to an elderly slave of portly figure who was in attendance. After a short interval had been allowed for the washing and changing which are so grateful after a voyage, the party was summoned to the dining chamber. They would gladly have been alone, but Marius saw that the notary expected an invitation, and was too kind-hearted not to give it. The repast, for the meagreness of which the man of business thought it necessary to apologize, was yet sumptuous enough to astonish our friends, accustomed as they had been for many years to the simple fare of their country home. There were six kinds of fish, dressed with various sauces, and their attention was especially called to an unusually large turbot which had been caught, they were told, by a fisherman of Barium, and sent by special messenger as a present to the Lady Philareté. A fat goose, a couple of guinea-fowl, a score of thrushes, a dish of sow's udder, and a quarter of lamb, were among the other delicacies provided, Philareté mentally resolving, as dish after dish was presented to her, that she would have less profuse housekeeping in the future. On the subject of wine the notary waxed eloquent. " That, sir," he said, pointing to a flask of ample proportions which stood at Lucius' elbow, " is the wine of the country, and the best that can be got. It is considered patriotic to have it on one's table, but I cannot unreservedly commend it. Our southern suns make it somewhat fiery. After all, there is nothing like Falernian and Setine. Our dear friend who is gone did not agree with me, I know. He was a true Tarentine, and would seldom drink what he called Roman wines. But he always kept them for his friends, and of the very best. We have — Pardon me, sir ; I should have said you have casks in your cellar that, I venture to say, are a good deal older than yourself, but I thought that to-day an ordinary vintage would suffice."

" I am very much obliged to you for all your care," said Marius, "but the truth is that I seldom drink any wine, be the vintage good or bad. My son is still more abstemious, and the ladies never touch it by any chance."

" My dear sir," said the little man, "you astonish me. A very few of our most aristocratic ladies are water-drinkers. It is a tradition in our best Greek families; but among gentlemen the habit is unknown. You and your son are likely to be the only water-drinkers in Tarentum, except, it may be, one or two Jew merchants."

Not long after he took his leave, disappointed of the long carouse which, on the strength of his acquaintance with the well-filled cellars of Plautinus, he had promised himself. The family, not a little relieved at his departure, looked at each other for a little while in a silence which Rhodium was the first to break. "This is awful," she said. "If this is a meagre dinner, for so the little man called it, what must a full one be like? How shall we live through it?"

" My dear Rhodium," her mother replied, "we won't be made the slaves of our riches; but we shall have to submit to go through a good deal that will be very tiresome. I sometimes wish that the old man had found some other way of disposing of his money. Still there are consolations, and one of them I may administer at once. Your father and I have made up our minds that though we must live here for several months in the year we will pay a long visit every year to our old dear little home in Scyllus. With summer and autumn there we can very well get through winter and spring here. After a while, I dare say, you will find riches more tolerable than you think. Take care that their charm does not grow upon you."

The room in which the party was assembled might well indeed have done something to reconcile one to wealth. The prospect from the windows was glorious; the famous bay lay stretched before the eyes almost as calm as a lake, and now brightened with the long lines of the latest sunbeams glistening upon it. Three windows occupied the whole of one side of the room, and made a prominent bow, with the left side almost facing the east, the right just catching the sunset. The opposite wall, in which were doors leading to the kitchen, and to two or three sleeping and sitting chambers, was wholly covered with a rich purple curtain, one of the finest products of the dyeing-works of the town. The western wall was covered with a fresco, "The Gods Feasting in Olympus," a copy of one of the best pictures of the palmy days of Greece; on the opposite side of the room the patriotism of a native artist had pictured one of the victories of Pyrrhus, the friend whose help had cost Tarentum so dear. It was a spirited battle scene, in which the elephants, the "huge earth-shaking beasts" that had more than once broken the Roman line of battle, were conspicuous. The floor was tessellated. Heads of Ceres the corn-goddess, and of Pomona the fruit-goddess, fish with scales of gold and silver and purple, pheasants with all their gorgeous colors, and doves with their sheeny plumage admirably represented, were among the patterns. The couches and chairs were of ebony, picked out with gold; every coverlet and cushion was of Tarentine purple. The library, besides its books, which Marius afterwards found to be admirably selected, was adorned with priceless marbles and bronzes. Every chamber was appropriately furnished. It was evident, in fact, that Plautinus had had not less taste than wealth.

Our friends, on separating for the night, agreed to meet for an early morning walk. To give this as much as possible the interest of an exploration, it was agreed that they should go without a guide, and take the direction that chance suggested. 'The result, we shall see, was curiously interesting.

"Which way shall we go?" said Marius to his wife and children as they met in the vestibule. " Say, Rhodium; we leave the choice to you."

"With the wind," cried the girl; and as she spoke there came a light breath, carrying with it a delicious remembrance of the sea from the gulf. Obedient to the guide thus chosen, the party turned their faces northwards. A walk of a few hundred yards brought them to the north gate of the city, through which the women from the neighboring villages were now thronging with their baskets of poultry, fruit, and other delicacies for the insatiable town. The country immediately under the walls was flat, and, to all appearance, somewhat neglected; and the walk did not promise much interest. But a sudden turn in the road changed the prospect. An enclosure of some six or seven *jugera* (a little more than four acres) in extent, surrounded with a low hedge of privet, which was in full bloom, lay before them. The garden, for such it evidently was, was a perfect blaze of color. On the north side, where they would not hinder the sunshine, was a row of young plane-trees.

Apple, pear, and plum trees, planted so as to leave ample room for air and sunshine, reached in orderly array to the southern boundary, where a long line of bee-hives was set, skilfully placed so as to be sheltered but not shadowed by the hedge. A narrow path divided the garden into two parts, which seemed severally devoted to profit and pleasure, one being stocked with every variety of vegetable, the other variegated with flower-beds of every variety of hue and fragrance. Over the gate was an inscription in Latin, a couple of verses inviting the passer-by to enter. Close by, busy with a rose-tree which, early as it was in the year, already promised to be a mass of bloom, stood an old man, who was evidently the master of the place, and who, hearing the sound of footsteps, turned round and courteously re-peated the invitation of his inscription. This done, he turned again to resume a conversation which the arrival of the strangers had interrupted.

"No, sir," he said, "there is no one in Italy who can bring roses into the market earlier than I can, but they import them from Egypt and beat me. They have abso-lutely no winter there — I knew the country well when I was young — while here the spring frosts are cruel, positively cruel. I thought that this year we should never have been quit of the north wind, and it was cold as if it blew straight from the Alps, which, they tell me, are covered all the year round with snow."

"My good friend," said the person whom he addressed, "if you had lived as near the Alps as I have you would be better content than you are. In my country I have seen the little pools positively frozen as late as this. I never felt safe about my fruit blossom till long after the middle of the month. Some years it would come almost to nothing, while your trees, as far as I have seen, have about as many apples, and pears, and plums upon them in the autumn as they have had flowers in the spring."

The speaker was a noticeable person. His figure was tall and slight, with something of a stoop; his face pale, dark in complexion and irregular in feature, but lighted up with a pair of singularly brilliant eyes. His voice was peculiarly sweet and gentle, and his accent, as Marius immediately perceived, that of a cultured man.

"Ah, sir!" replied the old man, "frost is only one of the gardener's enemies, and the less we have of that the more we are pestered with weeds and live creatures of every kind. I can hardly look round but I find the whole place choked up with a fresh crop of thistles, and darnel, and burrs, and caltrops. As for the caterpillars, the mice, the beetles, and above all the birds, they are past all bearing. I spent three *drachmas, denarii* you call them, on that Priapus there — they told me that it would frighten the birds, and I see the little rascals picking the fruit under his very nose."

"My friend," said the other, "I feel for you. I, too, was a farmer, till I took to a worse trade. But I must not keep you any longer from your work. Give me a bunch of roses, and mind that you keep your first strawberries for me. I have to leave for Rome to-morrow, but I shall be back in time for them." And with a kindly farewell to the old man and a courteous salutation to our party, he turned away.

"That, sir," said the old gardener to Marius, "is, they tell me, a great man at Rome; a poet they call him; gets

as much for a score of verses as I can earn in a year. But
I don't grudge it to him. He made that inscription for me
that you see over the gate — I am told it is very fine — and
would take nothing for it but a little twig of olive. That
was his fancy, sir. He said it was the best pay he could
have. He comes from the north, I understand ; had his
farm taken away from him by a soldier, and was very near
being killed when he tried to get it again. He lives here a
good deal in the winter, and I see him most days. He is
always asking me questions about my flowers, and about my
bees too, sir. He is never tired of talking about bees. I
tell him what I notice of their ways, about their following
their king, and sharing their work and helping each other.
And he has taught me one or two things worth knowing.
But he is not quite practical, to my mind. He told me the
other day how I was to get a new stock if I should want it.
I was to kill a young bullock without breaking the skin and
shut it up for a month, and at the end of the time I should
find the carcass full of bees. They did so in Egypt, he
said. That may be, sir, but I doubt whether here one would
get any thing but a stock of flies. If I want a new stock,
sir, I shall go and buy it. That will be better, I take it,
than risking the value of an ox. No, sir, I doubt whether
he is a practical bee-master, but he has a better trade than
that, for all he says. But excuse my chattering. It is the
way of old men. Let me just finish with this tree, and
then I will attend to you."

Marius had long been struck by something that seemed
familiar in the old man's face, and still more in his voice,
especially when he had grown excited in discoursing on the

wrongs of gardeners, but he could not succeed in remembering who he was. Unconsciously the old man helped him
out of the difficulty. Taking off his broad-brimmed felt
hat he showed a curious scar that seemed half the length
of his forehead close under the hair. In a moment there
flashed upon Marius, vivid as if he had been present at it
but the day before, the scenes of long-past days. He
resolved to feel his way by a few questions.

"Have you always been a gardener? I heard you say
something about Egypt. Did you follow the same trade
there?"

"No, sir; I learned the business here. Began it five-and-
thirty years ago come next autumn."

"And you saw something, I dare say, of the world in
your youth. A sailor, perhaps?"

"Yes, sir, I was a sailor;" and the old man gave a suspicious look at his questioner.

"Did you ever happen to see the great harbor of Syracuse; see it, I mean, from the water? And do you know
an island somewhere off the north-east corner of Crete?
And do you remember a young Roman, one Lucius Marius,
who owes you something which he never can repay, and
certainly will never forget?"

The old gardener had listened with something like dismay
to the earlier questions, but at the name of Lucius Marius
his anxious gaze relaxed into a smile. "And you"—he
said.

"I," replied our hero, "am Lucius Marius."

For a few minutes the old man seemed unable to speak.
Recovering himself a little he said, "It is not many of my

old acquaintances that I should care to meet. But you — the gods be thanked for sending you in my way."

"Come," said Marius, "tell us your story from the day that we parted. Up to that time my wife and my children know it, I may say, by heart. It was always the tale that the little ones would choose when they were to have a special treat."

"You shall have it, or as much of it as is worth telling. But come and sit down on the bench yonder under that pear-tree, for it won't be finished in a moment or two."

CHAPTER XXVI.

THE PIRATE-CAPTAIN'S STORY.

"IT must be four-and-thirty years," said the old man, after considering a while, "since I saw you last, and there has much happened in that time that I should not like to tell, nor you to hear."

It was curious to observe what a new dignity the speaker seemed to assume. He was no longer the old gardener, with no interest beyond his flowers and fruits, speaking a rude dialect which was only saved from being vulgar by its being manifestly foreign. He was a chief, a ruler of men, one who had commanded fleets and matched his power with Rome itself.

"It is true," he continued, "I was never quite the same after seeing and knowing you that I had been before. I don't think that I had ever felt for a prisoner what I felt for you. I had spared their lives often enough, but it was when it was not worth while to kill them. I never was so bad as some even in my worst days, never liked killing for killing's sake, or when I hoped to get a good ransom for them, or when, for any other reason, it paid me better to keep them alive than to put them to death. But you were, I think, the very first that I ever positively spared for pity's

sake ; ·but you were not the laſt. My men often thought
me a fool, and could not imagine what I meant. I had
some ugly quarrels about it, and should have had worse, but
that they knew pretty well that, whoever I might spare, I
never spared a mutineer. Yes, a good many citizens and
strangers owe their lives to you, and I am glad to think of
it. I don't pretend to be much troubled by remembering
what I once was. I was brought up to the business. It
was my father's before me, and my grandfather's, and his
father's, and so on for I don't know how many generations.
To this day I don't see but what it is as honest as the
trades that some very respectable persons get their money
by ; and I always behaved in it as an honest man should.
You laugh, sir, but you know what I mean. I divided
things fairly, and never kept a prisoner when his ransom had
been properly paid, and so forth. But I must confess that
what I like to think of, when I do go back to those days, is
what I was able to do for you and for others like you. But
you want to hear my story. Well, you know, I dare say,
that after you and I parted we had it our own way more
than ever in the Mediterranean. I am astonished that we
were ever allowed to do the things we did ; and not for a
few months, mind you, but for years. I did not know in
those days what Rome could do if she chose. I was fool
enough to think that she hadn't the power to crush us, but
I know better now. You have seen a little dog teasing a
big one, snarling and barking at him, biting his heels, and
so forth, till at last the big fellow gives him a shake and has
done with him. So it was with us. But I am, as I said,
amazed to this day when I think of what this great empire,

with legions and fleets and money, and the best generals
and commanders in the world, put up with. I suppose the
Romans were too busy quarrelling with each other to give
us a thought. They have, and from what people tell me
they always have had, a terrible way of quarrelling among
themselves. They have conquered pretty nearly the whole
world in spite of it. Without it two worlds would not have
been enough for them. Maybe you have heard of some
of the things we did. I reckon that some day people will
hardly believe them. They positively had to keep their
armies waiting, when they wanted to send them across the
sea, till we had gone into harbor for the winter. Who
could have believed that? And yet, as you may perhaps
have heard, it is a positive fact. I can tell you things, too,
that I did myself, that would make you stare. Why, sir, one
day when I was lying off the coast not very far from here,
with four or five ships, we saw two officers, *prætors* they call
them, going along the road. They had some five or six
thousand men, bound for Sicily or Asia, somewhere in the
neighborhood, but just then they were out of reach of the
army. There they were marching along the road in great
state, with their robes and ornaments, and their twelve lictors before them. Well, sir, I sent four or five boat-loads
of men ashore, laid wait for them in a place where the road
came close down to the sea, and positively carried off the
whole company. You should have seen their astonishment.
I cannot help laughing even now when I think of it. I
didn't hold them to ransom. My men did not understand
why, but I knew better; it would have been venturing too
far. Rome could not put up with such a disgrace; and we

should have been put down before we were. As it was, the crash came the very next year. No, I put them ashore, after giving them a good dinner on board, and only kept the axes out of the lictors' bundles as keepsakes. But we got some heavy ransoms too when it was safe to stand out for them. There was a lady, for instance, whom we carried off from near Misenum. I dare say that you know the place ; a great favorite it is with the rich Romans. She was on her way to a country house in the neighborhood, and had a whole troop of serving-women with her, and a party of slaves armed. The slaves did not make much fight — what should they fight for? We took their arms and let four or five of the sturdiest take service with us. The women I left on shore ; I never would cumber myself with them. We knew we had got a prize in the lady, but we did not know all. The fact was, that in one way that was the best thing we ever did. Why, sir, she was the daughter of a man who had fought against us, and conquered us — so, at least, he said. He came with a great fleet, and sent home fine despatches about what he had done, — he was a great speaker, I have heard say, Antonius was his name — and now we had his daughter, quite elderly she was then. A brave woman — the Roman women all are — she never shrieked or so much as shed a tear, but treated us all as if we were so many dogs. We got fifty pounds weight of gold for her. But the best thing of all — you must excuse me, sir, but when I get talking about these days, a thing I very seldom do, I feel as if I were on the deck of my own ship again — well, the boldest thing we ever did was when we actually sailed into Ostia — yes, into the port of Rome itself. There

was a fleet in the harbor nearly ready for sailing, and the
great man who was to take the command had just arrived.
Well, just about sunset, when more than half the crews were
on shore, drinking in the taverns or bidding good-by to
their friends — for they were to sail the next day — we
made our way into the harbor. Some of the ships were too
near to the piers to be meddled with; but the rest we either
burned or sank, or made off with. The men on board were
mostly slaves, the rowers, you know, sir, and they had not
much heart for fighting; and we were always ready to let
them escape as best they could. As for the officers and
sailors, many of them were asleep or tipsy. I never saw
such a sight. All the piers were crowded with people looking on; and there was the great man himself in a most
furious rage, stamping about and giving orders which there
was no one to listen to. They positively could not find
sober men enough to man the boats, and we were well out
of the reach of their javelins and slings. At last they
brought down some catapults, but by that time our work
was pretty well finished. We burned thirty ships and scut-
tled as many more, though we could not wait to see them
all sink; and ten we took away with us; we could not spare
crews for more.

"The end of it was, we grew too bold. It seemed as if
nothing could rouse the Romans; and I began to think that
they weren't *able* to put us down. It was a great mistake,
sir, and I ought to have known better. Well, at last we
began to lay hold of their wheat-ships from Egypt and
Utica and such places. You know, sir, they don't grow
much corn in Italy; vines and olives, and fruits of all kinds,

and flowers, pay much better, and a vast quantity of land is taken up with parks and the like. My kind friend, the poet, says that he is going to write about it, and see whether he can't bring back the old ways into fashion again. Things had not gone as far then as they have now, but still a great quantity of wheat had to be imported into Rome; so when we began to cut off the ships that brought it the people felt the pinch, and got really in earnest about it; and when the Romans are in earnest they do a thing pretty quickly and thoroughly. We heard all about it from our friends in Rome — we had very good friends, people in high place some of them, so high that you would scarcely believe if I were to tell you, and they got good pay from us. The best general in Rome was to have absolute command, with about as many ships and as many men as he chose to ask for. There was still a chance that it might not be done. There were other great men, or those who fancied themselves such, and they did not like the idea of all this power being given to somebody else. But before long came the news that the thing *was* done. Most of us were not afraid; they thought that the storm would pass over as it had passed over before. But I knew better; and yet I did not see what was to be done. At one time I thought of advising the others to make their submission, but I soon saw that it would be as much as my life was worth to hint at it; and besides, we had no regular authority among us. Every captain of a ship was independent in his way. They obeyed commands when actually fighting; but at all other times it was mostly a man for himself; so there was nothing for it but to fight, and that they were all ready to do; and I did my best to get ready, though I must own that I had very little hope. I am speaking, you will understand, of my own people, the Cilicians. We held together in a way. As for the rest, they were scattered just like a flock of sparrows when a hawk comes in sight. There was nothing, you see, to bind them to each other, for they came from every country under the sun, and some had no country at all. It would be a very strange thing, would be a true list of the free-booting ships that there were in those days, and of their owners. You would not believe it, sir, but there were rich men in Rome who had ships of their own in the trade; and a very good trade it was. They were ship-owners themselves for the most part. You look surprised, sir; but this is the way they managed it. A man would have the sixth part, say, of a merchant ship, or twenty merchant ships. Now, if he kept a freebooter at sea, and got half the profits of what it took, it paid him very well to lose the sixth of what was taken, particularly if he got something out of the treasury and something out of the associations they had, I was told, to protect themselves against loss. Well, sir, we Cilicians made up our minds to fight, and we had not long to wait. We had got together about a hundred and fifty ships of all sizes, and we lay off a harbor there is somewhere opposite the east end of Cyprus. It must have been about a month after midsummer when the Roman fleet came. We had men on the lookout along the coast, and were ready as far as we could be for them. It was, I remember, a little after sunrise that the ships came in sight, sixty of them, not more, so that we had double their number. But this was the only thing we beat them in. Better ships could not have been than these sixty, in fact they were picked for the work, and the crews were picked too. They had not a single slave on board; all the sailors above deck and below were free men, Italians many of them, others from Rhodes and Byzantium and the other great trading towns, for all were ready enough to follow when they saw that Rome was really in earnest. I did not know all this at the time, but I saw from the look of the ships, and the way they came on, that we had a hard piece of work before us. And the day was against us; I should have liked a brisk wind, the brisker the better; that would have given us a chance to show our seamanship. Our enemies could not touch us there. We could have sailed round and round them if there had only been some wind, but there was not a breath. It was a dead calm from the beginning of the affair unto the end.

" Well, sir, they came on in the shape of a half-moon, with the round of the curve, you will understand, not the hollow, towards us; and on the stern of the leading ship, which had a great flag hanging from its main-mast, stood the general, as I took him to be, with a number of men round him, who took his orders and made their signals accordingly. I never saw any thing like the regular sweep of their oars. The best harp-player in the world could not have kept time better. The forepart, too, of every ship was covered with a regular mass of men. They had locked their shields together over their heads, just as they do when they are at work on the walls of a town. Well, sir, of course we did not wait to be attacked. We lay close together in two lines, and I gave the word, for I had some sort of command, though it was not acknowledged as well as it might have been, that our ships were to scatter and ram the Romans, taking them as much as we could on the side. But we did very little good; they were too strong for us to hurt them much; indeed I heard afterwards that they had been specially strengthened; and then, though they were heavier than we, they faced round and met us with wonderful speed, thanks to their good crews, so that we really got more damage than we gave. And then when one of our ships did get a fair chance against one of theirs, and struck her, say amidships, before ours could clear again down came a heavy grapnel from the Roman's mast and held her fast; and then in a moment the sailors had a bridge up between the ships, and the soldiers poured over it, men in heavy armor with their pikes and swords, and boarded our vessel and swept its deck clear — for how could our light-armed fellows stand against them? — before you could count a hundred. The sea was so calm that the men could move as easily and regularly as if they had been on land. If there had been a wind they would have been staggering about, and we might have had a chance. But it was not to be, and on the whole, sir, I am not sorry. And this, the being boarded and taken, was just what happened to me. It was my business of course to set an example, and I made at the commander's ship. But first I thought I would disable her oars; so when we were just upon her I gave a turn to the rudder, for I was at the helm myself, and crashed in upon the left-side oars. Then, sheering off, and backing water till I had put a hundred paces' distance between my enemy and me, I came on again at full speed. My men could not have done better; they rowed as hard and as well as ever they did in their lives, but it was like knocking one's head against a wall. The place we rammed — they knew the place for which we were likely to make pretty well — had been made prodigiously strong, and we hardly so much as dented it; and then down came the grapnel, and we were fast. The sailors had their bridge out in a moment, in fact they were a little too quick, for we managed by lurching our ship down, which was done easily enough as we were all on that day, to get clear of it. I remember seeing two or three of the soldiers slip off into the sea. They went too, poor wretches, in their heavy armor without a struggle. You could positively see them at the bottom of the water, which was not more than forty or fifty feet deep and very clear. But we escaped only for a moment; the grapnel held us fast, and we could not cut the chain, for it was of iron. They soon had the bridge out again, and this time they made it safe enough, and the soldiers poured across it. Of course we did not give up without a fight; I had the picked men of the whole country about me, sir, good swordsmen all of them, and as strong, sinewy, determined fellows as ever you saw. But it did not last very long; it could not have lasted long in any case, for the odds were all against us, but as it turned I brought it to an end very soon; and a very happy thing it was for me and my people that I did. This was how it happened. There was a gallant young fellow among the enemy, one of the commander's *aides-de-camp*, and a cousin as I afterwards heard. Well, nothing would satisfy him but he must have, as he would say, the pirate-chief's head; and he made straight at me. He was a fair swordsman too, but no match for me as I was in those days. After a few passes I twisted

the sword clean out of his hand. He had his dagger out
in a moment and rushed at me — a braver and readier
young fellow I never saw — but his foot slipped and he fell
at full length at my feet. The general was watching us from
the other ship, and I heard him cry out. And then it
flashed upon me — the gods be praised for putting the
thought into my mind ! — that I would spare him, and so
perhaps earn my own life. I could have killed him at a
blow. There was an open space between the helmet and
the cuirass, always a weak spot in the best armed men. But
what was the good? It was all over with us, and we should
not have been the better if I had struck, and there had been
one Roman the less. So I dropped my sword, lifted him
from the deck, and said, ' We are conquered ; I put myself
and my people under your protection.' Then I shouted to
the crew to surrender ; and this, I take it, they were glad
enough to do, for they saw that there was no hope. The
end of it was, that our ships could make no head at all
against the Romans ; and they could not fly. The fact was
that there was no place to fly to. We were fighting like a
rat in its hole. And the Romans, too, had sent a squadron
round by the south side of Cyprus to keep any of us from
going eastward. It hove in sight an hour or two after the
battle had begun. It was admirably managed, I must say,
though there was some good luck, too, especially in the
weather. But then I have always heard say that Pompey —
that was the general's name, sir, you know — had the best
of luck all his life, till it turned against him. Before noon-
day some fifty or sixty ships had been taken, and about
thirty sunk ; the rest were run aground by their captains,

and the crews made the best of their way to the ports in the hill country. That of course was no use. If we could not hold our own by sea, we were not likely to do it by land. Long before the month was out they were all taken; indeed most of them surrendered. Well, we prisoners were kept in camps strongly guarded with soldiers till the whole business was finished; and then it was to be settled what was to be done with us. We didn't expect much mercy; indeed, I doubt very much whether any other general but Pompey would have shown it. You must pardon me for saying it. I seem to forget, when I am speaking to you, that you are a Roman, but mercy is not what we expect from your people; but then Pompey was not quite like others; and then he had the deciding about every thing in his own hands. It had been all left to him, how to manage the war and how to finish it. It is a different thing, sir, I take it, when a man has twenty thousand men under his very eye and has to decide whether they shall live or die, and when he has to refer it to other people a long way off and only carry out their orders. The senate sitting in judgment on us a thousand miles away at Rome might have ordered us to death, but Pompey, who was on the spot, couldn't do it, and, as I have said, he was not like the others.

"Well, I was told one day that I was to go before the great man. He was on board ship. The shore is not healthy when the weather is very hot, and the great officers did not see any more of it than they could help. He was sitting on a chair with his people about him, the young fellow that I had surrendered to being just behind him. He was a man of about forty, with a pleasant face, dignified enough, but not quite so great a man to look at as I had expected.

" 'You are a chief among these people?' he said.

" 'I am, sir,' I answered, 'as my father was before me, and his father before him.'

" 'What have you to say for yourself? You know what a pirate deserves;' and he made a sign with his arm which I understood well enough.

"Well, I thought for a moment what I should say, not that I hadn't thought of it before over and over again, but I never could quite make up my mind. Should I be humble or bold, throw myself at his feet and beg for mercy, or brave it out? When one *has* to make up one's mind, one does it quickly enough. What you have spent hours and hours in thinking over, and only made it darker than ever, comes out as clear as the light in a moment. 'May I speak frankly, my lord?' I said.

" 'As frankly as you will.'

" 'My lord,' I said, 'there is a story in our family which I should like to tell you as you give me leave to speak. We have been pirates, as you call us, for I do not know how many generations. Well, my lord, a far-away ancestor of mine was brought up before the great Alexander. He had been caught exercising his trade somewhere near Egypt, and he had to answer for himself. 'What do you mean,' said the king, 'plundering peaceable persons in this way?' 'Great king,' he answered, 'I do not see but what I have as much right to the seas in these parts as you have to the land. If I am a plunderer you must be the same. But you have a great army, and generals, and fleets, and armor of gold in battle, and a robe of purple in peace, and so they call you a great man, a conqueror, a son of the gods, and I know not what; I have nothing but a little ship and some threescore men, and they call me a pirate.' The great Alexander looked at him for a moment, almost as much astonished as if some one had struck him in the face. Then he burst out into a laugh. 'Take the fellow away,' he said, 'and give him a hundred gold pieces to shut his mouth.' That is the story, my lord, that they tell in my family, and we keep one of the gold pieces made up into a ring as a remembrance of it. Greece had only one Alexander, my lord, but Rome has had many, so much the worse for the world.'

"He smiled; I could see that he was pleased with the compliment. 'Ah!' he said, 'you think that Rome is the big robber, and you the little one. Well, it may be so; I won't argue the matter with you. You know the proverb, "Two of a trade never agree." And the one that has the upper hand has a way of keeping it. But hark! you have been pirates, freebooters you prefer to call it, for many generations. You have been brought up to this trade, and though I cannot allow you to go on with it I shall not be hard upon you. You shall have an opportunity of being honest men, as we count honesty, you know. This is a barren country of yours, and can't support you; but there is plenty of land for you elsewhere, and I shall settle you in it. To you I owe a special favor. I saw when you had my young cousin here at your mercy, and I have been making inquiries about you, and find that he is not the first Roman whose life you have spared. I shall take you to

Italy, for you are best a long way off from your old haunts, and you shall swear to me by all the gods, or give me your word, which I dare say will be just as good as your oath, that you will never set foot on a ship again, and we will find a place for you somewhere and the means of earning your bread. Is there any way that you would choose rather than another?' 'Well, my lord,' I answered, 'there are only two honest ways of making a livelihood that I know of — the sword and the plough — and as I must have nothing more to do with the first I choose the second.' 'So be it,' he said. 'My cousin here will see to it.'

"To make a long story short I came to Italy in the general's ship. By rights I should have followed in his triumph, but he excused me from that for his nephew's sake, and I set to work to earn my bread honestly. I did not exactly follow the plough, for I fancied that in a new country, with new ways, I should make but a poor hand at that business. But I had always had a taste for flowers and fruit, and I bought this little piece of land with some money that the general's cousin gave me. Pretty well waste it was at the time, but I liked the aspect of it. Indeed it only wanted labor; that I have given to it, and it is as pretty and profitable a little garden to-day as there is in Italy. Here I have been these thirty years. Many changes I have seen in them. Politics are nothing to me, but I could not help being sorry for the great man who was so kind to me, when I heard of his miserable ending. To be murdered by a slave and buried in the sand after all that he had been! And I hear them talk of his son as a pirate now! That is the strangest of all. How the world does come round, to be sure! But

I must not talk of these great matters. I hope, sir," he continued, returning with a smile to his old manner, "that you will give me your custom when you want any thing in my way, if you are going to live at Tarentum."

The old man's story finished, Lucius Marius had, as may be supposed, something of his own to tell. Heracleo had long since given up all hope of seeing his son again. He had gone back to his native village the winter after it had been harried by the troops of Tigranes, to find his home in ashes. Some wretched survivors had by that time crept back to their old abode. From them he learnt of the death of his wife and daughter. Sad as was the news it was better than to hear that they had been carried into captivity. About his son he had been able to learn nothing. What Lucius Marius now told him was therefore almost a relief. The young man was dead, but at least he had died nobly. To the story of the finding of the treasure he listened with a smile. "These are my riches now," he said, pointing to the garden beds and fruit-trees, "and I care for no other. But I am glad that the things are not lost to the world, and that you, sir, have your share. On the whole, it was not an unlucky day that put you into a pirate's hand — I am afraid that few can say as much."

We shall not follow any farther the fortunes of our hero and his family. They never quite ceased to feel that the great wealth which had devolved upon them was something of a burden, and always enjoyed the quiet retirement of Scyllus when the time came round for them to visit it again. Lucius Marius and Philareté lived to a good old age, and passed away quietly and without pain on the same day and almost at the same hour. Rhodium in due time made a very happy marriage, being fortunate enough to find what does not always come in the way of great heiresses, a man who loved her for herself and not for her fortune. It was said in the family that the great Agrippa, afterwards the son-in-law of the emperor, admired her (he saw her the year following the end of my story, when he was on his way to take command of the fleet against the younger Pompey), and that he would gladly have made her his wife. Fortunately for her his friends had a more splendid alliance in view for him, and Rhodium, who had not been particularly flattered by his preference, though he was a brave soldier and an honest man, was left to obscurity and happiness. The younger Lucius never took any part in public affairs, beyond being senator and in due course prætor of Tarentum; but he did his duty to his generation by a wise and liberal management of the great wealth which ultimately came into his hands. Our old friend the pirate-gardener ended his days in the house at Tarentum. His garden outside the walls became too much for him, and he let it for a handsome rent, not without many groans over the incapable way in which he was sure it would be managed by his tenant. But to the day of his death he was never too feeble to tend the shrubs and flowers in the open court of the mansion. He had the honor of having his epitaph written by Virgil, but unhappily both it and the inscription over his gate have been lost.